D1742829

THE
Pain Bearer

THE
Pain Bearer

KENDRA MERRITT

Eldros Legacy Press
P.O. Box 292
Englewood, Colorado 80151

THE PAIN BEARER
Copyright © 2023 by Eldros Legacy

Trade Paperback Edition

All rights reserved. No part of this publication may be reproduced, distributed or transmitted in any form or by any means, including photocopying, recording, or other electronic or mechanical methods, without the prior written permission of the publisher, except in the case of brief quotations embodied in critical reviews and certain other noncommercial uses permitted by copyright law. For permission requests, write to the publisher, addressed "Attention: Permissions Coordinator," at the address below.

Eldros Legacy Press
P.O. Box 292
Englewood, Colorado 80151

EldrosLegacyPress.com

This is a work of fiction. Names, characters, places, and incidents are a product of the author's imagination. Locales and public names are sometimes used for atmospheric purposes. Any resemblance to actual people, living or dead, or to businesses, companies, events, institutions, or locales is completely coincidental.

Cover Art by:
Jake Caleb

Cover Design by:
Rashed AlAkroka, Sean Olsen, Melissa Gay & Quincy J. Allen

Map Design by:
Sean Stallings

Ordering Information:

Quantity sales. Special discounts are available on quantity purchases by corporations, associations, and others. For details, contact us at the address above or via our website.

The Pain Bearer / Kendra Merritt — 1st ed.

ISBN: 978-1-959994-30-5

DEDICATION

To the pain bearers.

What is Eldros Legacy?

The Eldros Legacy is a multi-author, shared-world, mega-epic fantasy project managed by four Founders who share the vision of a new, expansive, epic fantasy world. In the coming years the Founders committed themselves to creating multiple storylines where they and many others will explore and write about a world once ruled by tyrannical giants.

The Founders are working on four different primary storylines on four different continents. Over the coming years, those four storylines will merge into a single meta story where fates of all races on Eldros will be decided.

In addition, a growing list of guest authors, short story writers, and other contributors will delve into virtually every corner of each continent. It's a grand design, and the Founders have high hopes that readers will delight in exploring every nook and cranny of the Eldros Legacy.

So, please join us and explore the world of Eldros and the epic tales that will be told by great story tellers, for Here There Be Giants!

We encourage you to follow us at www.eldroslegacy.com to keep up with everything going on. If you sign up there, you'll get our newsletter and announcements of new book releases. You can also follow up on FaceBook at:

facebook.com/groups/eldroslegacy.

Sincerely,

Todd, Marie, Mark, and Quincy
(The Founders)

MAPS

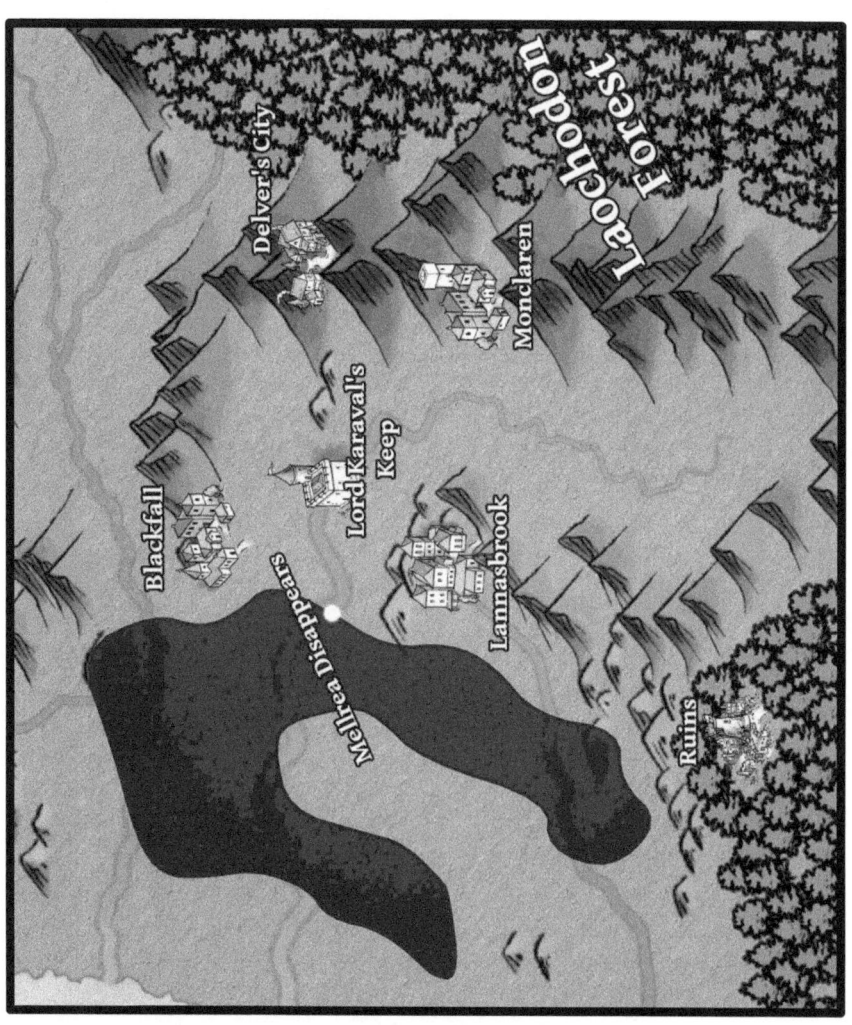

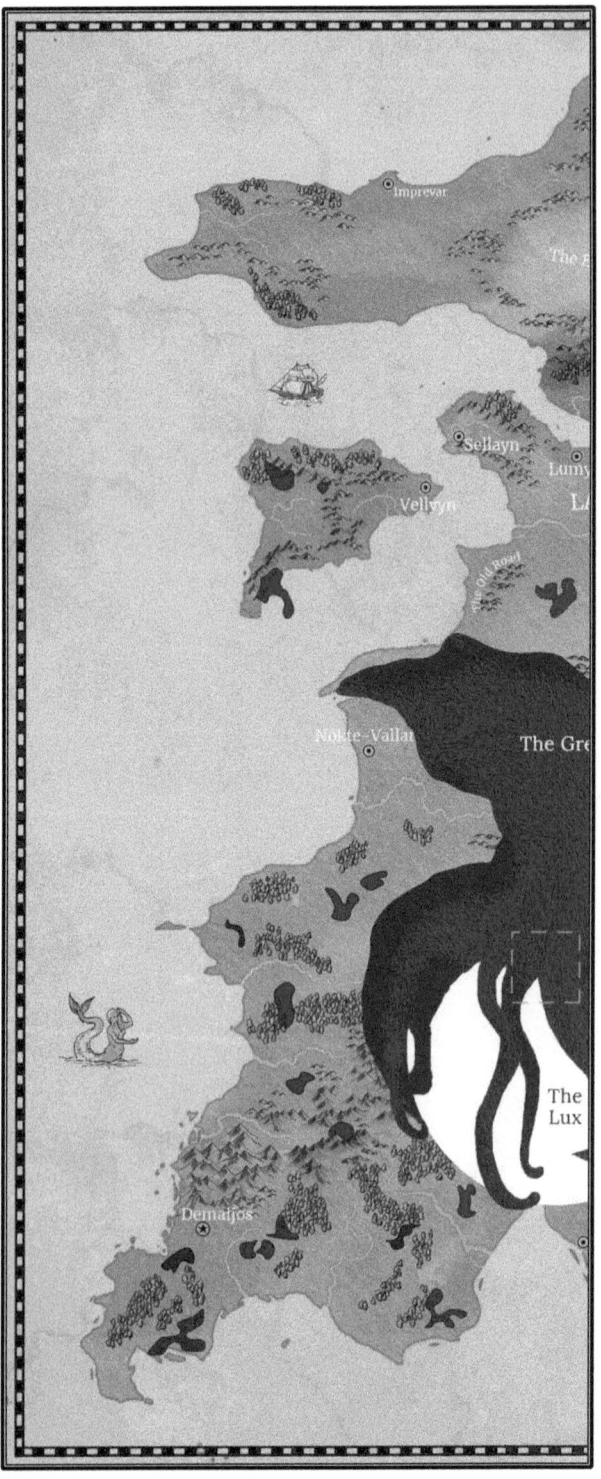

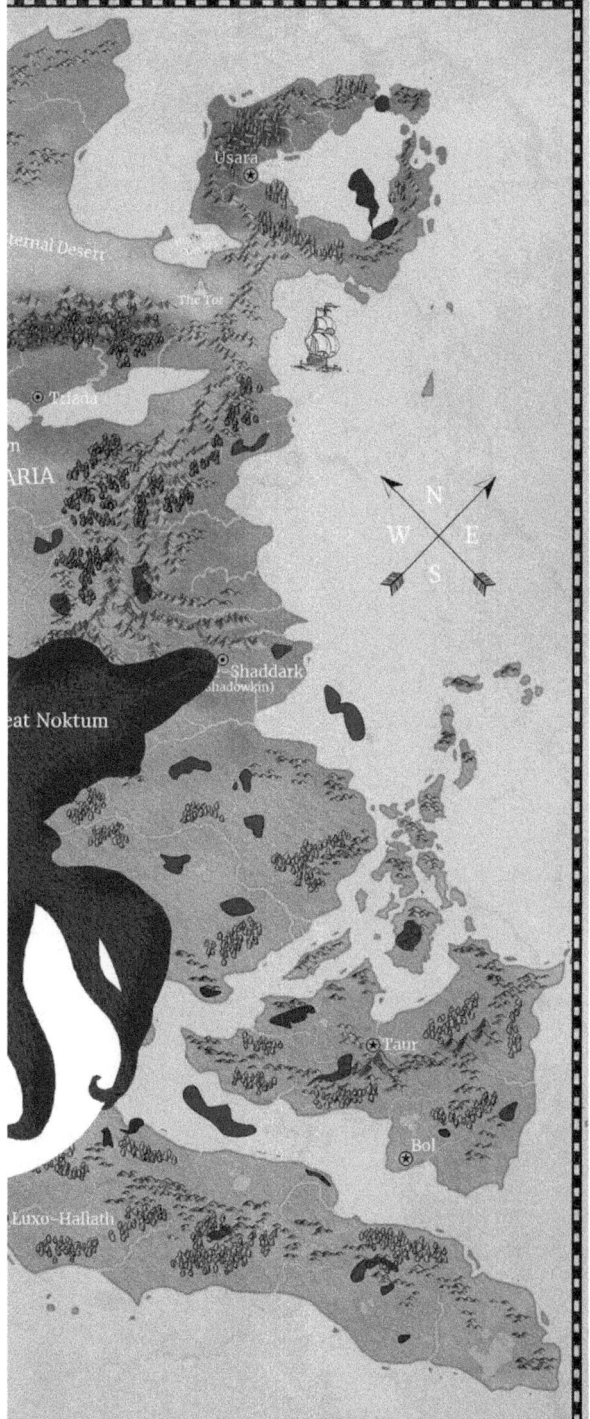

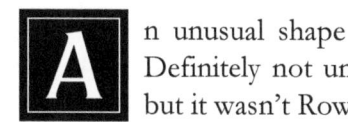

CHAPTER ONE

ROWAN

An unusual shape mounded the dirt at Rowan's feet. Definitely not unheard of for a dig site like this one, but it wasn't Rowan who usually found them.

She set aside the leather folio full of expensive parchment, balancing it and the little bottle of ink on an outcropping in the tumbled stone wall. Then she knelt and started scraping away the soft earth with her hands.

Jannik would be expecting the maps she'd made that morning, and she'd been excited to show him the drawing of the archway behind her. But on her way back to him, this bit of ground had caught her eye. A little mound two feet long was humped like a curtain draped over something long and skinny.

This is stupid, she told herself. *Jannik's been looking for this famous artifact for years. Almost his entire career. What are the odds that I would trip over it on my way through the ruins?*

But she couldn't help the thrill that raced along her neck and made her catch her breath.

She could just imagine the look on his face if she was the one to hand him what he'd been searching for. She could imagine his smile, his words, and if she stretched, she could even imagine a future where she didn't feel guilty about everything he'd given her so far.

This was a chance to repay him.

The sounds of the dig echoed around the crumbling walls which were just high enough to hide her where she knelt. Picks and shovels rang, and men's voices called to one another from the central chamber where Jannik had directed the workers to start today. The autumn sun beat down on the back of her neck and little curls had escaped from her bun to stick in the sweat.

Her fingers bumped something solid, and she pulled a large brush from its place on her belt.

With quick yet gentle hands she brushed away the remaining dirt.

And then spent a solid minute laughing at herself.

The broken handle of a shovel lay in her neatly excavated hole obviously left over from when they'd exhumed the chamber just days ago.

Oh, wonderful find, she thought as she fought to catch her breath against another flurry of giggles. She could imagine the label they'd affix to it. "Discarded excavation equipment, found by Rowan Norasdatter 1711 MG."

Stick to your maps and drawings, Rowan. Jannik actually wants those. He doesn't need another digger.

She stood with a wince and tried to stretch out her back. *Especially not one with a twisted spine and weak arms.*

The ache along the bottom of her ribs didn't disappear, but she'd grown used to ignoring the pain. She brushed her hands off along the canvas apron that protected her tunic, leaving streaks of dirt. Then she tucked the brush back in her belt and reached for the folio of maps, now that she was sure she wouldn't smudge them.

A shout carried across the ruined walls, and Rowan turned toward the central chamber. Another yell—this time it was Jannik's voice raised in triumph.

The diggers must have found something. Probably something far more interesting than a shovel handle.

Rowan tucked the folio under her arm and hurried through the maze of half-tumbled walls and broken archways.

Who would have thought a two-thousand-year-old structure could buzz with so much activity? Two workers dropped their tools and raced for the central chamber. Another trundled by with a wheelbarrow full of gravel. He stopped to tip his hat to Rowan as she passed, and she gave him a smile. Not all the diggers were so polite.

The walls around her rose tall enough to obscure the way, but Rowan had spent the last three months mapping the site as Jannik and the others excavated the rooms. She knew the way even in the dead of night.

Here was the only archway in the site that was complete, standing twice as tall as most men and as broad as two donkeys yoked together. There was the hallway that led through the middle of the facility. And through this window she could see the top of the stairwell a digger had unearthed just a few days ago.

The place might have been ruined, but a surprising number of walls remained tall and intact. Although, it wasn't hard to be taller than Rowan.

Even here in the most traversed parts of the dig, she watched her feet as she walked. Her first day at the dig, she'd tripped over a support beam and fallen into a newly excavated pit, and she had to be rescued. Jannik had laughed it off, saying, "I've been pulled out of so many pits now that it's a rite of passage." But Rowan had decided then and there never to make that mistake again. She was here to help Jannik pull history out of the ground. Not be pulled out of the ground herself. He was very generous with mistakes, but there was only so much kindness one person could repay in a lifetime, and she was reaching her maximum.

Rowan stepped around the tumbled corner of a wall and into the central chamber. Her boots sank into the soft dirt the diggers hadn't cleared away from the underlying flagstones yet. All that remained of the ceiling was a pile of smooth tile and broken stones standing in the corner waiting to be ferried out to the trash pit. Now the room stood open to the elements and who knew how tall it had been originally.

Jannik stood in the center of the chamber where the flagstones had been cleared, a piece of tarnished metal in his hands. It looked like brass or copper so badly corroded and misshapen Rowan couldn't even guess what it had been. The diggers all stood around him, craning to see.

She stepped closer, and one of the workers startled back like she'd stabbed him.

"Godsblighted," he muttered not quite under his breath.

Rowan raised her chin and stared straight ahead. She'd had plenty of practice ignoring the whispers, but the little stab of pain in her chest never lessened.

"If a curse could rub off on people, you all would look a lot different," she muttered under her breath.

"What did you say?"

"Hmm?" She met his eyes, then said with a purposely blank stare, "Nothing. What did you say?"

The man subsided, grumbling.

At the edge of the chamber, where the door had collapsed and created a wide opening, Rowan caught sight of Esrell. Her sister gave her a little wave and gestured behind her to a young man who shifted from foot to foot.

Darryn. Rowan would have sworn her brother had been half a head shorter when she'd left home at the beginning of the summer, but now he towered over both of them, even though he was younger by years.

Esrell had been at the dig for two weeks, but Rowan hadn't seen Darryn for months. She would have rushed to greet him if Jannik hadn't chosen that moment to look up and see her.

She gave Darryn a little wave that said "later" and turned from her siblings. She straightened her shoulders as much as she could.

"What is it?" Rowan asked, pushing through to stand at Jannik's side. "Is it the artifact you're looking for?"

He huffed a little laugh. "I have no idea."

The workers joined him in a chuckle.

If Jannik didn't know, none of them would. He was the only one this far west of the capital who even bothered to study the ruins of the Giants. The only one who saw value in knowledge and history. Too many people looked at the surface of a thing and saw how pretty it was or how much it could do for them. They didn't see what was underneath, at the heart.

Not the way Jannik did.

"What do you think?" he asked. He glanced at Rowan and cocked his head. He'd tied his silver hair back in a neat tail, and his freshly-trimmed beard bristled as he pursed his lips.

Rowan blinked, her mouth parting in surprise. "You're asking me?" She cleared her throat. "I mean... let me check your notes. I can make some quick sketches, and we can cross-reference where it was found with my maps and decide on a theory once we know a little more about the site."

"Actually," he held the lumpy bit of copper out to Rowan, "I was thinking of something a little less mundane."

Rowan's chest seized and she swallowed. "Your notes..."

He shook his head. "No. Could you please identify it? With your gift?"

"You know it's not much," she whispered. "It's never been enough to—" She cut herself off. He knew as well as she did the uselessness of that tiny bit of magic. He had to be asking her for a reason.

"I think in this case it might be helpful," he said, answering her unspoken question. "Perhaps it will give us some clue."

The workers stared at her curiously. None of them knew the disappointment that lay in her blood, though Esrell and Darryn did. Her siblings had lived through most of it. She just hated to remind them, especially when she thought she'd finally left that disappointment behind.

Jannik's encouraging smile didn't waver. He just waited, hand extended long enough for the moment to become awkward.

He'd stood like that the day he'd asked her to be his assistant. After the mage who'd tested her had left, Rowan had seen her life stretching on in unbroken misery. Two weeks later, Jannik had asked if she wanted a job and waited with a raised eyebrow as all the emotions had crowded through her, each one taking more than its fair share of space in her mind.

"All right," she said, both then and now. And she took the object from him. It looked like the handle of a hammer, but who knew yet if it was a true artifact? She'd treat it gently, as if it were.

She could imagine Esrell and Darryn holding their breath behind her, or maybe she was holding her breath enough for all of them.

Rowan ran her hands over the rough nodules and bumps, trying to make out the shape underneath. It was long and skinny, but that was about all she could tell under all the corrosion. She pushed all of her focus into her fingertips and searched for the telltale bits of heat that only she could feel that showed her where someone had once handled the object.

With this much junk between her and the actual surface of the object, the touchpoints faded to mere pinpricks of heat.

This wasn't usually the tricky part. With everyday objects that were handled over and over, warmth covered them. A million little passageways into the past.

But this hadn't been handled in millennium, and it had gathered a thick crust of minerals in the intervening time.

There. A tiny warmth flared under her middle finger, and she sought the spot again.

The spark that lived just behind her eyes responded, and she let it spread and fill her vision with darkness. It wasn't like the darkness of night or like a room with the light just doused. It pressed in on all sides, hot and heavy like a layer of dirt. A mountain of earth covering the object as it had for the last few centuries.

It was over in an instant. The barest glimpse of a thing's past. A random image gone in a few moments.

Normally she saw a memory, like looking through someone's eyes, the Life Magic in her creating a bridge to the person who had once held the thing in her hands. If she even saw that much. But this time had felt like reaching too far and falling somewhere in the middle.

"I'm sorry," she murmured, blinking the dark spots from her eyes. "It's been too long since someone touched it. I can't see more than darkness."

Jannik's mouth drew down and his shoulders drooped before he covered his reaction with a smile.

"I'm sorry," she said again, her knuckles tightening around the unidentified object. He hadn't said a word, but that quickly hidden twitch had cut as deep as the sharpest admonishment. "Maybe if it wasn't so old or so damaged..." She bit her tongue. Or maybe if she wasn't a failed kurios. If her magic was a blaze instead of a spark. But she kept her lips clamped tight on the excuses.

"I can identify it with your notes," she said instead, straightening up as much as she could. It only made her slightly less hunched. "I can remove some of the buildup and compare the shape with other artifacts we've found. Maybe we'll eventually be able to tell what it is."

"Don't worry about it, Rowan," Jannik said, reaching for the object. "It's probably nothing important."

Her fingers wanted to clench on it one more time, but she forced herself to let him take it.

Esrell came close to put her hand on Rowan's low shoulder as Jannik stepped away again. Darryn gave her a lopsided smile.

The diggers watched Jannik as Rowan turned to follow Esrell.

"What are you looking for?" one asked. The one who'd insulted her under his breath. "Treasure?" Most of these workers were new, fresh from the mines and quarries on Lord Hax's properties.

Jannik tapped his forehead. "History could be considered treasure to some. Knowledge is treasure. But for me, I want to find the artifact my great-grandfather searched for."

Rowan had heard the story from him many times, but she paused to listen anyway.

"Over a hundred years ago, he walked these hills looking for something of great historical value."

"What was it?" the worker asked.

Jannik chuckled. "I don't know. He never returned."

The workers shared his chuckle.

"My patron would love to know the answer to that question as well," Jannik said. "Lord Hax will be coming to inspect the site and our progress here soon. I'd love to show him something tangible."

Rowan winced. He didn't mean it as a blow. She wasn't responsible for making sure the dig was profitable. But what if the little unidentified tool had been something important and she could have changed the course of the dig?

"I need to find the artifact," Jannik said. "But I would settle for finding out what happened to my great-grandfather. My great-grandmother is long past caring, but I'd like to prove he didn't run off and jilt her anyway."

The workers all laughed.

"Wait, I haven't gotten to the best part. I've set aside a significant portion of my resources, and I'm offering a reward to anyone who finds evidence of my great-grandfather and the artifact he was hunting."

The workers let out a cheer that rang from the crumbled walls.

Rowan's heart leaped. She hadn't heard that part before.

And in the next second, her shoulders slumped. The chances of her finding the artifact herself had been slim when it was just her wandering the ruins while she drew maps. Now they'd be even worse with all the diggers trying their hand at digging up antiquities.

Darryn practically vibrated as Esrell linked her elbow with Rowan's and drew her away from the dig site where the workers renewed their efforts with vigor.

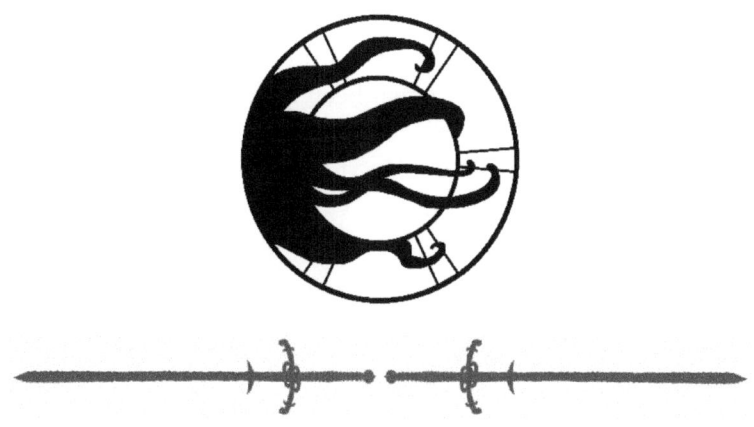

CHAPTER TWO

ROWAN

On the far side of the ruins, where the hills began to rise out of the dell, five sturdy tents surrounded a fire pit. One for Jannik, one for Rowan and Esrell, and three for the workers to share. Crates full of straw were stacked between them, waiting for the treasures they would eventually unearth, and a table stood at the far end of camp heaped with sawdust.

The homey little camp sat between the crumbling walls of the ruins and the first of the trees that surrounded the hollow in the hills. A donkey lipped at the dry grass, straining at the tether that kept her bound to the nearest tent stake.

"How was your trip?" Esrell asked Darryn as they stepped out of the ruins and into the clearing. "You made it in one piece, so I'll assume it was uneventful. No bandit encounters or ruffians. How's mother doing? I still can't believe she let you out of her sight." Esrell was only two years older than Darryn, but she reached up to ruffle his hair like he was seven instead of seventeen.

He dodged her with an exasperated look. "She's fine. If you'd slow down for a second, I could actually answer some of your questions. Senji's breath, you'd think you've had no one to talk to since you left. Has Rowan been ignoring you?"

Rowan rolled her eyes. "I've been busy," she said and stepped across the space to greet the family donkey. The animal raised her head and butted Rowan's chest.

"Right, busy," Darryn said, combing his hair back into place. Clearly Nora, their mother, hadn't cornered him for a haircut before he'd come, since his shaggy, brown locks almost reached his shoulders. He looked more and more like their father, Stefan, every day with his wide smile and sharp nose. Esrell had inherited the blue eyes and most of the same looks from their father, but her hair was sleek and shining, and she kept it pulled back in a crisp bun while she worked.

Rowan took after their mother with flyaway curls that sat somewhere between blond and brown, but none of her siblings shared her twisted spine with the one shoulder that humped too high and the other that sagged too low.

"Jannik must have lots of writing for you to do." Darryn's voice trailed off as if he couldn't think of anything better to say. "I knew he was a smart old man, but I didn't realize this is what he did."

"Don't call him old." Rowan untied Darryn's bag from the donkey's harness. "It's not nice. Or accurate. He's still very spry for his age."

"Which is what? Ancient?"

Rowan scowled at him before she ducked into the tent Darryn would be sharing with the diggers. She unwound his bedroll and stashed his bag in the corner for him. When she slipped out of the tent, she caught Esrell punching Darryn on the shoulder.

"Ow. All right, all right." Darryn rolled his eyes. "I take it back. He's very young for a—what was that word you always use, Rowan?"

"Antiquarian."

"For an antique person."

Esrell doubled over laughing as Rowan heaved a gusty sigh.

"An antiquarian is someone who studies the past," she said.

Darryn nodded. "And digs stuff out of the ground."

Now he was just trying to get a rise out of her. So, she tipped back her head and smiled at him. *Healer's Ghost, he'd grown so tall.*

"Yes. He digs stuff up. Stuff the Giants left behind."

Darryn grew still, catching the nuance in her voice. "Giants?" he said. "They're a myth."

"Not according to Jannik, and he's the expert."

"You believe him?"

She gestured him over to Esrell's table and cleared away some of the sawdust so she could lay out her maps and the latest drawings she'd done. "Here. All you have to do is look at the layout of this place and the size of the doors and stairs. One of the workers found a stairwell the other day with steps taller than would be comfortable for a Human. Everything's built on a bigger scale. Bigger and taller."

"Everyone's taller than you," Darryn said.

She flicked his ear. "Don't sass your big sister. I'm important now."

"Right… as an assistant."

"One day I might be a partner." And she would have earned it too. It wouldn't be some sort of gift.

Can't he see how important this is? How I fit in here?

Yes, some of the workers still whispered "godsblighted" behind her back, but it was much better than at home where she had to rely on her family to shield her from the disdain of the villagers.

Darryn stared down at her maps, mouth twisted.

"Jannik finds the artifacts," Rowan said. "And Esrell packs them so they are protected. Then he sends them to his patron, Lord Hax. That's where you come in."

Darryn threw his arm around her shoulder and pulled her in close. "That I can understand. Just point me at a crate you can't lift, and I'll do it for you. Just like at home."

Rowan opened her mouth to protest. This wasn't just like home. There were lots of delicate parts, schedules that needed to be organized and surveys to be finished. He didn't know how the dig worked yet, and she did.

He picked up one of the big copper plates and held it up to his nose as if admiring himself in the grimy surface.

She snatched it away from him and laid it back on the pile of sawdust. "Please be careful," she said as she pulled out her ink so she could label the plate for Esrell to pack.

"Relax, Rowan," he said. "I'm here to help now."

She bit her tongue. She'd been the one to convince Jannik to hire both Esrell and Darryn. And she had the sneaking suspicion that Darryn had been an easy sell because he came with the donkey. Cart animals ate into Jannik's budget by quite a bit, but they'd need one to ferry crates back to Lord Hax.

And it didn't matter who had gotten whom a job. She was just glad Darryn was here now. Lord Hax had started conscripting young men for his personal guard again, getting ready to march on his neighbors. As long as he kept his disputes to this side of the mountains, far-off King Vamreth didn't care about Lord Hax's campaigns. But the last time he'd gone to war against another noble, so many of the boys from their village had left to fight and had never come back.

Rowan took a deep breath and steered Darryn away from the table of artifacts. The plates weren't exactly exciting, but they represented her work so far, and she was proud of them.

Esrell gave her an understanding smile and slipped in to start packing them into their crate.

Darryn didn't seem to notice. He squeezed her tight, and she winced, her back twinging after her exertion that morning.

"Sorry," Darryn said. "Are you all right?"

She shook herself free from his grasp and gave him a tight smile. "Fine." It was a familiar pain, nothing new or alarming.

"You're sure you're not overdoing it? Jannik wasn't very detailed in his messages."

Rowan straightened up too fast, and her back twinged again. "Messages? He's been sending messages about me?"

It was Darryn's turn to wince. Behind him Esrell stiffened.

"Not very detailed ones," he said, his face going red.

"But he's been talking about me."

"Ma asked him to," Esrell said. "It was her condition for letting you come."

"Condition?" Rowan's voice rose to an embarrassing octave. She closed her eyes and breathed. *Letting* her come?

"We just wanted to check up on you," Darryn said too quickly. "We wanted to make sure Jannik understood how much pain you could hide before you collapsed."

"So, the only reason you all let me come was because you knew someone would be taking care of me," she spat the words out like a bad taste.

"Don't be like that, Rowan," Esrell said. "We're just looking out for you."

They *were* just looking out for her. Because they cared. She should be grateful, not angry. And it wasn't their fault she carried this much pain. It wasn't their fault she couldn't plow or sow the fields back home. Anyone would take that as proof she'd never be useful.

Her mother had told her long ago that she'd cried when Rowan had been born twisted and different, positive she would die before she could grow out of her crooked spine. She hadn't died, but she'd also never grown out of it. Her body had stooped to accommodate the curve of her back. She'd lived with it her whole life. Her family had wrapped themselves around her to protect her, making it impossible to forget.

It wasn't their fault that she felt their care like alcohol poured over an open wound, burning and healing at the same time.

But she'd thought that here she could be different. Here she'd thought she could prove that she didn't need them to take care of her. She hadn't realized they'd already decided she'd never get that far. And they'd taken steps to ensure it.

Darryn stared at her, perfectly reasonable. "Rowan, you know we just want what's best for you."

She swallowed down the bitter taste in her mouth and choked back the argument that she was years older than him.

She should be taking care of him. Not the other way around.

"You still have your place here with Jannik," Darryn said. "It's not like we've taken that away from you."

No, they'd just made it mean something different. She gave him a tight-lipped smile. "That's true. It's not like you can draw his maps."

He laughed. "Right. Everyone's good at something. Even if it's just writing."

He didn't even see the insult in that. Her ink-stained fingers might have been a good thing for Jannik, but around her family, it just reminded them that all she was good for was writing things down.

Scribes weren't exactly a commodity back home. Their father was a farmer and so was their neighbor and so was his neighbor. No one needed anything written except when it came time to send the taxes to Lord Hax, and most of them just used tallies. When her mother had found her a tutor to teach her to read, Rowan had been so proud. She'd thought it made her special. She hadn't realized yet that she needed to read because she was good for nothing else worthwhile.

He clapped her on the shoulder, lightly so as not to make her wince. "Hey, if you make all the maps, that means you can help us find that artifact?"

Rowan froze, the fake smile turning to a grimace on her face.

Esrell laughed. "What? You think you're an antiquarian now?"

Darryn shrugged. "Jannik said he'd give a reward to anyone who found his great-grandfather and that artifact. He didn't say you had to be an antiquarian. And that reward will be enough to send home, right?"

Jannik must have devoted most of his slim salary to the reward he was promising for whoever found evidence of his great-grandfather.

Darryn whistled through his teeth.

"There's still a lot of digging left to do," Rowan said, quickly. "Before we can really start looking."

"We?" Darryn said, tilting his head.

Rowan flushed. "They," she corrected. "And it could take ages."

A tiny, selfish piece of her wanted him to shrug and give up on the idea before it had settled in his mind.

Rowan hauled herself to her feet, ignoring the hand Darryn held out. She took it once she was standing and squeezed. "You can help Esrell tomorrow. That will teach you a little more about what we do here."

"And what are you going to be doing?"

"Jannik has me mapping the site," she said. "More writing. You'd be bored."

Exploring the ruins and digging through the debris weren't part of her duties. But mapmaking was. She already had a clear understanding of the ruins and their layout. Maybe even better than Jannik. If she could find the likeliest spot—if she found the artifact—it wouldn't just mean impressing Jannik. That money would help her family in a way Esrell and Darryn never could.

Maybe then they'd see how she fit here.

She didn't smile as she turned away from Darryn and Esrell, but a fierce hope beat in her chest.

CHAPTER THREE

ROWAN

After the digging crew was fed the next morning, Rowan gathered a sheaf of parchment and slipped it into the folio she'd made and hung it from her belt. Next came her quill and the bottle of ink, both she tucked carefully in their own places. As the diggers began filing into the ruins, following Jannik's excited voice, Rowan stopped by one of the crates near the far end of camp.

"What's that?" Darryn asked when Rowan cracked open the lid of the crate. Jannik had asked him to clean up the breakfast dishes, and while Darryn had rolled his eyes, he hadn't dared complain to his employer.

"Never you mind, Little Beast," Rowan said. Little clay disks inscribed with three concentric circles filled a small compartment of the crate. Rowan slipped a couple of the fire charges into the pocket of her apron and replaced the lid. It didn't fit well and slid home with a loud thump.

Darryn frowned and cast a quick glance at the retreating backs of the other workers. "Don't call me that. Just because I ruined your doll picnic once when I was three."

Rowan hid a smile. "I'm sorry. It was just for fun."

"I know. But I don't want to be known as Rowan and Esrell's little brother, here. I just want to be Darryn."

She bit her lip and patted him on the head. "All right, Darryn."

He batted at her hand and went back to his dishes, completely forgetting about the crate—as she'd intended.

She wasn't likely to need the disks. But *if* she happened to find anything, the small Land Magic blasting spells would help her exhume it. Because it wasn't like she could swing a pickax, and her fine-haired brushes and the chisel on the other side of her belt might not be enough.

She left Darryn puttering over the cook pot and Esrell yawning over her crates, and Rowan climbed into the ruins. This early in the day, the hike to her vantage at the top of the hill wasn't so hard on her back. She'd slept well enough that she'd woken without pain, and she quickly scaled the peak to look out over the dig site. From here she could see well enough to draw a new map, but this one was different from the rest. This time she sketched landmarks and marked the places she thought were the most promising.

She could see the facility laid out below her with its open rooms and half-tumbled walls. The long hallway led to the central chamber where Jannik directed the diggers, and the sun picked out lighter bits in the stones of the outer rooms. She could imagine the facility and the Giants who had once walked between them. The place was bigger than her village, but overall, there couldn't be more than ten chambers.

At least on the surface.

To the east of Jannik's now-concentrated efforts in the central chamber, stood the stairwell they'd found. It led down into the earth but had been blocked when the ceiling collapsed.

How much of the complex stretched under their feet, hidden and waiting?

Rowan climbed down the other side of the hill and headed for the stairs. That stairwell nagged at Rowan like the beginning of a toothache. Maybe if she poked at it enough, something significant might happen.

It could just be a basement for storage. Maybe they'd find some rotting barrels of ancient mead or root vegetables. That's what their mother had kept in their cellar.

Or it could be something more, the rooms above serving as an antechamber to what was below. An entry hall for the more important underground chambers.

She started from the collapsed stairwell and worked her way out. At first, she'd thought she might be able to blast her way through with the fire charges. That was what they were for after all, used in mines or quarries to break apart rock, but Jannik's patron had sent a few along to expedite the digging in certain places. Obviously, they wouldn't be useful anywhere there might be delicate artifacts, but for clearing rubble, they were ideal.

Except who knew how far the blockage extended down the stairwell. As soon as she drew even with it enough to peer through the cracks, Rowan realized there was an entire hill's worth of rock in her way. She wouldn't be getting through that with what was in her pockets, and the blast would bring the rest of the workers, plus Jannik, before she even knew what was down there.

No, she needed to find another way down.

She moved in concentric circles, marking off the areas she'd already searched on her map so she didn't backtrack by accident. She looked for anything that might lead downward. Stairs, drainage pipes, air holes. She even looked for collapsed tunnels or rooms where the roof had caved in.

No such luck.

The sun had started descending toward the opposite end of the ruin when she paused to rest her hip against a moss-covered stone. She scrubbed her sweaty forehead with the back of her hand and spat stray curls out of her mouth.

Well, she'd learned one thing today. How to feel foolish in just a few hours. Had she really expected to find Jannik's great-grandfather and his famous artifact on the very first day she'd been looking? Jannik was a seasoned antiquarian and had been searching for years, exhausting site after site before finally arriving at this one. Rowan had only been his assistant for three months.

The sounds of digging lessened over at the other end of the ruins and Rowan could imagine they were taking their lunch break, a chance to rest against the stones and pass around some bread and cheese. Her mouth watered.

She straightened up with a groan and stepped across the lumpy ground, avoiding the obvious rubble covered with moss and grass. Ahead, the walls fell away and the ground smoothed a little between her and the next ruined wall, leaving a much easier path. She gravitated that way, but the moment her boot fell on the slightly depressed ground, it seemed to give a little under her feet.

Her heart plummeted. Soft ground at a dig site signaled danger to anyone with an ounce of sense.

Rowan threw herself backward, but not before the ground fell out from under her feet. She plummeted fast enough she couldn't even scream.

* * *

For three full heartbeats, Rowan thought the earth had swallowed her, boots, belt, and all. Then she landed with a bone jarring thump, and all the breath raced from her lungs. She didn't have the time—let alone air—to scream.

Pain radiated out from her spine, and her fingers clenched involuntarily at the soft, sifting dirt beneath her. Even more alarming were the sparks flitting across her vision, like fireflies across the sun.

Finally, she sucked in a breath. She blinked away the flashes of light until she realized that she was staring up at a Rowan-shaped hole in the ground.

Up. Not down. Ground was not supposed to be above anything. That was kind of the point.

Rowan groaned and tried to roll, finding that her body still worked, and she hadn't actually broken anything. A huge blessing considering how she'd blundered into an excessively stupid mistake. She'd guessed there were underground chambers, and she hadn't waited for the workers to make sure the site was stable before tromping around looking for a way down.

Well, she'd found a way down all right.

She stifled a moan and pushed up on her elbows, ignoring the new twinges in her back. Then she put a hand to her head and peered at her new surroundings.

She'd fallen into a long, narrow hallway, and from the looks of it, the ceiling had collapsed long ago, leaving only a deceptively thick carpet of moss and grass to cover the gaps.

The hallway stretched in front of her and behind in an unbroken line, and the walls rose above her, smooth and twice as tall as Darryn.

There was no way she was climbing out by herself. She opened her mouth to yell for help and hesitated.

The hall led from the same direction as the stairwell she'd been surveying, and the afternoon sun streamed through the hole she'd made, providing light. The hall continued on behind her, an unknown portal that could lead to anything.

This was what she'd wanted. She'd found what she was looking for, even if it had been by accident. Surely it wouldn't hurt if she explored just a bit before she called for a rescue.

Rowan climbed out of the dislodged dirt and grass and faced the open hallway. With one hand on the wall to steady herself, she crept forward. Her shadow stretched long ahead of her, disappearing into the gloom beyond.

She counted thirty steps before her shadow blended into the darkness around her and she had to squint to see anything ahead of her.

Just a little bit more, she told herself. *Why didn't I think to bring something as simple as flint and tinder?*

Thirty more steps, and her eyes had adjusted enough to see the edges of the hallway.

Rowan bit her lip. Hallways usually led somewhere. They had rooms leading off them, or they opened onto other passageways. But this one remained straight, as if leading to one place.

It ended in a door of stone, tall enough to admit a draft horse.

Rowan's heart thumped. This had to be important. Someone had built this hallway to lead to this room for a reason.

The door sat in its frame, a solid piece of rock set perfectly flush with the wall.

Rowan ran her hands over the polished surface, looking for a handle or latch, but it was unbroken and unyielding. Pushing on it did nothing, though that wasn't surprising given her lack of strength. Her seeking hands found a panel beside the door, as smooth as glass, but it didn't seem to mean anything. There was no etching on it, and the door remained firmly shut no matter what she did.

She ran her fingertips along the joint between the door and the door frame and didn't even find a crack.

This door was sealed. Not like rubble had blocked the stairwell. This seemed sealed on purpose.

Just like a hallway had to lead somewhere, a sealed door had to be sealed for a reason.

Now she really should call for help, but something stopped her. Something more than just the curiosity she'd been following. A feeling tugged in her gut, uncomfortable and compelling. She needed to see what was behind the door.

She drew the little clay disks from the pocket of her apron. The fire charges carried a blasting spell laid there by a Land Magician. The most expensive equipment at the dig, but if the door really was guarding something important, it would be well worth it.

She hadn't used one before, but the concept was simple enough even for the workers. And Rowan had been on track to become a mage, even if she'd failed.

She shook her head, and before she could think better of it, she broke the first disk in half, severing the bonds on the magic inside.

Then she dropped the two halves at the bottom corners of the door and ran for it, each step jolting in her spine.

Halfway down the hall, she crouched and covered her head, and a second later a bang echoed up the corridor as the magic arced between the two halves of the fire charge.

The spell resulted in a disappointing hairline crack across the otherwise smooth door.

She'd give it one more try. And if it didn't work it would be time to call for help. Perhaps patience and pickaxes would work better.

She broke another fire charge and sprinted down the hall again.

This time a crack and a muffled thud followed the bang, and she returned to the door with her heart in her throat.

A chunk had fallen out of the door, leaving a hole large enough Rowan could squeeze through.

She took a deep breath and ducked her head, sticking her shoulder and one leg through the hole, shimmying through until she spilled out on the other side.

Only when she straightened did she realize she could see better than in the hallways.

A steady glow came from the back of the small room, through another hall. It illuminated the walls and rubble piled in the corners of the antechamber. The remains could have once been barrels or furniture, but now it was just burned and blackened debris. An ancient fire had stained the walls dark with soot and left a coating of ash over the floor at her feet.

She shuffled forward, holding her breath as she moved into the hallway beyond. The tug in her gut turned into a knot of anticipation.

Another room opened before her, lined with stone tables and benches, all built for someone taller than even her brother. The fire hadn't reached here, but tools lay scattered across the tabletops and floor as if blasted back.

It looked like a workroom or maybe a mage's laboratory, left spotless except for the dropped tools.

Her boot stirred a pile of ancient dust strangely incongruous in the otherwise stark room.

Against the far wall, a black, metal arch framed a pedestal which held a gold and silver lantern glowing with a cold, white light. Where the sun painted the world in yellow and gold hues, this washed the room in a sickly silver unlike any lightstone she'd ever seen.

Hanging beside it in midair, as if floating in a spell, was a young man.

Stefan had told them stories at bedtime of princesses cursed to sleep for a hundred years until someone woke them.

But no one would be waking this young man. His lips were blue with death, and one blemish marred his skin, an open sore on his neck. His chest had certainly been still for years, decades, maybe centuries, but he looked like he'd died yesterday.

Rowan had to swallow several times to clear the lump in her throat. Then she turned around, squeezed back out through the crack in the door, and made her way to the jagged hole in the ceiling.

Only then did she start yelling.

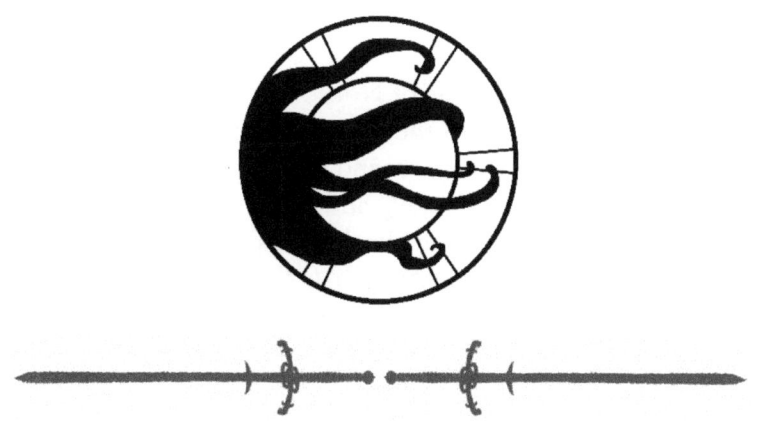

CHAPTER FOUR

ROWAN

The laboratory seemed much smaller with Esrell, Darryn, Jannik, Rowan, and all five workers squeezed between its walls. Their voices rang with wonder and excitement as Rowan stood back and surveyed her find.

"It's... strange," Esrell said, peering over the shoulder of a worker who examined the lantern and the pedestal it rested on. She glanced at Rowan's face. "Beautiful," she added quickly. "But strange. Never seen a lightstone like it."

"There's something about it," Darryn said. He waited by the door. The others seemed wary of the young man floating in the archway, and Darryn had refused even to come into the room with the rest of them. "Why is it still glowing? Shouldn't the flame have gone out a million years ago?"

Rowan scoffed. Hadn't he ever heard of magic? But before she could defend her find, Jannik looked up from the archway. "The Noksonoi have not been gone for nearly that long, Darryn," he said. "A mere seventeen-hundred years compared to a million."

Darryn rubbed his hands together, a nervous habit leftover from childhood. "Oh, right. I know my lamp oil lasts that long."

"Noksonoi?" Esrell said.

"That is what the Giants of Noksonon were called. And sites like this—" he gestured to the laboratory around them "—their strongholds and places of study and residence were nuraghis."

Rowan knew this already, and it didn't answer the real question burning a hole in the back of her brain. *What did I find? Is this the artifact Jannik was looking for? Is this his long-lost forefather?*

"Why is he floating like that?" Darryn asked, and Rowan bit her lip to keep from snapping at him to hold his tongue. Jannik couldn't concentrate if her brother kept prattling.

"It's a stasis spell. Designed to preserve things exactly as they are for centuries. It seems he found something the Giants were trying to protect and was caught in the trap."

Rowan's chest swelled. If the Giants were trying to protect the lantern, then it must be important. "Will you be able to get the lantern out?"

Jannik tapped the side of his nose. "Fortunately, I am familiar with many Noksonoi traps, and I believe we've found the trigger for this one. If you press here and here simultaneously..." He gestured to two of the workers who coordinated their efforts on either side of the archway. As they touched the gleaming black metal, something flashed under the archway, and the body of the young man slumped to the ground.

The workers all stepped back with matching grimaces.

Rowan expected Jannik to rush for the lantern, but he turned away, leaving it on its pedestal as he ran his hands along the tables, squinting at each tool.

"Jannik?" she said.

He waved a hand without sparing her a glance. "Go ahead. I don't see any more traps."

He didn't want to do the honors? Maybe he wanted her to feel in charge. It was her find after all.

Rowan held her breath and stepped forward. She hesitated before placing her hands on the handle of the lantern and lifting it free of the pedestal.

Her first find. She turned to beam at Jannik.

He pushed on the edge of a table as if trying to move it, but it was attached to the wall.

What was he doing? Everything important was right here.

"Can we see it?" one of the workers asked, holding out his hands.

Rowan fought the ridiculous urge to clutch her find to her chest. She looked at Jannik, certain he wouldn't want this thing passed around like some cheap novelty.

But Jannik poked at the stones of the wall as if looking for hidden compartments or passageways. "It's all right, Rowan. They won't hurt it, I'm sure."

"You don't want to look at it first?" She released the lantern to the nearest worker with a swiftly hidden wince. "You're the expert. I don't even know what it is."

He laughed, short and loud. "It's a lantern. A light source. A magical one at that, one much more long-lasting and powerful than lightstones."

She blinked and her cheeks burned. Of course, it was a lantern, but surely there was more to it than that?

She tried to smile as the workers passed the pretty, golden thing from one to another, each exclaiming and admiring as it went around the room.

Rowan glanced between Jannik and the lantern and the young man, teeth clenched tight enough to hurt. "What about the body?"

"What about it?" Jannik whirled on her, brows coming down in a heavy frown. "Can't you see I'm looking for something here, Rowan?"

She jerked back, mouth snapping closed on her arguments.

This… this wasn't his artifact then. If he was still looking for it, then she hadn't found what he'd been searching for.

She swallowed back the bitter knot in her throat and knelt beside the young man who lay forgotten by the pedestal.

"Don't touch him," Darryn hissed from the doorway.

She pursed her lips, ignoring her brother and fought not to show her disappointment.

Jannik ran his hands over his hair and took a breath. Then he hunkered down beside her.

"I'm sorry, Rowan. I'm just… I thought maybe this was it."

She nodded, not trusting herself to speak yet. She had too.

She cleared her throat and nodded to the young man. "I thought this might be your great-grandfather."

The young man looked like he could have been asleep, but she didn't need to check to know he was long since dead. A stasis spell preserved things like fruits and vegetables for a time, or it could trap a person in one place, but that person would not survive the experience.

He chuckled, but his eyes were sad. "No. Hardly. My great-grandfather was almost fifty when he disappeared. This fellow couldn't have been much more than twenty." He gestured to the young man's worn tunic. "Not much to go on by his clothes, but he could have wandered in here anywhere from fifty to two hundred years ago. An unfortunate treasure hunter who got caught in a Noksonoi trap."

Rowan held her breath, guarding against the sharp stab of disappointment in her chest. "Then the lantern really isn't what you were looking for," she said so only he could hear. "It's not the artifact."

"No," Jannik's eyes flicked to the others where they laughed and passed the lantern over to Esrell. "I may not know much about what he was hunting, but I know my great-grandfather wasn't looking for a light source. It's still an incredible find, though, Rowan. You should be proud."

Rowan's lips thinned, but she tried to smile at him. It wasn't herself she wanted to make proud.

"Leave it to me," Esrell was saying as she took the lantern in her hands. "I don't trust you clumsy louts to get this thing to the surface in one piece."

"Come," Jannik said, his hand squeezing Rowan's shoulder. "You can help me search the room. Let's see if there's anything we missed before we get back to the sunlight."

Rowan let him help her off the ground and followed as the others left and Jannik hurried from wall to wall, tapping over and over again, looking for something that wasn't there.

● ● ●

In the evening, as the sun sank behind the hill and spilled shadows through the ruins, they buried the young man from the laboratory. The diggers had rigged a blanket sling so they didn't have to touch him and only stuck around long enough to help lower the body into its grave. None of them wanted to stay to say any words.

"What's wrong with them?" Rowan asked Darryn who picked up the shovel to start filling in the grave.

Darryn glanced at the workers heading back to camp. "Well, I don't know about them, but I know I don't really like this fellow."

"Why not? It's not his fault he's dead."

"How do you know?"

She put her hands on her hips and stared down at the young man lying lonely at the bottom of the hole. "Well, I guess I have no idea, but it seems cruel to judge someone who's not around to defend themselves."

"It's just… creepy," Darryn said. "He's a million years old—"

"Two hundred at most," she corrected.

"—but he looks like he stuck around after he was gone. Maybe he's watching us now." Darryn gave a theatrical shudder.

Rowan made a face. "That's ridiculous."

Darryn shrugged. "I'm just saying, that's why no one likes him."

"I feel kind of sorry for him," Rowan said as Darryn stuck the shovel into the mound of soft dirt.

"Why?" he asked with a grunt.

"Because the only two people here at his funeral don't even know who he is to mourn him. Wait a second."

Rowan squatted beside the grave and swung her legs over.

"What are you doing?" Darryn cried, tossing aside the shovel.

Rowan slid to the bottom of the hole, ignoring the ache in her spine. "I just want to know who he was. I want someone to mourn him."

The young man's dark hair fell across his forehead, overlong like Darryn's. Someone so young surely still had a mother when he'd died. How long had she waited for him to come home? Did he have any brothers or nephews who'd looked for him like Jannik had been searching for his great-grandfather?

She had no idea if he'd believed in an afterlife or if he prescribed to the idea that he'd be reborn, like the villagers she'd grown up with. But it seemed wrong to pile dirt on top of him without any sort of acknowledgment.

"I'm sorry," she whispered. "Rest well, finally."

A polished wooden ring adorned his finger still. They'd left it alone because the simple carved band wasn't worth anything, and no one would admit to wanting to rob the dead, but maybe Rowan's gift would be able to tell her a little about his life before he'd died so unceremoniously and went into the ground to be forgotten.

She pulled it from his hand, and as it slipped off his finger, his entire body collapsed, falling to dust. Even his clothes disintegrated before her eyes.

Rowan gasped and lurched back.

From his vantage Darryn cried out. "What was that?"

Rowan fought to keep her breath even. "I think he was very, very old. Maybe his body finally realized how old, now that he wasn't in the spell anymore."

"Well, get out of there. Come on, Rowan. I'm not letting you sit down there with a disintegrating corpse."

She held up her hand, and Darryn helped pull her from the grave.

"You're crazy," he told her as she dusted her hands off on her apron.

"He's gone, Darryn. He can't do anything to me now. Do you need any help with this?"

Darryn tossed the first shovel full of dirt into the hole. "Definitely not from you. I'm filling this in, and then I'm forgetting all about it. Go back to your own thing."

She hesitated. For a moment she could feel what Darryn was talking about, as if someone watched the back of her head, making her neck prickle. She stuck the ring in her pocket, promising herself she'd investigate further when she had a chance.

Then she shook the feeling off and went to find Jannik.

He stood in his tent, bent over a table strewn with her maps. A lantern—a normal one—illuminated his work against the coming night.

"We buried our unknown man," she told him quietly.

"Thank you," Jannik said, giving her a warm smile before going back to his maps.

"There's more. He... he collapsed into dust when I touched him."

Jannik's wide mouth dipped in a frown. "Interesting. I wonder if that was a delayed effect of the stasis. Or a reaction to its disruption. The body held together for long enough to move him out, but no longer. I suppose we're lucky he didn't disintegrate on our way back to camp." He shrugged. "Well, he's gone now, and I don't have time to dwell on who he was."

Rowan touched her pocket where the ring sat. She would have to be the one to care about the young man. "What are you working on?"

"Trying to decide where to concentrate our efforts tomorrow. Maybe there are more underground tunnels. Though the last one didn't seem to lead anywhere else."

Rowan's brow drew down. "You didn't want to study the lantern?"

He blinked at her. "Why would I? It's not my great-grandfather's legacy."

Her mouth opened and closed before she found the words she was looking for. "Because it's clearly important. This whole facility was built to house that one laboratory. I mean, I *think* it was. Surely it warrants some examination."

Jannik rubbed his hands over his face. "It's a lamp. And I'm sure it has an interesting story, but I need to concentrate my efforts to find my great-grandfather and his artifact. That is what Lord Hax pays me for. And I would like to show him some progress when he visits."

It wasn't like Jannik to turn away from an interesting problem. She remembered countless nights around their family table as he helped her stepfather with a tricky engineering problem. A water wheel that spun too slow, or a plow that broke too often.

"I thought Lord Hax paid you to find Giant artifacts," she said. "What's so important about this one that it supersedes everything else? How do you know the lantern isn't it?"

Jannik blew out his breath and turned to rest his hip against the table. "I haven't told this to the diggers. I don't want anyone getting the wrong idea, but my great-grandfather was looking for a weapon. Something the Giants called the Grief Draw. It sounds fearsome. As if it brought them much pain. My great-grandfather promised it to Lord Hax—the current lord's grandfather—over a hundred years ago. Then he disappeared."

Rowan waited.

"When he failed to deliver this great weapon, my family bore the shame of his broken oath. We've been beholden to Lord Hax and his sons ever since. He's not my patron because he chose me. He's my patron because I'm still trying to pay him back for that failed promise so long ago."

"So, you want to find that weapon," Rowan said.

"I have to redeem my great-grandfather. Prove he didn't just run away from his obligations. Or worse, take the weapon for himself. If I can redeem that old man, then my family will be free of his debt."

Rowan's fingers ran up and down the length of her arm, a frown pulling at her eyebrows. From everything she'd heard of Lord Hax, she thought it was probably a good thing he didn't have this mystical weapon. Too many older boys from her village had marched off to fight the little battles he'd picked with his neighbors and never come home.

But if Jannik was beholden to this man, then he would never let this go. Even when there was a magnificent discovery staring him in the face.

"I understand," she said quietly. She almost didn't say the next part, remembering how he'd snapped at her in the underground laboratory when she'd pushed him about something he considered unimportant. "But would you mind if I looked into the lantern? Maybe it can help you."

He'd gone back to the maps she'd drawn, but he waved a hand at her. "Of course. Take my notes. Maybe something in there can be of assistance."

She slipped the notebook off the table beside him, honored that he'd let her handle it, then she let herself out of the tent without bothering him further.

A white glow led her to the table where Esrell usually worked. Her sister stood with the lantern in her hands, frowning into its light.

"I'm going to take it to make some notes, all right?" Rowan told Esrell.

Esrell blinked as if coming back from some distant thought and held the lantern out to her. "Of course. Gladly. I think the light is giving me a headache."

"Oh no. Are you all right?"

Esrell rubbed her forehead. "I just need to lie down. I think I'll make it an early night."

Rowan nodded. "Good idea. I'll take this somewhere else so the light doesn't bother you."

"Thanks," she said and headed for their tent, her hand still to her head.

Rowan frowned down at the lantern. "Now," she said. "Let's figure out why you're so important. And maybe we can come up with some other way to repay Jannik's debt to Lord Hax."

CHAPTER FIVE

ROWAN

Rowan hunched over the makeshift table she'd erected in the shade of one of the ruined walls. The wall kept the sun from washing out the light of the lantern, and since that was the part she wanted to study, she needed the shadows. She would have used their tent, but Esrell had slept in this morning and Rowan didn't want to wake her.

She nibbled on the end of her quill before adding a detail to the sketch she'd made. She was having a hard time depicting the abstract design that decorated the cap where the handle connected, the interlocking pattern detailed enough to tax her drawing skills.

She stretched out a fingertip and tapped one of the five glass panes that covered the flame. The fire hung in the center, burning with a steady, white light far clearer than any candle or fire, without a wick or wax or oil to consume.

"What is keeping you lit? No lightstone I've ever heard of lasts for centuries," she whispered and rested her chin on her hands to peer at it. The light might not have been giving her a headache, but the mystery of it would soon.

The ruins around her bustled with activity, the workers clearing the site and laying down boards as pathways to the different parts of the dig. Lord Hax would arrive at any minute, and Jannik wanted everything perfect.

Rowan had cleaned up as much as she could around camp before deciding she'd better make way for the others to do the heavy lifting.

Her lips twisted in thought, and she glanced at Jannik's notes open on the table next to hers. But she hadn't found any mentions of a light source.

As far as she could see, there was no way to open the lantern to tend the flame. The glass panes stretched unbroken between the gold and silver supports, though there were ridges on either side of each pane.

She added to her notes.

> *No way to open.*
> *Flame constant.*
> *How would you relight it if it went out?*

Not that it had gone out, and she couldn't see any way to douse the light either. Last night she'd had to throw a blanket over it to hide the light so she could sleep.

Rowan could see the usefulness of a light that never went out, but surely not being able to control it would get annoying sooner rather than later.

She tapped the glass again. Maybe it was some kind of failed experiment. But then why leave it in its own facility?

"Rowan!" Darryn's voice broke her concentration. "What are you doing over here? Lord Hax just arrived." He took her elbow and tried to steer her away from the table.

Her breath caught, but she resisted him long enough to tuck the lantern and her notes into the empty crate sitting beside the table.

Jannik stood at the far end of the ruins beside their little camp. Several men and half a dozen horses milled around the tents, and Jannik bobbed his head at one in particular, a tall, broad-shouldered figure dressed in crimson and amber brocade.

She slipped in beside Jannik, folding her hands in front of her clean apron. Darryn joined the workers who were headed into the ruins looking busy and profitable. Esrell packed a crate at her table, looking pale even in the bright sunlight.

"My lord, I thought you'd stay for longer. To observe the site and inspect our work," Jannik said.

Lord Hax raised his chin and gave the site a cursory glance. "A day is all I can spare for something so small. I wouldn't have stopped at all except it was on the way. And you promised me results."

He speared Jannik with his steely gaze. Rowan had never seen eyes that color, a curiously light blue, the same color as a winter sky.

Rowan ran her thumb over her knuckle, watching Jannik.

"Digging takes time, my lord. Digging carefully takes even longer."

Rowan glanced between Jannik's panicked expression and Lord Hax's frown. "We have found some things," she said, steeling herself to speak. "If you'd like to take a look…"

Lord Hax turned to her with a scowl. He looked her up and down, eyes lingering on her high shoulder. "Did you say something, godsblighted?"

Rowan jerked back a step. Her jaw clenched.

"It's no wonder you haven't found anything useful to me. The gods are punishing her for a past life and now she's spreading her bad luck here."

Rowan bit her tongue hard enough to taste blood. She absolutely could not say what she was thinking. Not to a baron. And definitely not to someone who held so much of Jannik's life in his hands.

Jannik's eyes flicked to her and back to Lord Hax. "My lord, you know that's a silly superstition. Rowan is a valuable member of my team."

Gratitude swelled in her chest, but Lord Hax continued to scowl at her.

"I think you should see our lantern, my lord," Jannik said. "At the very least it is interesting—"

"Interesting will not get you anywhere," Lord Hax said. He turned his shoulder to exclude Rowan completely. "You promised me a weapon, the same as your idiot grandfather. I have wasted enough time and money indulging you with this, but no more. If you do not deliver on your promise in the next two weeks, I am scrapping the whole project, and you will become the custodian for my personal collection. No funding, no assistants, and no redemption for your family."

Lord Hax spun on his heel, leaving Jannik gaping behind him.

"My lord!" Jannik scrambled after the baron, casting Rowan a panicked look. "Two weeks is just not reasonable..." His voice trailed off as they moved out of sight.

Healer's Ghost, had she made that worse? Or had Lord Hax come here specifically to deliver his ultimatum?

Either way, the dig was thrown into a frenzy for the rest of the day. The diggers rushed to excavate the central chamber and the surrounding rooms while Jannik paced from one end of the site to the other, watching their progress with too-bright eyes.

Rowan worked late that night trying to keep Jannik's notes up to date but his clipped answers to her suggestions made her finally realize he just wanted to be left alone to supervise the digging. Any other thoughts or study could come later when he'd secured what he needed.

Rowan remained subdued the next morning when she took the lantern from its crate and set it back on the table.

She placed both hands flat on either side of the lantern.

Lord Hax had dismissed it out of hand. Jannik didn't have time for it. But something had made the Giants lock this thing away in that laboratory. Something made this lantern important and if she could get Jannik to see it for just a second, maybe she could save him from Lord Hax's threat.

She had one last choice if she wanted to learn more about the lantern. She didn't love using her gift, since it had failed her so often, but maybe just this once it could pull Jannik out of his panic.

Before she could talk herself out of it, she traced a finger down the glass and felt for the traces of heat left behind by hands. A few touchpoints gathered around the panes of glass, but the most concentrated flare of warmth came from the handle.

Well, that made sense.

The spark behind her eyes responded, reaching out to form a bridge with the heat on the handle, and a black wave crashed across her vision, drawing her into a vision of the lantern's past.

The darkness flashed to life in a smear of color, and she saw the shining edge of something sharp slash down.

Rowan flinched, but the vision was just an image, and even if it startled her, it couldn't hurt her. A light flared, replacing the black, and with it came a piercing scream. It tore into Rowan's heart, and her breath caught in her throat as panic coursed down her limbs, urging her to flee. Her mouth went dry with a clear and sudden certainty.

This was her end. Under the fear and the panic, flowed a sense of inevitability. There would be no escape as a dreadful acceptance made her limbs heavy.

And suddenly it was done. Rowan found herself on her hands and knees beside the table, panting, the lingering sense of dread crowding her thoughts and the taste of blood gathering on the back of her tongue. Her breath came in uncontrolled gulps, and she clutched at her heart, willing it to stop thundering in her chest.

"Healer's Ghost, what was that?" She stared at the lantern, hands trembling.

The visions, the tiny little glimpses of the past had never come with *feelings* before. They'd always been little bits of an image, a split second of time that she had to mull over to make sense of. If she ever made sense of it at all.

This... this had felt like a sliver of someone's life.

No, not life. This had been a sliver of death.

Rowan tried to climb to her feet, but it took several tries before she could get her shaking limbs to cooperate and her cramped back to unbend. She braced her hands on the table, gripping the edge to steady herself. The lantern sat unmoved in the center, completely oblivious to the anguish it had just caused.

So, what had she seen? The blur of colors could have been anything, and there was no way she was going to try touching it again to see more. But the bright edge had clearly been a blade. That would explain the terror and the sudden finality.

Rowan swallowed. Dread filled her gut like a stone when she glanced at the lantern. She wanted to bury it. To throw it back into the pit she'd taken it out of and shovel the dirt and grass and stone over top of it.

Rowan shook her head. Why did she feel that about an inanimate object? Especially one so valuable. It might not be what Jannik was looking for, but as soon as he could see past his obsession, he would realize what they held. He would be able to find the words to convince Lord Hax that this magical artifact was enough to pay his debt.

Wouldn't he?

Jannik was the smartest man she knew. He was just letting other things get in the way right now. A baron would surely be interested in the lantern once its value was explained to him.

And this dread is just imaginary. What harm could a lantern do?

She drew in a deep breath and forced herself to reach for the lantern. To convince herself that it was innocuous.

As her fingers touched the gleaming metal, a voice speared into her head, fragments of words jumbling together so that nothing made sense.

"He-me... Hoo-poss-pa-lp-no!"

Rowan winced. The voice had edges sharp enough to cut while the rest was muffled and broken, like pieces of a glass ornament tumbling around in a sack.

She snatched her hands away from the lantern and stuffed them under her armpits. Was she hearing things now? Random voices were never a great thing.

Healer's Ghost, she was going mad. Her gift must have shattered and left her holding the pieces of her mind.

None of this made sense. Her gift wasn't about voices. It didn't let her hear the past. And besides, this had been different. Something else entirely.

Esrell had claimed the light gave her a headache. Rowan could feel the edges of her own headache coming on. Maybe her sister had experienced the same thing. Maybe the lantern wasn't just a light. Maybe it was designed to drive people insane.

Rowan grabbed the blanket she'd used the night before and tossed it over the lantern. She wasn't touching it with her bare hands again until she figured out what it was.

Then she tucked it under her arm and went to find Esrell.

CHAPTER SIX

ROWAN

The silence of the ruins registered just before Rowan stepped into camp. The usual sounds of digging and the calls of men working were absent. Rowan's brow drew down as she came around the corner of the first tent and nearly ran into Darryn, who carried a shovel over his shoulder.

"Where are you going?" Rowan asked, readjusting the lantern under its blanket.

Darryn cocked a thumb at the ruins. "Jannik asked me to dig," he said. "Does this mean I'm getting a promotion?"

"I don't know." Rowan squinted around camp. "Why are *you* digging? Did he find something and he needs more workers?"

Darryn shook his head. "Some of the others came down with something. One threw up last night. They're sleeping it off today, so I'm filling in. I don't want to be late." He started walking backward. "See you at supper time?"

"Sure," she said with a distracted frown.

Usually when everyone woke up with a stomachache, it meant something was wrong with the meal the night before. But

Rowan felt fine, and she'd eaten from the same pot as everyone else.

Esrell wasn't at her usual table.

Rowan lifted the flap to their tent and peeked inside. She recoiled with her hand over her nose. Whatever the problem was, Esrell had it too. The acrid smell of vomit came from a pot at the head of Esrell's bedroll.

Her sister winced away from the light spilling in from the tent flap.

"Healer's Ghost, are you all right?" Rowan asked before she could bite the question back. She hated when anyone asked her that, especially when the answer was obvious.

She knelt beside Esrell and put the back of her hand to her sister's forehead.

"Don't," Esrell said, her voice a croak. "You might catch it."

Rowan wanted to argue that she didn't care, but she was only good to Jannik if she was well enough to work.

"When did this start?" she asked instead.

"Last night."

"Is it just the vomiting?" Rowan wasn't as clever with healing as her mother was, but she'd watched Nora nurse nearly everyone in the village. So she at least knew the right questions to ask.

"Yes," Esrell said, but Rowan caught the way she hesitated before answering.

Esrell's skin was clammy, but that could be the nausea as much as it could be fever.

"Is there anything I can do?"

Esrell started to shake her head then paused. "Water?" she said.

Rowan found a cup and filled it at the water barrel before returning to the tent. When Esrell reached out to grasp the cup, she winced, and Rowan bit her lip at the sight of blisters on Esrell's palms. The moment she'd taken a sip, Esrell put the cup down and hid her hands again.

Rowan's face must have given her away because Esrell tried to smile. "It's fine," she said. "I'll be fine. I just need to rest for a bit, and then I'll be up and working again. I promise."

Rowan cupped her elbows as she sat on her heels beside her sister. The words were so familiar they bit at Rowan's resolve. She knew exactly what it was like to hide her pain so her family wouldn't worry.

She should insist Darryn take Esrell home. Blisters, fever, and nausea? Rowan didn't know anything that would cause all that, but their mother might.

But she didn't want to humiliate her sister by making them leave. That's how Rowan would feel if it was her. She'd feel like she'd somehow failed.

"Go on," Esrell said. "I don't want you to get sick too."

Rowan gathered the lantern against her chest and chewed her lip.

She wouldn't insist Esrell go home. She'd respect her sister when she said she just needed rest. Of course, that didn't mean she had to abandon Esrell completely.

"All right," she said. "But I'm coming back to check on you later. I'll just be right outside, so yell if you need anything."

Esrell nodded, her eyes already closing in sleep.

Rowan backed out of the tent and let the flap drop. She stared at the weave of the canvas for a long time, the faint sounds of retching coming from some of the other tents.

Just the day before, Lord Hax had stood there at the corner of Jannik's tent and browbeat him about not having any results yet. And with Esrell out of commission and the rest of the workers sick, his progress would slow to a crawl.

❧   ❧   ❧

Jannik hadn't returned from the dig by the time the sun started its descent, but Rowan couldn't imagine he was making a ton of progress with just Darryn digging for him. She hoped the two of them didn't run into any more problems like she had with the collapsing tunnel.

But Jannik had already proved he was experienced with Giants' strongholds. He knew better than to stumble around places where the ground was soft.

Rowan stared at the cloth-covered bundle standing on Esrell's table, her lips thin. She'd finished all the busy work around camp, plus she'd finished packing the crates Esrell had left undone.

There was nothing left except the lantern. And she'd never figure out why it was so important if she kept it all wrapped up and never looked at it again.

She took a deep breath and steadied her hands against the table. "You'd better be worth something," she said.

In one swift move, before she could think better of it, she yanked the blanket from the lantern. The light sprang out, throwing her misshapen shadow across the canvas walls of the nearby tents. The lantern squatted there, like a beautiful mistake.

But she'd already made her decision. Wavering now was just cowardice.

She rubbed her hands together, preparing herself for the worst and placed her palms on the lantern.

The voice speared short and sharp and still jumbled into her head. Fragments of words and sounds raced through her, concentrating in the pain behind her eyes.

Rowan couldn't help yanking her hands back again. *What was this? Some side effect or leftover piece from my vision earlier? Is my gift growing? Or is it being corrupted?*

She hauled in a deep breath and glared at the lantern. "This isn't going to work if you keep yelling at me," she said as if it could listen to her. "Now, behave."

She gritted her teeth and placed one hand on the handle.

This time there was an entire breath before the voice came again, and when it came, it was the barest thread weaving through her thoughts. Like a whisper just too faint to catch.

"…pleassse…mmmeee…gainnn"

She leaned closer. That had sounded closer to actual words.

"Wait, can you actually understand me?" She crouched so her gaze was level with the constant flame inside the lantern. "Try it one more time."

"Please don't put me in the dark again."

Healer's Ghost, that was an actual sentence. But what did it mean about the dark?

Rowan's gaze slid to the blanket pooled on the dirt beside the table.

She gasped and stumbled back, a chill traveling down every inch of her twisted spine. Her fingers went to her cheeks. It was talking. The lantern was actually talking to her. It wasn't a figment of her imagination or a fragmented memory left over from her gift. It was talking to her, reacting to her actions and words.

Her heart raced in her chest. What had she pulled out of the ground? What magic gave life to gold and silver and glass? More than ever, she wished she hadn't failed as a mage. She'd have a much greater chance of knowing the answers to all her questions.

The voice had died away the moment she'd pulled her hands from the lantern. Clearly, she could only hear it when she was touching it.

Much less reluctantly, she grasped the handle again.

"Are you… are you actually talking to me?" The voice sounded inside her head, but she spoke aloud, feeling absolutely ridiculous.

"I think so," the voice said like a thought that wasn't her own. "I mean you could be a… a hallucination. That would be… new. But you don't feel like a hallucination. Do you think you're a hallucination?"

The voice had a tinny, far away quality, and she had a hard time placing its gender. It spoke in fits and starts with strange pauses between words, as if thinking in a foreign cadence.

"No, I'm not a hallucination." Hopefully no one would walk by and see her talking to herself. "I'm sorry, I've never spoken to an inanimate object before."

"Inanimate object?" The voice barked a laugh. "No. I'm not that… stupid hunk of metal. The lantern isn't nearly so e-eloquent. It mostly just sits there and shines."

Rowan's brow furrowed, and she cast a furtive glance around her, but she was still alone. She could hear Jannik and Darryn deeper in the ruins. They must have been on their way back, but they hadn't come into camp yet.

"Then, what are you?"

"Trapped!" the voice said. "Sorry, I've had loads of time to think up bad jokes. I'm inside the lantern. I'm Human. Was Human. Now I'm a lot... a lot less than that. A collection of thoughts and a name. I had a name. What was it? Gav—Gavyn! Yes, I'm Gavyn."

Rowan rubbed her eyes. On a scale of run-of-the-mill to strange, this had fallen off the other end into surreal, but the manners her mother had drilled into her long ago surfaced.

"Hello, Gavyn. I'm Rowan."

"Pleased to meet you," he said, his tinny voice tinged with palpable irony.

A person inside a lantern. She fought to control the hysterical laughter bubbling its way up her throat. Was this the sort of thing she'd have learned to deal with as a mage? It seemed out of the realm of normal, even for people who spent their lives steeped in magic. Or maybe she just lacked imagination.

"How did you get in there?" She tilted the lantern to peer at the light inside. It burned as steadily as it had been for the last day and a half.

"I can see you, you know. I have a... a fabulous view up your nose when you look at it like that."

Rowan glared at the lantern. "Hey, less about my nose and more about your problem, please."

"Sorry, it's just been ages since I had anyone or anything to look at but that laboratory. Even the inside of your nose is preferable."

"Gavyn, answer the question."

"Fine. How did I get trapped in here? A combination of stupidity and... cleverness."

"That doesn't actually answer my question."

"Fair. But the problem is I don't know the answer myself. Believe me, I... I've spent years—decades maybe—coming up with theories. Impossible to tell how long really. I couldn't exactly count the days underground."

Rowan tried to imagine a lifetime underground, trapped in a body that couldn't move or talk or even blink. How sane would she be when someone finally dug her up and carried her into the sunlight? She shuddered.

"Start at the beginning then. Who were you before?"

"A Land Mage. We were trapped for over a month," Gavyn said, his voice gone soft with memory. "Some madman captured eighteen—no twenty?—of us. He... wanted the lantern and made us work on it to make it safe for him. I figured if there wasn't a lantern anymore, then he wouldn't have a reason to hurt anyone ever again. So, I tried to destroy it."

"And it didn't go well."

"Absolutely awful."

Rowan bit her lip. "I'm sorry."

"The only good part is that the madman is no longer around to torment anyone else. Even if it means I spent... however long stuck in that basement."

Rowan's breath escaped with a soft sound as she made the connection between the voice and everything they'd found. "Oh."

"What?"

"Well..." She hesitated. "I'm not sure how to tell you this, but I think you might be dead. We found the body of a young man next to the lantern, trapped in a preservation spell."

"Oh, don't worry," he said, sounding weary. "I knew that part. I can see, remember? My body died but the rest of me didn't. Just out of curiosity, what did you do with me?"

"We gave you a decent burial." She dug in the pocket of her apron. "I did keep this. I thought it might tell me who you were." She held up the simple, wooden ring so that the worn material gleamed in the lantern light.

"A gift from my mother," he said, and she didn't think she was imagining the wistfulness. "She gave it to me when I went to study with my master. It won't tell you anything about me though."

"Well, that's the thing. I have this gift that can sometimes show me a memory of someone who touched something."

"Life Magic!" he exclaimed, the words spearing through her head. "I knew I felt Life Magic when you touched the lantern."

Rowan shook her head. "No, no. It's just a little useless gift. I'm not any kind of mage."

"Even little gifts come from one of the major disciplines. You sense memories?"

"I get tiny little glimpses if someone has touched an object."

"And what did you see when you touched the lantern?"

Her lips thinned. "A sword. I think. But more than that was the feeling of something horrible. It was like I knew I was going to die. There was panic and terror and just an awful sense of ending."

"Ah," Gavyn said, voice quiet. "That would have been me. There was definitely a sword and lots of panic and terror and death. Mine and the man who kidnapped us. Sorry you had to see that. But I think it connected you to me. You couldn't hear me before that, could you?"

"No."

"Ha, I guess that means I'm not exactly dead. Not exactly alive either, but halfway to life is better than no way. Maybe…" He made a noise like an intake of breath, but since a disembodied soul in a lantern didn't actually have any breath, it must have been habit. "Maybe you can help me get out of here. Life Magic might be able to give me new life so to speak. Or—" Now his voice fell. "No, actually that's a bad idea. You should put me back and forget you ever saw this thing."

She'd opened her mouth to argue that her gift would never be strong enough to create a new body. Did magic even do that? But the sudden change in the direction of his thoughts left her reeling.

"Wait," she said. "Why? At least with me you'd have someone to talk to."

"It's not worth it. I would have told you right away, but you started to actually talk back to me, and it was just so good to hear someone and actually be a person again."

"Gavyn, what are you talking about?"

"Right. The lantern. It's dangerous, Rowan. It's a weapon. It kills the people who touch it."

CHAPTER SEVEN

ROWAN

owan's hand slipped from the handle, and she stepped back with a gasp. As soon as her hand left the lantern, Gavyn's voice faded from her mind.

She screwed up her courage and grasped the handle again. "What do you mean?" she asked, voice sharp.

Jannik's weapon was the lantern all along?

"I mean, it kills people," Gavyn said, slow and deliberate. "The man who wanted it seemed to think that was its purpose, and I certainly saw enough death to believe it. Slow, painful death, but maybe it—"

"You're rambling again," Rowan said. "You do that a lot, but if this thing is dangerous, could we hurry it up, please?"

"Yes," he said simply. "Of course. There were mages with me in that laboratory. Almost a dozen. Mostly Land Mages, like me. A couple Life Mages, including a healer. To keep us going."

His voice went soft and gentle for a moment before gaining vehemence again. "Because the lantern kills anyone who spends time touching it. The truth is, I would have been dead anyway even if I hadn't gotten myself welded to the damn thing."

Rowan swallowed, her throat suddenly dry. She glanced at the tent behind her where her sister still lay, struck down by a mysterious malady.

"How does it kill you, Gavyn?"

"It gives you some kind of illness. Not like a plague or anything, but it makes your body sick. First comes the nausea and fever and aches. And then there are blisters and sores. Like your body is falling apart. We never did figure out why it happened. Or how to stop it. It killed everyone before me. I was the last one left, besides our healer."

Rowan's heart shriveled inside her chest. "Gavyn, my sister is sick."

"How so?" he said, voice sharp.

"She's been throwing up. And she has blisters on her palms."

"She held the lantern?"

Rowan nodded. "You see everything, right? She's the other girl in camp. She has long, dark hair, and she carried the lantern up from the laboratory. Did she hold it for long enough to feel its effects?"

A thoughtful pause. "I'm not sure. Time is a little disjointed right now. I'm having a hard time judging hours versus moments but... probably. It doesn't take long." Another pause. "I'm sorry."

Rowan shook her head. "How do I stop it?"

"I don't know. None of the others survived. Anyone who worked with it directly were the worst off. And you've been working with the lantern all day now."

"I feel fine," Rowan snapped. "But Esrell... How long does it take?"

"A couple of days to a couple of weeks depending."

"If we got it away from her, if she wasn't near it anymore, would she recover?"

"Maybe. I don't know." His voice went bitter. "None of us had the luxury to find out."

Rowan winced. Because they'd been locked in with it.

She straightened and then had to ignore the way her back spasmed. Behind her, she could hear Jannik bidding Darryn goodnight.

So many people she cared about were here in camp, where the lantern could kill them.

Where it already was killing them.

She could throw it back down the hole where she'd found it. Would that be far enough away from Esrell and the others to help them?

But what about Gavyn? She would be consigning him to the rest of eternity in the dark with no hope of escape. His voice had gone so bright with hope in those few moments when he'd thought she could help him, before his concern over the lantern had killed his joy.

She wanted to pull her hand from the metal and mitigate her own damage, but she couldn't leave him shouting into the silence without any way to communicate.

"I have to talk to Jannik," she said. She pulled the lantern from the table and swung around so the shadows jumped against the tents.

"You should throw me back into the laboratory and seal it." His voice wobbled. Who knew how much strength it took for him to argue for that?

"Jannik is the wisest person I know," she said. "He'll know what to do. I'm sure of it."

❦ ❦ ❦

Rowan met no one as she raced to Jannik's tent, the lantern clutched in her left hand. Everyone else was either too sick to venture out of their tents or had already gone to sleep.

"Jannik," she called as she pushed through his tent flap.

She startled him as he bent over his table. He dropped his notes, and they cascaded over the surface of the table and onto the ground.

"I know I encourage communication, Rowan," he told her with an indulgent smile, "but it's polite to give a body a little warning."

"I'm sorry, but you need to hear this."

His brow drew down in a heavy frown. "What is it? What's wrong?"

She shook her head, words crowding forward in a jumble so that she didn't even know where to start. She placed the lantern on the table and stepped back to stare at its unwavering light.

"It's not just a lantern," she said softly. "It's so much more complicated than that."

"Tell me." He leaned back against the table.

"The boy we buried. The one we found with the lantern. He's not... completely gone." She gestured to the artifact. "He's trapped inside."

Jannik's mouth fell open, and his eyes flicked between the lantern and Rowan. "What—How do you know this?"

"I can talk to him. Or he can talk to me. I tried to use my gift to show me some of the lantern's past, but I think it connected me to him. He was very hard to understand at first, I think because he's been in there for so long, but his name is Gavyn, and he's been telling me about the lantern's history."

"Extraordinary." Jannik turned to gaze into the light. "To be able to glimpse the past like that with your gift is incredible in and of itself, but to be able to talk to someone who was actually there." He gave her a broad smile. "Your gift is proving invaluable."

Her lips thinned. He was missing the point.

He reached out to touch the pane of glass. "Does he know how to work it?"

"Don't touch it." She barely kept herself from screaming it.

He stepped back, alarmed.

She kept her voice as level as possible. She needed him to listen, not worry if she was unhinged. "Jannik, it kills people."

He glanced at her sharply. "What do you mean?"

She took a deep breath and repeated what Gavyn had told her about the mages who had died, the way the lantern had slowly burned them up and then consumed him.

Jannik crossed his arms over his chest. "Are you sure?"

"I only know what Gavyn's told me, but it sounds bad. Like mass murder through horrible illness."

"It's the weapon," he whispered.

She winced. "Jannik…"

"It's the Grief Draw. You were right all along." He gripped her hands and swooped in to kiss her on the cheek, the bristles of his beard pricking her skin. "You found the artifact."

Rowan's hand crept to her cheek as Jannik spun away. He gathered the notes on his table and snatched up a nearby quill.

"Yes, but—"

"The reward is yours obviously. I imagine you'll want to send it to your family? I hope you will stay on as my assistant. We work very well together, and I need you more than ever now."

He was proud of her. She could read it in his eyes. Esrell and Darryn would be proud too. Nora and Stefan and their little brothers, they'd all *see* Rowan finally. Not as the twisted older sister too stunted to take care of herself, but as someone who could care for all of them.

As much as she wanted it to be that simple, the rest of the truth burned in her throat.

"It might be the weapon," she told Jannik. "But it's not what you thought. It's killing people right now." She reached out to touch the handle of the lantern. "Gavyn, are you still there?"

"Where else would I be?" His tinny voice radiated sarcasm.

Jannik watched her, head tilted.

She met his gaze. "We'll all die just from touching this thing."

"Nonsense," Jannik said. "You look perfectly fine to me."

"Esrell doesn't." Rowan's breath hissed between her teeth. "The other workers don't."

Jannik paused, his lips parted as some thought flickered behind his eyes. Then he shook his head. "They'll all be better with some rest. I'm sure it's nothing serious."

Rowan's knuckles tightened on the handle of the lantern. "The mages weren't. Esrell's symptoms match Gavyn's description, and his friends were all dead within days."

Jannik reached for Rowan's shoulder and gently pulled her aside so that her hand fell away from the lantern. When he spoke, it was under his breath, as if that would keep Gavyn from hearing.

"Rowan, the Grief Draw is a very powerful artifact. We know that much from my great-grandfather's research. There will be lots of people, friends and foes alike, who want its power and will try to take it from us. You need to learn how to discern friend and foe now. Who actually has your best interests at heart and who is working toward their own interests. This Gavyn sounds like he might be addled at best and manipulative at worst. He wants you to believe him so that you will help him."

She recoiled under his rebuke, glancing between him and the lantern. "Of course I want to help him. I'd think less of anyone willing to leave him in there alone, but I don't think he's trying to manipulate me." She pulled away from Jannik and stepped back to the lantern so she could place her hand on it.

Gavyn's voice came into her head. "I'm pretty sure I don't like that guy."

Rowan glanced at Jannik, but her mentor didn't give any indication he'd heard or guessed at Gavyn's comment. He watched her with a frown.

"I know it sounds… bad," she whispered, struggling to find words that would help her make sense of Jannik's words and actions. "He's just used to thinking about all sides of an issue. It can be off-putting to some people, but it comes from being highly intelligent."

"I know—knew—plenty of intelligent people. Gods, they're probably all dead by now, aren't they? But most of them were smart enough to listen when someone was trying to warn them."

Jannik raised his eyebrows. "Rowan. I'm not sure you should talk to him anymore. Unless he's going to tell you how to work the weapon, he's really no more help."

"Help?" Rowan said, her breath hitching. "He's a person, not… not a tool."

"He is a voice from a different time." His eyes softened. "I know it's confusing, but I need you to listen to me. I'm the one here, right now. I'm the one whose life you can change with this."

Rowan bit her lip. The first time Jannik had told her the story about his great-grandfather, she'd been riveted by the awe in his voice. It had been so easy to get swept into the story of the noble treasure hunter, the selfless patriarch who had disappeared trying to bring their family wealth and fame.

"Jannik," Rowan tried again. "I know this is important to you, but we need to figure out a way to keep the lantern from hurting anyone else. And if we can get rid of it without getting rid of Gavyn, too, then that would be so much better."

Jannik jerked and his eyes widened. He shook his head hard enough some of his hair came loose from its tie. "Get rid of it?" Horror crept into his voice. "Oh, no. We are not getting rid of it."

"But it's killing people," Rowan cried.

"That is what it is built to do," Jannik said, his voice rising to match hers. "It's a weapon built by the Giants. Of course it is going to be dangerous."

He paced close to her, making her lean back without thinking.

"That's part of our job. Digging up artifacts that can help humanity. Rowan, I thought you of all people would understand how valuable this is. After all this time you've spent studying with me, I really thought you would be the first to help me."

Rowan's mouth worked, trying to give voice to her argument, but his words had knocked her off course.

He gripped her arms. "Rowan, my family went into so much debt hoping my great-grandfather would come back with something amazing. Something life-changing. We outfitted him with a king's ransom of equipment. Weapons and armor to keep him safe. An amulet that detected magic. That alone cost as much as a small house."

"What?" Gavyn said, his voice cutting through Rowan's thoughts.

"Then he disappeared, leaving us in debt and beholden to the lord for his broken promises." Jannik let her go and turned away, shaking his head. "This will free us, finally. This will make all of that worth it."

"What is he talking about, Rowan?" Gavyn asked sharply.

Rowan swallowed. "Jannik's great-grandfather was a treasure hunter. He disappeared almost a hundred years ago looking for the Grief Draw."

Jannik shook his head like he couldn't believe she was still listening to this voice inside a lantern.

Gavyn laughed in the back of Rowan's mind. The sound rode the edge of hysteria and rage and sent a tingle down her spine. "Treasure hunter? More like murderer."

"What?" She stared at the lantern.

"The man who kidnapped us?" Gavyn's voice grew heated. "The one who captured us and locked us in that basement and forced us to work on an artifact that killed us? He called himself a treasure hunter. And he wore an amulet that detected magic."

Rowan's throat went dry.

"That's how he tracked down young mages. The ones like me who were powerful enough to do what he wanted but unpracticed, so we couldn't defend ourselves. And any time we tried to use magic to fight back, he knew. He knew before we could get organized. And he'd kill us. He murdered children right in front of us, so we would know not to thwart him."

Rowan's free hand crept to her mouth in horror. "Healer's Ghost."

"What is he saying to you?" Jannik said, mouth pulled tight and flat.

Rowan swallowed and tried to translate. "He... he says your grandfather was the one who captured the mages and forced them to work on the lantern. He says... he killed them."

Jannik's mouth pulled tight, and his eyes hardened. "That's not right."

"It is," Gavyn said in her mind.

"He was a treasure hunter," Jannik said. "Not some mercenary."

"A kidnapper and a murderer," Gavyn cried. "He killed them all. He killed Keinwen. He killed *me*!"

"Jannik, he killed them." Rowan couldn't keep the horror out of her voice.

"No."

"He wasn't going to return the lantern like he promised," Gavyn said. "He said he wanted to make it safe so *he* could use it."

"You think he would have betrayed his family like that?" Rowan asked him.

"Why wouldn't he? He murdered children for his own gain. Why wouldn't he have condemned his own offspring?"

"Enough!" Jannik's voice cut through Gavyn's words. He braced his hands on the table in the sudden silence and closed his eyes.

Rowan kept her lips pinched tight, and even Gavyn was silent in the back of her mind.

Jannik took a deep bracing breath. "No."

"No?" Rowan said, and Jannik straightened up to glare at her.

"My great-grandfather was brave. And noble. His discovery would have elevated my family alongside Lord Hax's. He was not an oathbreaker. Not a murderer. I will not believe anyone who says he was."

"Jannik. Gavyn is—"

"A liar. I'm sending the lantern to Lord Hax. To repay my great-grandfather's debt and to prove he was a man of his word." Jannik went on, as if refusing to leave room for Gavyn's pain. His clenched his fist and clunked it against the edge of the table to emphasize each point. "I will redeem his promise, and my family will finally be free of his patronage. Darryn will carry it until then. To save you the trouble. He is proving to be a hard-working young man."

He turned, dismissing her as easily as he'd dismissed Gavyn.

A cold, hard knot settled in Rowan's stomach. He was really going to send something as powerful and awful as the Grief Draw to that man? She couldn't shake the goosebumps that rose when she remembered Lord Hax's eyes as he'd said "godsblighted."

She swallowed. "What about the deaths? What about the danger?"

"What about it?"

"The lantern clearly kills people. Darryn will be at risk if you make him hold it. And then Lord Hax will use it against his enemies."

Jannik spun, his hand slashing through the air. "It is a weapon, Rowan. Its purpose is death. Lord Hax can use it for whatever he sees fit."

"Don't we have a responsibility as antiquarians?" she asked quietly. "Don't we have a responsibility to the history we dig up? To use it to help people?"

"Or at the very least not kill them?" Gavyn muttered in her mind.

"We don't even know that it kills people the way you think," Jannik said. "This Gavyn is lying about my great-grandfather. He could be lying about the rest."

Rowan took an involuntary step back.

She'd known Jannik almost her whole life. He'd been a friend of her mother's. She'd only just met Gavyn an hour before, and she couldn't even see him. She had only his voice to gauge the truth of his words.

Would it be so bad to trust her mentor who'd given so much of himself so she could have a future? She could give Jannik the lantern. If he trusted Lord Hax, shouldn't she trust him too? The reward would be hers as would the recognition. Esrell and Darryn would never ask if she was overdoing it again. They'd never linger in the background to make sure she was taken care of.

Jannik wouldn't feel like he'd made a mistake giving her this chance because she would have found the thing he'd been looking for. And maybe he was right. Maybe Gavyn was lying.

But... Esrell was still sick.

And Jannik didn't seem to care. He didn't care that Gavyn was stuck in the lantern. He didn't care that he might endanger Darryn too.

Even if Rowan let him take the lantern to Lord Hax, he wouldn't move it fast enough to save Esrell. Especially if he didn't believe her about the danger.

I have to get this as far away as I can.

"I can't let you take the lantern to Lord Hax." She stared at the Grief Draw as if that would make her words less of a rift she'd never be able to fix.

"What?" Jannik's nostrils flared.

She raised her chin. "I can't let you take the lantern. I have to get it away from Esrell."

"My dear," Jannik said. "You act as if you had any choice in the matter."

Rowan's heart pounded. *He's taking my discovery?*

This was not the man she'd revered for so long. Had he changed? Or was she finally seeing who he really was under all the jovial smiles and self-deprecating jokes?

"It's not yours," Rowan said. "I was the one who found it, and I've decided not to give it to you." The words tried to stick in her dry throat.

Jannik snorted and reached for the lantern. Ignoring her again.

In her head, Gavyn cried out. In fear or anger, it didn't matter. What would it be like to be held by the relative of someone who had tormented you until your death? Someone who refused to acknowledge you and your pain?

Rowan yanked back, pulling the lantern out of reach. Jannik's mouth pinched, and his eyes blazed. He lunged for Rowan, but she stumbled back, twisting to keep the lantern away from him.

Jannik hauled on her arm, bringing the lantern closer to him, and she did the only thing she could think to do. She bit his hand right on the meaty part by the thumb.

Jannik yelled and backhanded her across the face with his free hand.

Rowan gasped and fell back, her cheek burning from the blow. The lantern went flying, bouncing against Jannik's bedroll and rolling across the ground to the corner of the tent. She lay at Jannik's feet, her hand against her burning cheek.

Angry tears pricked her eyes as Jannik huffed above her. He'd struck her. Her mind stuttered on that one fact, playing it over and over again.

Jannik stepped toward the lantern lying in the corner, disregarding her anguish, disregarding the danger to her sister and Gavyn and himself.

She sobbed and kicked at the back of his legs. Jannik stumbled. Then he tripped two paces and careened headfirst into the table.

He hit with a meaty thunk. And then lay still.

CHAPTER EIGHT

ROWAN

Rowan stared, her mouth falling open. "Oh, no," she whispered. "Healer's Ghost, what did I do?"

He'd... he'd hit her, and then she'd kicked him, and... it had all happened so fast.

She scrambled across the ground on her hands and knees and rolled him onto his back. A large, red mark marred his forehead, and his eyes were closed, but his chest still rose and fell with shallow breaths.

She sat back and pressed her hand to her heart. *I didn't kill him. Thank the Healer, I didn't kill him.*

Her heart still thudded under her palm, a wild beat urging her to her feet, to run, to do something, anything besides sit there like a ninny. If she could just wake him up, she could apologize. She could still make this all right, and everything could go back to normal.

But no. If his eyes opened, it wouldn't be forgiveness she saw in them. He'd just take the lantern, and everything would be horrible again. Esrell would still be sick, and Jannik still wouldn't care.

Esrell!

Rowan didn't have time to sit here and dither. The lantern was killing Esrell with every moment she delayed. Who knew how much time Rowan had to escape with it? She could drop dead from carrying it, at any time.

Rowan crawled to the corner where the lantern had come to rest, and she snatched it up by the handle.

"Gavyn," she whispered. "Are you all right?"

"Your concern is touching, but I am a disembodied voice bound to a piece of malevolent metal. I am both completely unharmed and far, far from all right."

A little laugh escaped her lips, and she clamped down on it before it turned hysterical. "You know you can just say yes."

"Don't worry, you'll get used to my sense of humor."

Rowan held the lantern up level with her eyes. The metal itself gleamed even in the dim tent, reflecting its own light the way it had since they'd pulled it out of the underground laboratory. But a hairline crack ran directly through one of the panes of glass.

Hopefully the damage was minimal. What was done was done, and she couldn't fix something made by the Giants.

She climbed to her feet with a grimace. Her spine felt more crunched than normal, and she struggled to straighten up. Then she stared down at Jannik where he lay.

Gavyn was silent in her hand, and she got the impression he was staring at her old mentor as well.

Rowan pushed down the misery, swallowing against the thick, wet feeling in her throat until she could breathe a little easier.

She lifted her arm to give the lantern a significant look. "All right. Let's get you as far from my family as possible."

"And the fanatic antiquarian," Gavyn answered. "It's funny. By stealing me, you'll be saving his life too."

Rowan pulled aside the tent flap and peered out into the darkness before she brought the lantern around enough to illuminate the camp. No one lurked there. They were all still tucked up in their tents.

She stopped long enough to snatch her satchel from the tent she shared with Esrell. Her sister still slept, eyelids shadowed in her pale face.

Rowan bit her lip hard enough to hurt, refusing to think about the fact that this could be the last time she saw Esrell. She would have woken Darryn to explain everything, but it would have taken too much time. He'd never just let her be right without asking a million questions and testing every possible choice and outcome for himself.

And Rowan had already wasted too much of Esrell's time fighting with Jannik.

She couldn't leave him a note since he couldn't read, so she just had to hope he had enough sense to get Esrell to a healer. Or home to their mother.

Rowan slipped the strap of her satchel over her head and hurried to the barrels and crates that Darryn had stacked behind Jannik's tent.

"What are you stopping for?" Gavyn said. "You're taking forever."

"You might not need to eat, but I do. And if I'm already a thief for taking you, then I might as well feed myself."

The barrels contained some dried meat and fruit. Things that would keep just as easily on a journey as they did on a dig. She had no idea where she was going or how long it would take her, but she could fit enough for a couple of days in her satchel.

The crates held pickaxes and shovels. Brushes and fire charges. All the things Lord Hax had sent to keep the excavation going. Rowan hesitated a moment before she grabbed a handful of fire charges. She left the other tools alone. A pickax could be a weapon, depending on what you swung it at, but it was also heavy. She couldn't imagine carrying it for very long, let alone swinging it at anyone. She'd just have to make do with the things that wouldn't slow her down.

Without even thinking about it, she tried replacing the lid of the crate. Her job was to keep the camp and the dig site tidy after all. But the heavy lid had never sat right and slid back into place with a jarring thump.

Rowan winced and then froze as Darryn's voice came out of the night. "Is someone there?"

"Sorry about this, Gavyn," Rowan said under her breath. She could just reach the blanket she'd left on Esrell's table, and she snatched it up to fling over the lantern. Its light disappeared.

"Rowan?" Darryn called. "Is that you?"

She held her breath and gathered the lantern up in her arms, blanket and all. Then she looked for a path of escape.

Straight up the hill was her only option if she didn't want to cross through camp. Hopefully the trees would hide her from sight before long.

"Jannik?" Darryn's footsteps headed for Jannik's tent, and Rowan realized that for a few moments the bulky canvas stood between her and her brother.

She took advantage of the moment and ran, holding the lantern so it didn't clank. Within moments, she had disappeared into the trees.

Chapter Nine

GAVYN

Muffled darkness surrounded Gavyn, and with no sight and little sound, he couldn't even be sure he still existed. Rowan's hand wasn't on the lantern anymore, so all he could do was scream into the silence.

You would think that after staring at the same surroundings for the better part of an eternity, darkness would be welcome.

It wasn't.

He'd learned long ago that time went loopy the longer you stared at it. There'd been plenty of moments in his youth when his mother had sat him in the corner for being bad and the minutes had ticked by, endless in his boredom. Apparently, he'd grown used to it, and now he couldn't hold onto the passage of time. It slid by him in fits and starts.

He sank into the blur to protect himself, to shield his mind from the gnawing terror that she would never let him out again, never speak to him again.

Abruptly the blanket was swept away, and Rowan's pale face peered in at him. "I'm sorry, I'm sorry. I wanted to be sure Darryn couldn't see the light."

Gavyn stifled the screams and tried to focus on the trees, the branches against the night sky, and the face before him.

The last finally settled him. Rowan's features were already growing familiar, and there was something calming about her eyes.

"'S all right," he said. That was all he could manage in the moment. If he tried to add any more, she'd be able to tell it was a lie.

The corners of her mouth drew down, but her eyes darted behind her, and she started moving again.

He concentrated on her profile. The lantern let him see in all directions, but he preferred to focus on one side. Like a Human.

When she'd first pulled him from the ground, there'd been so many faces and features, and his mind had forgotten how to process them. Her voice had been his anchor.

Now, every time the world started going blurry and his thoughts tried to float and let time flow past, he memorized the shape of Rowan's nose. Curly hair tied in a practical braid fell over her shoulder which was oddly sloped and uneven with the other side. A good portion of her spine bunched, making her look lopsided. He let her worried eyes ground him in the knowledge she was there.

I'm not alone anymore.

Gavyn couldn't exactly feel the night air against the skin he didn't have, but he could imagine it well enough. The longer he went being able to see and hear, the further from the edge of panic he moved. He rejoiced in the feeling of movement, even if it made his head hurt a bit. The sight of trees swooping past and the night sky stretching above them didn't send him into a panic but actually made him feel... free.

A hundred years, Rowan had said. Had it really been so long? He hadn't really noticed while staring at the same walls over and over and over, but above ground time kept trying to skip forward.

He was pretty sure he had it under control now. Pretty sure. Of course, who knew if he was entirely sane after all that time? How did you know when you'd gone crazy?

What did madness look like if you just went quietly insane in your own head?

Gavyn realized he'd drifted again and fought to pull himself back. To focus on his surroundings. The trees around them grew denser as they moved up the hill and away from the ruins in the dell below. Mostly dark bark and wide leaves, but here and there a silver trunk stood out, like the one he'd left Keinwen under so, so long ago.

Keinwen. Gods, what had happened to her? Had she survived after he'd gotten her out? There'd been a moment when Rowan's Life Magic had first touched him when he'd thought she was the healer, but with a hundred years between them, there was no chance she was still alive now. How long had she survived after he'd been sucked into the lantern? So much of what had happened he'd done for her, so she'd be safe.

He needed to know if it had worked. The uncertainty would kill him faster than anything else would. Or drive him deeper into madness.

But finding out was going to be hard without his own body. Arms were overrated, but he at least needed legs. As it was, he was entirely dependent on Rowan and wherever she decided to take him.

She held the lantern out at arm's reach to light her way through the forest, so he had a good view of her face. Layers of fright drew deep lines on either side of her mouth and eyes, but over that lay a fierce determination. He could only guess at what was going on under her surface. She'd trusted that man, Jannik. He'd read it in her words and her face, but her mentor had let her down in a big way.

Gavyn knew what it was like to be so frightened for someone you cared about that you threw away all thought of your own safety.

They had something in common, along with their connection and the security he felt in her hands.

But even a hundred years distance couldn't dull the ache of Keinwen's fate and his memory of all the others who had perished in that laboratory. He couldn't endanger Rowan by asking her to carry the lantern longer just so he had someone to talk to. Even if it meant he'd never learn about Keinwen. Even if it meant he'd go back in a hole for another hundred years. Or a thousand. Or an eternity.

He couldn't watch another friend die while their body betrayed them.

Even if the lantern didn't seem to be affecting Rowan yet…

Come to think of it, why isn't the lantern affecting her yet?

CHAPTER TEN

ROWAN

 owan walked until she collapsed. She slept huddled amongst the roots, her head propped on the bunched-up blanket. Then she woke and walked some more.

Every time her weary limbs and aching back urged her to stop, she remembered Esrell's pale face, and she pushed on just a little further. She couldn't be sure how far was safe, which meant finding just a little more energy to keep going.

Was Esrell even still alive? She might not have left in time. Horrible images of Esrell and the workers kept floating to the front of her mind, her sister and people she'd known dying in pain and fear.

"Rowan."

Just a little further, then she could sit.

"Rowan!" The voice yelling inside her head finally made her jump. She squinted down at the lantern, its light washed out under the afternoon sun.

Gavyn called to her, "Rowan, you have to stop."

She blinked at the lantern. "What?"

"You have to stop. You have to rest. You're killing yourself."

"I'm dead anyway, right?" she said, the thought leaving little inflection in her voice after the exhaustion had taken everything else. "If it's going to kill me anyway, I might as well get it as far away from my family as I can first."

"Rowan, how long have you been holding the lantern? Total. Since you pulled it out of the ground?"

"I don't know. Hours? Off and on over days?"

"Longer than Esrell? Longer than the others who were sick?"

"Yes," she said, certainty returning to her voice. "Esrell held it for a couple of hours while we climbed out of the ruins and while we buried you. But I've been working on it since then."

"And how do you feel?"

"Awful," she snapped.

"Tired like you just spent all night walking without eating? Makes sense. But are you nauseous? Are your hands blistered? Are your insides liquefying?"

Rowan pulled a face, but she traded which hand she held the lantern in and looked at her palm. Sweat made it sticky, and black dirt gathered in the creases but...

"No," she said. "I'm hungry. Starving but I don't feel the way Esrell looked."

"That's what I thought," Gavyn said, the words thoughtful and drawn out.

"Is that normal? From what you remember?"

"No. For those who didn't actually work with the lantern, maybe. But for someone who held it as long as you have? No. This is different."

Rowan pressed her hand to her head as she staggered. "What does that mean?"

"Sit down. Eat something. I'd tell you to sleep but you don't strike me as sensible enough to sleep when you've got that much on your mind."

She huffed a laugh but did as he said, sitting right there on the roots of a nearby tree. She hadn't really been paying attention to her surroundings, concerned more with getting away, not with the actual direction. She'd walked them deep into the forest that bordered the ruins. Somewhere to the south, lay the dig site and somewhere to the west, was the road that eventually led to her home village.

The moment she stuffed a bit of dried meat in her mouth, her appetite yelled at her for ignoring it for so long, and she couldn't shovel the food in fast enough.

A few minutes later, she leaned her head back against the trunk and closed her eyes to take a second and breathe.

"Are we far enough?" she asked quietly. "Will Esrell be all right?"

Gavyn remained silent, and she realized she'd taken her hand from the lantern in order to eat. She snatched it up again.

"Sorry."

"The constant pawing should be annoying, but you are my only access to anything resembling communication, so I find I don't mind."

"Why do you talk like that?"

"Like what?"

"You don't talk like our neighbors or my da. You talk like Jannik."

A split-second pause. "Not sure I like the comparison right now, but I've always talked like this."

"I take it you didn't grow up on a farm."

"Oh. No. My father was a merchant. I was apprenticed to a Land Mage when I was twelve. I studied with him until I was kidnapped by the treasure hunter."

"He went after Land Mages specifically?"

"We work primarily in metal and rock and glass. I guess he figured we'd have the best chance of making the lantern work for him. There were a couple of Life Mages in the mix, maybe because we weren't getting anywhere. And a healer to keep us alive longer."

Rowan wrapped her free arm around her knees. His voice went particularly soft when he mentioned them, and it wasn't the first time she'd noticed. "You've mentioned the healer before. What was their name?"

He hesitated for a moment. "Keinwen."

"Did she die too?"

"I have no idea." His voice went heavy with frustration. "I tried to get her out. We were the last two, and I knew I was going to die, but I wanted to save Keinwen, at least. I got her free and left her at the edge of the forest but... she'd overextended. She'd used too much magic trying to keep us alive and... I don't know if she made it. I left her there and went back to destroy the treasure hunter and the lantern, and that's that. She never tried to come back for me, so I have no idea if she survived."

Rowan raised the lantern as if to look in Gavyn's eyes, but all she saw was the unwavering flame. "Gavyn, the room you were in was sealed. The stairs were blocked, and the whole place was locked up tight. I needed fire charges to get in, and I only found the door because the floor caved in at the right place. If she was alive, she probably couldn't get to you. She could have spent years trying."

Gavyn was silent a moment. "That makes me feel better. And somehow worse."

"It means, she could have survived. You don't know. My village isn't that far. Maybe she walked there."

"Yes," Gavyn said, and his voice gained strength. "She was the strongest of all of us. Even among a bunch of Land Mages. A month of work and all of us were dead except her."

Rowan held her hand up to stare at it. "So, what does it mean that it's not killing me?"

"I don't know. If I had any idea, I would have used it to save us all back then."

Rowan bit her lip. "I'm sorry. I'm sorry this happened to you. And to them."

"I guess that makes two of us. I did this to myself—tried to destroy it—so the treasure hunter would never be able to use it or torment other mages with it again. Guess it didn't occur to me to wipe out his whole family."

Rowan fell silent. Jannik had made a choice she couldn't agree with, but he *had* given her a chance. He'd given her a purpose and a job that she could do when her whole family had assumed she'd spend her life on their charity. She couldn't hate him for that.

She could see his face in her mind, wounded and betrayed.

"Healer's Ghost, Gavyn. I'm not dying." Her voice rose.

"No," he said, clearly waiting for the catch.

"I thought this was a one-way trip. If I'm not dying, then what will Jannik do? What will Esrell and Darryn think of me? I struck Jannik and stole his artifact." Her hands crept to her cheeks as the implications of her actions crashed around her. "I'm a criminal, and he's going to hate me."

"He hit you first," Gavyn said flatly. "He hit you so he could take something *you* found. He would have taken me and relegated me to silence forever. Forgive me if I think that means you were justified."

"What do I do now?" she whispered. She stared at the gleaming lantern. "I have the lantern just like I wanted. I'm not dying. Which I didn't think to hope for, but it's a welcome addition. So, what do I do? No one will trust me ever again."

"I trust you," Gavyn said.

Rowan sucked in a breath.

"You believed me, and no one else did. That… means a lot to me. I'm not in a position to promise much, but I'll help you. You're not alone, all right?"

She laughed around the lump in her throat. "From one useless person to another, let me just say that's a pretty good promise."

Gavyn snorted. "Useless how? You pulled me out of the ground. You saved me from an eternity of boredom and then a fanatic antiquarian. You are my hero."

She shook her head. If he was too polite to point out the obvious then she wouldn't either.

"There is one thing," he said.

"Name it."

"Help me find Keinwen? Or at least, what happened to her."

"Of course," she said without really thinking about how hard it would be to find a woman who'd been dead for nearly a century.

Gavyn *needed* her. No one had ever needed Rowan before.

She scowled at the light. "But Jannik was right. If this really is the Grief Draw, then he won't be the only one who'll come after me. How do I keep it safe? I'm not some mercenary who can protect it."

"You were the one who recognized its danger and did something about it," Gavyn said. "That counts for a lot. And you seem to be immune to its effects. Or at least resistant."

"So, it might be killing me, just a lot slower?" She snorted. "That's comforting."

"I didn't really mean it to be comforting. More like a clue to the mystery."

Rowan tilted her head back toward the sun that filtered down through the leaves. "Keeping the lantern safe will be hard enough, but maybe solving the mystery will help."

"So, keep ahead of all the treasure hunters and antiquarians," Gavyn said as if making a list. "Find out why you're immune. And find out what this thing actually does besides kill people. Sounds like we have plenty to do."

⬠ ⬠ ⬠

Gavyn finally persuaded Rowan to lay down among the roots of the trees and sleep. Jannik had to be out looking for her by now, but she had a pretty good head start and he didn't know what direction she'd headed. So, she should be safe enough to rest.

So why were her shoulders tense and quivering like she expected to hear someone coming out of the woods any second?

"I can see in all directions," Gavyn told her. "I'll keep watch."

"And how will I know if you see something?"

His voice gave her the impression of a shrug. "Keep your hand on the lantern while you sleep, then I can wake you if I see or hear anything. The hearing part is actually more interesting, though, isn't it? How does one hear without ears?"

"Gavyn."

"Of course, I'm seeing without eyes, too, so…"

Rowan lay down and pillowed her head on her blanket, Gavyn's babble subsiding into the exhaustion clouding her mind.

She had to admit, she felt much better when she woke up. Gavyn hadn't sounded the alarm so she could only assume that they were safe for now.

She stretched and her back twinged. At the dig, she'd slept on a cot shoved into their little tent for just that reason. Sleeping on roots was going to take its toll sooner rather than later.

The sun sank behind the tips of the distant mountain peaks as she rubbed the grit from her eyes.

"Better?" Gavyn asked the moment she put her hand back on the lantern.

"Better," she agreed. "But I'm going to have to find someplace to sleep at night if we're going to keep moving. I can't sleep on the ground often, or I won't be worth much of anything during the days."

"Did you happen to steal any money while you were escaping?"

Rowan made a face. "No, but maybe I'll be able to trade some cooking or cleaning for a bed in an inn."

"Do you think Jannik would be able to find you if you stay at inns?"

Rowan chewed her lip. "Good point. I'm rather noticeable already even without a conspicuous lantern."

As she sat, she changed which hand she was touching the lantern with and shook out the other one.

"What's wrong?" Gavyn asked.

Rowan squinted at her hand, searching for blisters or any of the other symptoms Esrell had, but her skin was healthy if dirty.

"When you were alive," she said, slowly. "Did the lantern ever… buzz?"

"Buzz?"

"Like holding a handful of bees."

"No. But then, no one I know ever held it as long as you have. Including me."

"Maybe there are side effects to it not killing me."

"Being alive seems like a pretty good side effect."

She still didn't trust the thing, but there was also a part of her that couldn't just leave it alone. It drew her, like the pull in her gut that had led her to the laboratory in the first place.

"Make a note, but if the worst it does is buzz, you're doing a hell of a lot better than me," he added as she dug in her satchel for parchment. The ink and her quill still rested in their place on her belt.

"Yes, if it's a competition, you win. I'll never be able to say a magical lantern tried to kill me and sucked my consciousness into it. Hopefully. Huh."

She drew out a leather-bound journal.

"What's that?"

"Jannik gave me his notes while I was studying the lantern. I must have forgotten to give them back."

"Hmm, is it petty of me to hope he spends ages looking for them?"

"Probably." She turned the journal over in her lap and sighed. "He trusted me enough not to wonder where they were."

"Why did you respect that man so much?" Gavyn asked softly.

"I've known him my whole life," she said. "He always had time for children, and there were a lot of them in my family."

He remained silent, and she realized she hadn't really answered his question.

"He was the one who gave me a job when no one thought I was good for anything."

Gavyn snorted. "You have Life Magic. That's good for a lot more than nothing."

Rowan rolled her eyes. "Spoken like a true mage. Sorry, but the rest of us have to live with the fact that we're not all powerful. I think I'd rather have no magic than this little spark."

"All right, forgetting for a second that you're talking to someone whose magic got him trapped in a metal body that can't *do* anything, I'll admit I liked magic quite a lot. So, that begs the question, why would you throw away even a portion of that gift?"

"Because it didn't solve anything for me. It raised my hopes and then didn't give me any of the things it promised."

"And what was it supposed to promise?"

"Strength?" she said. "Independence? I was always smaller and weaker than everyone else. I couldn't even do the same chores as my siblings, but then I started seeing things when I touched objects. Everyone thought I was going to be special. My mother called in so many favors to get a mage to come look at me. To take me away as his apprentice."

Rowan rubbed her free hand up and down her other arm. "But it turns out that those little glimpses into the past is all I can do. I can't heal. I can't grow things. I can't even control the things I do see. It's just random. The mage left, and I went back to being nothing. Jannik saved me from that. He made me his assistant, and he never acted like he was doing me a favor. Apparently, he was supposed to be keeping an eye on me. Making sure I didn't overdo it. But he never let on. He made me feel—" She stopped. She was going to say "valuable," but he hadn't done more than treat her like a Human being. "He made me feel normal."

She shrugged. "It doesn't excuse what he did, but—"

"But we can't completely erase everything he gave you either."

She nodded, glad he saw that it was more complicated for her than just escaping someone who'd hurt her.

She opened the journal. Maybe he'd found something before she had even arrived and had neglected to mention it to her.

She passed the notes she'd already read and a couple of rough diagrams of the early dig site and a map. Most everything was familiar.

Rowan turned back to the very first page where Jannik had written out the story of his great-grandfather. It was the same one he'd told her, including the details of the noble treasure hunter. Though it left out the part where he'd kidnapped a bunch of mages and trapped them with a murderous artifact. Unsurprising. The story spanned three pages and didn't offer anything new.

She almost closed it again with a sigh, and then a note written in the margin caught her eye. The page listed possible dig sites and other well-known nuraghis where he might find evidence of the treasure hunter. Her name was scrawled across the corner as if an afterthought.

Rowan? Could be useful in the ruins. Right heritage.

"What is it?" Gavyn asked. "You stopped."

Rowan's finger traced the words written in Jannik's looping hand. "He wrote about me."

"Checking up like you said?"

"No." This was different. This was before she'd ever come to the dig. He'd thought of her, maybe even sought her out especially. "It says I could be useful in the ruins. Something about having the 'right heritage'?"

"Right heritage? What does that mean?"

"I have no idea. He never mentioned it."

Gavyn paused a moment. "Maybe he wasn't doing you a favor. Maybe you were doing him one. What *is* your heritage?"

Rowan remained quiet, thoughts spinning through her head.

"Rowan?"

"I didn't think it was anything special. My mother is the village healer. She makes poultices and teas. Her family has lived in our village for generations. She learned her craft from her mother and grandmother but it's nothing special. Nothing like magic."

"And your father?" Gavyn prompted. "You said he's a farmer."

"Actually, that's my stepfather, Stefan. Esrell and Darryn and the rest of my siblings, he's their father. Mine, I never knew. My mother married Stefan when I was so young, so he's always been my da. I don't even know the other one's name."

"You never even asked?"

She cast the lantern a sharp glance. "I did once. I asked Stefan who my 'real' da was, and he went quiet and sad. Like I'd hurt him just by asking. So I never brought it up again."

Stefan had always been Da. He'd played with her the same as the others. He'd swept her up in hugs, even after Esrell had been born. He'd taken turns tossing Darryn and Esrell and Rowan high into the air before they'd gotten too big to lift. And even when he and Nora had worried deep into the night about how to feed them all, Rowan had never felt like Stefan resented her.

It was strange now to think of whoever had come before him. Someone with the "right" heritage. Whatever that was.

"Jannik knew," Gavyn said. "He knew who your real father is."

"So does my mother, presumably." She and Jannik had been old friends. Who knew what she'd confided to the old man?

He'd known and he hadn't told her. Whatever it was made her useful to him, and he'd brought her to the dig, not because she would make a great assistant. Not even as a favor or some altruistic gesture. He'd needed something from her.

All those little compliments and kindnesses, had he meant any of them? Or had they just been a way to manipulate her into sticking around? A way to make her like him and do what he wanted. He'd certainly been quick enough to throw it all away when she wasn't willing to give him the lantern.

Rowan snapped the book shut and tucked it into her satchel, then she slung the strap over her head and secured the blanket so she could walk with one hand free.

"At least we know where we're going next," Gavyn said. He didn't need her to fill in the blanks. "How far is your village?"

"It's the closest bit of civilization to the dig. Darryn did it in two days, but it'll take me at least three."

"I'd ask if you're sure you want to go home. Jannik will surely think to look for you there, but—"

"It's our only clue. And it's important. Jannik wouldn't have mentioned it if it wasn't. I just don't know why yet. And Ma can tell me why. As long as we go now, we can beat him there."

A myriad of questions and possible answers spilled through her head, but one circled back to the fore over and over.

Why didn't Ma tell me before?

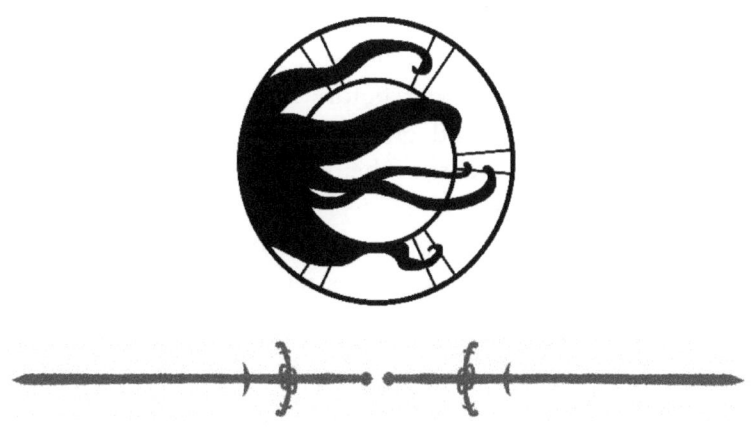

CHAPTER ELEVEN

ROWAN

When we get there, I'll leave you outside the village. In a tree or something."

They'd been walking for most of a day, with Rowan napping every time they found someplace a little flatter with less roots. But her body wasn't used to this. It was going to take its toll eventually.

"You'd trust me with the squirrels?" Gavyn said with a scoff.

"It's not you I'm worried about. It's the lantern. I'd rather it killed off a nest of squirrels than my family."

"Obviously I don't want it to hurt your family, but I don't think you should just leave it lying around. Someone might find it and take it, no matter how well you hide it. And on a personal note, you're my only connection with the world. I don't like being left behind."

She blew out her breath. His words might have seemed calm, but she could imagine the undercurrent of tension easily enough. And she hated the idea of leaving him all by himself. She hadn't forgotten the first thing he'd managed to say to her. "Don't put me in the dark again." And being left without a voice probably felt a lot like the dark.

Rowan stopped to survey her surroundings. They'd broken from the forest just an hour before and the hills rose to her right, growing steeper and grander before turning into sharp peaks. The road ran parallel to them and would take her straight to her village at the end of the range.

As she walked, a black patch of darkness grew opposite the mountains. It looked like a shadow stretched across the land, but Rowan had been this way before. She knew better.

The mountains forced the road close to the black curtain here, shrouding the landscape beyond in impenetrable darkness. Thick tentacles waved from its surface, questing through the air as if seeking someone to grab.

Rowan and Gavyn both grew quiet as they hurried by. She didn't have to ask if they'd had noktums during Gavyn's time. The noktums were eternal. Every child in Usara—likely every child on Noksonon—grew up knowing to avoid the patches of darkness. People disappeared into the noktum and never returned. There were tales of monsters coming through, drawn into the daylight world by blood and the scent of prey.

Her shoulders didn't relax until the edge of the noktum had retreated far, far to the west and faded into the black of normal night. By then the muscles of her back were cramped from being held so tight for so long.

She switched hands with the lantern again and shook out the one that tingled. Her knuckles were starting to ache from being clenched around the handle so long.

"Still buzzing?" Gavyn asked gently.

"It's getting worse. Like pins and needles after your hand has fallen asleep and is just waking up."

He hesitated. "I think as long as we make our visit quickly and don't let anyone touch the lantern while we're there, your family will be safe. I don't want to put them in any danger either, Rowan."

Her shoulders slumped. "I know. It will have to be enough. Unless we come up with some other trail to follow."

Lightning flashed overhead, lighting up the dark. The road made the way smoother, but it was very open. She could see anyone coming for miles, but that meant she had less places to hide. It made the back of her neck prickle.

Fat drops of rain splatted in the dirt. Her feet began to drag, and her back tensed again as cold raindrops slid down her neck. She shivered and found she couldn't stop.

"Are you all right?" Gavyn asked.

"I'm going to have to find somewhere to sleep that isn't the ground."

"You think that's a good idea?"

"I think it's the only idea." She would have snapped at him, but all her energy was going into keeping her eyes open and her feet moving. "I can't spend another night on the ground, Gavyn. Especially not in the rain. Otherwise, I won't be able to move tomorrow." And she hadn't grabbed a cloak on her way out of camp. The autumn night had been so mild it hadn't even occurred to her.

At least the lantern functioned as an actual lantern, and the magical flame didn't sputter in the wet. Its cold light kept her from tripping over her feet or any bumps in the road. She was so focused on the path in front of her that she almost missed when the light of the lantern blended with the warm, yellow glow of firelight.

"Rowan," Gavyn called as she struggled to take another step. "Rowan, look up."

Rowan raised her head and blinked the rainwater from her eyes.

A little hut stood on the side of the road, firelight leaking through the cracks in the shutters. It was a wayrest, a tiny building with firewood stacked to one side under a roof to keep it dry. Inside there'd be a couple of cots and a fireplace. They were often built along the roads in areas where inns were few and far between.

From the look of this one, some other traveler had already found it for the night.

Rowan was beyond caring. She stumbled up to the door, but just as she reached for the handle, it burst open, and Rowan tripped backward with a cry. She fell on her back in the road, her hand clenching around the lantern to keep it from rolling away.

"I thought I heard someone out here," a voice said. "I'm so sorry I startled you, honey. Here, let me help you."

A woman, bent with age, stepped out into the rain and reached for Rowan's free hand. She had no choice but to take it and let the old woman help her out of the mud. The woman squinted, the seams in her face deepening as she brushed ineffectively at the mud matting the back of Rowan's tunic.

"It's fine," Rowan said. "It's fine."

"Well, no, it's not," the woman said, drawing on her arm so that she finally passed into the warmth of the wayrest. Shelves lined the far wall flanking a merry little fireplace, each one covered with dried foodstuff and kindling. "You're lucky old Midge was here restocking. The fire's already going, and you'll be dry in no time. Then that mud will flake right off."

The woman finally let go of her arm to close the door, and Rowan's free hand went around the lantern, hugging it to her chest. The motion drew Midge's attention, and her brow furrowed.

"What do you have there?"

"Nothing," Rowan said too quickly. "It's nothing."

"Right, good cover," Gavyn said in her head. "She'll absolutely believe that."

Midge peered at her, eyes nearly disappearing into her drooping eyelids. Maybe the old woman was so nearsighted she'd completely overlook the gleaming bit of gold and glass.

Gavyn was right, she'd already screwed this up.

"A lantern?" Midge said. "That's beautiful workmanship. But odd. May I see it?"

"No," Rowan said. "I mean. No, thank you. I'm carrying it for…"

Healer's Ghost, she'd never been good at lying. What would keep the old woman from looking any closer?

"I'm carrying it for Lord Hax. Delivering it, I mean. I don't think he'd want me passing it around."

Midge blinked at her. Hopefully it was enough. Lord Hax had never been known for his patience or benevolence.

Finally, she smiled. "All right. It's not my habit to pry. You set yourself by the fire, and I'll find a clean bowl for the soup."

"Thank you," Rowan said. "But I-I'd just like to rest. I've been walking—" A fortuitous yawn interrupted her, nearly cracking her jaw.

"Say no more, honey." Midge held up her hands. "Just take that tunic off first so you don't muck up the bed, thank you. Then I'll leave you alone. Old Midge knows when to pester and when to shut up."

Rowan almost argued, but it would be a lot nicer to sleep without the heavy wet garment tangling around her. And if Midge was kind enough to keep this wayrest stocked and clean, then Rowan wasn't going to be the awful person who messed it up.

She stripped the wet tunic off and draped it over the hook by the fire, leaving only her linen shift underneath. But Midge didn't seem to mind, bustling around the hearth. Rowan stumbled to the bed nearest the fire and fell into it. She placed the lantern under the edge of the rough cot, and she rolled onto her side so she could keep her hand against it.

Gavyn might have murmured something to her as she closed her eyes, but sleep fell over her, insistent and urgent.

A crusty film glued her eyelids together when she finally woke. She blinked, trying to bring the room into focus. From the dim light coming in through the cracks around the shutters, she realized she'd slept for hours, but the rain still pattered against the roof.

Rustling came from the other side of the wayrest and the whisper of a voice.

Rowan took a deep breath to clear the rest of the sleep from her mind and reached under the bed for the lantern.

Her fingers closed over empty air.

Her heart hammered as she sat up and peered over the side of the cot at the bare floorboards.

Rowan spun to survey the rest of the room and gasped. Midge sat by the fire humming to herself while a large man stood beside her, turning the lantern over and over in his hands.

He wore his light hair cropped short, and a sword hung from his belt.

"What are you doing?" Rowan snapped. She swung her legs over the edge of the cot and then realized she still wore only her shift. She clutched the blankets around her and glanced desperately at her tunic hanging across the room.

"Relieving you of your burden, honey," Midge said, perfectly calm. "What do you think, Verron? Will you be able to sell it?"

The man used his nail to tap the glass. It made a sharp little *tink, tink, tink* noise. "Might be hard to find a buyer."

"You think? Even for a pretty lamp like that?"

"It's clearly magic, Ma," Verron said. "Valuable though. I'll have to find someone who'll pay."

"You're thieves," Rowan said flatly. The doddering old woman had thrown her off her guard, and she'd been so tired...

Midge snorted. "You're one to talk. Don't try to tell me Lord Hax just gave this thing to you to carry around. Take it from us, honey. If you're going to lie to cover up theft, think of something a lot more believable."

"Please don't touch it," Rowan said, standing with the blanket wrapped around her. "It's dangerous. It hurt my sister." She edged toward the hook where her tunic hung.

"What did it do? Spill burning oil on her?" Midge said with a chuckle. "You'll have to do better than that."

Verron held the lantern closer to his face. "It doesn't have any oil in it, Ma," he said with an uncertain frown.

"Please, I'm just trying to protect you," Rowan said. She grabbed her tunic from the hook and slung it over her arm with the blanket still clutched tight around her. Her satchel hung from the same hook. Its contents had been rearranged, but apparently Midge hadn't found any value in the notebooks or the dried food, and she likely had no idea what the fire charges were.

The fire charges. Could Rowan use those to get Gavyn and the lantern back and then escape?

She winced. Probably not. Unless she wanted to blast herself with the spell as well as Verron and his mother.

"Don't do anything you might regret now, honey," Midge said as if reading her thoughts.

Rowan glared at her. "What? Like steal something that doesn't belong to me?"

Midge chuckled and turned back to her pot. "Squawk all you want. You can't fight my Verron to get your pretty bauble back."

Rowan glanced at the hulking brute. He might have been the old woman's muscle, but he was glancing between Rowan and the lantern like he had a mind of his own and he was rethinking his mother's plan.

"Do you know anything about magic?" she asked him specifically, already knowing the answer. "I do. A little. I know enough to regret that little bit. It's changed my life. I know enough to recognize a curse when I see one."

"Curse?" Verron said.

"Don't listen to her," Midge said. "She's just trying to scare you into dropping it."

"Yes, curse." It was close enough at least. "That thing made my sister sick. It made our whole camp sick. I'm trying to get it as far away from them as possible, so it doesn't hurt anyone else."

"Step away from him, girl," Midge said, her voice going far less friendly now, and Rowan took it as a sign that she was getting somewhere with Verron.

Midge stood and stepped up to Rowan and nudged her back, away from her son.

Rowan put a hand out to steady herself and touched the mantle over the fireplace. A bit of warmth flared under her fingertips, different from the heat of the flames. A touchpoint.

"Look, Ma, maybe she has a point. Why else would she be out here in the middle of nowhere with a magic lantern?"

"Because she's a thief like us, you nitwit."

Rowan had nothing to lose and no other ideas, so she let her gift flare and reach for the touchpoint on the mantel.

Black swept her vision for that one second then was replaced with an image of Midge standing over her pot, holding her forearm and cursing.

It was gone in the next instant, and Rowan shook the vision from her eyes.

"I'm just saying we can be careful," Verron said. "I don't want any magical curses on me or mine."

"Oh, give me that." Midge snatched the lantern from him, making it swing wildly and cast flickering shadows over the interior of the wayrest. "If you're too scared to hold it, I will. We'll take it to your buyer, and it'll be out of our hands before any curse comes down—"

Rowan snatched up the poker beside the fireplace and brought it down swiftly on Midge's forearm where she'd seen her burn herself.

Midge cried out and dropped the lantern.

Rowan dove for it, her back twinging wildly. The blanket dropped from around her, but she caught the lantern and stumbled back away from Verron and Midge.

Midge crouched, cradling her arm and cursing, but Verron blocked the door.

"Thought you said you didn't want to hurt us," he said with a grim tilt of his mouth.

Rowan mirrored his expression. "Trust me, this is me keeping you alive."

Verron's gaze flickered between her and his mother, and his mouth hardened.

"Gavyn, do you have any ideas?" Rowan said.

"Me?" Gavyn's voice was welcome after so many moments when she couldn't hear him. "What in the cursed hells am I going to do?"

"I don't know, the lantern does things, right?" She didn't want to tell complete strangers that it was some sort of weapon. They already wanted it badly enough as it was. "Maybe you can control it."

"Who is she talking to?" Verron muttered to his mother.

"No one." Midge narrowed her eyes. "Not only is she a liar, she's a madwoman as well."

"Gavyn!"

"I'm stuck in here, I'm a prisoner. I'm not the master of the lantern! I can't affect anything. I can see and I can hear and can think; there's nothing else, Rowan!"

The light pulsed in time with the words that resounded in her head, and she fought down a brief grin of triumph.

"I think you're holding out on me, Gavyn."

"Why? Why would I do that? You think if I could do anything I would choose not to?"

Verron clenched his fists and stepped toward Rowan.

And just then the lantern flared in her hands. Rowan squeezed her eyes tight, warned only by the sliver of hope she'd had that this would happen.

Verron and Midge cried out in unison.

The flash of light subsided, and Rowan lowered her hand. Verron stumbled blindly, and Rowan took the chance to dart around him to the door of the wayrest.

Cold rain pattered against the roof, and she ducked out into it without a second glance behind.

She didn't stop running until she couldn't breathe anymore, and she collapsed to her knees in the middle of the muddy road.

When she took stock of herself, she realized she was still in her shift with her tunic slung over her arm and her satchel over the other shoulder.

She paused long enough to wrestle the wet fabric over her head. "So much for getting warm and dry."

"I hope the good night's sleep was worth nearly losing the lantern," Gavyn said acidly once she'd picked it back up.

Rowan's shoulders slumped. She didn't dare rest the way she wanted to. Who knew how long Verron and Midge would remain blinded? They could be coming up the road after her at any moment.

"I'm sorry," Rowan said. "But I can't go on and on forever. I have to stop. I have to sleep."

Gavyn hesitated long enough for her to start sniffling in the rain. "No," he said. "I'm sorry. I shouldn't have snapped. Never thought I'd forget what it was like to be Human with a body and everything."

Rowan resettled her satchel—at least she'd had the presence of mind to sling it over her shoulder after checking it—and stepped off the road. The way would be a lot slower going in the foothills, but at least there she had some cover from other thieves or from Verron and Midge if they caught up to her.

"What are we going to do, Gavyn?"

"I don't know. That was exactly what we were worried about. Someone saw something valuable and tried to take it, disregarding the danger."

"Thanks for saving me."

Gavyn snorted. "You saved us. How did you know I could do that? Use the lantern's light like that."

"I hoped." Rowan rubbed the rainwater from her face. "You obviously created some kind of connection with it when you tried to destroy it. You magically welded yourself to it. So, it stands to reason that it's not just your prison. There's a part of you that is the lantern and a part of the lantern that is you."

"So, I can control it."

"Or at least a part of it. We still don't know what it does or how. But maybe now you aren't as helpless as you thought."

"Woohoo, I can make light," he said wearily. "Do you know how many years I spent in that basement not being able to do anything?"

"Nearly a hundred," Rowan answered before she realized it was probably a rhetorical question.

"It's... a lot of time." Another pause and Rowan got the impression he was shaking the melancholy from his thoughts. "All right, so what did we learn?"

"Don't trust strangers?"

"Right. The Grief Draw is too conspicuous."

"We need a way to hide it or disguise it, but without actually leaving it somewhere."

"I'd… rather not go in the dark again, but I will if it will keep that sort of thing from happening again."

Rowan stared down at her belt with all its little pockets and cases for ink and quills and parchment. It would have been easy to leave it behind by accident, but it had been tucked in the folds her tunic where it had hung from its hook.

"I think I might have an idea about that."

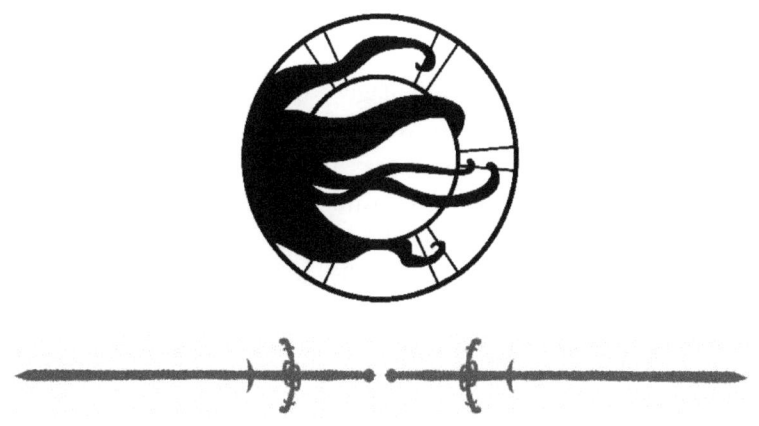

CHAPTER TWELVE

ROWAN

Lannasbrook sat nestled in the foothills at the end of the western mountain range with the rising peaks on one side and fields along the other. Late morning sun gilded the thatched roofs, the rain from the previous two days finally gone.

"This is your home?" Gavyn said.

She'd pulled apart her satchel to make a leather case for the lantern. It covered the glass panes from the bottom all the way to the metal cap with holes poked in a pretty pattern to look decorative but also so Gavyn could see out. It wasn't the best view, he'd said, but it beat having a blanket thrown over him. Straps connected the lantern to her belt at her hip, and with the cap free of leather, Rowan could rest her hand on the top of the lantern to hear him speak.

"Yes, this is Lannasbrook." She surveyed the first couple of cottages. The foothills flattened out to give way to fields, leaving the road to meander through the center of the village. "The last village in Lord Hax's lands. Everything beyond belongs to Lord Karaval."

"If you say so. I honestly have no idea where we are. When the treasure hunter kidnapped me, I spent most of the time traveling unconscious."

Rowan pointed past the village. "If you keep going another couple of days, you'll get to Monclaren, a bigger town up in the eastern range. Even further east is the capital."

"That's where I'm from. I wonder if any of my family is still around there." He paused as if taking stock of her village and everything beyond. "This is actually quite far from the ruins. I don't know if Keinwen would have made it this far."

Rowan didn't answer. Keinwen sounded remarkable, but if she had been weak or sick from her experience, Lannasbrook would have seemed a million miles away. And even if she made it, finding any trace of her now would be next to impossible.

Rowan blew out her breath and squared her shoulders toward the settlement. She was stalling, and she knew it. She jerked her chin up in the old habitual gesture and started down the road toward her home for the first time in three months.

Her feet dragged a little, and not just from the last two nights she'd spent sleeping on the ground. Her back ached, and her hips hurt, but neither compared to the tightness in her chest.

In the first field she passed, an old woman and a younger man straightened to shield their eyes, peering at the visitor coming down their road. Rowan could tell the moment they recognized her.

The old woman spit and turned her back, then she picked up her scythe again to swing it in a wide arc.

The man glared as she made her way along the edge of the field. Rowan remembered him as a boy, kicking her game pieces into the pond and screaming at her back, but he'd grown tall and broad now.

Her shoulders twitched as if she could dislodge their disapproval, but it worked about as well as it had when she was a child.

She knew better than to hope that Rona and her son were the only ones out and about today. Autumn meant the grain had to be harvested, threshed, and winnowed before it could be hauled off to the market at Monclaren. Everyone would be outside, and Rowan had to walk the gauntlet of the road.

"I should have gone around back," she muttered. It would have been twice as long to go around the fields, and she hadn't been able to stomach the thought of more walking, but then she wouldn't have had to endure the looks.

An old man with a red rag tied around his head leaned on his scythe beside the crumbling stone wall dividing his fields from the road. He narrowed his eyes as Rowan passed.

"Keep moving, blighted," Bellrand croaked even though Rowan's pace hadn't slowed at all.

"Soo, did you trample these people's crops or something?" Gavyn said as she left the old man's stare behind. "They don't seem to like you very much."

"If it was something I could apologize for, I would have done it long ago," Rowan said through clenched teeth. "This is normal, just ignore it."

A man trundling a wheelbarrow down the road gave her a wide berth and spat in her shadow.

"Rowan, this is not normal."

"Maybe not for you."

Coming home should have been full of joy. She should have felt like she was walking into a cocoon of safety. At least that's how others always described a homecoming, but the village had never felt safe. Even as a child, before she knew why, she'd walked this road with her shoulders tensed and an extra eye behind her. Now she was old enough to know why.

As she came into the village proper, where houses lined the road and the fields stretched out behind them, a group of children screeched past. They swerved around her shouting, "Blighted, blighted!"

Rowan sighed. "It's just normal for me. They've always called me 'godsblighted.' They think the gods cursed me for something I did in another life."

"Do you believe them?"

No. The answer was absolutely no, of course. How many times had her mother tried to convince her the villagers were wrong? How many times had she gone home crying, wondering what she'd done wrong?

"Nothing, little Row," her mother had always said, voice gentle even as her lips went white with rage. "There is nothing wrong with you. I love you, and I will always protect you."

And later her mother would whisper to Esrell and Darryn, "We must care for Rowan. It is our job to protect her from the world."

And Rowan, pretending she couldn't hear, would grit her teeth and think, *If there was nothing wrong with me, then I wouldn't need to be protected.*

"I don't believe in gods who would punish someone for something they don't remember and didn't choose," Rowan told Gavyn.

And in the end, she cared very little what the villagers thought. It wasn't their opinion that mattered. They weren't the ones who coddled and shielded and tried to wrap her in cotton lest she cut herself on the realities of her body and its limitations. They weren't the ones she had to convince that she was capable and competent.

And it was so much harder to do the convincing when you had your own insidious doubts.

She kept her hand casually pressed to the cap of the lantern, maintaining contact without drawing attention to it.

"It must have been very uncomfortable," Gavyn said. "Growing up with people who think you're a monster."

"I don't blame them," she muttered, trying not to move her lips. If the villagers didn't already think she was cursed, talking to herself would certainly convince them she was possessed. "Not anymore. To others I look monstrous." She could say it now with only a little bit of bile creeping up the back of her throat.

"Actually, you *can* blame them. Living out in the middle of nowhere is no excuse to wear your ass as a hat."

Rowan couldn't help snorting. "You might be more enlightened than most. For good reason." She tapped the metal with her fingertip, though the late morning sunlight washed out the white glow of the lantern.

"Ha. Good one. You at least seem to possess some good sense, though you were born here."

Rowan shrugged, ignoring the pack of children who followed her shouting nasty names. "I feel sorry for them actually. They're afraid. It's easier for them to believe that something bad only happens to you if you do something to deserve it, rather than face the fear that we're all at the mercy of chance."

"How noble of you. Are those your own words of wisdom?"

A smile played with her lips. "My mother's, but I'd rather believe it than spend my life angry."

"Then I'll be angry for you."

Rowan had nearly reached her parents' house at the very end of the village when a stout housewife blocked her path.

"We don't want you here, blighted," she said, planting her hands on her broad hips. The basket hanging from her elbow swung with the movement.

"You've always made that clear, Helana," Rowan said, voice flat. "But I live here."

"No more you don't. We won't stand for it."

Rowan's lips thinned. "What are you talking about?"

"It weren't enough you were born blighted; you defy the gods and tempt them to make your next life worse. We all work to please them so we can be born again, better. But you made yourself a thief. You took a thing that doesn't belong to you."

Ice raced along Rowan's arms, leaving goosebumps in its wake.

"Jannik beat us here," Gavyn said in the back of her mind.

Rowan shook her head at Helana. "You don't know what you're talking about. This is more complicated than—"

"Theft is theft. You always did have your nose in the air. Thinking you were better than the rest."

Rowan huffed a disbelieving laugh and put her hand to her chest. "What? After all the time you spent telling me I wasn't worth anything?"

Helana sniffed. "You're not, but you always defied the gods' will. Flaunting your fancy writing in our faces. Flaunting the job you got. It went to your head, it did, and now you're trying to get away with something that's not yours."

Rowan cast a quick glance around the village. The others had drifted in from the fields, gathering down the road. She didn't see her parents.

"Liar and a thief," Bellrand muttered.

"What did Jannik tell you?" Rowan asked.

"You made up lies about him," Helana said. "Telling the diggers he didn't care when they got sick. He found something powerful, and you decided to take it for yourself. Weak, Rowan, you were always weak, so you wanted that power."

"It was dangerous," Rowan said. "He didn't tell you everything. He's the liar, not me." Healer's Ghost, did he manipulate everyone this way? How much of who he was was true and how much had he convinced people to believe?

"They're not going to listen," Gavyn said. "Rowan, this is going to get ugly."

"I have to talk to my parents." Rowan tried to move past Helana, but the housewife used her bulk to block Rowan and thrust her back a step.

"Maybe the gods put you here so we could prove our faith," she said.

Bellrand stooped to pick up a rock.

The old tingle ran down Rowan's crooked spine. The one that told her to watch behind her as she walked down the street.

"Get out of here, Rowan," Gavyn cried. "Run."

Rowan spun, but the crowd had closed in behind her, carrying scythes and sickles in white-knuckled grips. The children cast about on the ground for stones as big as Rowan's fist.

Her breath came in great gasps as panic rose in her chest.

"Hey. Hey!" A figure pushed through the gathered villagers, and Rowan sobbed in relief.

Her stepfather, Stefan, took her arm and turned himself so he stood between her and Helana. There were still more behind her, and her neck crawled, but Stefan's bulk felt like a bulwark. A shield against everything else.

"Healer take you, what do you think you're doing?" Stefan's voice had always been so gentle with her and her siblings, but now it held an edge that cut through the villagers' noise.

Even Helana glanced up at Stefan's broad face and wide shoulders and winced. "You can't protect her forever, Stefan. The gods want her punished."

"The gods?" Stefan said. "Or you? Be careful you don't make a mistake that lands *you* crippled in another life." He glared down Helana and Bellrand as the two most vocal of their neighbors. "Now get out of the way. I'm taking my daughter home. Unless you think stoning *me* will go well for you."

He didn't flex the muscles he'd earned over a lifetime in the fields, and he didn't brandish the pitchfork he carried low at his side. But Helana took a step back under the force of his stare. She and Bellrand exchanged a look and stepped aside, leaving a narrow aisle for Stefan and Rowan.

Rowan's skin crawled as Stefan drew her forward through that passage of hate and loathing. She stayed in his shadow and let him lead.

"Go home," Stefan said as Rowan darted around him and reached for the latch. "I won't ask again."

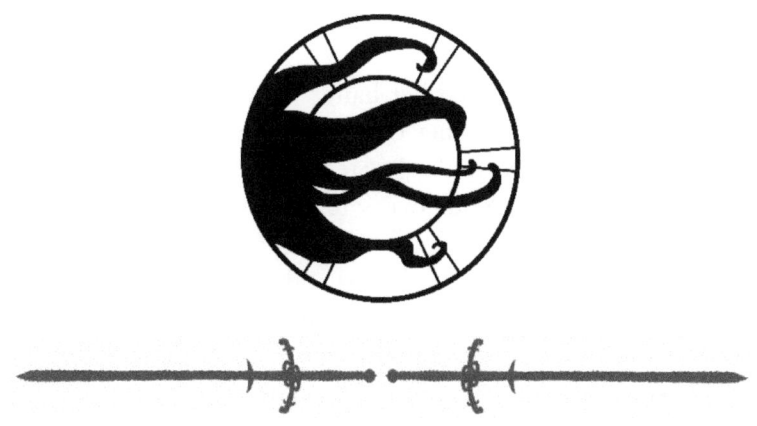

CHAPTER THIRTEEN

ROWAN

With her parents' solid wood door behind her, her shoulders sagged, the tension bleeding away until she nearly collapsed on the floor. The sharp scent of willow pervaded the house, and something bubbled softly over the fire.

Rowan's littlest brothers, Onrick and Verner, raced to clutch at her knees shouting, "Rowan, Rowan!"

Her throat closed up. At least it hadn't been *their* voices shouting "blighted!"

She hugged them each around their shoulders, before shooing them away with a tight smile. The lantern still hung at her hip, and now that she'd actually made it home, she had a time limit to how long she knew she could stay.

"You shouldn't have done that," Rowan said quietly to her stepfather. "Who knows what they will do to you now."

Stefan's mobile lips thinned, but he met her eyes with his. "They still respect me. We'll be safe as long as that's true. And so will you. You will always be at home in my house, Rowan."

Rowan slid down the door and sat on the floor, arms around her knees. Stefan knelt in front of her.

"Are you all right?"

"No." Rowan scrubbed her hands over her face, thinking of the stones and how close they'd been. "Where's Jannik?"

"He was here yesterday," Stefan said. "He and Darryn brought Esrell home. Your ma is tending her at the sick house now."

She buried her face in her hands and wept at the words.

Stefan wrapped her in his arms and let her cry.

"She's all right?" she said between sobs. "I thought she was going to die. This whole time I didn't know if she'd survive."

"Your ma says the vomiting stopped yesterday. She'll be all right eventually. Nora knows more than I, and I trust her when she tells me things like that."

"Getting her away from the lantern helped," Gavyn said as Rowan's elbow brushed the handle.

She nodded and wiped her eyes. But Stefan was still there with his hands on her shoulders, and the lantern still hung within reach. She cleared her throat and stood so Stefan had to move away.

"Where is Darryn?"

Stefan hesitated, caught between standing and crouching. Then he straightened and went to close the shutters. As if barring them in the middle of the day was completely normal.

"He's out looking for you. He believed the things Jannik was saying. About you stealing something. I trust Jannik, but you've never taken something that didn't belong to you in your life."

Rowan drew herself up. "I did take it," she said, voice fierce. "But I did it for a reason. The artifact was making Esrell sick, and Jannik didn't believe me."

Stefan drew back, his brow coming down, and he blinked at her. She'd always thought of his brown eyes as huge and trusting. Stefan spoke kindly of people even when they'd wronged him; he laughed in the face of anger and eased Nora's more volatile worries. How much of that would be tested by

Jannik's lie? Rowan's story barely made sense to her. What would her parents make of it?

Rowan opened her mouth, but the door banged open, making her start.

Her mother thumped in, her boots clunking on the floorboards as she knocked the door back and tossed her healer's bag to one side.

Nora wore her curly hair pulled back from her face, but just like Rowan's, stray strands had escaped to frame her eyes. She tossed aside a stained apron, but her tunic remained clean.

She caught sight of Rowan, and for a split second, Rowan waited to see the doubt creep into her gaze. Jannik was Nora's oldest friend.

"Rowan," her mother breathed, and then she was across the room, sweeping Rowan up into her arms.

Even in adulthood, Rowan barely came up to her mother's shoulder, and she buried her face in Nora's chest. Nora's arms closed around her like a shield, and for once, Rowan didn't resent it.

"Helana said you'd come home," Nora said, pulling away to search her face at arm's length.

Stefan growled under his breath. "Did she tell you about the stones too?"

Nora looked at him sharply. "No. She left that part out."

"How is Esrell?" Rowan asked before they could pick apart Helana's actions. Her time was limited, and she wouldn't give any more to that woman than she already had.

"Recovering," Nora said. "She was struggling, but I believe she's past the worst of it. I'm keeping her at the sick house for now."

Years before, Nora had browbeat the villagers until they'd pitched together to build another hut on the edge of town. A place where she could tend those who fell ill without having to keep them in their own homes. They'd ignored her until, over time, they'd finally come to realize that most of Nora's patients survived.

She'd spent a lot of time observing, and while healers in Monclaren drained their patients of blood, Nora had noticed that clean hands and clean bandages kept wounds from festering. And isolating coughs and sniffles kept them from spreading.

"The quiet is probably good for her," Rowan said softly as she took her seat on the stool again. "But you don't have to worry about anyone else getting sick."

Nora sat opposite her while Stefan puttered around the hearth, keeping Onrick from playing in the ashes. "What do you mean? How do you know?"

"It was the artifact we found," Rowan said. "*I* found. Esrell touched it, and it made her sick. It made everyone sick except Jannik and Darryn, who never actually handled it."

"How can an object make someone sick?" Nora said, shaking her head.

Rowan spread her hands. "How can dirty hands and bandages make wounds fester? Trust me, Ma. It happened before, but when I tried to tell Jannik, he didn't believe me. I knew the only way to keep Esrell safe was to take it away."

"I trust you," Nora said, without another breath of disbelief. She took Rowan's hands in hers and turned them over to examine her palms. Her mother's eyes rose to search her face. "But you touched it, Esrell said. Will I be tending you now?"

Rowan schooled her expression to keep from grimacing. She'd held the Grief Draw more than any of them knew, even Esrell. And she very carefully didn't keep from mentioning that the object in question hung from her hip, even now. She didn't want them worrying about what it might do to them, and as long as it stayed in its case and no one touched it, they should be safe. She would *make* them safe.

But her mother's concern led right into why Rowan had risked coming here in the first place.

She turned her hands over again to show her mother she didn't have the same blisters Esrell had. "I seem to be immune."

Nora's brows drew together, a sure sign her thoughts were working through Rowan's words. "Why wouldn't it hurt you, too, if it's that dangerous?"

Rowan held her gaze. "I don't know. Maybe because of my father."

Nora and Stefan both fell still, Nora's hands still clasping her fingers and Stefan straight and silent by the hearth.

"I'm sorry," Rowan said, turning to Stefan. "You're my da more than anyone else, especially someone I never met, but there *was* someone before." She turned back to her mother. "We all know that."

She kept her breath moving in and out as steady as she could manage as Nora's lips turned down. Was that sadness? Regret? Disgust? Rowan could only tell that she'd made her parents unhappy, but not exactly how.

"I need to know."

Nora took a deep, bracing breath. "You really think it's important?"

"Jannik seemed to think so, and he's still the expert." Rowan's teeth clenched. "Why did he know, and I didn't? Why would *anyone* know before me?"

Her voice rose unexpectedly. She hadn't realized the burning feeling in her chest was betrayal until it came roiling up her throat.

"He knew because he was there, Row. It wasn't as if I went around talking about it with just anyone." Nora's lip twitched. "He's been a friend for longer than you've been alive, so yes, he knew your father."

Rowan's shoulders drooped. "Who was it, Ma? Why is he so important that Jannik would think I'd be useful? What heritage did he give me?"

Nora licked her lips, face tight. "I don't think it's *who* he was so much as *what* he was."

"What does that mean?"

"Don't make that face," Nora said quickly. "This is why I didn't want to tell you when you were little. It would have just made you feel more different."

"Then maybe you shouldn't have had a godsblighted child." The heat rose, making the words come out in short, sharp bursts, far hotter than she meant them. "Maybe you shouldn't have taught me to read. Or raised me with people who called me 'monster.'"

"I didn't let you call yourself that when you were little," Nora said, voice fierce. "I won't let you do it now either."

Stefan moved to stand behind Nora, placing his hands on her shoulders. She reached up to clasp his fingers.

"I'm sorry I've made mistakes, but I will not regret the one that made you."

Rowan reeled on her stool, faced with the meaning in her mother's words. She gulped down a breath and forced the questions to calm underneath the certainty she'd held for so long. Her mother loved her. Little else mattered after that.

Nora patted Stefan's hand and twisted her head to gaze up at him. She didn't have to say anything.

His lips quirked, and he kissed the top of her head. "I think I'll go play with the boys for a bit."

He gave Rowan a wink and swept Onrick up in his arms before herding Verner to the other side of the room where the basket of carved horses sat.

Rowan swallowed. "What was my father, then? The longer you take to tell me, the worse things I'm going to make up in my head."

Nora snorted. "That I can believe. He was a Delver, Rowan. Do you even know what a Delver is?"

Rowan blinked, trying to form a clear picture from the snippets of myth and gossip she'd heard around the village and in Monclaren. "The dwarves?"

Nora nodded. "They come out of the mountains sometimes to trade with the smiths in the mountain towns. This particular Delver was aiming for Monclaren and missed the mark. You know the ravine past the foothills where the blood blossoms grow?"

Rowan remembered the steep hills covered in crimson flowers where her mother gathered the ingredients for many of her poultices and nodded.

"He broke a leg and two ribs and lay in the bottom for nearly a week before I found him."

"And you tended him."

A smile flitted across her mother's face. "I did. He was…"

"Short?" Rowan raised her eyebrows.

Nora gave her a mild glare. "Strong. Handsome in his own way. More importantly, he was kind. And funny. He made me laugh. Mostly on purpose and sometimes because we were so different."

Rowan could imagine it now. The recovery. The laughter. The brief romance. "He… didn't want to stay?" Her voice broke on the last word.

Nora ducked her head to meet Rowan's gaze squarely. "He had no idea about you, Row, and Delvers aren't too comfortable above ground. Once he was gone, and I knew you were coming, I didn't have a way to contact him. I sent a message once, through the Delvers in Monclaren. When I never heard back…" She shrugged. "I assumed that was my answer."

Rowan bit her lip. She wasn't the only one who might have been hurt in all this. "I'm sorry."

Nora shook her head as if to clear it. "Maybe *I* should be sorry." For once, she wouldn't meet Rowan's eyes, and her throat bobbed as she swallowed. "I always wondered if it was his blood and my blood at war that made you the way you are."

Rowan's back hurt. So did her heart. She could see her mother almost as clear as if her gift had given her the vision, cradling a tiny, twisted baby and crying as she wondered how long the little girl would live and what kind of life something so broken and malformed could look forward to.

At the far side of the room, Stefan sat on the floor with his long legs sprawled in front of him, dancing a wooden horse for Onrick. Beside him, Verner hopped from one foot to the other in time with a nursery rhyme.

> *"Healer, healer, why do you sigh?*
> *Remember to laugh, so you don't cry.*
> *Light against the dark and time too long to mark.*
> *Healer, healer, save me please try."*

It was a familiar song she'd sung herself when she was little. Grim in the way most nursery rhymes were. Verner upheld the local tradition and spun in a circle before falling to the ground with a giggle on the last line.

Rowan rubbed her chest over her heart, thoughts moving too fast to capture. Like she was spinning too and would collapse to the ground under their weight at any moment.

So much knowledge she hadn't had an hour ago. So much pain she hadn't carried until just now. Hers. Her mother's. Even Stefan's and her unknown father's out there somewhere.

"Did he have a name?" she asked. It seemed so petty and so important at the same time.

"Lynnock," Nora said.

Rowan opened her mouth just as a sharp knock rattled the door. Rowan jumped, her stool rocking.

"Nora," Jannik's voice called. "Open up. I know she's in there. All she has to do is give it back. You hear that, Rowan? All is forgiven if you just give me the lantern."

CHAPTER FOURTEEN

GAVYN

Even from his spot on her hip, Gavyn could see that Rowan's home was clean and cramped and well-loved. Generations of soot blackened the mantle over the fireplace, and Gavyn caught sight of an ancient mortar and pestle propped up there in a place of honor.

Rowan had mentioned she came from a long line of healers. Perhaps it had belonged to some grandmother nearly forgotten in time but honored just the same.

Melancholy settled in his thoughts as Rowan spoke with her parents. Had Keinwen found a place like this to belong? A village where her magic would be appreciated? How would he ever find out?

Rowan had cut holes for him in the lantern's case, and while he didn't have as wide a view as he used to, he could still piece together the scene around him through his little peepholes. From the front, he could make out Rowan's mother with her curly hair and delicate features. Rowan might have been short and a little hunched, if they were honest, but he could see the strong resemblance to Nora in the lines of her face and jaw.

But there were also some missing pieces there. Rowan's features had been smoothed and spread out by a different source.

Clearly the unknown father.

The Delver.

Gavyn had never met a Delver. Even before he'd lodged himself in this cage of metal and light. He really only knew about them from stories and the occasional peddler who claimed to have one of their trinkets. Personally, he'd always assumed the peddlers were charlatans.

But Gavyn wouldn't have dared call Nora a liar. Besides, her story was plausible. He could think of several reasons beyond the ones she stated for why she'd never told Rowan about her father. For one, the villagers already seemed a little backward. He couldn't imagine they'd welcome a romance with someone who was not even Human.

Rowan sat frozen, and Gavyn didn't press her to respond. He couldn't imagine what was going through her head right now.

A sing-song voice threaded through the farmhouse, providing a homey backdrop incongruous with Rowan's shock.

Behind them, Stefan sat on the floor with his offspring, the picture of patient fatherhood. The littlest boy sat on his lap, gnawing on a wooden horse while the older one spun in dizzying circles across the flagstones.

> *"Healer, healer, why do you sigh?*
> *Remember to laugh, so you don't cry.*
> *Light against the dark and time too long to mark.*
> *Healer, healer, save me please try."*

If Gavyn had had lungs, he would have held his breath. Like most nursery rhymes, the words barely made sense, just bits of nonsense strung together in song. But that line. *Laugh so you don't cry*. That carried across the small house and rang in his head like a bell.

Laugh so you don't cry.

"If we're not laughing, we're crying, Keinwen. And I don't know about you, but I'm tired of crying."

He'd said that. Those were some of the last words he'd ever said to her.

So many years stood between him and that moment in the past, but he could still see her face, her golden skin, dark with exhaustion, her eyes hopeless, staring at him as he tried to make her smile.

It had been so important to him.

This wasn't a fever dream from years underground staring at the same four walls. This was a memory.

He'd said that to her.

Why would his words be in a nursery rhyme sung by Rowan's little brothers?

"Rowan."

She wasn't listening. She didn't even have her hand on the lantern.

"Rowan! Rowan!"

How could he get her to hear him? How could he get her to answer him?

"Rowan, the rhyme! What is it? Listen to me!"

A knock rang through the house, making the hinges rattle.

"Nora," a voice called.

Senji's spit, it's Jannik. Gavyn's thoughts wavered.

"Open up."

Stefan clutched his son tight enough to make the boy squirm, and the farmer lumbered to his feet.

"I know she's in there. All she has to do is give it back. You hear that, Rowan? All is forgiven if you just give me the lantern."

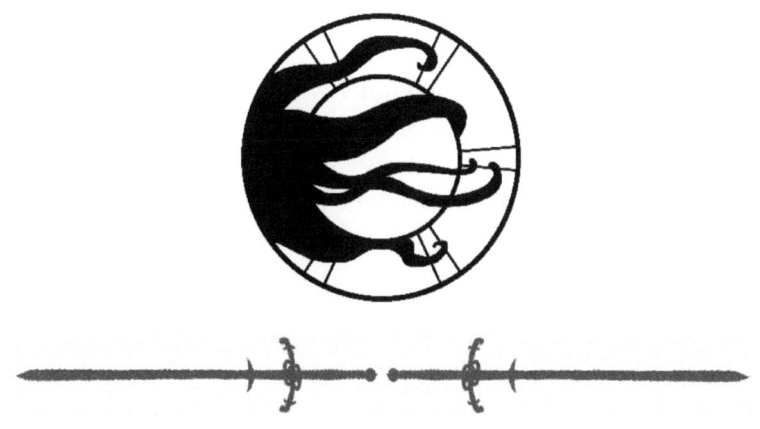

CHAPTER FIFTEEN

ROWAN

ealer's Ghost, Jannik's returned.

H"Rowan?" Jannik called through the door, voice even and reasonable. "That power is not yours. I told you people would come after the lantern, seeking to use it for their own ends. I never expected you to be one of them."

"That's not—" Rowan said, but her voice squeaked. She knew no matter how hard she argued, he'd turn her words around just like he'd done in his tent when she'd tried to get him to see the danger to Esrell and Darryn. Like he tried to do when he told her Gavyn was a liar.

"Nora," another voice called, and Rowan recognized Helana. "She's godsblighted, you know this. You can't protect her from the gods' curse forever."

Something thumped the closed shutters and made Nora jump. Voices called back and forth outside, greater in number than just Jannik and Helana.

Rowan's hands crept to her cheeks. They'd finally come for her. This was the reason her skin crawled every time she walked down the street. Because all this time they'd been just an insult away from violence. Right now, they were just yelling, rattling at the door and the shutters, but what would they do when Nora and Stefan refused to hand her over? What would they do when Rowan refused Jannik a second time?

"What do you think you're doing?" Stefan said through the door, settling Onrick on his hip. "This is our home. You can't just come here demanding whatever you want."

"She's a thief, Stefan," Helana said. "Bring her out, or we'll come in there and take her out."

Rowan's heart clenched. This wasn't just a threat to her. If they broke the door down, Nora and Stefan would be directly in the way of their hate. Onrick and Verner too. Esrell wouldn't be safe, isolated as she was. They'd go after her entire family. Just because of Jannik's lies.

"Jannik," Nora said evenly, moving to the door so he could hear her ringing voice. "You would let them do this?"

Jannik didn't answer. Either he couldn't hear her over the growing rumble of the crowd, or he didn't care.

Rowan's eyes darted between her mother and stepfather. She took in the way Stefan clutched Onrick and the way Verner hid behind his father's legs. She surveyed the little house with its loft where she'd slept with Esrell and Darryn.

She could easily imagine the villagers bursting through the door, breaking the table and its chairs on their way in, smashing her mother's poultice bottles, setting fire to the bed and the loft as they dragged Nora and Stefan and the boys outside.

She'd been a fool to come here. She'd been a fool to think she could protect them from the damage of her choices or even that the damage was limited to the lantern and Esrell's blisters.

Rowan's hand crept to the Grief Draw. Was keeping it really worth sacrificing Nora and Stefan and Onrick and Verner?

"I'll give myself up," she said. "If I go with Jannik, maybe they'll leave you alone."

Gavyn remained silent, but she could guess at his fear.

She lowered her head to speak directly to him. "Maybe he'll let me hold it for him, so it won't hurt anyone else." And so she could continue to talk to Gavyn.

Stefan stepped up beside Rowan as Nora's lips thinned. "No," he said.

She craned her neck to look up into his face.

He smiled down at her. "Even if we were willing to let you go—which we're not—we can't trust him anymore."

"Not when his words brought this mob here," Nora added.

Rowan's fingers clenched on the lantern. "But they might hurt you."

"And you think they'll just let you walk over to Jannik?" Nora said. "If they were willing to throw rocks before, what do you think they'll do now? No. You're not going out there."

Rowan bit her lip hard enough to sting. Their support meant everything to her, but their danger was her fault. What other option was there? What other option would they accept?

Her gaze flicked to the back door. "Maybe I'm not going out the front. But I *am* going."

Nora's lips thinned as she followed her daughter's glance.

"I'll go out the back and cause enough commotion that it'll be obvious that I've left. That will draw Jannik and the villagers. They won't have any reason to bother you if they think I've escaped."

"No." Nora stepped across the flagstones to seize Rowan's hands. "Not alone. I don't want you out there by yourself."

Rowan pulled herself gently from her mother. Her hands still shook, but she steadied one on the top of the lantern.

"Let's get out of here." Gavyn's calm voice came into her head.

"I'm not alone, Ma. I have to go," Rowan told Nora and Stefan. "I don't want this mess to hurt any of you, so you can't come with me, even if Esrell didn't need you."

Rowan moved toward the back door. Stefan set Onrick down and hurried to the shelves beside the hearth where he snatched up a sack.

Nora followed Rowan. "I need to know you have a plan. That you'll be safe."

The door cracked under someone's blow, and they all winced.

"Distract them, Ma. That's what will keep me safe right now."

Nora's mouth twisted, but she finally seized Rowan in a fierce hug and kissed her forehead. "Be safe," she said. Then she hurried back to the door.

"Fine, fine!" she called. "Rowan's coming out, but you've cracked the door in its frame. You have to step back so we can open it."

Rowan spun to the back door. She had very little time to make this work.

Stefan was already there with the sack. He'd shooed both boys under the table and told them to wait.

"Take that," he whispered, handing her the sack. "I hope I didn't forget anything. Now wait."

He put his ear to the back door and listened, his finger to his lips. Then he opened the door with a quick shove.

There was a cry, and Rowan darted out the door and dodged around Bellrand who'd been standing on the step. The old man rolled in the dirt and tried to grab at her feet as she passed, but Rowan sprinted for the stone wall separating their yard from the first field.

She wasn't exactly graceful as she tumbled over the top, and she hit the ground with a jarring thud that shot pain up her spine, but she was out of sight of the house for the moment.

"Here!" Bellrand cried. "She's here at the back."

Healer's Ghost, I need another distraction. Something to draw them off the wrong way.

Her hands fumbled at her belt where she'd stored everything that went in her cannibalized satchel. Ink, quill, parchment, lantern.

Fire charges.

Without thinking twice, she snatched one of the clay disks out of its pocket and snapped it in half, activating the spell.

Then she chucked the two halves toward the lane at the edge of the field.

The blast echoed from the foothills, and dirt pattered around her as calls and cries came from the front of the house.

Rowan twisted and ran crouched over in the opposite direction, toward the gap in the mountains.

At the edge of the trees, she turned, her hand on the rough bark of a beech. The mass of villagers converged on the lane across the field. None looked back at the forest.

The house remained locked up tight, her parents probably hiding for now until tempers in the village settled. They wouldn't know what had happened to her. They wouldn't know if she was all right or where she was going. But they would be safe.

The lantern buzzed under her hand, sending pins and needles across her palm, and she turned to disappear into the foothills.

● ● ●

Rowan knew these hills even better than the road to the ruins. She hadn't been a particularly adventurous child, but she'd spent enough time up here with her brother and sister. She kept away from the road for now and cut through the foothills to the very end of the mountain range. Her legs ached from the constant climbing but far ahead of her, across the sloping valley, another range stood even taller than the western peaks where her village lay.

"Where are we going?" Gavyn asked her as the sun disappeared behind them and the shadows chased them under the trees that dotted the foothills.

To him it probably looked like they were just running in a panic, but Rowan kept her eye on the hill beside them, measuring it against the distant peak, and as soon as it lined up perfectly, she turned until she heard the stream burble in the distance.

Her feet ached and her back sang with pain by the time a little charcoal burner's hut materialized out of the darkness. The kilns stood cold and empty beside it.

"Here," Rowan said. She pushed the door open on its leather hinges and nearly fell inside. The dark closed around her, hiding her from anyone else in the woods, and she let out a sigh she hadn't realized she'd been holding in.

"We should be safe here. No one comes up this way around this time of year. And I think we should stay away from places where I might be recognized."

"Probably a good idea," Gavyn said.

"I didn't expect Jannik to get ahead of us so fast." Rowan spoke to the inside of the door. Then she squared her shoulders and turned.

She pulled the lantern from its case at her hip, letting its light spill over the interior of the hut. A cobweb hung in the corner, but the rest of the tiny space was tidy enough. A bare cot stood along the left wall, opposite a little fire pit. A hole in the thatched roof would let out any smoke, and there was some wood stacked in the corner to aid the men and women who stayed here while tending the kilns outside.

The lantern gave her plenty of light but no heat, so Rowan squatted beside the fire pit and built herself a cheery blaze. Then she opened the sack Stefan had thrust at her and surveyed the contents.

Several days' worth of food—if she rationed herself—lay on top of a blanket thick enough she would be protected from the hard ground if she had to sleep outside again. And an enveloping cloak complete with hood was tucked beside that.

Rowan swallowed down the lump in her throat.

"Your stepfather is a thoughtful man," Gavyn said.

"There's no one kinder," Rowan said. She sat back, stretching her legs out in front of her, and she scrubbed her hands over her face. "I knew he wasn't my real father all this time. But the truth is even harder to imagine than I thought."

"Are you all right?" Gavyn said when she placed her hand back on the lantern.

"I don't know yet. I'm not... not Human."

"You are half Human," he said.

Rowan huffed a laugh. "And half something else."

"That's not necessarily a bad thing. Maybe it's the reason you're immune to the lantern."

Rowan held out her hands in front of her. Nothing had physically changed, but now the knuckles seemed too knobbly, the bones stretched strangely thin between them, and she closed her eyes before she imagined something freakish and alien where her own flesh and blood had been before.

She'd never seen one of the Delvers before. The most she knew about them she'd heard in rumors and cruel jokes.

Delvers are worse than moles, digging in the dark.

Delvers are stunted from all that time in cramped underground places.

Delvers eat rocks and are about as intelligent.

None of these could be true, based on her mother's account, but the truth was still strange. She'd been sired by a reclusive miner who hardly ever ventured out of his mountains.

Rowan opened her eyes again and squinted into the light of the lantern. She picked it up and held it in front of her with both hands.

"What do Delvers have to do with something the Giants made?" she asked, mostly to herself.

"I don't know," Gavyn answered her anyway. "I've never met one. They don't come out of their caves often, and they come down to the lowlands never."

"And we found the lantern down low. So why would it have anything to do with them?"

"Maybe the Giants stole it from them," Gavyn said. "Or maybe they made it to give to the Giants. Who knows? But if it's your heritage that makes you immune, and your heritage is Delver heritage..."

"Then the Delvers have to know more. At the very least, they'll know more than me." She settled the lantern in her lap and stretched her back. That twisted spine made her stand out in Lannasbrook. She'd never fit in there, but maybe it was more than just her physical differences. Maybe there was a place where her more unusual traits would be considered normal.

"I have to find a Delver to talk to."

"How far is Monclaren?" Gavyn asked as Rowan pushed herself off the floor with a groan.

"Far enough." She pulled the blanket from Stefan's sack and spread it out on the cot, one-handed. "But they might know what this thing actually is and how it works. They might be able to keep it safe. They might know my father." She added the last part under her breath, but Gavyn surely heard it anyway.

"Healer's Ghost," Rowan said with a groan as she lowered herself to the cot and grabbed an apple from the sack. "This just gets more and more complicated. A lantern with a man stuck inside, a weapon with no instructions, a sickness with no cure, and now Delvers."

There was a moment of silence while Rowan bit into the apple, one hand on the top of the lantern.

"What's that phrase you use?" Gavyn said into the quiet.

"What phrase?"

"Healer's Ghost. It's not a curse I've ever heard before."

Rowan cocked her head. "It's not really a curse. It's more like a prayer or asking for a blessing. I've only ever heard people around here use it. It's a local legend."

"Does it have anything to do with that rhyme your brother was reciting?"

Rowan had to think back. Verner's game had faded into the background; just a child's song, nothing special or worthy of notice.

"I don't know. I've never connected the two, but I guess they could be talking about the same healer. That would actually make a lot of sense."

"What's the legend?" Gavyn said, voice rising. "Tell me the story."

She was about to tease him for needing a bedtime story, but something in his voice stopped her. Whatever his interest, it was serious to him, and she couldn't make fun of something that made him sound that desperate.

"The way my grandmother always told it, and she was the storyteller of the family, there was a healer once who roamed the woods around our village. Some people said she was looking for a lost child. Some said she'd misplaced a necklace, but my grandmother knew the truth." Rowan tried to moderate her voice, mimicking her grandma's dramatic tones. "She was searching for her wounded lover. She knew she could save him if she could just find him. But…"

"But what?" Gavyn said. "What happened?"

Rowan's mouth fell open, pieces falling into place. "Someone stole him. Again, the stories vary, but Grandma swore the Giants came back and stole him away so the healer could never find him. She wandered the woods for the rest of her life looking. It consumed her until she died. And now, even in death, you can still catch her wandering the forest, looking for her stolen lover."

"Keinwen," Gavyn whispered.

"I…I think so." The pieces of the story were so similar.

His voice rose. "It's Keinwen. Rowan, that story is about *Keinwen!*"

"The Giants didn't steal you," she said, her excitement meeting his. "You never escaped from their trap in the first place."

"Your grandma knew it. What else did she say?"

"That's it. People think it's just a story, but my grandma heard it from her grandmother who says she saw the Healer's Ghost many times. The ghost always appeared the same time every month, like she followed the same path through the woods, over and over, between the ruins and the village and Monclaren."

"She was looking for someone. She was looking for me!"

Rowan bit her lip, the implications swirling around and around. "You were the lover in the story?"

Gavyn stammered, and she could just imagine his flush. "Well, I-I… no. Not like that." He grew quiet. "I loved her, but we were captives. We never had a chance to… We were only free for a few moments, and then I had to go back to destroy the lantern so Keinwen would have a chance to live. The treasure hunter was dead and gone so I thought she'd have a chance. I thought… but I didn't know."

"I'm sorry," Rowan said. How awful would it be to feel that way for someone and to never be able to tell them? Never be able to show them and never even know if they lived?

"Could you sing the song?" he asked. "The rhyme?"

Rowan felt a little silly, trying to remember the whole thing from her childhood, but she wasn't going to deny Gavyn this brief flare of hope. So, she sang it for him. All the verses she remembered.

> *"Healer, healer, why do you sigh?*
> *Remember to laugh so you don't cry.*
> *Light against the dark, and time too long to mark,*
> *Healer, healer, save me, please try.*
>
> *"Healer, healer, where do you go?*
> *Dark in broad daylight will bring only woe.*
> *Teeth on the hill, bells silent and still,*
> *Healer, healer, black hides your foe.*
>
> *"Healer, healer, glass bound with gold,*
> *Mind your hands for danger you hold.*
> *Pieces together, unique in their measure,*
> *Healer, healer, complete you are bold."*

As she fell silent, Gavyn hummed the last bar over again.

"I told her that if we weren't laughing, we were crying. And I was tired of crying. It's my words echoing back over a hundred years. Keinwen leaving me a message."

"What does the message say?"

"I have no idea," he cried, seemingly delighted by his ignorance. "But it means she lived, Rowan. She didn't die there in that valley."

It also meant that she had spent a lot of her life trying to find a man who was trapped beyond her reach, but Rowan didn't say that part out loud. If he was right, it meant Keinwen had enough hope to leave him a message in something more indelible than ink. A nursery rhyme passed down over and over.

Hopefully the message hadn't been distorted over the years.

"All right." She nodded, catching his enthusiasm. "We have to go to Monclaren then. Not just because of the Delvers. We have to find out what happened to her. The legend says that was the way she walked. Between the ruins and Lannasbrook and Monclaren."

"Maybe someone there knew her. Maybe there are more stories. Healer's Ghost, ha!"

It was the brightest she'd ever heard his voice, a lifetime of promise held in his tone. Her heart ached with hope that he was right. For his sake.

CHAPTER SIXTEEN

ROWAN

Light against the dark and time too long to mark," Gavyn said as Rowan trudged up the road, huffing with every breath. "That has to be talking about the lantern and all the time I spent trapped."

"We covered that already," Rowan said as she huffed along. Peaks rose on either side of the road which followed the winding valley between.

Personally, Rowan thought the line was talking about all the time Keinwen had spent looking without finding Gavyn, but Gavyn had his own theories, and they'd been over each and every one in detail the last two days. She knew them by heart now and was tempted to take her hand away from the lantern and just let Gavyn chatter away without her input.

"The next verse though, talks about dark in broad daylight or whatever. Is that another clue? Where do you get dark during the day? A noktum?"

"I hope not," Rowan said for the third time. "I'm not braving a noktum based on a nursery rhyme."

The rocks to the left side of the road dropped away into a river valley. The ribbon of bright water splashed below, twisting around the boulders as it burbled its way out of the mountains and into the foothills behind them.

"Yes, well, nursery rhymes all seem to be nonsense until you know a little more of the story behind them. Do you know the one about the cow and the pitchfork?"

"I know one about a cow dancing with a pitchfork. And I know one where the cow eats the farmer with a pitchfork. Which one are you talking about?" Rowan stopped to stretch her spine and wince.

Gavyn paused. "The cow *eats* the farmer? I always thought he was just chasing him. That's especially morbid."

"Yes, well, nursery rhymes also tend to be warnings. 'Black hides your foe'? Keinwen was warning you of something."

"So, what's the warning in the cow one? Don't let your livestock eat you?"

Rowan had walked so much in the past week, she'd nearly worn through her boots. She'd never done that much traveling before. When Stefan had brought her to Monclaren before, he'd always insisted she ride in the cart. Her back ached at night when she lay down to sleep, but it hurt less and less to sleep on the ground.

She was thinking to herself they had to be getting close, when she came around a bend in the road and finally caught sight of Monclaren.

She stopped to whistle between her teeth.

"They picked a hell of a spot, didn't they?" Gavyn said.

The town had been built against the side of the mountain, straight up the steep slope, with the road winding through it to come out the other side, halfway up the peak. Each tier of houses and shops sat almost directly above the one before it.

This high in the mountains, Rowan's breath came out in clouds of fog, even this early in fall, and little heaps of snow lived in the shadows of the buildings where the sun never quite reached.

A couple flakes drifted down, and Rowan shifted her cloak on her shoulders to keep the chill out. She'd perfected the move, flipping the right edge behind the lantern on her hip so it stayed pinned back and Gavyn could see better.

They'd made it to town, but they still had to find the Delvers, and who knew how hard that was going to be?

She passed the mill beside the river and started up the winding road. Shops and houses lined the road on the left, and a sheer cliff face topped with more buildings stood on her right. She watched for anything useful, eyes cataloging the signs hanging out over the streets. Here was a butcher and a grocer. She would stop at the cobbler to fix her boots, except the funds Stefan had stuffed in the sack would dwindle fast if she wasn't careful. She had enough to buy food to replace what she'd used already, and that was it.

"Do you know where we're headed?" Gavyn asked from her side. "You've been here before, right?"

Rowan's lips pulled down, and she spoke quietly so the shoppers passing by wouldn't think her mad for speaking to herself. "Yes, but I want to stay away from anyone I might know. We don't need to repeat our mistakes."

Jannik could just as easily have gotten here before them again. Not that he knew for certain they were headed for Monclaren—and Rowan trusted her parents wouldn't tell him—but it was a decent guess if he knew she would be investigating her heritage.

"Fair enough." Gavyn remained quieter than he'd been for most of the last two days, probably absorbing the sights and sounds of the town.

At the first switchback, where the road turned abruptly to head straight up to the rest of the town, more space had been carved out of the cliffs to form a sort of square. From the heaps of marble and granite outside the shops, this section of town catered to the quarry workers who made Monclaren their home.

Rowan passed a building with a pickax and another tool she didn't recognize nailed over the door. A mason sat on the stoop, chiseling his mark into the corner of a rough-cut block of marble.

"Excuse me," she said, standing to one side so her shadow wouldn't block his work. "Do you know where the Delvers are?"

The man looked up, his bushy eyebrows bristling as he squinted at her. "Delvers?"

"They come here to trade, don't they?" Rowan said. She chewed her lip, waiting for his response.

"They usually end up with the blacksmiths and miners up the road. They don't have much use for cut stone. Probably make their own just fine."

"Thank you," Rowan said and turned to let him get back to his work. She would have kept on up the hill but something made her pause.

The sun peeked between clouds, glittering from the few snowflakes in the air, and hit a statue that stood in the middle of the square.

"Rowan," Gavyn said, voice tight. "Go around to the front of the statue."

"Why?"

"Just do it, please."

A woman stood, chin held high, curly hair spilling down her back. Three figures sprawled at her feet covered in veils, and even enveloped in stony cloth, Rowan could see they held their hands up to the woman in supplication. The statue stared up the road, as if waiting for something. She held one hand to her chest, but the other reached down as if to pull the nearest figure to its feet.

"What is it?" she asked as she moved closer.

"It's Keinwen."

A woman bent with age sat at the statue's base, sorting yarn into a basket at her feet. She raised her hand to Rowan. "Admiring our healer?"

Rowan moved closer. "You have the legend of the Healer's Ghost too?"

The woman nodded, making gray tendrils bounce around her face. "Oh, yes. She's very famous in Monclaren."

"It's her," Gavyn said into her head. "They got her nose wrong, but whoever carved this knew Keinwen."

Then the healer really was Gavyn's lost friend. She'd lived and made an impression on the locals here as well.

"We have tales of her, too, down in my village. I think that's where she's from."

The woman scowled. "No, no. She's ours. Everyone knows the Healer of Monclaren."

Rowan hadn't known, but she wasn't about to argue who loved Keinwen more. They would all lose to Gavyn.

"Do you know the story?" Rowan asked. "About how she was looking for her wounded lover and ended up wandering for eternity when she couldn't find him."

"Half right," the woman said, holding out her hand and tilting it back and forth. "Someone stole him out from under her. That's why she couldn't find him. But she freed Monclaren from a corrupt lord, and we in turn helped her find what she was looking for."

Rowan bit her lip. They knew the end of the real story. At least Gavyn's half of it, and Keinwen had never saved him. So, who knew how much of the rest of the story was true?

"I like your ending better," Rowan told the old woman.

She snorted. "Of course. It's the best because it's the truth."

Rowan gave the woman a respectful nod and moved away up the street. "Keinwen's tale traveled further than I thought," she said.

Gavyn remained quiet for a moment. "It sounds like she had an eventful life."

"Why do you sound sad?"

"Not sad, just melancholy. She lived, and that's the important part. But…"

"She lived without you," Rowan added softly.

"That's good," he said, and Rowan realized that she might never have said the part about Keinwen roaming forever looking for him, but he'd been thinking about it anyway. "She went on to have a life. Maybe she fell in love, had a family. Rescued a town."

He fell quiet, and Rowan bit her tongue to keep from filling his silence.

She wanted to promise him everything in that moment of sadness. She wanted to promise him his own life and family. But how would that even be possible?

What had Keinwen been trying to communicate with her rhyme? The old woman's version of the story hadn't given them any more clues, but Gavyn didn't voice any more guesses.

The next switchback opened into the square, where most of the town's grocers and market stalls stood. Stefan ran a stall here when he came with his harvest.

Rowan hurried by before anyone could recognize her.

One more switchback up and they found the square lined with smiths. Hammers rang, echoing off the buildings, and the heat from the forges warmed the air enough that Rowan could throw her cloak back over her shoulders. To the side, an archway led to the first blacksmith, his forge open to the square. The air above it shimmered with heat, and Rowan's nose tingled with the smell of hot metal.

The smith stood beside his forge, pulling a glowing rod out of the coals. Rowan didn't want to interrupt him while he was working, but luckily an apprentice manned his counter.

"How can I help you?" the boy asked, wiping sooty hands down an equally sooty apron.

"I'm looking for the Delvers," Rowan said, stepping up to the counter. "Do you know where they trade?"

The boy's brow came down under his slightly singed bangs. "Delvers?"

"The dwarves? One of the masons told me they're usually found here with the smiths and miners."

"I guess they are, but they aren't here right now."

Rowan's shoulders drooped. "Oh. Do you know when they'll be back?"

The boy's face screwed up in thought before he turned. "Oy! Master Noral!"

The burly smith smashed the glowing metal with his hammer one last time before tossing it into the flames and spinning to acknowledge his apprentice. "What?"

"You know when the Delvers are supposed to be back?"

The smith came to the counter, towering over Rowan and the apprentice alike. "Not sure. They don't generally tell us their business, but they were here only a couple of weeks ago, and it's usually months in between visits."

"Months?" Rowan said, heart plummeting.

The smith's gaze softened, and he leaned down on the counter so he wasn't quite so tall. "What do you need, sweetheart? The Delvers might be good miners and craftsmen, but we aren't exactly nothing when it comes to metalwork." As he spoke, the apprentice stepped back to the forge to take up the smith's hammer.

She gave him a reluctant smile. "I'm sorry. I'm not really looking for something to buy. I'm looking for my... my father. And they're the only ones who might know where he is." A half-truth but she wasn't sure how people would react to learning she was only part Human. It would be better to play it safe. And she definitely wasn't going to whip out the lantern, even for a smith who might be able to tell her something about the craftsmanship.

The smith's lips twisted in regret. "Sorry they're not here then." His gaze lightened. "But you could try Penrill if it's important enough to seek them out before they get back."

"Penrill?"

"He's a trader. Has a storefront up the way. He deals in all sorts of things, depending on the season and the demand. He claims to travel to the Delver city regularly. Some of the rest think he's carrying tales, since he's a strange sort, but he brings me metals I don't see anywhere else except when the Delvers come to town."

"Thank you," Rowan said.

"Tell him Master Noral sent you, and maybe he won't be so squirrelly about it all," he called as she left the forge.

"Squirrelly?" Gavyn said. "Do you suppose that means he likes nuts?"

Rowan snorted as she stopped at the corner just outside Master Noral's shop, rubbing her hands together. The air outside bit a little harder after the pleasant heat of the forge.

She glanced up at the peaks around them, her brow furrowed. "I was really hoping to find the Delvers here. How far can I really go on my own?"

She shut up as a woman passed her, swathed in a thick, well-made cloak. Rowan glanced at her surreptitiously. She'd never seen anyone with such dark skin before. The woman wore her curly, black hair tied back in a tight bun, and a curved short sword swung from her hip. Rowan caught the flash of a noble's coat of arms on her shoulder.

The woman barely glanced at Rowan as she stepped inside Master Noral's forge.

"One day, someone is going to notice you talking to yourself," Gavyn said as Master Noral rumbled a question Rowan couldn't quite catch to the newcomer. "And then we'll really be in trouble."

"I'm not talking to myself, I'm talking to you. If you didn't chatter in the back of my head so much..."

She trailed off as the woman's voice carried through the open archway.

"—looking for a lantern."

Rowan flattened herself against the wall of the forge, her mouth going dry.

"Lantern?" Master Noral said. "I've done some in my time. The fancy work isn't really my thing, but I have some that are perfectly serviceable if you're going digging."

"I'm not looking for a common light source. My Lord Karaval wants something specific. A gold and silver lantern with a flame that never dies. He knows there's one in the area."

"That sounds magical. You'd do better to find one of the mages up the hill. They'll be able to—"

Rowan didn't wait to hear the rest. Master Noral might not recognize what the woman was after, but Rowan did.

"Lord Karaval?" Gavyn said. "Who the hell is Lord Karaval?"

Rowan shook her head. "His lands neighbor Lord Hax's," she whispered. "One of Lord Hax's rivals."

"A rival? Well, then we know why he'd want the Grief Draw. Let's stay out of her path."

"You don't have to tell me twice. How does he know about the lantern?"

"Like Jannik said, power attracts all sorts of people, and Jannik is spreading tales about what I stole all over the place."

Rowan bit her lip. She'd been worried enough about keeping ahead of Jannik. That woman had looked plenty capable, with good quality weapons and a sharp expression.

"Find that shop," Gavyn said as Rowan pulled her cloak over the lantern's case to hide it. "Let's get off the street."

"I'm working on it," she murmured.

Master Noral had said "up the way" so Rowan raced up the road, examining the signs. Few of them had any lettering on them. Most just had a picture of their wares out front. But there, five shops down, was one with the eclectic collection of an apple, a hammer, and a book. And painted along the top were the words:

Penrill's Particular Properties

Rowan pushed through the door and let it close behind her, muffling the noise of the street.

Barrels lined the walls filled with dried fruit and meat. The scent of spices she didn't recognize tickled her nose, heralding a sneeze. The goods in the shop really were eclectic. Alongside the foodstuffs stood racks of tools, a few children's toys, and a lone shelf of books.

"Hello?" Rowan called.

A head popped up over the counter at the back of the shop. "Oh, sorry. Didn't hear you come in."

The man stood, unfolding his long, awkward length until he stood nearly as tall as Master Noral but a quarter as wide. The effect made him look like a stork as he stalked around the counter.

"What can I help you find today? A bushel of apples? A crosscut saw? I have one around here somewhere."

"Actually I—"

"Fabric? I do carry bolts of whole cloth."

"No, I—"

"Maybe you'd like a set of dice for your da."

Rowan planted her hands on her hips. "Do you actually sell *anything* when you bombard people like this?"

The man froze in the middle of the floor and blinked as Gavyn snorted in her head.

"You'd actually be surprised what works," the man said.

Rowan rolled her eyes. "Would you like to hear what I actually need?"

"I would love to." He folded his hands in front of him. "How can I help you?"

"Are you Penrill?"

"I am."

"Master Noral said you might help me. I need to find the Delvers."

Penrill hesitated the barest moment before he strutted back behind the counter. "Ah, can't help you there, I'm afraid. I have several of their trinkets, of course, but no Delvers themselves in stock, haha."

"All right, squirrelly means he *is* nuts, not that he likes nuts," Gavyn said.

Rowan stepped to the counter where Penrill was pulling out several strange-looking apparatuses. One had a crank and several gears attached to a plate. Another held three glass tubes affixed to a long stand.

"Please, I came here looking for the Delvers, and now I've learned it might be months before they come back. Master Noral said you've been to their city."

"Many times," Penrill said. "But that won't transport one here."

"No," Rowan said, holding onto her calm with both hands and teeth. "Do you know if any might be heading back this way sooner?"

"Delvers are very punctual people. They stick to their schedule, or they die trying. They won't be back till spring." Penrill spun the crank, and the gears on the little gadget made a humming noise. He held out his hand and wiggled his eyebrows. "But here's one of their machines. Like it?"

"I'm sure it's lovely," she said without looking.

There was nothing for it then. She couldn't stay here in town, not with this Lord Karaval looking for her along with Jannik. She had to keep moving, and the best way to go was forward.

"Can you take me to their city?" Rowan said before thinking it through. She hid a wince when she remembered the tiny stash of coins in her sack. There was no chance it would pay for a trip into the mountains.

"I cannot," Penrill said, and he stopped cranking the mechanism. Finally, his eyes rested on her face, and the frenetic energy that filled him seemed to slow.

"Why not?" Rowan asked.

"The Delvers don't like outsiders. They don't want people to know too much about them or where they live."

Rowan frowned. "But you *have* been to their city, yes? They let you in."

"Do you know how long it took me to build enough trust with them to get that far?"

"Then you would be able to introduce me."

Penrill threw up his hands. "They trust me to bring them supplies and things from town they wouldn't otherwise get until they come themselves. They also trust me not to abuse the privilege. It's a very tenuous and unique arrangement, and I will not jeopardize it."

"You haven't even asked me why I want to go. Maybe it would be worth it."

Penrill replaced the apparatuses back under the counter. "Doubt it. But feel free to try to convince me. Talk is free."

"One of them is my father."

Penrill stilled, and he stared up at her.

Rowan took a deep breath. "My mother says I'm half Delver. And I'm in some trouble. I think the Delvers can help, but I have to find them first. If you could just tell me which direction to try."

She'd already walked this far. What was another mountain or two? And at the end of it was a family member she'd never met. One who could help her or could convince the rest of the Delvers to help her.

"You wouldn't even get up the first peak," he yelped. "I'm not letting you kill yourself."

"Well, now that's your choice, isn't it?" she said, leaning on the counter. "I'm going. I can either do it with your help or without."

The shopkeeper blinked.

Rowan turned and tapped her teeth. "Now do I need climbing gear? A tent? What does a climbing axe look like?"

Penrill made a pained noise in the back of his throat. "You're joking."

"I am not."

He shook his head. "I think this is blackmail. Or some kind of extortion."

"Would it help if I said 'please' again?"

Penrill sighed, his shoulders lifting with it. "Well, you're telling the truth about being part Delver."

"Yes. I am," Rowan said, with a frown. "But how can you tell?"

"They're the most pig-headed, stubborn people I've met."

Rowan raised her eyebrows, sensing an opening in his defenses. "Yes?"

"I leave at the end of the week," he said.

Rowan took a deep breath, a smile spreading across her face.

"You can't convince me to go any earlier," he said, waving a finger in her direction. "So don't try. Delvers expect their associates to be punctual as well. Passage will cost twenty silver."

"Or…" She drew out the word. "That's a week's salary. So, a week's worth of work if, say, I couldn't pay?"

He heaved another sigh. "Of course you can't. Another reason you're coming on my regularly scheduled trip and not getting special treatment. Fine, but I'm going to work you most unfairly the whole week."

"Thank you, Penrill," she said. Laying low in a shop sounded much better than trying to find a place to hide from all the people looking for her. Maybe she could convince him to give her a pallet in the back room to sleep too.

Penrill grumbled. "And if you lose me my arrangement with the Delvers, you'll be working for me for free for a lot longer than that."

"I'll tell them I browbeat you and that you have nothing to do with me or my search. How does that sound?" she asked, skipping to keep up with him as he walked down his shelves.

He sighed again. She had a feeling she'd get tired of that after a while. "Like I'm going to regret this."

CHAPTER SEVENTEEN

ROWAN

Rowan walked alongside the wagon, keeping one hand on the side and one on the lantern. The placid donkey wended his way up the path and hardly needed Rowan to keep the rig steady, but there was a steep drop on the other side, and she felt better with her hand on the wagon.

Snowflakes mixed with freezing rain pattered around them, and Rowan pulled her cloak tighter. Tonight would be a lot colder than the last couple of nights they'd spent in the mountains.

"Penrill?" she called toward the donkey's head where her guide walked. "Are we going to have to sleep in the wet?"

Penrill cast a glance up at the clouds and then peered ahead of them at the path winding up the side of the mountain.

"Hopefully not," he called back. "There's a good chance we'll be under the mountain by nightfall. But only if you don't slow us down."

Rowan rolled her eyes. She could walk faster than this tired old donkey could run, and after the last few days Penrill knew it.

Just like she in turn knew that his favorite pastime was complaining.

She'd spent the first day in his shop organizing his goods into categories, and he'd spent the next day arguing that he couldn't find anything anymore. As soon as he'd realized she knew how to read and write, he'd set her to cataloging his books and then complained that her writing was too cramped.

"I think it's his way of saying thank you," Rowan told Gavyn the third night. "He can't bring himself to say the actual words, so he makes sure you know he noticed by making a big stink about everything you do."

"Or maybe he's just grumpy you do things better than him," Gavyn said.

"Probably both." It didn't matter to Rowan. She just smiled at him sweetly whenever he grumbled, and by the end of the week, he was using her system to do things twice as fast.

And despite Penrill's attitude, hiding out in the shop was considerably better than trying to dodge all the people looking for her. She hadn't seen any sign of Jannik yet, but she knew he couldn't be far behind, and she'd had to avoid Lord Karaval's woman three times that week.

It had been a relief to get on the road, even if the road was little more than a gravel path up through the peaks.

Rowan pushed ahead so she could walk on the other side of the donkey's head. "You make this trip every few weeks?" she said, squinting into the sleet. "It's so long."

Penrill glanced at her. "The Delvers like their privacy. You don't bother them, and they don't bother you, you know?"

"Are they that unfriendly?" Rowan bit her lip.

"Well, they put up with me, so that should tell you something."

"Ah, that makes me feel better."

He shot her a quizzical look.

"Anyone who puts up with you has the patience of a saint." She grinned at him.

He snorted. "Or a sense of humor." He looked at her sidelong. "So, are you finally going to tell me why you want to find them so bad?"

She blinked at him. "I told you, my father—"

"That's what you keep saying, but it's not everything is it? If it was just meeting your old man, you could have waited till spring. It would have been more comfortable." He gestured to the sleet. "And that wouldn't have come with the risk of annoying them. There's some reason it has to be right now. Something important enough to extort innocent traders into doing your bidding."

Her teeth clenched, and she stared down at the path in front of her feet. She trusted Penrill—to a degree—but there were too many rumors circulating Monclaren about the lantern Lord Karaval was looking for. None of them got very close to the truth, but all of them featured a valuable magical lantern.

Penrill was frenetic. Not dumb.

He humphed when she took too long to answer. "You're not going to tell me, are you?"

She winced. "I'm sorry."

"Does it have anything to do with the way you talk to yourself constantly?"

Her mouth dropped open.

"He has you there," Gavyn said in the back of her head. "I knew that would come up someday."

Rowan would have snapped back at Gavyn, but that would have just proved Penrill's point. As it was, he glanced at where her hand rested on the lantern cap.

She let it drop abruptly.

"How did you—Why would you say that?" she asked Penrill, mind racing.

He smiled and turned back to the path. This was the sort of wet snow that sheeted straight down instead of swirling around in drifts.

"I know a lot of Delvers who talk to their devices when they're working," he said.

"I'm only half Delver," Rowan said. "And I don't have any devices."

Penrill shrugged and kept trudging. The path had gotten steep, and the soles of Rowan's boots slid against the wet rock.

She liked Penrill. And she did trust him. But she'd also trusted Jannik.

Every time she pulled out the blasted lantern and its light shown across someone, things changed. Things got harder or more complicated. People became entirely different.

The sting from Jannik's blow had long since faded, but her fingers crept to her cheek anyway.

She pulled her cloak tighter around herself. Would the light change things when she got to the Delver city too? She didn't want to coerce anyone into doing something they didn't want to, but wouldn't a father be willing to help a daughter? Lynnock was her best chance at convincing the Delvers to manage the Grief Draw.

Rowan tried to think of something to distract Penrill, some story about why she talked to herself, but the merchant's gaze darted across the path in front of them, his mouth a tight, little line of worry, and she kept quiet. The next bend of the path had disappeared behind the shifting gray wall of sleet and ice.

"Careful now," Penrill said. "This is going to get slippery."

"Should we stop?" Rowan pulled her hood up to keep the sleet out of her eyes.

Penrill looked back at the wagon and then up at the path. "I try not to come this way when the weather's bad. But at this point, I think it would be better to get to the other side before it gets worse."

Rowan shivered, her back starting to cramp in the cold, but she tried to pick up the pace, her boots sliding with every step.

The path grew narrower, falling away into a rocky gully on the left and rising too steep to climb on the right. Without needing to be told, Rowan fell back behind the wagon as Penrill stepped out front to lead the donkey.

Rowan put one hand on the back to push. She might not have been making a whole lot of a difference, but it made her feel useful, and the wagon helped steady her too.

"It's barely fall," Gavyn said in the back of her mind. Even with the sleet hissing down, she could hear him clearly. "Is this normal?"

"We get early storms down in the foothills sometimes," she said through her teeth. "It's not unheard of."

"I hope Penrill knows what he's doing," Gavyn muttered.

Rowan did too.

As if in answer, she heard his voice from over the wagon. "We need to get off this slope," he said. "Then we'll find shelter where it's not so steep."

He had to yell over the wind now. It lashed at Rowan's cloak and spat freezing rain into her face, making it sting. She kept her head down and concentrated on her feet.

Ahead, Penrill swore.

A rock slid under Rowan's boot, making her stumble, and she slipped when she tried to catch her balance. Her heart lurched as she wobbled toward the deep gully. Her hand clenched on the back of the wagon, and she hauled herself upright with a yank, then checked the lantern was secure.

"Careful," Gavyn said.

She was too winded to tell him how stupid that sounded. At least now she was upright again.

There was a snaky, slithering sound, and Penrill cried out. The wagon shifted under Rowan's hand.

"Get back," Gavyn called.

Rowan gasped and straightened as the path slid out from under the wagon. Like a river of rock and gravel, the ground itself shifted and tumbled downward. Her feet skidded, and she threw herself backward.

Penrill screamed, and the wagon fell away from Rowan, down toward the gully. A rumbling followed, and Rowan looked up to see the steep slope above them plummeting, as if the earth itself folded toward the path. Stones as big as Rowan's head rolled past.

Rowan scrambled back, out of the rockslide, but not fast enough. Her legs went out from under her, and she slid, the gravel and rock tearing at her hands and clothes as she reached to stop herself.

A boulder bounced an arm's length away like a pebble against the ground, and Rowan winced. She stopped trying to break her fall and flung her arms over her head.

Finally, the rumbling died away, and Rowan lay still, waiting for the world to stop spinning. She opened her eyes and found herself curled up among the rocks with her heart pounding hard enough she could hear it in her ears.

"Rowan!" Gavyn called. In the slide, her elbow had ended up wedged against the top of the lantern. "Rowan, are you all right?"

Rowan took a deep breath and tried to take stock. Her arms and hands stung, feeling raw and bruised. Her back was a knot of misery, and her legs were sore. But there was no shattering pain of broken bones. She could breathe, as long as she ignored the panic that threatened to seize her lungs.

She blinked and pulled her arms from her eyes.

Sleet obscured the world, shrouding everything in gray mist and white curtains. Tumbled rock and stone lay at a steep angle, covering the slope of the mountain and destroying any trace of the path they'd been following. Rowan squinted upward. She had no idea how far she'd slid.

"I'm all right," she told Gavyn. "I think."

He made a relieved noise in the back of her head.

A quick survey told her she'd been extremely lucky. She lay at the back edge of the slide, her cloak caught between stones, but she was mostly unharmed.

She saw no trace of Penrill.

"Penrill?" she called.

There was no answer. All she could hear was the wind and the deafening hiss of the sleet.

"Penrill? Keep a look out," she told Gavyn. "Tell me if you see anything."

"I doubt I can see more than you at this point," Gavyn said as she climbed carefully from the rocks that had cradled her. But his voice strained as if he tried anyway.

Rowan placed her feet carefully, terrified she'd start another slide. Some of the smaller pebbles and gravel shifted and skittered down the slope, but the bigger boulders stayed put. She had to clamber on hands and feet across the steep, rocky terrain.

"Penrill?" Sleet stung her eyes, and she blinked, forcing down the black feeling that climbed up her throat.

"There," Gavyn called. "To your left."

Down the slope from her, a wheel lay crushed between two rocks.

Rowan's jaw clenched, and she scrambled down toward it, trying to gauge how far Penrill had been from the wagon when they'd slid.

Here and there she found shattered wood and the broken curve of a barrel.

She kept going, her face freezing and her hands leaving bloody marks on the stones as she climbed.

Finally, she found an arm and then a shoulder and cleared away enough debris that Penrill blinked up at her.

"Rowan?" he said. Then he grimaced.

Rowan blew her breath out. He was alive.

"Hold on." She cleared away the smaller rocks that she could fling down the slope and then started in on the stones that pinned him to the mountain. She wiggled her fingers into the cracks between, heedless of the pain and heaved until they rolled away.

She cleared his torso so he could lay there, breathing heavily, but his legs remained trapped under boulders she couldn't budge.

Rowan fell back to catch her breath.

"This isn't going to work," Gavyn said when she brushed the lantern.

"What would you rather I do?" Rowan snapped. "Leave him? I'm not doing that."

Penrill blinked at her. Then his eyes closed.

"Penrill, stay with me." She slid over to him to pat his face. Sleet froze to his eyelashes and the ends of his hair. "Wake up."

Penrill groaned. "But my bed is so comfortable," he said and cracked a grin.

Her lips thinned in a pained smile. Her breath came in shuddering gasps, and she stared up the slope toward the hidden path, then back down at Penrill and the shattered pieces of the wagon.

She swallowed.

"Penrill, how far to the Delver city?"

His head lolled, and she caught it gently in her hands.

"Penrill."

"I don't know… maybe a few hours," he gasped.

Every time he closed his eyes, she held her breath, convinced he'd never open them again. "How do I get there?" she said, giving him a gentle shake.

He tried to raise his arm and point up the slope and the rest of the mountainside. "North," he grated. "You come around the point of the mountain and—they might like to stay out of the way, but they have a flair for the dramatic. There's an entrance in the side of the cliff. Can't miss it." He lay back, blinking up at the clouds, his chest laboring for breath.

Her jaw ached from clenching her teeth so hard.

"What are you going to do?" Gavyn asked.

"I've only got two options. Stay here and try to dig him out." She kicked at the boulders keeping his legs pinned to show how futile that was. "Or try to find the city and bring back help."

"Alone? Without a guide? In this weather?"

"What else am I going to do, Gavyn?"

"I don't know," he said, voice quiet. "I just want you to know what you're up against."

She huffed a laugh. "Believe me, I know."

Penrill stared at her, eyes a little bleary but still following the one-sided conversation.

Rowan clambered across the rocks to sift through the wreckage of the wagon, looking for anything useful. Very little was accessible. All the dried fruits were buried. And the tools which might have helped her could have been anywhere under the stretch of rock and stone. But she did find a bolt of bright red fabric.

She scrambled back to Penrill and unwound the cloth so she could drape it around him. It might keep him warmer and hopefully would help her find him again.

"Penrill, I'm going for help. Don't you dare die on me, all right?"

His lips twisted in a desperate smile. "Wouldn't dream of it." He craned his neck around to peer through the sheets of ice and snow which fell even faster now. "Rowan, I hate to say don't do this, but it's going to be dark soon. You can barely see now as it is."

"Don't worry." She gave him a grim smile and pulled the lantern from its case. The light sprang out, illuminating the rocks around them, casting jumping shadows across the slide.

Penrill's eyes widened, and his gaze flickered between the lantern, with its alien workmanship, and her face, which she hoped reflected her resolve. Questions and speculations lined up behind his eyes, but she didn't have time to address any of them.

"Darkness won't be a problem," she said.

CHAPTER EIGHTEEN

ROWAN

Rowan scrambled up the steep, tumbled rocks toward where she remembered the path being. She winced as the handle of the lantern dug into her damaged palm, making it sting.

She had to pause every third or fourth step to catch her breath.

"You climb," Gavyn said. "I'll look for the path."

She didn't bother answering, just cast the lantern a strained smile.

Concentrating on her free hand and her feet only made the way slightly easier. Too often a boulder shifted under her weight, and Rowan froze, trying to keep her balance, praying she didn't start another slide. Sharp edges of rock cut into her free hand and her knees anytime she slipped or skidded.

Sheets of gray and white hid everything more than a few feet away, and the lantern's light seemed to bounce from the sleet, creating a bright but nearly opaque bubble around her.

After ten minutes of climbing, she had to stop and shake out the hand that held the lantern.

"What's wrong?" Gavyn asked.

Rowan tried to catch her breath before answering. "It hurts," she said. She held out her hand to examine her palm, but lacerations crisscrossed her skin. That alone could be the source of the pain, but if there was anything worse—like blisters—then the blood hid it.

But now wasn't the time to toss the lantern, even if she was ready to be rid of it.

She traded hands and started upward again.

Her foot slipped, and the rock cut into her worn boot sole, tearing a jagged hole in the side. Rowan cried out.

"There," Gavyn called. "I think that's what's left of the path. Just a little further, Rowan."

Rowan squinted but couldn't see anything past the white. Still, she trusted Gavyn, so she forced her feet to move again, ignoring the pain.

She crested another rock, and yes, the way did level out here. This must have once been the path even if it was concealed now.

If she kept the slope of the mountain to her right, then she should be going in the right direction. She scrambled and slid, and finally the boulders became gravel which became the stone and dirt path they'd been following.

At least now she could walk instead of scrambling over rocks. She wrapped her cloak around her, holding it closed with her free hand and raised the lantern to cast its light across the path and shield her face from the wind at the same time.

They were so close to the city. A few hours? Penrill couldn't die only hours away from his goal. And he especially couldn't die when she could make the difference for him.

How long had she been walking already? It felt like forever, but she had the sinking feeling it had only been minutes. Who knew how long it had taken her to get clear of the rockslide?

The freezing rain left a layer of ice across the path, and she had to place her feet carefully.

Rowan stumbled over her frozen toes and fell. She paused there on her knees, one hand bracing her, the other resting the lantern on the rocky ground.

"It's all right," Gavyn said. "You can do this. Come on."

His voice sounded warm, and a part of her resented the fact that he couldn't feel the cold, even while she tried to take comfort from his words. She climbed to her feet and pressed on, her face ducked to avoid the worst of the sleet.

"You can do it. One more step. Now another. You can do one step at a time. That's not so bad, is it?"

Her legs burned like she'd climbed a million stairs, and she bent over to gulp for breath again.

She blinked away the frost forming on her eyelashes. Beneath her feet, the path had changed to rocky scree, little tufts of dead grass sticking up between the stones.

Path? No. The path wouldn't be overgrown like this.

Rowan spun, holding up the lantern.

"Gavyn," she cried, staring at the steep slope around her. "Gavyn, I'm not on the path!"

"What?"

"I don't see it. I've lost the path. Which way do I go?"

"I-I don't know. I was concentrating on you. I'm sorry." He hesitated. "Down the slope. Right? You probably went up without realizing it?"

She scrambled back the way she thought she might have come, loose stones skittering away from her feet to bounce into the hidden gully below.

"Careful," Gavyn cried. "You'll start another slide."

There was no way she'd climbed this far without realizing it. She turned and tried to go back, maybe she'd gone down the slope without knowing, and the path lay above her.

The cold air burned in her lungs, and she didn't seem to be making any progress upward. She scrambled and crawled and climbed endlessly, but the terrain never changed.

Rowan stopped and curled up around the lantern. Its light gave off no heat. Just another way the stupid thing was trying to ruin everything. Panic made her limbs shake. Or maybe that was the cold.

"I'm just wandering blindly," she told Gavyn. "Healer's Ghost, we're not going to find the city. Are we?"

Her shoulders shook, and she could barely draw breath. She was going to let Penrill down. He'd die down there half-buried, thinking she had abandoned him. And she would die here on this slope, and her family would never learn what happened to her.

She turned to plop her butt on the rocky ground, resting her legs. It didn't help. Everything burned. Except her feet which had gone past numb to feeling deceptively warm.

She tipped her head back to stare across the empty space filled with undulating curtains of sleet and snow. The wind made waves of them in the air.

One wave curled and dissipated, leaving a clear patch of darkness for a moment, and Rowan could see the lantern's light bounce from the opposite peak. It was a lot closer than it felt like in the enveloping whiteness.

Just as the snow blew past and closed in again, she made out dark figures trudging across the opposite slope. Her breath caught.

"People!" she cried and sprang to her feet. The muscles along her back seized, but she didn't care for once.

"What?"

"I saw people, on the other slope. Gavyn, they're not that far from us."

"Can you make it over there before they're gone?"

"Never, but..." She raised her voice and her hands in the air. "Hey! Help! Help! Over here! Can you hear me?"

Rowan strained her ears, but nothing came back to her through the storm. Not even an echo.

"The wind's too strong," Gavyn said. "And all this snow and ice muffles sound."

"We have to get their attention. Before they're out of range. Hey!"

She screamed herself hoarse, but still no one responded.

"They're going to get away," she croaked. "What else can I do?" She glanced at the lantern in her hand and gasped. "Gavyn, make the light brighter. Like you did with those thieves."

"I don't know how I did that the first time."

"You're connected to the lantern. It's a part of you. You can control it, at least a little bit."

"That's all well and good to say. But how do you actually do it? I didn't mean to make anything happen that first time. It just did."

"What were you thinking?"

"Why does that—"

"Thinking is about the only thing you can do. So, what were you thinking?"

"I was angry at you." He sounded like he was getting angry again.

Good.

"I was angry, and it just happened."

"So, you have to be emotional," Rowan said. She gestured to the storm and the sleet raging down around them. "How are you not emotional right now?"

"I am."

"Penrill will die," she shouted. "I'll die. And when that happens, you'll be stuck on this mountainside for another hundred years! No one to talk to. Nothing to do. All alone with your thoughts and your memories. Again."

Gavyn cried out, and the lantern flashed before flaring into a blinding white light. Rowan threw her free arm in front of her face to protect her eyes.

Finally, she heard something through the storm. Faint calls that were nearly whipped out of existence by the wind.

"Keep going," Rowan called. "They can see us."

She kept the lantern raised and her arm over her face until the voices got closer, and finally, she let her trembling arm fall.

Gavyn let the light go, and it dimmed to its normal glow.

"Are you all right?" Rowan asked, shaking so hard, it made her teeth chatter.

"I don't know. If you're going to cause me emotional damage every time we're in a tight spot, I might just have to walk away." His voice had gone thready and exhausted.

She winced. "I'm sorry, but it worked."

Dark shapes coalesced out of the sleet and morphed into concrete figures.

Short, stocky figures with broad shoulders and wide features. Delvers. They were Delvers.

Rowan sagged with relief.

"I am so glad to see you," she told them as soon as they were within hearing distance. "Penrill is trapped. There was a rockslide." She tried to point and realized she had no idea which direction she should direct them. "Along the path somewhere. I got lost trying to find help."

The Delver in the lead jerked his head to two others behind him, and they disappeared down the slope as if they knew where they were going without her.

"Thank you. I don't know how long it's been or how hurt he is."

"We'll find him either way," the lead Delver said. He had short hair and a bristly beard frosted over so badly with ice she had no idea what color they would be normally. "Are you hurt…"

His gaze locked on the lantern.

Rowan's heart skipped. The open concern in his face flitted away, replaced by wary hostility.

"You carry a Giant's artifact." The Delvers behind him closed in, their brows drawing down in suspicion.

"Yes," she said simply.

"Drop it," he said. "Drop it now."

"I can't—"

"You do not comprehend the dangers you are carrying around like a common torch."

"Actually, I do."

"Just like a Human. Arrogant and ignorant in turn. You're going to get yourself and others killed just for a stupid piece of treasure."

"It's a lot more than that, but if you'd just listen—"

"No, you listen, Human. If you want to play with things that you don't understand—"

"It tried to kill my sister," Rowan shouted. Then she swallowed as he retreated a step. "You don't have to convince me how dangerous it is, because I know, all right? But I've been carrying it for half a month now, and it hasn't killed me yet, and I think you're the reason why."

She settled a grim look on the lead Delver who had shut his mouth. His gaze raked her up and down, taking in her stature and the crook of her spine.

"I brought it to you because no one else down there seems to comprehend what it is or that it might kill them. Apparently, you do. So, stop yelling at me and help me."

She raised her eyebrows but was afraid the nuances of her expression would be lost in the storm. She tried to raise the lantern again, but her arm trembled, and her palm burned. She couldn't hide her wince.

The Delver saw. "You're not fully Human, are you?"

"No," she said, arguments skittering away in favor of simplicity. She was so tired.

The lead Delver jerked his head again, and one of the others behind him stepped up to sweep an extra cloak around her shoulders.

"Come then," the Delver said. "Even *I'm* freezing my ass off, and we can argue well enough in the warm, little sister."

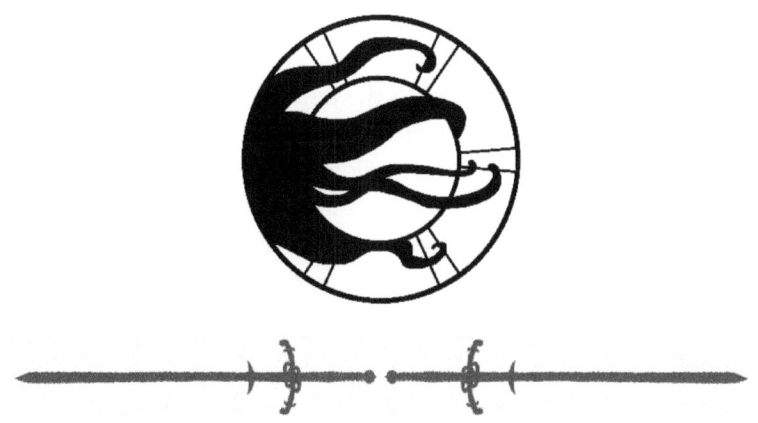

CHAPTER NINETEEN

ROWAN

Rowan was happy to put her head down and stumble along as the Delvers kept her safely between them. She pulled the extra hood down as far as she could to keep the sleet out of her eyes and concentrated on putting one foot in front of the other.

The Delvers moved so carefully that she barely registered when they stopped for more than a moment. When she lifted her head blearily, she noticed rocks and gravel spread out from their feet.

They'd found the edge of the rockslide again.

Shapes came through the storm, two upright with a long, low bundle slung between them.

Rowan cried out when she saw Penrill's pale face through the sleet.

"Found him, Byrson," one of the Delvers said.

"Alive?" the lead Delver with the frosted beard asked.

Rowan held her breath.

"For now. Looks like he'll need Lynniki as soon as we get back though."

"Then hurry. Or he'll need the morgue."

The two Delvers shifted Penrill's weight between them so they could move quickly, then they started back up the trail. They had no trouble keeping to the path even in the storm.

The Delver with the beard—Byrson the other had called him—turned Rowan by the shoulder and then tucked her hand firmly under his arm and towed her along after him.

She let him shield her from most of the wind and sleet, and with her hand firmly trapped, she wouldn't be able to wander off the path, even with her eyes closed. Which they threatened to do with each step.

The world around them blurred, and Rowan's focus narrowed to her feet and keeping her boots from sliding across the rocks. She had no idea how long they walked after finding Penrill. Reality wavered in and out of focus, her icy nose and toes taking more than their fair share of her awareness. The surrounding peaks blended with the foggy shapes of half-captured dreams.

The wind stopped abruptly, and warm darkness surrounded Rowan. She had the brief impression of harsh edges of light and enveloping dark that extended into a vast open space. Then pain speared through her feet as they tingled back to life and warmth.

Gentle hands put her to bed even as she whimpered, and warm compresses were laid on her feet, and furs tucked up around her chin.

She came awake with the sluggish thoughts and fuzzy head that told her she'd slept too long. Some heavy blinking brought an unfamiliar room into view, and she rubbed her eyes before looking again.

Stone walls seemed to be hewn out of the rock itself with no visible tool marks or striations. But intricate bronze and copper accents had been set into the stone itself, and decorative corner pieces ornamented where the walls met the ceiling.

The bed was also stone but had a deep well stuffed with straw and topped with leather and furs to create a cozy nest.

The lantern sat beside the bed on a little shelf, and Rowan reached for it before really thinking about it.

"Are you all right?" Gavyn asked. His voice sounded sluggish.

"Better," she said. "Were you sleeping?"

"Can't really sleep inside this thing. But long periods without contact tend to stretch and make me go fuzzy."

"Where are we?"

"In a city under a mountain," he said. "Wait till you see it. I can't imagine how long it took to carve all this out of the stone."

"What about Penrill?"

"They brought him in, but I don't know where he ended up."

Rowan pushed back the furs and swung her legs over the side of the bed. She'd expected the air to be chilly after the comfort of her nest, but it felt pleasant against her skin. In the corner, between the walls and the ceiling, hung a copper pipe. Little streams of steam escaped from the joints, and Rowan guessed that was the source of heat.

Someone had wrapped her feet in thick, leather slippers lined with some sort of fleece, and she found her now-dry tunic draped over a stand in the corner. Considering the state of her boots, she was happy to keep the slippers on for now.

A hiss and a creak made her jump before she noticed a square opening in the wall. A little platform carrying a tray of bread and cheese came into view, traveling on a complicated system of wires and pulleys. Rowan laughed and snagged a piece of bread. It was dark and dense and tasted faintly of herbs.

Water stood in a shallow stone basin against the opposite wall. She braced herself to splash some on her face and gasped when the water ran warm and soothing down her cheeks. Even the stone of the basin was warm against her hands.

She turned them over to examine her palms. The angry red abrasions had receded and faded, leaving pink, healing skin.

But when Rowan picked up the lantern, she hissed in pain. The metal burned like cold fire, despite the fact that her hands didn't seem injured anymore.

"More pain?" Gavyn said.

"Yes. But still no blisters." And an internal check convinced her that she was hungry, not nauseous.

Gavyn remained quiet.

Rowan tucked the lantern into its case at her hip. She was finally in the place where she would get answers. As long as she wasn't going to drop dead in the next two steps, her questions could wait a little longer.

There was no door, just a wide archway that led out to a featureless stone corridor. When Rowan poked her head around the edge of the doorway, a Delver pushed up from where he'd been leaning against the wall.

Without the frost in his hair and beard, it was hard to tell, but Rowan was pretty sure it was the same one from the mountainside. Byrson.

She blinked at him. "Have you been waiting for me?"

He jerked his chin up to look at her. She stood more than a head taller than him. A unique experience for her.

"Nothing personal," he said. His voice was deep and rich. "We didn't want that," he pointed a thick finger at the case on her belt. "Walking around without supervision. And we wanted you to have someone here in case you woke confused. Do you feel better?"

"I do, thank you. Have you… been here the whole time?" She glanced back at the open archway into the room.

His lips quirked in a grin. "I've stood out here to give you privacy." He cocked his head. "Do you always talk to yourself?"

Rowan sighed. "It's a long story. Where is Penrill?"

"Penrill rests and recovers. He had more to recover from than you did."

"Is he going to be all right?"

"Possibly, but I am not the one to answer your questions. Will you come?"

He turned and swept a hand out, asking her to follow him. As if she had a choice in the matter. If they didn't want the lantern wandering around, then she was a sort of prisoner here anyway. Albeit one who was treated very politely.

She fell in beside him as he strode down the featureless hall. He wore a fur-lined tunic with no sleeves, leaving his arms curiously bare. Tools and a couple of weapons hung from his heavy belt.

"I'm very glad you found us when you did," Rowan said.

Byrson glanced at her. "It was a lucky thing."

"I doubt you usually go for pleasant walks in the middle of storms."

He snorted. "No. That one caught us off guard. My team and I are in charge of maintaining and guarding the road to our city." He waved a hand to indicate the thick stone walls around them. The copper pipes continued even here, keeping the air pleasant and balmy. "We clear off most dangers so the few we trust—like Penrill—can make it through, but everyone else is directed away. The storm crept up on us like it did you, I imagine. Penrill is too crafty to travel the mountain paths when a storm is threatening."

"We were so close, I think he thought we could make it."

Byrson pursed his lips and grunted, avoiding judgment either way.

He led her to a room a few doors down from where she'd awoken. Another open archway led into the space where benches stood in rows marching up to a low desk. The furniture, Rowan noticed, had been built for shorter legs and backs than hers. Kind of like the ruins where they'd found the lantern but in the opposite direction.

No one sat at the desk, but a couple of Delvers waited on the benches, listening to a young woman who stood in the aisle. Despite the fact that they all sat, one stood out to Rowan among the rest. His lined face radiated concentration as he listened, and he folded his knobbly fingers before his stark white beard. He wore a sleeveless, maroon robe over a blue tunic embroidered with bronze thread.

The woman was even more interesting. She stood at the same height as Byrson, only slightly leaner. All Rowan could see of her from the back was her bushy, roan-colored hair tied into a complicated braid, but her belt also bristled with tools much smaller and more varied than Byrson's.

These were her father's people. It was strange to think of herself that way. As someone who belonged here.

"So, the merchant will live?" the Delver in the robe was saying as they walked in.

"Oh, yes," the woman said.

Rowan's jaw unclenched. She hadn't even realized she was gritting her teeth.

"Just in time," Byrson said. "Our visitor is awake." He nodded between Rowan and the older Delver. "This is Elder Modral and the rest of our council."

Rowan ducked her head, not sure if she should wave or bow or what. "I'm Rowan Norasdatter," she said. The woman had turned as she'd entered, and Rowan met her dark eyes. "Penrill's all right?"

"He's resting comfortably, though I'm not sure yet if we'll be able to save his leg. It was shattered in the rock fall."

Rowan winced.

Elder Modral held out a hand to the woman. "Rowan, this is Lynniki. Our resident expert in many things." He returned his gaze to the woman. "What is your plan?"

"I'll try replacing it, of course. As long as he'll let me."

Replace it? How did someone replace a leg?

Lynniki raised a hand to sweep some hair back from her face in what seemed like a nervous gesture. It was only as the light gleamed against her fingers that Rowan noticed the hand was made entirely of metal. Joints broke the smooth stretch of bronze, making the contraption surprisingly lifelike.

Rowan fought not to stare. She hated when people stared at her humped shoulder, so she figured she could extend this young woman the same courtesy.

"I will let you get back to your patient then," Modral said. He looked at Rowan. "You're very lucky Byrson found you when you did."

"I know. And thank you. Penrill said you don't really like visitors."

"We prefer to keep to ourselves. We'll come down to your towns for trade, but we like to control who we see and when.

What made you try to find us despite Penrill's warnings?"

Rowan's lips thinned. He had to know the answer to that already. Byrson would have had speculations, and Modral was looking at her like he was waiting for her to fail some sort of test.

Well, she'd fought so hard to be here where her questions could be answered. No point in holding anything back anymore.

She pulled the lantern from the case at her hip and set it on the nearest bench.

The Delvers all drew back, faces twisting in a variety of horror ranging from mild worry to outright hostility. All directed at the lantern, thankfully and not Rowan herself.

"I suppose that's one way to answer the question," Gavyn muttered before Rowan pulled her hand away.

Modral looked long and hard at the lantern, its light reflecting in his dark eyes. Finally, his mouth firmed, and he fixed Rowan with his stare. "Do you know what this is, young Human?"

Rowan could just imagine the outrage and lecture if she said no. So she didn't.

"The Giants called it the Grief Draw. I know it's dangerous," she said. "I know it killed many mages over a hundred years ago. I know it tried to kill my sister and several others." She held out her hands. "But I don't know why or how to stop it. No one down there wants to believe it's dangerous. And even if they do, they want to use it anyway."

"Use it for what?"

"I don't know," Rowan admitted. "They think it's some sort of weapon. They know it's powerful, and they want that power. All I know is that it gives off light, it trapped a mage's consciousness inside, and it eventually kills anyone who holds it more than a few minutes."

"It trapped someone's consciousness?" Lynniki said. She bent to peer at the lantern.

"Lynniki, don't you have a patient to see to?" Modral said.

"I can't do anything until he wakes up." She reached out to tap the glass with her fingernail, and Rowan just kept herself from lunging forward to grab her. "Is he still in there?"

"Lynniki," Modral said. His voice wasn't unkind, but it had gone firm and unyielding.

"Fine, fine. I'll save my questions." She stood with her cheeks puffed out like all her words were trying to burst free.

Rowan blinked and returned her gaze to the elder Delver.

He glanced at the ceiling, as if asking for divine patience, and finally looked back at Rowan. "Where did you find this?"

He reached out, but his hand stopped just before touching the lantern, fingers twitching.

"A ruin south and west of Monclaren. There are crumbled walls and buildings at the bottom of a wooded dell, as if hidden there. And below it there are passageways and tunnels all leading to what looks like a mage's laboratory. That's where the lantern was."

Modral exchanged a glance with Byrson. "The Anklassan Nuraghi."

"You know it?" Rowan said.

"We know *of* it," Byrson rumbled. "We keep track of the lairs across Noksonon, but we know enough not to venture into them."

Rowan raised an eyebrow. "It would be nice if you would warn the rest of the world then."

"What happened when you found it?" Modral asked.

Rowan took a deep breath. "Nothing at first. It seemed to just make light, but then people started getting sick, and my mentor, Jannik, decided it was a weapon." She swallowed. "He wanted to give it to someone who would use it against other people, and I couldn't let him do that. So I took it. But Jannik isn't the only one after it now, and I don't think I can trust anyone else."

Modral tilted his head. "But you trust us. Why do you think we would be able to help you?"

Rowan's lips thinned. "Because I'm half Delver, and the lantern doesn't seem to affect me. I knew those two things had to be connected."

Modral's expression didn't change, but Lynniki snickered. "Clever reasoning."

Modral glared at her, and Lynniki just shrugged.

"Then I'm right," Rowan said. "Delvers do have something to do with it all."

Modral's lips twitched like he was trying to decide what to say. "Yes. In a way, but it's complicated."

"So is everything that is worth thinking about." She gestured to the lantern. "So what does it do?"

Modral jerked his chin. "What makes you think it does anything? It's a lantern. It shines."

Rowan snorted. The Delver elder asked questions designed to make a person think. He knew the answer, he was just getting Rowan to defend her own thoughts. "It was locked away in a laboratory that seemed to be built just to hold something dangerous like this. Why would anyone, let alone the Giants, go through all that just to store a glorified lamp? It has to do something. Something I don't understand yet."

Lynniki laughed outright, making all of them jump. "Another clever conclusion. She's sharp. Makes sense, if she's one of us."

"One of you," Rowan murmured. Her gaze traveled to and from each face in the room. They didn't seem so alien or otherworldly.

"You did say you were half Delver," Modral said, tilting his head.

Rowan gulped. "Do you know if my father lives in your city? His name is Lynnock."

The young woman went still, and Modral blinked. They exchanged a look.

"He does, doesn't he?" Rowan said quietly.

Another Delver trotted into the room and pulled on Lynniki's shoulder so she bent to hear what he had to say.

She blew out her breath. "Penrill's woken up. I have to go."

She hurried for the door but paused to glance back at Rowan. "You can visit him in a bit if you'd like." Then she was gone.

Rowan returned her gaze to Modral. "Lynnock?" she said again.

His mouth drew down. "He was one of ours, yes."

"Was," she repeated, voice flat.

"Lynnock was a wanderer. He never stayed in the mountain long. But he hasn't returned in many years. We believe he must have met an accident out in the world. There aren't many who are friendly to our kind."

Rowan sucked in a breath. "He's... gone, then."

"I'm sorry."

The pain didn't burn or flare like she would have expected from grief. It left a piece of numbness in her chest. It wasn't like she'd known Lynnock. She'd only known *of* him for a couple of weeks.

Now she would never know him. Never have the chance.

But he'd been her plan. The Delvers could help her with the lantern, but she'd counted on having her father there to ease the way. It would have been much easier to ask a favor of family rather than complete strangers.

Her gaze went back to the lantern. Her problem, glowing as baleful as ever.

Modral exchanged looks with the rest of the council and Byrson. Without a word, the others stood and stepped from the room. He gave her a sad smile. "Come. We will talk, you and I."

CHAPTER TWENTY

ROWAN

owan slipped the lantern back into the case at her hip and followed Modral. Byrson came too, but he stayed a few steps behind, as if to give them space.

"I'm sorry about your father," Gavyn said as she stepped after Modral.

Rowan gave a shrug with her high shoulder. "I knew the chances of finding him were low. I just thought maybe..."

Maybe it would have been a little piece in the puzzle of herself. Knowing Lynnock was a Delver had completely reshaped her image of herself, but who had he been as a person? What kind of a man—er, dwarf—could she have counted as family?

"At least I'm here now," she told Gavyn. "Maybe I can get to know him by getting to know his people."

Modral raised a quizzical eyebrow as she drew even with him, and then he glanced at the lantern. "The mage inside. He talks?"

"Yes." Rowan ran her fingertips around the smooth rim of the lantern. It buzzed against her skin and sent pins and needles through her even with that small touch. "I seem to have created a connection with him. So far, I'm the only one he's been able to talk to in a hundred years."

"That sounds truly terrible." He gave a little bow directly to the lantern. "I am sorry."

Rowan could feel Gavyn's surprise. "Thank you," he said.

"I think you might be the first person, besides me, to address him directly." Rowan smiled at Modral.

Modral nodded. "It is never nice to meet another victim of the Giants, but we understand the pain they've left behind and respect anyone who lives with it."

"I never really thought of the Giants as my problem," Gavyn grumbled in the back of her mind as she trotted to keep up with Modral. "But maybe I should have if it was their creation that caused all this."

The old Delver led her to the end of the hall. As they approached, Rowan couldn't see much beyond. The hall seemed to open into an empty space, dim and dark.

Only once they had passed through did she see why it seemed so deserted.

An enormous cavern fell away from them, as if the entire inside of a mountain had been hollowed out to make room for the city within. All the buildings marched away below them, half a mile of empty space between the roofs and the cavern ceiling. Houses and streets and towers all jumbled together so Rowan couldn't even see the cavern floor.

Huge oil lamps strung across the open air, lighting the city with a steady orange gleam. Bronze and copper roofs spread below, some gleaming in the light and others fading to a nice, soft green.

"Welcome to our city," Modral murmured beside Rowan.

They stood on a walkway carved out of the side of the mountain, hanging above the city itself. If Rowan craned her neck, she could see it winding away from them, down to the streets below.

"I have never seen anything like this," she said, unable to keep the awe from her voice.

The Delver city might have been the only city she'd seen in her life, but she couldn't imagine anything would outshine this, even if she traveled the world for the rest of her years.

"How did you build this?"

"By hand," Modral said, surveying his city with visible pride. "Shovelful after shovelful. Delvers are not gifted with an overabundance of magic. And our technology—well, we did not have a head start."

He turned with a gesture and stepped down the walkway.

Rowan followed, though she found herself peering over the edge to the buildings below. A thin railing of bronze was the only thing that separated them from the empty air.

"Could you not stand so close to the edge?" Gavyn said, voice strangled.

"What?" Rowan said. "Don't tell me you're afraid of heights."

"If you go over, I go over."

Rowan bit down a smile but took pity on him and stepped back a pace to follow Modral.

He led her around the walkway, and as she followed, bright colors caught her eye. All along the wall of the cavern were murals, starting near her feet and spreading up the wall nearly to the ceiling. Huge swathes of red and green and blue that her eyes couldn't even make sense of until she tilted her head back and let her gaze go distant to take in as much as she could.

Here was an enormous painting of a man with Delver proportions: broad shoulders, narrow hips, and short legs. He wore a gold-edged blue tunic that fell to his knees, leaving his legs bare beneath. His sandals were nearly as tall as Rowan.

Beside him was a depiction of the city, all gold and bronze and green with an open triangle surrounding it, representing the mountain that sheltered it.

Modral stopped in front of a line of Delvers. They wore white garments around their waists, but Rowan couldn't tell if they were supposed to be short trousers or if they were some sort of primitive skirt. Each one raised their hands over their head as golden chains fell away from their wrists.

"I would ask if you know the history of the Delvers, but considering most of the people below still consider us fairy stories, I don't think you would have had much opportunity."

Rowan shook her head. "Even the ones in Monclaren who see you every now and then don't know much. And my mother didn't have time to tell me what she knew." If her father had bothered to tell Nora about his people in the first place.

"We are created beings. Built and bred by our creators to mine and handle the dangerous materials used for their magic."

Rowan licked her lips. "Created by who?"

"The Giants. They called themselves the Eldroi. And we were once Wergoi."

Rowan's gaze flicked up to the mural. There were no Giants painted on the wall, but the chains gleamed bright gold in the light from the oil lamps.

"They made us for a specific purpose. We unearthed the pitchblende for the Mavric iron they used in their tools and homes and sometimes their strongholds. Among other things just as deadly and dangerous."

"That's why you're immune." Rowan ran a finger over the lantern's top. "That's why *I'm* immune."

"Resistant," he said. "Which is not quite the same thing, but yes. We were designed that way. Created as tools that could withstand stronger things than Humans. Our bodies do not fall apart after handling Mavric iron. We do not get sores the way Humans do or die in blood and vomit and feces with what we call Mavric sickness. But their creations are still dangerous in and of themselves. The Eldroi were not known for their caring."

Rowan gritted her teeth and placed her hand on the handle of the lantern. "It... hurts to hold now," she said. "Like a burn that is only growing worse and worse, never healing. Is that an effect of the lantern? Or is it because I'm only half Delver?"

Modral's white brows drew down. "It could be either. While we are immune to most side effects, the pain of the metal builds up over time. A Human would barely notice it, because a Human would be dead before it grew enough to feel it."

The lantern stung her fingertips, and she let her hand fall back to her side. "That is oddly comforting," she muttered. It meant that her heritage really was protecting her. At least as much as it could.

She craned her neck back to stare up at the painting. "Why aren't there any Giants in your pictures?" she asked. If these were supposed to be depictions of history, she would have expected the creators of the Delvers to feature somewhere.

Modral's mouth twisted like he gritted his teeth. "We do not depict our creators because we do not revere them. They might have been the origin of our race, but that does not make them something to be respected. There are Wergoi still deeper underground who remain intensely loyal to the Eldroi. They wait in the darkness for the return of their *masters*," he spat the word, "but we broke from them centuries ago."

That explained the broken shackles on the wall.

She could never match his vehemence, but she could understand it. "I've walked the halls of a nuraghi. I've held the lantern. And I've felt that creeping dread from their places in this world, but were the Eldroi themselves all so evil?"

"Evil or careless. What is the difference when the thing you are careless with is people? We were treated as slaves, little more than tools. Do you feel sorry for the hammer? Or the chisel? Or do you pound it and use it and replace it when it is used up?"

He threw back his head. "When the Giants fell, we were finally free. We carved out our mountain and built our city. We remade ourselves without the Giants' influence. Without their corruption or their taint in our culture. We created our own art and music and tools. We abandoned the technology and magic of the Giants and started over with our own. We rebuilt who we are."

He blew out his breath. "Perhaps there might have been some that were different, but even their benign magic hurt and killed living creatures. Evil? Maybe, maybe not. Careless and arrogant, yes. It's easy to judge a race based on the majority and hard to judge it based on a few."

"So, you purged them from yourselves," Rowan said and gestured to the wall. "And from your history."

He turned to her, gaze intense. "This is why what you carry is so dangerous. Not because it will make us sick like your kin down below. It is a piece of Eldroi influence. Our clan has worked too hard for too many centuries to obliterate the mark they left on us." He gestured to the lantern. "This could be the undoing of all of us."

Rowan's lips thinned as she followed his pointing finger. "Do you know what it is exactly?"

Modral tucked his hands into his belt. "We remember enough of the Eldroi to know it's not a creation from this continent. This workmanship is not dark enough or dense enough for the Noksonoi."

Rowan blinked. "There were other Giants elsewhere?"

"Many. They ruled this world, not just Noksonon. And like any fallible creatures granted too much power, they squabbled. Only their squabbles murdered millions. This, I can tell was made by the enemies of the Noksonoi, but that's all."

"So, you don't know what it does." She tried not to let her disappointment show. She didn't want to use the Grief Draw, but it would have been nice to know what she'd sacrificed everything for.

"No. Only…"

"Only what?"

"Only that if it was created by Giants to war against other Giants, and it was locked away because even the Noksonoi were afraid of it, then it is better left to mystery."

Rowan pursed her lips, and her brow furrowed. She could see his point. But wasn't it better to understand what could hurt you? Wasn't it better to understand so you could control the things that you *could* control?

"I admire everything you've done here," she said slowly. "The way you've redefined yourselves is amazing. That's why you're the best ones to help me. You understand the constructs of the Giants better than anyone. You can keep the lantern here so it can't hurt anyone and out of reach of the people who would use it. You can bury it where it will be safe."

Modral's eyes remained on her face as his mouth hardened. "No."

"But—"

"We cannot—we will not risk everything we've built. We will not allow anything of Giant make to remain in our city."

"I—"

"You may rest," he said implacably. "You may ask your questions and receive answers and get to know your father's people. And then in three days, we will ask you to leave. With the Grief Draw."

CHAPTER TWENTY-ONE

ROWAN

They were going to throw her out. Politely, of course, because she was beginning to realize the Delvers were meticulously polite about everything. But in three days, her welcome would be worn out, and they'd make her leave with the lantern.

Even though she was part Delver. Even though she was family.

Modral had walked her back to the room where she'd woken up, ignoring her arguments. When they'd reached the open archway he'd said, "This is not a punishment, Rowan. This is for the better."

And then he'd turned and left.

Rowan had fought the urge to throw the lantern after him. Better for who? Better for them surely. But he couldn't possibly mean better for Rowan or even better for the rest of the world, because she had no idea what she was doing.

But Modral clearly was done talking. Rowan spent that first day trying to track him down again, but he wasn't in any of the rooms along her hallway. Byrson trailed her but refused to answer when she asked him for Modral's whereabouts. He was a guard for the lantern, not Rowan herself, but since she was the one stuck carrying it, that made them one and the same.

Byrson didn't stop her from venturing into the city, and Rowan took the chance to explore a little while she tried to find the elder. He kept a few paces to her left as she walked the streets, staring up at copper-roofed buildings.

The stone rang with the sound of Delver voices and industry. Workshops bustled, and short, broad figures trotted down the streets, but Rowan walked in her own little bubble of quiet. Where she passed, silence followed, and other Delvers skipped back to avoid her. She'd worry that she smelled, except for the frightened gazes that locked on the case at her hip.

News must travel fast through the city, Rowan thought sourly.

"Flee before the fearsome beast," Gavyn said, but his laugh sounded weak in her head.

Rowan walked until she was exhausted and her back ached. Then she returned to her room at the top of the walkway encircling the city. All without talking to another living Delver. Or finding Modral.

Here it was obvious the Delvers had planned for visitors, despite what Penrill had said. Her room was one of several along the hall, built to accommodate people apart from the city, and the room where she'd first met the council had been arranged as a space to meet with anyone entering the city with business.

But that didn't mean much to Rowan, after the frightened looks and frantic scuttling of the Delvers down below as they'd avoided her. The comfort of her bed had gone cold with the light of the lantern gleaming from the shelf beside her.

Rowan woke on the morning of the second day with the prickly feeling along her neck of someone watching her.

She sat up, but her abrupt movement didn't startle the woman leaning against the doorway. Her thick roan-colored curls were tied into a fat braid that draped her shoulder, clashing awfully with the orange of her tunic. A metal arm gleamed from her right sleeve.

The woman who'd been with the elders yesterday. The one in charge of Penrill.

"Hello," she said with a wide grin the moment Rowan made eye contact. "You're awake finally."

Rowan blinked. "Were you watching me sleep?"

"Yes. Why? Oh wait, is that creepy to Humans too?"

Byrson saved her from answering by sticking his head in the doorway to say, "Yes."

The woman just rolled her eyes. "Well, how else do you know when someone wakes up if you don't watch them sleep?"

Rowan swung her legs over the edge of the bed and grabbed her tunic as Byrson rumbled, "You wait for them to tell you they're ready for visitors."

The woman made a sound like "pfft" and tossed her braid over her shoulder. "That wastes so much time. You're awake now, right?" she asked Rowan.

Rowan nodded. "You're Lynniki?"

"I love smart people. I came to ask if you wanted to see Penrill, now that he's up for it."

"Yes." Rowan hurried to snatch up the lantern, ignoring the way it stung, and stuffed it into its case. "Yes, of course. Just let me eat something quick."

The little moving platform in the wall had produced another tray of bread and cheese.

Lynniki eyed the fare and sniffed. "You don't want to eat that. Come with me."

"I don't?" Rowan said, but the woman had already left.

"I'll take her from here, Byrson," Lynniki called over her shoulder as Rowan trotted to catch up.

A quick look showed Byrson glancing at the ceiling for patience, but he didn't follow them as Lynniki led Rowan out of the hallway and down the winding walkway into the city proper.

"That's the city entrance, officially," Lynniki said, pointing up the other end of the path where it disappeared into a huge recess lined with oil lamps. "The big one we let outsiders see. When outsiders see anything at all. There are other littler entrances and bolt-holes throughout the mountain, but there are some people who might actually kill me if I showed you any of those."

Rowan blinked as she realized she was getting a real tour finally. Lynniki didn't seem to be a Delver who stood on ceremony.

"That way is a lot of our craftsmen. It helps to keep them all in the same area. Sound gathers and adds up really quickly when you're surrounded by rock, so we keep them segregated off to the side to save our ears."

Rowan glanced down the street Lynniki had indicated to see open shop fronts where Delvers plied glowing metal with hammers or bright-colored garments came together under needle and thread. Most everyone around her seemed to be wearing an eye-smarting shade of orange or red or blue. A startling contrast to the drab colors sported in Monclaren and Lannasbrook.

They passed a massive wheel set into a tower that vented steam. As the wheel spun, it turned a cylinder, and a set of gears whirred into life. Rowan tried to follow the apparatus with her eyes to guess what it did, but Lynniki had pulled ahead, and she had to leave the strange contraption or be lost.

The next street over sat under a faint haze of greasy smoke, and the sizzle of fried food filled the air. Rowan's stomach rumbled.

With a sniff, Lynniki passed three stalls selling breakfast that looked perfectly acceptable to Rowan before stopping in front of the fourth. Stacks of flat, fried cakes lined the countertop interspersed with bowls of dark, glistening preserves, melted cheese, and savory-smelling meat.

Lynniki held up four fingers, and the vendor slapped two fried cakes in two different baskets. He handed them over with a wary look at Rowan.

Lynniki ignored him and handed one of the baskets to her. "Breakfast."

"Thank you," Rowan said. "But I can't pay you back."

"Pay?" Lynniki said. "What—Oh you mean trade like in the Human towns. With coins and stuff. Don't worry about that."

Rowan's brow raised. "You don't have money?"

Lynniki shrugged. "It's more complicated than that. We have an intricate system of barter and exchange based on each person's contributions to the clan and our society. The best part is that everyone is clothed and fed regardless of their usefulness. The bad part is that further contributions are judged subjectively by the council. They decide what's worth pursuing and what's just a selfish hobby." Her voice had gone bitter and sharp.

That sounded like an old wound.

"So, this is going on your tally," Rowan said. "Or do I have one too?"

"Like I said, clothed and fed. My guess is they just assumed you knew you could ask for something more interesting than the plain stuff you were given yesterday."

Bread and cheese had seemed a little tame for her first visit to a foreign city, but Rowan hadn't even realized she'd had other options.

"Thanks," Rowan said. "How do I eat this?"

Lynniki showed her how to spread cheese and the unidentified meat in the center of the thin, fried cake and wrap it up so she could eat it with one hand and not drip cheese all down her front. She handled the bundle of cake and filling as if her metal hand were made of flesh. Rowan wasn't sure if her dexterity came from some magic in the joints or if it was just due to long practice. Each finger bent independently but Lynniki also twisted her wrist to keep everything balanced on her palm instead of relying solely on her ability to grip.

Rowan realized she was staring and went back to her meal.

"And for dessert," the Delver said and slathered preserves all over her second cake before topping it off with a sprinkle of sugar.

"Dessert?" Rowan asked with a laugh. "For breakfast?"

"You have to start the day the way you intend to finish it, otherwise what's the point?" She shoved the last of her breakfast into her mouth and licked her fingers.

This seemed like plenty for Rowan, but Lynniki held up another two fingers to the vendor and took the basket he handed her. Instead of eating it, though, she dished up some cheese and meat on the side and tucked it under her arm.

"Finish that up," Lynniki told her. "The sick ward is just down this way."

Rowan wolfed the rest of her meal—she hadn't even realized how hungry she'd been—and followed Lynniki to the end of the food vendor's street.

The Delver ducked down another road much smaller than the first, and Rowan counted off the doors until they reached the fifth one.

Lynniki strode inside as if she owned the place.

The first room held four chairs and an open archway. Beyond the arch, beds lined a long, wide hall, separated by hanging tapestries of bright orange and blue.

Penrill lay in the one closest to the archway. The merchant sat against a straw-stuffed pillow, his legs straight out in front of him, covered by a sheet. He spooned up thin gruel and let it run back into the bowl, an expression of puzzled disgust on his face.

Rowan rushed up to him. "Penrill!"

A grin replaced the disgust, and he plopped his spoon back in the bowl. "Rowan."

"I'm so glad you're all right. The last time I saw you—"

Penrill waved a hand to cut her off. "I was nearly dead? I thought so too," he said, voice free of bitterness or fear. "But thanks to you and Byrson, I'm not. So, thank you."

"What else could I have done? I wasn't going to leave you there."

"And I wasn't going to make it out without help, so... thank you again."

Rowan pulled up the little stool that stood next to the bed. One of the few things actually made with wood she'd seen so far in the city.

"How do you feel?"

Penrill frowned. "Fragile. Banged up. But that's a great deal better than dead, so I'll take it. Lynniki even says I'll walk again."

"It takes practice," Lynniki said from the foot of the bed. She held up her metal hand, and the fingers bent and flexed. "But you're my best work so far."

Penrill eyed her askance. "Not sure how I feel about being someone's project or some kind of half Delver device but..." He shrugged.

"It's better than being dead on a mountainside?" Rowan asked.

"Exactly."

Lynniki snorted. "Here you go, project. I brought you breakfast." She plopped the second basket of cakes on his covers.

Penrill's face lit up. "Oh, much better. You're forgiven. Tinker away, creator." He held the basket up allowing access to his legs.

Lynniki flipped the edge of the blanket back deftly, revealing the bright metal of Penrill's new leg where it met his flesh just above the knee.

Penrill turned from her with the barest wince as Lynniki worked, and he concentrated on his breakfast.

Rowan swallowed. What would it be like to have to choose between a useless limb that at least belonged to you and an alien creation of metal and magic? Penrill seemed to take it in stride, but he also seemed to have a hard time looking at it.

Rowan leaned forward to catch his attention. At least she could distract him while Lynniki worked.

His eye caught on the case at her hip. "You know, I always thought that was just another tool on your belt, but back on the mountain you pulled out a light. And there were all those rumors about a lantern before we left Monclaren."

Rowan bit her lip. She owed Penrill a great deal more than just rumors and prevarication. "There were."

There wasn't anyone else in the hall except for a couple of Delvers down at the other end who weren't paying any attention to them. So she pulled the lantern from its case.

Penrill's eyes widened.

"Don't touch it," Rowan said. "It keeps killing people."

"The thought hadn't even crossed my mind. It's pretty enough, but it gives me the quakes if you know what I mean."

Rowan pursed her lips. "You have good instincts."

Lynniki's gaze had alighted on the lantern. Rowan half expected her to shuffle away like the other Delvers had, but she leaned forward for a better look.

"Definitely not Noksonoi workmanship. Fascinating. I wonder where it's from," she murmured.

"So that's why you were trying to find the Delvers," Penrill said, drawing her attention back.

"I thought they could help. Too many people seem to be trying to take it so they can use it. But it's dangerous. I just wanted to find someone who understood that and would help me keep it safe."

"And they won't?" He gestured vaguely to the city.

"Modral says they don't want the lantern here at all. They won't let it stay."

"What about your father?" Penrill said. "Won't he argue for you?"

Rowan glanced down. "That's what I'd hoped for, but apparently he's been gone for a long time."

"I'm sorry."

"Gone doesn't necessarily mean forgotten," Lynniki said, her gaze on Penrill's knee joint. She pulled out a tool that looked like nothing more than a thin, metal stick and stuck it in the joint and twisted. There was a click, and Lynniki nodded, satisfied. "Is that the only reason you wanted to find your father?"

Rowan fiddled with the edge of her ragged tunic. "No. I wanted to know who he was. And I guess I wanted to know who *I* was. I never really belonged in my village. Maybe... maybe I could have belonged here if it weren't for the Grief Draw."

Lynniki's lips twitched and thinned before her expression smoothed. Then she sat back and pulled the blanket back over Penrill's leg.

"You're coming along a lot faster than I expected. I think you can start walking on it the next couple of days. I'll keep an eye on you, but as long as you're willing to work and practice, you're past the dangerous part."

"Thank you, Lynniki," Penrill said, and for once, his voice was quiet and serious.

Lynniki jerked her chin in a nod. "Rest for now. Practice tomorrow."

Rowan said goodbye to Penrill and followed her out. At the door, she slipped the lantern back into its case.

Lynniki watched, eyes never leaving its gleaming surface. "You said there was a man trapped inside."

"Yes." Rowan cocked her head. "His name is Gavyn."

"Hello, Gavyn."

Gavyn made a surprised noise in the back of Rowan's head before responding. "Er, hello."

"He says, hello. Are all Delvers so polite?"

"Polite enough to address someone to their face? Of course. Why? Aren't Humans?"

Rowan winced.

"I like it here," Gavyn said. "Have I mentioned that I like it here yet?"

"Most barely believed he was actually there. And the rest... we didn't think it was a good idea to tell everyone everything about the lantern."

"Makes sense," Lynniki said. She knelt right there on the step of the sick room to peer through the holes in the case. "I'd love to ask you some questions about your experience. Like, can you see and hear everything around you? Do you still have feelings? Can you still do magic?"

Rowan swayed backward a little.

"Uh," Gavyn said.

"Maybe one thing at a time," Rowan said.

"Of course, of course. I need paper and pencil anyway. What does it do though, do you think?"

"I don't know." Rowan bit her lip. "Modral didn't think it was worth investigating. He said if it was made by the Giants, then it wasn't used for anything good and wanted to leave it at that."

Lynniki made a rude noise and stood. "Well, that's stupid. I mean, he's probably right, at least a little, but just because something wasn't made for good doesn't mean it has to be bad.

And you can learn a lot about something just by studying its construction."

"You mean, you think you might be able to tell what it's for?"

Lynniki grinned up at her. "I can at least try. Unlike the elders. You can come with me to my workshop. We'll examine it together, and when I have questions, you can translate Gavyn's answers for me."

"You're willing to help me?" Rowan said as Lynniki stepped off the doorstep and headed down the narrow street. "Why?"

Lynniki paused and said over her shoulder. "Because you were right. Family does mean something here." She turned enough to meet Rowan's eyes squarely. "Lynnock is my brother. I think he'd want me to help my niece."

CHAPTER TWENTY-TWO

ROWAN

ith that bit of news, Lynniki headed off into the city, and Rowan had to chase after her. She was getting the impression that the Delver never wasted time when she could be moving or doing.

Lynniki led them to the crafters' side of town and down another smaller street to a workshop with a pair of double doors. She threw the doors open to reveal a wide room lined with benches and a broad table taking up the center of the space, all lit by hanging lightstones. The first Rowan had seen in the city. Tools hung from the walls, and clutter crowded the bench tops with everything from hammers and screws to bent metal pieces clipped into precise shapes.

It reminded Rowan of the laboratory where they'd found the lantern, only much more welcoming. Like someone actually lived and worked here on projects that they loved.

Lynniki gestured to the lantern and then slapped the tabletop before she puttered around lighting more lamps.

"You're my aunt?" Rowan said, taking the lantern from its case and placing it on the table. "Why didn't you say something?"

Lynniki paused for a moment, her gaze fixed on the wall. "You're the first Human I've met besides Penrill. Well, part Human. The elders always tell us how much Humans fear what they don't understand. I guess I didn't know how you'd take learning you're related to us. To me."

Rowan ran a hand up her arm. "It was a shock, but like I said, I never fit in while growing up. You all seemed like the answer to that."

Lynniki turned, her lips pulling in a grin. "You're kind of a shock to me too. Not an unpleasant one, of course. I just never really thought of Lynnock as the family type. Yet here you are."

"I don't think he had the chance to be the family type. I don't think he even knew about me. My mother sent a message, but if Lynnock was as much of a wanderer as everyone said, he probably never got it."

"Probably not, then."

"Do you think he is actually dead?"

Lynniki sighed. "Because he hasn't been back in a while? He could be. Or that could be Modral and the elders being alarmists. But I'm not going to give up on my only brother until I have proof he's gone."

That was more hope than Rowan had had yesterday. Lynnock obviously wouldn't be able to help her here, but maybe one day she'd get to meet him.

Rowan cocked her head at her new aunt. "So I don't have any more aunts or uncles?"

"Nope, sorry. Delvers can't really have large families. The fact that there were two kids in our family is actually a bit rare."

"Oh, I actually just thought you seem a bit young to be Lynnock's sister. I thought maybe there might be more in between." She looked nearly the same age as Rowan, and compared to the others—Byrson and the elders—Lynniki had the air of repressed youth.

Lynniki tilted her head. "Actually, Delvers live a really long time. Get used to that, by the way. Your lifespan is probably double most Humans'. It can be really hard to judge age."

Rowan blinked, trying to wrap her thoughts around that while Lynniki stooped to examine the lantern.

"It's just me," she said. "And I'm not exactly a shining example of Delver solidarity. In case you thought I could help you find a home here."

Rowan bit her lip. It occurred to her that she'd been hoping to get to know her father, but here was a living breathing relative who had a lot more in common with her than an unknown parent.

She leaned her elbows on the table to join Lynniki in her study of the lantern. "Delver solidarity seems overrated, if they're all afraid of me. What do you think of the Grief Draw?"

Lynniki tapped the glass, noting the long, hair-thin crack from the fight with Jannik. Then she took the lantern in both hands and turned it this way and that.

"Still fascinating. No discernible power source. Has the flame ever gone out?"

Rowan shook her head. "Not since I've had it."

"Hmm. Can you describe the nuraghi where it was found again?"

Rowan did her best to describe the laboratory, as Lynniki sketched a rough diagram on a piece of parchment.

The Delver had even more patience and attention to detail than Jannik. By the time she moved on to different questions, she could probably visualize the nuraghi as well as Rowan who had been there. While she asked Gavyn about his experience and perception of the world, she was busy drawing detailed diagrams of the lantern, even going so far as to picture it from different views.

Rowan craned her neck to see over Lynniki's shoulder. Clearly the Delver was used to building things, if her arm and Penrill's leg were an example of her work, but she was also a fair hand at history, from what Rowan could tell.

"Do you have any ideas yet?" Rowan asked.

"Plenty." But she didn't elaborate.

When Rowan raised her eyebrows, Lynniki's face brightened. "Oh, you mean useful theorems. No. Well, not exactly. There's a lot going on up here." She twiddled her fingers around her ear. "Eldroi artifacts are many and varied, but I don't think I've ever heard of one sucking someone into it. I wonder if Gavyn is the power source. Do you feel like a power source?" she asked the lantern.

Rowan could almost imagine him glancing down at himself. "I don't... think so? What would a power source feel like?"

Rowan shook her head. "Modral said he could tell it wasn't from around here. That maybe it was made by the enemies of the Noksonoi. Maybe they built things that sucked people in."

"True, true." Lynniki nodded. "This definitely isn't a Noksonoi device. That just makes it all the more fascinating."

"Is your expertise with Eldroi artifacts?"

Lynniki straightened with a huge sigh. "It would be, but the elders don't allow it. They're too worried that the closer we get to the Giants, even after this long, the greater the possibility of corruption."

Rowan raised her eyebrows. "What do you think?"

Lynniki flashed her a grin. "I think all knowledge is useful. Either as a way to move forward or a way to avoid past mistakes. Burying our heads under a mountain won't help us build ourselves a new culture and society for very long. Eventually we will have to come to terms with where we came from and learn how to use the traits the Giants bred into us. Is that so awful?"

"I think it's admirable, as long as you're careful." Rowan gestured at the lantern. "I got stuck with the Grief Draw because I wasn't careful."

Gavyn snorted. "Same here."

Lynniki threw her hands up. "Obviously, I'm careful. It's not like I've learned nothing in all my research. But there are so many useful things buried in the ruins left by the Giants, and not all of them will kill you. We should be able to study them, pick them apart, until we can recreate their effects without the danger, but if the elders even suspect I might have gotten an idea or a part from a Eldroi device, they shut me down with a lecture and a black mark on my tally. Even if I declawed the original inspiration and re-purposed it into something new and valuable."

She subsided, glaring at the lantern like it had personally offended her.

"Well, now's your chance," Rowan said. "I have no idea what I'm doing with this thing. So speculate away."

"In other words, stop moaning and get to work?" She laughed. "I get it, but I would really love some more to work with. Something from the Eldroi themselves. Or even some vague hypothesis from someone who's seen the thing work."

"Keinwen's rhyme," Gavyn said. "Tell her the rhyme."

"Oh, yes. We think one of Gavyn's fellow mages left him a message after she escaped. She's featured in a nursery rhyme that was popular in the surrounding towns for the last hundred years."

"Well, tell me. Tell me!" Lynniki said, pulling forward a clean sheet of parchment.

Rowan recited the verses for her while she transcribed.

"We think the first verse is talking about Keinwen. It's a clear reference to something Gavyn told her before they escaped. And the 'light against the dark' is definitely referring to the lantern."

"And I think in 'time too long to mark' she suspected I might be stuck for a long time," Gavyn said.

Rowan related that thought even though it seemed a little far-fetched to her. "Or it's a metaphor for how she was feeling about searching her whole life," she added.

Lynniki screwed up her face. "I hate metaphors. I much prefer absolutes. Why couldn't she just say, 'hey, Gavyn, if you get this, look here'?"

Rowan chuckled. "I imagine that sort of message wouldn't have been interesting enough for other people to withstand the test of time. This way, children have been singing these words and passing them down for years."

"Hmm, so it could be subject to a shift in language and perception over time too," Lynniki muttered. "Wonderful. I'm more interested in that third verse, though. What was it again?"

"Healer, healer, glass bound with gold
Mind your hands for danger you hold

Pieces together, unique in their glow
Healer, healer, complete you are bold."

"All right, well once you know what it's talking about, 'glass bound with gold' and 'danger you hold' are obvious. The lantern's reputation precedes it."

"Keinwen spent a long time trying to keep us alive down there," Gavyn said in the back of Rowan's mind. "She would know how dangerous the lantern was."

"Yes, but what does the rest of it mean?" Rowan asked out loud.

"That's the part that seems straightforward to me," Lynniki said. "Finally we're talking about form following function."

Rowan gave her a puzzled look.

Lynniki slid the lantern across the table to her. "Look closer around the glass."

Rowan leaned down to peer at the lantern. "All right?"

"See around the edges. They're raised. Those are clamps meant to hold something."

Rowan took a deep breath. "Healer's Ghost, there are more pieces for it."

"Yes!" Lynniki cried. "More pieces with unique functions. I'd guess the lantern doesn't even work until all the bits are put together. That's why it mentions being complete in the last line."

She pulled the lantern back across the tabletop and picked it up between her hands. "From the shape and size and placement, it looks like they might be panes of more glass designed to fit over the existing ones that protect the flame. And as the light shines through, something happens."

"What?"

"That's the best part! We'll have to figure it out."

Rowan would argue that that seemed like the most *frustrating* part, but who was she to ruin Lynniki's fun?

"Keinwen spent so much of her life trying to figure this out," Gavyn murmured in the back of Rowan's head.

"Hmm?"

"She escaped. She had a life and her magic. Maybe she had a family and children. Maybe her ancestors are running around out there now. But she spent so much of her life trying to understand the lantern. Just on the off chance that understanding it might help me. Even when she knew she probably would never see me again."

Rowan remained quiet, unsure if he needed or wanted comfort or was just working through his thoughts on his own.

"I've spent a long time feeling trapped, but I think it's time I did something to change that. I want to honor Keinwen's sacrifice."

"How will you do that?" Rowan asked quietly.

"It's time I started helping myself. I need to get out of here."

"What's he saying?" Lynniki asked.

"He wants to be free of the lantern."

Lynniki clapped her hands together and rubbed them. "Another puzzle!"

"You'll need a body," Rowan said. "A disembodied mind needs a home."

Gavyn snorted. "How am I going to do that? It's not like I have one lying around anymore. It was dead. You buried it, remember?"

"All right, yes," Rowan said with a wince. "Minor problem number one. I buried your dead body. Sorry."

Lynniki cocked her head. "Actually. I've been thinking about that."

"You have?" Rowan said.

Lynniki shrugged. "I have about thirteen problems running around my head at once. I just let them do their thing until one of them jumps forward to say 'look at me!'"

"So what are you thinking?"

She held out her metal arm, a slow smile spreading across her face as she bent each finger individually. "If I can make limbs, a body should be easy enough. It's transferring him that's going to be the problem. That'll take magic, and Delvers aren't all that good at magic. Resistant to Giant magic means we don't have a lot of our own."

"We'll find something," Gavyn said, excitement lacing his voice. "Rowan is clever, and she hasn't let me down yet."

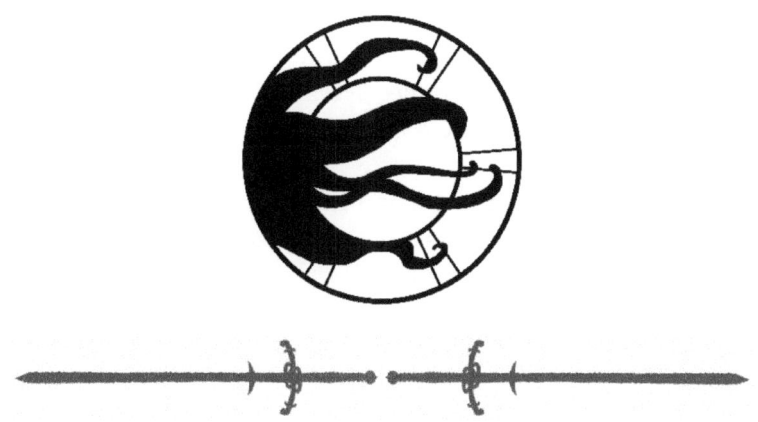

CHAPTER TWENTY-THREE

ROWAN

owan followed Lynniki as she scrambled across the surface of the mountain. Stones fell away from her feet, and she winced, unpleasantly reminded of the rockslide. But Lynniki seemed to know what she was doing, and today the sun shone down, giving them a clear, spectacular view of the rest of the range.

In the bright sunlight, it was actually much warmer than it had been the day she and Penrill had tried to reach the city. Rowan still wore her cloak—now a little ragged along the edge—but she was sweating as she tried to follow Lynniki's zigzagging path up the mountain.

"Here we are," Lynniki called and swooped down on a boulder that was half again as tall as most Delvers. She set her shoulder to the massive rock, and Rowan was about to snort. There was no way Lynniki would be able to move it.

But the boulder slid aside revealing two metal rails that glinted in the sun and a round hole lined with copper big enough to swallow Rowan.

"Why does your mountain have holes in it?" Rowan asked, stepping up to peer down the shaft.

"Vents," Lynniki said. "It's an intricate system that keeps air moving in and smoke and fumes cycling out. Otherwise, it would get very hazy inside, and we'd have all died of asphyxiation a long time ago."

Lynniki knelt on the rock and hung her head over the hole. "Although, I hear you pass out first, and it's a surprisingly peaceful way to go. Hold my feet."

Rowan lunged for the Delver's boots as she plunged inside the hole, her head and torso hanging down until she nearly disappeared.

"Healer's Ghost," Rowan gasped, "is that why you asked me along?"

"Not the only reason." Lynniki's voice rang from the wide copper tube. "Clever people are more fun to spend time with, and it's been ages since I had anyone clever enough to talk to."

Rowan would have been flattered, but she was too busy hanging on for dear life. The Delver might have been shorter, but she was a lot more solid than a Human, and Rowan worried that Lynniki had vastly overestimated her strength.

"Don't drop her," Gavyn said from her belt. "She's my only chance at freedom."

"Trust me, I know," Rowan said through gritted teeth. "I'd rather not drop my only aunt either. Especially not before I get to yell at her for this."

"You know," Lynniki said. "I think I'm getting used to hearing only half of a conversation. Aha! I found one."

"Can I pull you up?"

"Hang on, this could be useful too. There. Now pull."

Rowan strained, her back screaming at her, and Lynniki popped out of the hole like a cork out of a bottle and rolled a little way down the slope.

"Ta-da," she said and held up two mysterious bits of copper machinery.

"I'd be more impressed if I knew what they were," Rowan panted.

"This one is really good for the articulations we'll need for Gavyn's new body. And this one—well, I don't know yet, but I'm sure I'll need it at some point."

Rowan frowned at the hole. "Do you store things down there?"

Lynniki gave her a look. "What? No. I took them out of the fan for the vent."

Rowan squeaked.

"Don't give me that look. It'll still work just fine. I should know. I built it to have plenty of redundancies."

Rowan bit her lip and peered over the edge of the vent. She'd protest and say they didn't need to dismantle parts of the city to build Gavyn a body, but the truth was, she had no idea.

And she didn't have time to ask Lynniki to slow down and explain it to her. This was Rowan's third day in the city. She didn't see the elder actually throwing her out the city gates tomorrow morning, but she could imagine half a dozen polite ways he could make good on his threat.

Besides, Rowan really didn't want to outstay her welcome in a place that had been mostly kind to her.

But Lynniki hadn't even started building yet. There was no way she'd be done by morning. This project could take months.

If the elders didn't let Rowan stay for a little longer with the lantern, then she would have to ask Lynniki to come down to Monclaren or one of the other towns where Rowan could meet her once the body was complete. Then Rowan would be in charge of finding the magic to transfer Gavyn over to his new home, not that she had any idea what she was looking for in that regard.

Lynniki set her shoulder to the stone again and slid it back into place, the rails making its movement as smooth as the lantern's glass.

Rowan shaded her eyes with her hand. "Are there more nearby?" She tried to decide which boulders were the covers for more vents and which were just boulders.

Movement caught her eye, and she squinted down the slope.

In the sharp little valley between peaks, Byrson was waving wildly.

"What's wrong?" Lynniki said as Rowan stiffened.

"Trouble, I think."

They slid and skidded down the slope as Byrson hurried to meet them halfway.

"Get inside," Byrson said, before either Rowan or Lynniki had a chance to open their mouth. "We've got a party of Humans armed to the teeth headed this way."

"What?" Rowan said.

Lynniki snorted. "No one would be stupid enough to try attacking a Delver city. Would they?"

"I'm not going to wait around and give them an intelligence test," Byrson said. "They're on the path. They clearly know the city is nearby. We're buttoning everything up so that's as far as they get."

Rowan glanced down at the lantern, her mouth falling open. "Oh no," she whispered.

"What was that?" Byrson said.

"What did they look like? The Humans."

"They're led by a dark-skinned woman, armed like she knows how to use a weapon."

"Did you see her insignia? Who does she serve?"

"I don't know what all your symbols mean. The colors on her sleeve were red and blue. That's all I know."

Rowan sucked in a breath. "She serves Lord Karaval. She must have followed me from Monclaren. Healer's Ghost, she's persistent. Byrson is right," Rowan told Lynniki. "They're not here to say please and thank you. They're here for the lantern."

"How many are there?" Lynniki asked. "We've got all those traps that will drop boulders on their heads."

Byrson's lips thinned. "If we start killing Humans, we risk starting a war with all of them. We're safe enough as long as we're quiet and stay on their good side. But this could tip the balance and bring them into the mountains to hunt us down."

"Even if it's self-defense?" Rowan asked.

"That's never mattered to you Humans before. If you want to hate someone, you hate them."

Rowan flushed. Three days ago, she'd been "sister." Now she was back to being one of "you Humans."

Modral might not have been right about the lantern corrupting the Delvers, but the effect was the same. She'd brought trouble and violence to a peaceful city, and now they would have to pay for her problems.

"Get inside," Byrson said. "Tell Modral we'll close the gates. If they can't find us, they can't fight us."

Lynniki opened her mouth to protest, but Byrson took her shoulder and flung her toward the entrance to the city. Rowan stumbled after her. They weren't far from the massive opening to the city cavern, and Rowan tucked her hand under Lynniki's arm to haul her inside.

The roof of the cavern cut off the bright midday sun, plunging them into shadow, and Rowan blinked, willing her eyes to adjust.

Lynniki pulled her arm free and stopped in the middle of the passage. Rowan glanced back to see whatever had caught her eye.

Byrson stood silhouetted against the sunshine.

A huge grating noise made Rowan flinch and cover her ears. Then the ground rumbled under her feet, making them tingle and itch.

From either side of them, slabs of rock rolled forward, slowly and inexorably cutting the cavern off from the outside world. It seemed as though the entire mountainside moved in a creeping collapse, except that Rowan could see the rails laid into the floor.

Rowan and Lynniki stumbled back before the two halves met in the middle. Through the closing fissure, Rowan caught a glimpse of Byrson turning to face the threat they couldn't see yet.

Rowan tried to swallow down the knot in her throat.

The stone gates met with a thud that echoed in Rowan's chest. The rock blended with the walls and she could imagine that it looked like an unbroken section of mountain from the outside, hiding the city behind a door nearly ten feet thick.

"Nothing's getting through that," Gavyn said as her elbow brushed the top of the lantern.

"What about Byrson?" Rowan murmured.

Gavyn was silent.

Lynniki spun away from the solid rock wall, toward the tunnel into the city. "He'll be fine," she said. "He's craftier in the peaks than any Human. Get to Modral. Tell him the gates are closed."

"What are you—?" But Lynniki was already gone, her metal arm flashing once before she disappeared into the shadows of the tunnel where Rowan assumed there was another passage.

"I guess she has somewhere to be," Gavyn said.

"Knowing her, she probably has some device to bring the mountain down on any invaders," Rowan said. "I hope she knows what she's doing."

She stepped quickly through the tunnel to the hallway with the meeting room where the city elders convened.

A copper pipe was tucked into the corner between the wall and the ceiling. As Rowan passed under it, steam hissed and spat from the joints, and then, all of a sudden, a whistle at the end of the line shrieked to life.

Rowan winced and ducked into the meeting room.

Modral was on his feet already, the other elders clambering around him. He met her eyes.

"Unfriendly visitors?" he said, mildly.

Rowan gave him a short nod. "They're the ones who were looking for the lantern back in Monclaren. They followed Penrill and I. Byrson closed the gates."

"That is the best thing we can do for now. Sit quiet and tight. If they can't find the city, then they can't lay siege to it. And if they can't find any of our people, then we won't have to defend ourselves with force."

Rowan bit her lip. That woman had looked plenty capable back in Monclaren. She had the skill to track Rowan and Penrill through the mountains, despite the landslide. Even though the Delvers had done their best to keep its location hidden, the woman was practically on top of the city. *After all that, is it so far-fetched to think she might find some way inside?*

She nearly argued, to ask if he really felt safe behind their rock walls, but as their gazes locked, the corner of his mouth twitched down. An involuntary show of emotion quickly hidden.

Modral was worried.

Rowan had spent the morning rehearsing the words to ask him to let her stay longer. To let her and Gavyn live in the mountain until they could build him a new body and figure out how to transfer him into it. She would have promised to keep the lantern away from the Delvers as much as possible. To minimize their contact with it.

But the damage was already done. She'd already disrupted their lives and threatened their peace.

"I'll leave," Rowan said before she'd even realized she'd made the decision. "I'll take the lantern and get out through one of the other entrances. If I'm not here, then they have nothing to look for, no reason to break in. You'll be safe from the lantern and any other trouble it might bring."

For a second, Rowan expected Modral to protest. He opened his mouth, then hesitated. When he spoke, he said, "Thank you. We will provide provisions of course."

"Right," Rowan said, staggering a little. She wouldn't take back her offer, but she had to take a moment to breathe. To steel herself for what she was about to do.

"I'm going with her," Lynniki said from the open archway.

Rowan spun. The Delver stood there, weighed down by a pack that was nearly as big as she was, and holding another in her hand. Bits of copper hung from one side, and tools clanged against the other.

"Lynniki…" Rowan started, a tide of relief rising in her chest.

Lynniki met Modral's eyes. "I'm going with Rowan. Gavyn still needs help, and I know the Eldroi's technology better than anyone. *They* need me."

Modral's mouth tightened. "You will corrupt yourself. Don't pretend you're not using this as an excuse to touch and fondle things you shouldn't, Lynniki. You will lose yourself in this misplaced obsession."

Lynniki threw the extra pack down. "You think I don't know enough to be wary of Giant artifacts? I've studied them more than you have. I know what they're capable of more than elders who make judgments based on fragmented memories. But being wary is not the same as being afraid, and ignoring something isn't always the best way to guard against it."

Modral lifted a hand as if to discount her, but Lynniki jerked her chin up to glare at him.

"I'm going to help Rowan. For Lynnock's sake, but also for her own. She's stuck with this burden, but she doesn't have to be stuck alone."

Rowan swallowed. She was glad to have the Delver along, and not just for Lynnock's sake either.

"And your particular interests have nothing to do with it, I suppose?" Modral said with a sour smile.

"Of course they do. I'll be out of the mountain finally. Away from your strictures, so I can finally study the Eldroi and everything they've left behind. I can figure out how to use what they left to help us. Without corrupting us. And if you can't see that I'm trying to help, well, I'm done trying to prove it to you." She turned her face away. "At the very least, this means you won't have to argue with me anymore."

She snatched up the extra pack again and handed it to Rowan.

Rowan took it with a warm smile. "Thank you, Lynniki."

She shrugged into the pack, wondering what the Delver had time to pack in that brief few moments. Maybe she'd been planning on leaving for a long time, and this was just the first chance she'd had.

"We'll stall them as long as we can," Modral said, though neither of them looked up. "To give you a better chance."

Lynniki's shoulders stiffened, then she trudged into the hall.

Rowan cast a glance back. His offer was a bandage applied much too late to stop any sort of bleeding, but he'd been kind to Rowan, despite their disagreements.

"Thank you," she said. Then she followed her Delver aunt, feeling a lot lighter about leaving than she'd expected.

Lynniki gave her a twisted smile as she caught up. "I'm sorry I couldn't help you fit in here."

"I don't think either of us is supposed to. Let's go."

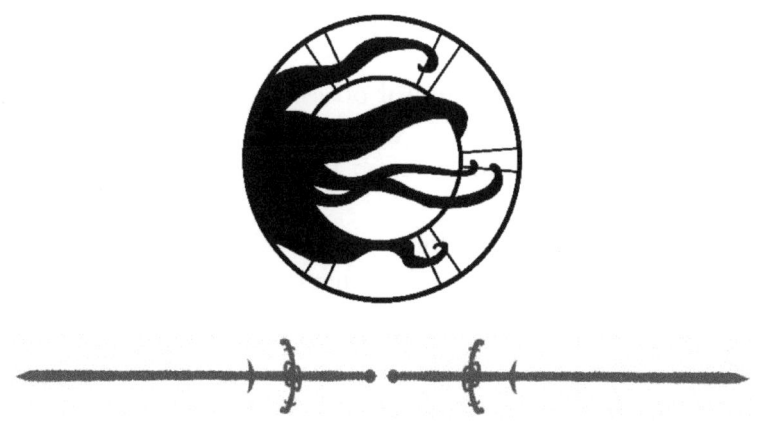

CHAPTER TWENTY-FOUR

ROWAN

Lynniki led Rowan to the very back of the city, where a grate covered the smallest passage Rowan had seen in the entire city. This took them to the far side of the mountain and a little gully that ran to the valley below.

They slid and skidded their way down, using its high walls to mask their movement.

"Where are we going?" Lynniki asked.

"Uh." Rowan had been about to ask her the same thing. "We need to find somewhere safe," she said, trying to keep her voice confident.

They paused where the gully grew a little less steep, and Rowan braced herself against the sloping wall. "Someplace no one will come looking for the lantern. The list of people I trust is growing very short, and the list of people who want to take it is growing longer."

"Most Human settlements will be out then," Lynniki said, her mouth screwing up in thought. "I doubt any other Delver clans will want anything to do with it. I wouldn't trust the

Wergoi, either, if we could even find them. They would just want to worship it or something stupid. They're obsessed with the Eldroi."

"I thought you were kind of obsessed with the Giants too," Rowan said, grinning.

"I have a healthy appreciation for their technology. I don't worship them."

Rowan snorted. "All right, so we avoid the Wergoi, the Delvers, and Humans. What does that leave us?"

"Not much. What about hiding where no one will think to look?"

Rowan frowned. "What are you thinking?"

"A nuraghi."

"That... might work. Most people avoid ruins. They think they're haunted, or they give them a strange feeling. Jannik might still think to look there, since he's used to them. But—"

Her hand brushed the lantern, and Gavyn's voice came into her head like he'd been screaming at her the whole time.

"Rowan! Behind you."

Rowan spun, as stones skidded past, bouncing from the walls of the gully.

High on the hill above, a woman appeared, one foot up on the nearest rock, a naked blade in her hand. She'd thrown her cloak back over her shoulders to reveal a leather jerkin, nearly as dark as her skin, crossed with a thick belt.

Guardsmen in Lord Karaval's colors appeared around her, staring down at them, trapped in the gully.

Rowan sucked in a breath of chilly air, her lungs burning with it.

"Eldroi curse me, it was a feint," Lynniki whispered.

Rowan seized her hand. "Run!"

Lynniki sprinted ahead, far faster than her frame and the bulky pack should have allowed for. She leaped down the steep slope between the gully walls, bounding over boulders with each step.

Rowan followed less gracefully. She slipped and slid, the cloth of her tunic tearing with a vicious ripping sound. The boots the Delvers had given her were of good quality, but they didn't fit her feet exactly, and she tripped over the loose toes.

"Gavyn," she gasped. "Are they coming?"

"I can't see," Gavyn said under her hand. "The walls are too high."

The enemy was between them and the Delver city. There would be no ducking back inside to safety, even if they were fast enough.

A stone rolled under her foot, and she crashed to the ground at a funny angle, jarring her spine.

She gasped, and Lynniki stopped her frenetic flight downhill. "Rowan?"

Rowan tried to stand, but her back spasmed, sending shooting pains down her legs. Her breath hissed through her teeth.

Up. Up. She had to stand. She had to get away. If Lord Karaval's men caught them, he'd have the lantern. All of this fleeing would have been for nothing.

She used the walls of the gully to lever herself to her feet as Lynniki raced to help her.

"Are you all right?" she asked.

"I have to be," Rowan said through gritted teeth. "Go."

Lynniki gave her a shoulder to lean on, extending her metal hand to steady them against the wall.

Rowan breathed raggedly through her nose, ignoring the pain in her back and legs. Forward. That was all she could do. Keep moving forward.

There was a sharp intake of breath from Lynniki, and Rowan looked up.

The woman stood on the lip of the gully just ahead of them. She pointed her sword at them. "Surrender your weapons."

Rowan laughed, short and sharp. She carried nothing except the lantern, and she didn't know how to use that except to goad Gavyn into blinding their enemies.

Lynniki pulled a hammer from the side of her pack and brandished it with a fierce, feral look. "Come and take it from me."

Rowan swallowed. Bold words, but they meant nothing unless Lynniki was prepared to defend them both with a blunt tool.

There was no change in the woman's expression. "Very well," she said.

Rowan opened her mouth to ask Gavyn to flare the light and blind the woman.

Something hit her from behind, sending a starburst of pain across her vision before the world went black. The last thing she heard was Lynniki cry out.

CHAPTER TWENTY-FIVE

ROWAN

R owan became aware of the musty smell of grain that was just beginning to go off before she even opened her eyes. She blinked, noting the way her eyelids tried to stick together. The world around her remained fuzzy.

How long had she been out? She didn't remember falling asleep. The last thing she remembered—

She sat up with a gasp. Her head sent a spike of pain down her neck, almost matched by the ache in her spine.

"Careful there," Lynniki's voice said.

Rowan put her hand to her head and groaned.

"They got you good. Both of us actually, but I think my skull is thicker. I woke up nearly an hour ago."

Rowan rubbed the stickiness from her eyes and found herself in a dim, little room, bare except for a couple of barrels in the corner and some musty rushes that covered the floor. A window stood high on the wall, letting a little stream of light through the barred shutters, illuminating Lynniki sitting opposite Rowan. She sported an impressive bruise across the side of her face, spreading from her hairline to her jaw.

Rowan pushed herself up on her hands and knees to balance against the barrels. "Gavyn?" She compulsively checked her hip and sucked in a breath when she found nothing except an empty spot on her belt. "Gavyn!"

"There," Lynniki said.

Rowan followed her gesture and found a gate barring the end of their dim little room, like would be found on a pantry or a wine cellar in a noble's house. Something to keep thieves away from the expensive cheese and drink. Except, right now, it was keeping Lynniki and Rowan in.

Just outside the gate, the lantern sat on a barrel, still in its case.

Rowan lunged to her feet and rattled the gate.

"I tried that already," Lynniki said.

The handle didn't budge. Rowan ignored the spiking pain in her back and head and reached her arm through the bars, straining for the lantern. Her fingers stretched just inches away, but no matter how she twisted, she couldn't get any closer.

"I know your arms are longer than mine, but I think they accounted for that."

Rowan sagged again, sliding down the grating, the metal biting into her forehead as she rested her head against the bars.

"Who?" Rowan asked.

"Not sure yet," Lynniki said. "No one's been by, but I'd bet the contents of my pack it was that woman. The dangerous-looking one."

"A good bet. Where are we?"

Lynniki's lips twisted. "I feel like all my answers are going to be 'I don't know.' I can't see much through the crack in the shutters." She flushed. "I'm not tall enough. But I can tell you, there's no mountains out there."

Rowan blew out her breath. "So wherever they've brought us is a long distance down." The guards had been wearing Lord Karaval's colors, but Rowan only knew that his lands lay north of Lord Hax's. Not much else.

They'd fallen right into the trap. The woman had made a clear frontal assault against the Delver city, forcing them to flee, and then caught them on their way out the back. Like a rabbit escaping the snare only to run straight into the hunter's hands.

Rowan pounded her head lightly with her fist. Stupid, stupid, stupid.

Beyond the gate, the rest of the pantry seemed mostly bare. Perhaps it had been cleared out just for them. How special.

The door beyond opened, and Rowan jerked up with a frown.

The first person through was the woman. She no longer wore her cloak, and her sword was sheathed. But her expression was as focused as it had been on the mountain. Her eyes flicked to the corners of the room, and in the light of the pantry, Rowan could see they were two different colors. One a deep amber and the other a murky green.

She raised the sharp edge of her nose. "My lord," she said and stepped aside.

Two men entered behind her, one in a dark blue robe, tied with a green sash, but it was the other who arrested Rowan's gaze. He was tall, though not monstrously so, with broad shoulders and a cleft chin. But it wasn't his size that made her sit up and hold her breath. It was the way he held himself, the way he seemed to fill the room as though it were an audience hall, not a pantry.

The woman and the robed man both held back, deferring to him as he stepped across the pantry.

His gaze raked over Rowan and Lynniki behind their gate before settling on the lantern. Rowan was expecting triumph or joy to light in his expression. Instead, his eyes grew tight, and his mouth twitched in a little grimace, quickly hidden.

"Good work, Captain Tera," he said. "That's it."

"Thank you, Lord Karaval," the woman replied. Her expression remained stoic despite the praise.

Lord Karaval. This was the man who had been chasing her since Monclaren. Lord Hax's rival.

Rowan's insides twisted in an uncomfortable mix of comfort and fear. He looked a little like her stepfather.

Lord Karaval's nose had been broken at some point in the past, leaving it crooked, and his face had seen more weathering than someone who'd spent his whole life indoors. Seams ran from the corners of his eyes and his mouth, though his hair remained thick and stark black, falling just long enough to brush his collar.

He jerked his head at the robed man. "Gillfry, it's all yours."

The other man stepped forward.

"No, don't," Rowan said. She reached through the bars as if that would do anything to stop them.

It did enough. Gillfry hesitated and cast a glance at his lord.

Lord Karaval turned eyes so dark they were nearly black on her, and Rowan gulped.

Her mind raced. He had the lantern. There was nothing she could do behind a locked gate.

All she had were words. She had to convince Lord Karaval that the dangers of the lantern weren't worth whatever it was he wanted it for. She surged to her feet with a wince.

"Don't touch it," she said. "Please, it will kill you."

Maybe this one would actually listen. Unlike Jannik.

Lord Karaval stepped closer and peered down at her. Rowan swallowed and took an involuntary step back.

"Gillfry is the most accomplished mage outside of the capital," Lord Karaval said, his voice rich and resonant even in this small space. "He won't do anything reckless."

"Just holding it is the problem," Rowan said. "Please believe me. You can't stop what it will do. Whatever you want to do with it, isn't worth it."

"That is a broad assumption," Lord Karaval said, raising his chin. "You cannot fathom the Grief Draw's worth to me."

"No, but I know all about its risks. Its dangers. It will melt you from the inside. Is that worth it to *you*?" She craned around to peer at Gillfry.

The mage licked his lips and glanced at Lord Karaval.

The lord nodded to his mage. "Proceed. Jannik made it clear she would say anything to keep her ill-gotten prize."

Rowan fell back another step, shock lancing through her chest. Jannik's lies had reached even this noble?

The mage took up the lantern without a second glance at Rowan.

"You can't use it." It was her last argument, and she flung it desperately like a thrown dagger. "Even Jannik didn't know how to make it work. You don't know what it is or how it works. And it could hurt someone."

Lord Karaval's jaw twitched. "I know enough. It will light up a noktum, and that is all that matters."

Rowan's jaw fell open. "A noktum?"

Like the swath of darkness she'd passed on the way home. Noktums didn't just swallow light. They swallowed people. And anyone unlucky enough to be snatched into one never came out again. Helana had told the village children stories about the monsters that roamed the perpetual shadows and the ones who slunk through into the daylight realm to kill and maim.

"How do you know?" Rowan whispered. It was more than she knew about the lantern, and she'd been carrying it for over a month now.

"A magical light for a magical darkness."

He didn't want a weapon. That in itself was refreshing, but it didn't justify what he was about to do.

"Just because it can be used as a light doesn't make it safe."

"It will get me through the black," Lord Karaval said, turning his shoulder as if to leave. "That is what matters."

"What could be so important inside a noktum?" Rowan called after him, gripping the bars that separated them. "What could you possibly be looking for in there? Weapons to defeat your enemies? Riches for your vaults? Treasure?"

Gillfry swept out the door.

Lord Karaval paused on the threshold. "Something like that," he said over his shoulder. Then he stepped through.

"Wait! Stop!"

Captain Tera followed her lord, shutting the door behind her with a very final click.

❦ ❦ ❦

Rowan's fingers gripped the bars of the locked gate, rough bits of metal digging into her skin. Her forehead fell against the bars, and she breathed through her nose.

She slid down the bars to land in a heap on the floor, head bowed.

"Are you all right?" Lynniki asked softly.

"I had one little thing to do. Keep the lantern away from Jannik and treasure hunters like Lord Karaval." She gestured helplessly through the bars. "You can see how well I did it."

She curled her hand into a fist and pounded it against the packed dirt floor. It didn't even make a dent.

Lynniki's lips thinned and twisted like she wanted to say something but couldn't think of anything.

"Healer's Ghost, I knew I wasn't going to be enough. From the moment I struck Jannik, I've been running because that's the only thing I could think to do. It just took me this long to prove it."

"Is that why you came to the Delvers for help? You didn't think you could carry the lantern on your own?"

Rowan opened her mouth, but she wasn't sure what she had to argue about. That was exactly what she'd been doing. Looking for someone else to take the lantern, despite all the anger she'd held toward her family for underestimating her. She'd burned with that anger when she found out Darryn and the others had conscripted Jannik to look after her.

But here she'd been running around trying to find someone to keep looking after her.

She shut her mouth with a click.

Lynniki shook her head. "We haven't failed yet, you know?"

Rowan jerked her chin up. "What?"

Lynniki shrugged and lifted her metal hand. It glinted in the tiny sliver of light that came through the shutters. "The first three of these I made all fell to pieces when I tried to use them. Failures, you might say. There's magic in the joints to translate my thoughts to movement. Magic I stole from nuraghis. But Delvers aren't great at magic. It took a while to figure out how to integrate it."

She flexed her fingers. "The first few failed, but I didn't stop. I kept going until one of them finally worked. That's the only failure. When you stop moving forward. Stop trying."

Rowan rolled her lip between her teeth as she stared at Lynniki's hand. "How did it happen?"

Lynniki huffed a laugh. "A few years ago I was excavating one of the tunnels for the vents. A section collapsed, and I lost my arm, much like Penrill lost his leg."

"I'm sorry," Rowan said.

"I'm not. Not anymore. I spent almost a year feeling useless and sorry for myself, and *that* was too long."

"What changed?"

Lynniki smiled. How could such a quiet expression look so fierce at the same time? "I woke up one day tired of it all. I decided I wasn't going to be useless anymore. I became something different."

Rowan wanted to curl up into a ball and let Lord Karaval learn the dangers of the Grief Draw the hard way. But Lynniki's smile made a little spark burn in her chest. It flared and flamed, searing through everything else until angry heat filled her.

How often had she believed her family when they'd told her she needed someone to care for her? How often had she believed the villagers when they called her blighted? How often did she believe she was worthless and useless every time someone dismissed her words and arguments? Each time she let the words in, they chipped away at the strength inside her.

She was tired of not being enough. Tired of people not listening to her. Tired of settling for being the useless sister.

So many of those things were her choices. And she was done making them.

"I'm going to be something—someone—different," she said.

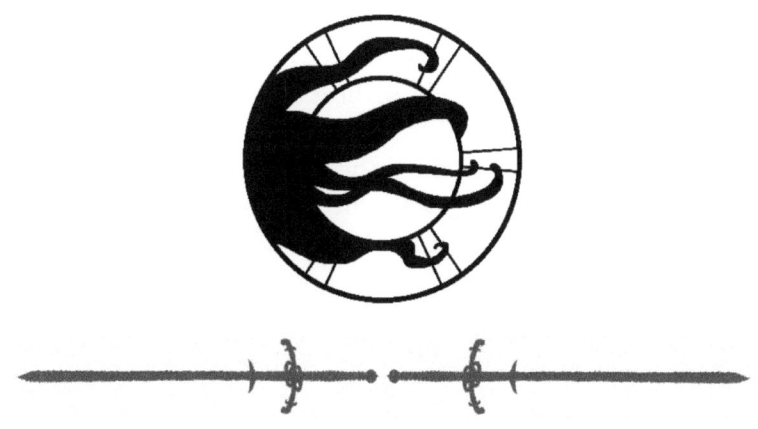

CHAPTER TWENTY-SIX

GAVYN

The mage peered at the lantern, his watery brown eyes inches away from its surface.

Gavyn screamed inside his prison. "Listen to her! Senji's teeth, why don't they ever listen."

Gillfry's hands touched the bare metal, completely oblivious to the fate he was inviting. Gavyn screamed the whole way up the stairs of the keep, ignoring everything except the mage's face looming over him. If he could ever get anyone else to hear him besides Rowan, now would be the moment. He wouldn't be responsible for another mage's death. Even a hundred years after all the others.

If he could just speak, maybe he could stop this, but even Rowan couldn't get them to listen, and she knew as much as he did.

The mage placed the lantern on a table in a workroom far different from the one in the Giant's laboratory. Tapestries hung over the stone walls, softening them, and colored bottles lined the work bench.

The place still filled him with that same cold dread as the bare walls he'd stared at for a hundred years.

"Please, listen," he pleaded as the mage puttered around the other side of the room. "Please hear me. I don't want you to die."

But the mage, Gillfry, didn't hear. He didn't stop. He came back and started fiddling with the top of the lantern where whorls of filigree wrapped around the handle.

What if the mage figured out how to activate the lantern when Rowan hadn't? Or worse—was it worse?—what if he broke it? Would Gavyn survive if the panes shattered, or the light went out? What would hold him to this world if there was no more lantern?

You would think after being so long imprisoned, a final death would seem like a blessing. An end to his years of boredom interspersed with terror.

But it wasn't.

He reached inside to the heart of the wickless flame and pulled.

The light flared outward, pure white and blinding, as it had in the wayrest. As it had on the mountainside.

The mage can't continue if he can't see. Could he?

CHAPTER TWENTY-SEVEN

ROWAN

Rowan kicked the bars. "Lynniki, you want to get out of here?"

Lynniki rolled her eyes. "Obviously. I was just waiting for you to decide you wanted to fight."

The old Rowan would have objected to the word "fight," but the new Rowan liked the sound of it. Her fingers were already curling into fists, and she could imagine swinging one of Lynniki's hammers at a certain stubborn lord.

"All right, how?" Rowan's eyes scanned the makeshift cell. The barrels held promise, but it turned out they held only moldy onions.

Lynniki's pack with all of her tools lay beyond the bars of their cage, next to the barrel where the lantern had sat. Much too far for either of them to reach. There was nothing they could use to drag it closer. The barrels were too well made to pull apart and the floor was packed dirt with no floorboards to pull up.

Rowan's frown deepened as her eyes traced the gate. She wasn't a craftsman like Lynniki, but doors and gates were pretty simple when you came down to it. Anyone who'd repaired a leather hinge or placed a hinge pin knew how they worked.

"Could we get the gate off its hinges, do you think?"

Lynniki knelt beside the bottom hinge and picked at the head of the pin with the fingernail of her good hand. "Probably not."

Rowan's shoulders sagged.

"Not without my tools. It's too well made. They flattened the ends with a chisel so it wouldn't come off again easily, but it's not a bad idea." Her gaze roamed the cell and lit on the window. A grin spread across her face. "And I'll bet no one has paid as much attention to the shutters."

She stood and stepped to the window. Rowan was already scooting a barrel across to it, leaving gouges in the dirt floor. Lynniki climbed atop the barrel and peered at its hinges.

"Well?" Rowan said.

Lynniki grinned at her under her arm. "Doable. This guy must have money. They're better made than I thought they would be, but they haven't been flattened like the gate."

It took most of the rest of the day. Lynniki couldn't get a good grip on either of the pins. Her metal fingers kept sliding off, and she spent so long trying with her good hand that her fingertips were red and raw and swollen. It didn't help that they had to keep stopping whenever they heard something outside the door.

The work went faster once Rowan took off her belt and pried the tongue of her buckle off to give to Lynniki.

By late afternoon, Lynniki had used the little strip of metal to pry the hinges out of their sockets. The window led out onto a courtyard drenched in afternoon sun. Rowan was glad for the warmth compared to the mountain's chilly heights, but broad daylight held risks.

She stood on a barrel and peeked over the edge of the window into what looked like a courtyard with a wide wall all around. Beyond the wall, she could see the peaks of roofs and the occasional bell tower.

Servants in brown and gray tunics pattered across the courtyard, calling to each other and carrying dishes or boxes. A group of guards in red and blue lounged against a nearby wall, laughing.

"We'll have to wait. Someone will see and stop us for sure," she told Lynniki.

The Delver nodded and flexed her fingers. Rowan winced. She could imagine they ached as bad as her head and her back did after the hours of work at the shutters.

Rowan chafed at the delay, staying perched on the barrel and counting the time as the shadows lengthened and the sun disappeared behind the city walls. Her fingers clenched on the sill as she surreptitiously watched the people in the courtyard.

One by one, the servants disappeared. Eventually the guards stood and stretched and shuffled off to wherever guards spent the night. By the time the courtyard lay in full dark, the flagstones were empty.

Rowan straightened on top of her barrel. Her tunic flapped without her belt, and the barrel wobbled.

"Careful," Lynniki whispered, though Rowan wasn't sure what else she would be.

From her perch, she could wiggle through the window, but there was a bad moment on the other side when she realized how high off the ground she was and that she was going to hit it headfirst. Lynniki grabbed her legs as she slithered down the wall and helped ease her landing.

Rowan brushed off her arms as she peered around the darkened courtyard. She stood in the shadow of the wall while torches and lanterns left pools of light across the broad flagstones at perfect intervals around her. Behind her, a huge, square keep rose several stories into the air, squat and ugly but incredibly stout.

A few guards walked the top of the wall, their gazes focused on the city and the lands beyond.

Rowan took a split second to be relieved that the window had let her out on the inside of the fortress and not the outside. She couldn't imagine sneaking into someplace so well fortified.

Lynniki huffed above her, and Rowan turned to help her aunt through the window. The Delver's broader shoulders got stuck, but she backed out again and came through with both arms over her head.

Rowan braced her as she fell down the wall.

They held their breath, sneaking furtive glances around the courtyard to see if anyone had heard them.

A door down the wall opened and a servant exited dressed in a clean, brown smock and carrying a stack of firewood. She crossed the flagstones without a glance into their corner and disappeared into a door at the foot of the keep.

Lynniki blew out her breath. "All right. Now what?"

"We find Gavyn and the lantern." Rowan peered up at the keep. "And I'll bet he's in there."

"Lead the way. I think we'd better avoid being seen. You could pass as one of Lord Karaval's servants, but I'm not going to blend in." She gestured to her height with a rueful grimace.

"We'll stay out of sight," Rowan whispered back. Hopefully, this late, Lord Karaval's retainers would be busy with supper and settling down for the night.

They slipped through the door they'd seen the serving girl enter.

A hall stretched to the left and the right, lit by softly glowing wall sconces. Rowan had expected rushlights or more torches sputtering in the halls, but these held expensive candles that burned with a clearer light than even Jannik could afford.

"Left or right?" Lynniki asked.

Rowan's lips thinned. "I don't know. Where would a mage's workroom be?"

Someone cried out, and Rowan instinctively flattened herself against the wall.

"What?" Lynniki asked, eyes wide as she surveyed the hall.

"You didn't hear that?"

"Hear what?"

There was another cry, and this time Rowan realized the voice was familiar. And she wasn't hearing it with her ears.

"Gavyn?"

Lynniki looked at her sharply. "You can hear him?"

"I... I think so?" Rowan pushed off from the wall.

"No, no. He's... melt... I told you. *She* told you. Why... listen?" His voice came in fragments and cut off bits of thought, like it had when she'd first heard him in the ruins. Panic laced his tone, making the hair on Rowan's arms stand up.

"Gavyn, can you hear me?" she whispered, feeling ridiculous.

"I thought you had to be touching the lantern to hear him." Lynniki followed cautiously as Rowan stumbled down the hallway, picking a direction at random, hoping it was the right one.

"I thought so, too. That's how it's always worked but I don't know. I'm learning more about it every day. Maybe we've built our connection over all these weeks. It was the Life Magic that connected us in the first place."

"What's he saying?"

Rowan grimaced and paused to concentrate.

"Oh gods. If anyone... he's dying. We told him and now he's dying. Melted. Why didn't... someone..."

"He's saying 'he's dying' over and over."

They exchanged a look.

"The mage," Lynniki said. "Eldroi take him. He should have listened to you."

They all should have listened. Every last one of them, down to Jannik. But it was too late for them now.

"I'm sorry, I'm sorry. I didn't know," Gavyn babbled in the back of Rowan's head.

Rowan spun. "I think it sounds like he's this way."

"You can tell which direction he is now?"

Rowan snapped over her shoulder, "You want to wander aimlessly?"

"Nope. Pick a hypothesis and test it. If it doesn't work, pick another. Lead on. I'll follow."

They came around a corner, and the wall beside them abruptly opened in an archway that led to a wide, long banqueting hall. Several retainers sat at the long table, trenchers full of stew.

Rowan leaped back before anyone could see them and pressed Lynniki to the wall.

"We have to chance it," Lynniki said. "Unless you want to retrace our steps. Just go quick and act like you have every right to be there."

"What about you?"

Lynniki shrugged. "Maybe they'll think I'm a child."

A really broad, squat child. There was no way that was going to work, but Gavyn's voice continued to babble in the back of Rowan's head, and she couldn't concentrate on anything except making it stop.

"All right, let's go."

Rowan scuttled across the opening, trying to look like she had somewhere to be. Mostly she thought she just came off as worried. A quick glance at the hall showed her the head table was empty. Lord Karaval either didn't dine with his retainers or he'd been called away.

Lynniki skipped after her.

"What are you doing?" Rowan whispered as soon as they were past.

"Acting like a child?" she said.

"You think children skip everywhere?"

"Don't they? I don't know many children."

Considering how few Delver youth Rowan had seen in the city, she could imagine that was true.

Lynniki paused at a table in the hall. Several baskets of bread waited there beside a stack of large metal serving platters.

Before Rowan could protest, Lynniki stuffed nearly half a loaf of bread in her mouth at once and then picked up one of the platters. She gave it an experimental swing. When she caught Rowan looking, she swallowed and held the platter out. "Want a weapon?"

It was better than nothing. She snatched it and tried to hold it like she knew what she was doing.

Rowan waited till they were around the corner from the banquet hall before pausing again. "Gavyn, Gavyn can you hear me?"

"Gods, I'm sorry. I'm sorry."

"Gavyn, please. Please, hear me."

"Rowan?"

Rowan's shoulders sagged, and she collapsed against the wall.

"Gavyn. Where are you? We're coming to get you."

"How—?" His voice faded in and out, like he fought to stay focused. "How are you even—"

"I don't know, but I'm not wasting it. Do you know where you are?"

"Near the top of some stairs. I... I think. I wasn't paying attention. Past a big hall with tables and then some stairs. Maybe. The mage has a workshop here."

"We're coming," Rowan said, pushing off the wall.

"Hurry," Gavyn whispered.

Rowan repeated the meager directions to Lynniki as they went, to help her remember. They'd been lucky so far. The hall was clear. Everyone seemed to be at dinner down below.

But at the top of the first set of stairs, their luck ran out.

A guard in a coat of dark mail stepped from a room just as they reached the landing.

Rowan gave him a desperate grin and tried to sidle past him, holding her platter against her hip.

He smiled back at her. Then his eyes slid to Lynniki.

She also gave him a friendly grin. But it couldn't disguise her height or shape.

The guard's eyes narrowed. "Hey—"

Rowan pounced. As the guard turned his back toward her, she swung her platter as hard as she could across the back of his head.

He cried out and fell to his knees, one hand raised to clutch his skull.

"Sorry about this," Lynniki said and bashed him over the head again.

He slumped to the floor with a clang.

"Healer's Ghost, we're in trouble now," Rowan said, staring at the sprawled body.

"Quick, roll him to the side," Lynniki said.

Rowan almost suggested hiding him in the room he'd just left, but they had no idea what was in there. Maybe it was a barracks, and guards were about to come boiling out to investigate the noise.

She managed to shove him into the corner with one arm over his head, so he looked like he slept.

"Come on," Lynniki said, racing for another set of stairs. "We have to hurry now."

Rowan followed, casting one last look behind.

At the top of the second set of stairs, the way branched. They could go straight, or they could go right.

"Rowan, Rowan. He's dying. He's gonna be gone. I couldn't stop it. I'm sorry. I didn't know what else to do." Gavyn kept up his litany in the back of her head.

"Gavyn. Please, I can't concentrate. I can't—" She gasped.

To the right, two guards and a manservant came down the hall. They spotted Rowan and Lynniki and gave a shout.

Lynniki glanced at her. "I'll take these. You get to Gavyn."

Without waiting for an answer, the Delver rushed the trio. With clumsy efficiency, she threw herself down in front of them, tripping all three at once. They went down with a cacophony of clatters and profanity.

Rowan wished her a silent "good luck" and raced ahead.

"Gavyn, how many doors? Which one is the workshop?"

"I don't know. He's here. He's here. It's over."

"What? Gavyn!"

These doors that she passed looked like bedrooms? But there at the end of the hall, one stood ajar, and a cold, white light spilled into the hall.

Rowan hit it running, and it burst open to strike the wall with a bang.

The lantern sat on a thick, wood table against the back wall. Someone sprawled on the floor, and Rowan only recognized

Gillfry from the blue robe now stained darker with blood and other worse things.

The mage's face was swollen and weeping awful fluids from blisters as big as Rowan's palm.

Lord Karaval knelt at his side, and he spun at the sound of the door, hand going to the dagger at his waist.

His dark eyes raked Rowan from head to foot, pausing on the platter she brandished in both hands. But his gaze didn't seem to register either her presence or her weapon. His eyes remained shocked and blank.

He swallowed hard and looked back at Gillfry's pitiful body.

Rowan lowered the platter. Gavyn was finally silent in the back of her head. He was right. It was over. They were too late. They might not have had a chance to save him at all anyway.

Rowan stepped closer to Lord Karaval whose face and hands were slack. Her mother had treated shocked patients often enough that Rowan could recognize it. Whether Gillfry had been a good friend or not, whether he'd worked with Lord Karaval for long or only a short time, a sight like this would make anyone go glassy and distant.

"I did this," Lord Karaval whispered.

Rowan bit her tongue against an "I warned you." From the look on his face, she couldn't say anything Lord Karaval wasn't already thinking.

He might have been her nearest threat but she just couldn't see him that way when he was staring at her like that. It hadn't been that long ago that she'd imagined finding Esrell like this.

She tucked the platter under her arm and put her hand on the Lord's shoulder. "I'm sorry."

CHAPTER TWENTY-EIGHT

ROWAN

 ord Karaval took those several precious moments to grieve, but by the time the two guards hauled Lynniki into the room, he was climbing to his feet.

The guards saw the body on the floor, and their eyes widened.

"Take these two," Lord Karaval said, gesturing to Rowan and Lynniki.

"Wait," Rowan said as the nearest guard reached for her arm. She nearly swatted him with the platter. She hadn't fought her way up here just to be dragged away and locked in the pantry again. "You have to give me the lantern before anyone else gets hurt."

"Trust me," Lord Karaval said, his face darkening. "I'm trying to keep as many people safe as possible, but I can't give it to anyone until I know what happened here."

"Trust you? After you didn't listen to me in the first place?" A guard grabbed her by the arm, and she tried to yank away, but his grip only tightened. "Lord Karaval!"

The lord turned away, back to his dead mage.

"I'm listening now," he said quietly. "It will have to be enough."

Rowan blinked, her mouth open on a half-breathed protest. His words had stolen her momentum, and she didn't fight the guard this time.

"Gavyn, don't worry. We're coming back for you."

Rowan caught the confused look Lord Karaval cast her as she let the guard tow her away finally.

This time she and Lynniki were taken to what was clearly a guest bedroom. A significant improvement over the gated pantry.

Lynniki tilted her head at the large bed with the brocade covering and canopy, then shrugged. "We should rest. Who knows when we'll get another chance?"

Rowan winced. "I can't even imagine sleeping right now."

Instead, she paced. Lynniki occupied herself going through the wardrobe in the corner and picking apart the expensive-looking clock on the mantel while Rowan counted the steps between the hearth and the door.

She wasn't sure how long it took, since Lynniki had the clock apart on the table, but it felt like less than an hour when the door opened and a guard beckoned them with a respectful bow.

"That's new," Lynniki said, hopping off her chair.

Rowan defiantly kept hold of her platter, though Lynniki had traded hers for a poker from the fireplace. The guard didn't bother confiscating their makeshift weapons as he led them into the hall, though Rowan wasn't sure if that was out of courtesy or because she wasn't a threat to him. Two doors down from the mage's workroom, the guard opened a door into a study furnished with walls of books and a large desk.

Lord Karaval waited behind the desk, hands clasped behind him. The lantern stood on top of it.

A large window, looking out on the lamp-lit city below, took up the entire wall behind him. Beyond the walls, lights reflected on the rolling plains, as if they were covered in a flat sheet of water, but Rowan couldn't tell in the dark what was land and what was river.

The door closed behind them, and Rowan glanced over her shoulder to see Captain Tera take her place beside it. She glared at Lynniki's poker until the Delver sheepishly tried to hide it behind one leg.

Rowan started forward, and Lord Karaval lifted his chin.

"Will this thing kill us just by being in the same room with it?"

Rowan stopped just short of the desk in surprise. She'd expected anger and arguments. Not a rational question.

"Not soon," she answered, matching his tone. "Physical touch seems to be the fastest road toward death, and symptoms tend to get better when isolated from it." She glanced between Lord Karaval and the lantern. "Did you touch it?"

His lips hardened. "No. I brought it here with a pair of long tongs, and I didn't let anyone else handle it after Gillfry... after Gillfry perished."

The knot in her stomach released. She hadn't even realized she'd been walking around with a gut ache.

"Then you believe me?" she said, and she couldn't keep the awe out of her voice.

He crossed his arms. "It's hard to argue when you're staring at a corpse."

Rowan blew out her breath. Maybe that had been her problem with Jannik. No one had died.

"Or possibly three corpses," Lord Karaval said, eyes boring into her. "There were two bodies found in a wayrest on the road between Monclaren and the western ruins. I suspected plague, but they looked just like poor Gillfry, and now I'm wondering..."

Ice crept up Rowan's spine. "Midge and her son," she whispered.

Lord Karaval raised his eyebrows, prompting her to elaborate.

She hesitated then took a deep breath. "Thieves who tried to take the Grief Draw from me. But they didn't handle it that long, and I took it away. They should have recovered if they even had any effects at all."

"The light." Gavyn's voice sounded weak and exhausted in the back of her head.

"What?"

Lord Karaval gave her a funny look. "I said nothing."

Rowan flapped her hands to shush him while Lynniki said, "She's not talking to you."

She placed both hands on either side of the lantern. "Tell me," she said gently. "Did you flare the light again?"

"I didn't know what to do. I thought the mage might break the lantern, and if he broke it, what would happen to me? Would the magic keeping me here and alive just go away? He couldn't hear me, and they weren't listening to you, and I tried to blind him. Just for a moment to get him to stop. But he didn't, and... and then he started melting. Going all bloated and runny and—"

She put her hand on the top of the lantern, heart trying to pound its way up her throat. It was silly and stupid. It wasn't like Gavyn could actually feel the gesture or take comfort from her touch, but she needed to do something.

"I'm sorry I left you so long," she said to him. "Maybe if we'd gotten there sooner..."

"Does she do this often?" Lord Karaval asked of Lynniki.

Lynniki grinned. "More than I think she realizes. Don't worry. You get used to it."

"You came as fast as you could," Gavyn said, sounding a mile away and as small as a mouse. "I made a choice. I just didn't realize what it would do. The mages that died with me a hundred years ago. They all died like that, but this was faster. A thousand times faster."

"May I interrupt?" Lord Karaval said, surprisingly polite. "Do you know what happened in there?"

Rowan raised her eyes to his. She sighed and patted the lantern—another silly gesture—before flopping down on the chair in front of the desk. Lord Karaval sat behind it a bit slower, his eyes still on her face.

"There aren't just two of us; there are three." Rowan pointed to herself and Lynniki and then to the lantern. "Gavyn, meet Lord Karaval. Lord Karaval, this is Gavyn. A Land Mage magically bound to the lantern almost a hundred years ago. He's been stuck inside ever since."

"Charmed," Gavyn said, a little of his normal wit seeping back into his voice.

"He says, 'nice to meet you,'" Rowan told Lord Karaval pointedly.

Lord Karaval looked between her and Lynniki and then at the lantern, trying to gauge if this was a joke. None of them were laughing.

Lord Karaval finally nodded to the lantern. "How do you do?"

Gavyn only growled in response.

"A bit traumatized, I think," Rowan said. "He thought your mage was going to damage him. So he flared the light. It's something we've managed to do twice before to get out of trouble. We had no idea it did more than make the lantern brighter. Midge and her son, we left behind. And the Delvers…"

"Wouldn't have noticed anything," Lynniki supplied from beside the bookshelf. She'd found an interesting section apparently and was pulling books down as fast as she could reach them.

Lord Karaval stared hard at the lantern. "So he reacted in self-defense. And it really is a weapon."

"It could just be that whatever it is that powers the Grief Draw is just as dangerous as the metal itself," Lynniki said, not looking up from her perusal. "And when the light flares, it's using more power and affecting a wider area."

Lord Karaval frowned. "You said you've done this before, and you've been carrying it for a while. Why aren't you affected?"

Rowan had a feeling she was going to get tired of the question.

"I'm part Delver," she said and gestured to Lynniki. "That's my aunt. Delvers were created specifically to mine and handle the metal the Giants used in their workings. We're immune to most effects."

He twitched. "Most?" he said.

She flexed her hand. "It hurts to hold, and it's getting worse. Every time I pick it up, it burns without leaving a mark."

"Better than Gillfry," Gavyn murmured.

"Yes," Rowan said under her breath. "Still better than that."

Lord Karaval had both hands flat on his desk as he stared at the lantern. Rowan wondered if he knew that he chewed his lip while he was thinking.

He'd taken in everything they'd said and was now mulling it over.

But Rowan was done waiting around for other people to decide she was worth listening to. "Lord Karaval," she said. "Why are we having this conversation?"

He looked up at her, surprised.

"I'm glad for it," she said. "But you had the lantern. You didn't have to talk to us again."

"I made a mistake, and someone under my care died for it. I won't let it happen again. Since you seem to know more about it than anyone, I would be a fool to ignore you."

"There are a lot of fools out there. If you believe me that it's dangerous, why aren't you throwing it off a cliff? Or burying it too deep to find?" Rowan knew why *she* wasn't doing any of those things. She wasn't about to condemn Gavyn to possible death or an eternity in the darkness again.

"Because it's still too valuable to him," Lynniki said. She snapped the book in her hand shut and turned to face them.

He sat back in his chair, eyeing them. Rowan noticed he didn't deny Lynniki's words.

"What's in this noktum?" she asked. "That's what you want the lantern for, right? Why is it so important?"

Lord Karaval blew out his breath and stood, as if he'd made a decision. Then he pulled a map from the table under the window and spread it on the desk.

Rowan moved the lantern over to make room.

"My wife and daughter were traveling this road almost a month ago," he said almost before Rowan could register that they were looking at a map of the mountains and the wide, flat valley west of the twin ranges. Monclaren was there in the middle. Rowan's village wasn't even pictured. A big, black splotch took up a large portion of the valley to the west.

Lord Karaval trailed his finger along the edge of the black. "They disappeared at the edge of the noktum. I can only assume Lord Hax's men forced them too close, and they were sucked in. He's been making threats for years now."

Rowan bit her lip and leaned forward. It was a very big splotch.

"I need the lantern because it's the only chance I have to get Patessa and Mellrea back."

"Healer's Ghost, I'm sorry," Rowan whispered.

"How did you even know about the lantern?" Lynniki said, stepping close with her books clutched in her arms.

"My daughter, Mellrea, studied with Jannik. She was one of his students until last year."

Rowan blinked. "Really?"

"She criticized him for his obsession and he dismissed her. A few months ago she proposed the idea that the weapon he was looking for might be a light source, given that the noktums played a pivotal role in Giant history. But she disappeared before she could prove her theory." He gave Rowan a rueful glance. "When he started looking for you, claiming you'd stolen some sort of lantern, I started looking as well."

He sat back in his chair, fingers laced in front of his chin. "I know why Jannik wants it so badly. I want it too. It could be Patessa and Mellrea's only chance."

He subsided, holding Rowan's gaze steadily.

Rowan let him stare, doing her own thinking.

Could she trust this man? He'd tried to take the lantern from her, just like Jannik, but now they sat here so he could explain himself. He looked at her like he was waiting for her decision. As if she had a choice in the matter.

She couldn't give him the lantern, and she wouldn't let him take it. But there might be another way.

She let her eyes follow the lines of his face before she glanced down at the spreading stain of the noktum on the map.

This Mellrea sounded smart. She might know things about the lantern that Rowan didn't. The chances of finding her were so slim they'd disappear if you looked at them too hard, but Rowan was done running away from things. She was ready to take a few chances.

She stood, startling Lynniki and the lord. "I have a deal for you, Lord Karaval."

His forehead creased. "Yes?"

She reached for the lantern and pulled it toward her before placing her hand possessively on the handle. She hid the wince of pain.

"The Grief Draw is mine. I'm the one who can talk to Gavyn, and therefore I'm the one carrying it. I will fight to keep it, but I don't think you will try to take it from me now."

His mouth twitched. "Which part of that is the deal?"

She ignored him. "You have resources I don't. Wealth and people who work for you. If you help me keep the lantern safe from people who would use it, then I will help find your family." She glanced at the map. "Even if that means heading into a noktum."

Lord Karaval needed her. Patessa and Mellrea needed her. The heady feeling filled her up and made the risks fade away.

Lord Karaval spread his hands flat on the desk top, eyes narrowing a fraction. "You'll help me?"

"Yes. If you promise to protect the Grief Draw. There will be others who want it for its presumed power. Jannik in particular. You'll be my best defense against them. You might have to fight for it. I would *expect* you to fight for it."

"And you think you can find Patessa and Mellrea?"

"I think I'm your best bet. And you're mine."

He looked between the lantern and Rowan's face.

He held out his hand. "I, Lord Vellwen Karaval, promise to aid you in keeping the Grief Draw safe. To the best of my honor and abilities. In return, will you do everything you can to find my wife and daughter?"

Rowan swallowed before taking his hand. "To the best of my honor and abilities, my lord."

CHAPTER TWENTY-NINE

ROWAN

Rowan wanted to go back to sleeping with the lantern in hand, but the burning kept her awake. Instead, she tucked it under the bed in Lord Karaval's sumptuous guest room, pulling the bed covers down until they hid it from view. Even without touching the handle, she could hear Gavyn singing Keinwen's nursery rhyme softly in the back of her head. It raised the hairs along the back of her neck, but she found she couldn't tell him to stop. If that was what he found comforting, she wouldn't complain.

He'd been quiet since Gillfry's death, and Rowan could think of a hundred reasons why. She wanted to be sure he was all right, but exhaustion crept up on her. She was asleep as soon as her head hit the pillow.

She woke with a start and fumbled for the lantern. Her heart rate slowed as her fingers closed around the handle and the now-familiar burn swept through her hand.

A part of her had worried that it would be gone, even after her agreement with Lord Karaval, but it hadn't moved.

The bed across the way was rumpled but empty, as if Lynniki had slept there and risen early.

Rowan rubbed her hands over her eyes and splashed some water on her face from the washbasin in the corner.

"Gavyn?" she said, knowing he would hear her, especially here in the same room. They should test how far they could be separated now.

"I'm here. I'm always here." His voice trailed away.

"Are you all right?"

"That… is an impossible question."

Her lips thinned. "I know, but I don't know what else to ask."

"You could try, 'how about you don't kill any more mages, Gavyn?' Or better, 'how would you like to get out of there?' I've noticed we haven't made any progress on that."

"We haven't exactly had time," Rowan said, voice rising. "Should we have stopped on the mountainside so Lynniki could build you a new body? Should I conjure you one with my failed magic?"

"Of course not! I just need to be doing something. And I can't do *anything*."

This time she bit her tongue, the argument bleeding out of her as she realized this anger was just a front for feeling helpless.

Gavyn stayed quiet too, and she got the impression of collapse. Like someone falling still after pacing for too long. "Would you just take me outside? I want to see the sun."

It was such a pitiful request that it made Rowan's chest ache, because that was the only thing he felt like she could give him.

"Of course," she said quietly. She slid the lantern into its leather case, which she'd retrieved from the pantry the night before, and made sure that the little holes were uncovered so Gavyn could see out.

Then she ventured down the stairs. The banquet hall stood empty. Either she was too early or too late for breakfast. From the way her stomach growled she was guessing too late.

Lord Karaval's keep was a fortress, so it didn't have many windows, and when she finally pushed through the door, the bright autumn sunlight hit her like a dagger to the eyes.

She held up a hand and peered around the courtyard. Big doors in the left wall were flung open to reveal workshops: a farrier, a blacksmith, and a fletcher, from the looks of it.

That's where Rowan found Lynniki.

"Gently!" the Delver yelled. "Eldroi stomp us, you wield your hammer like a hammer. Have you never even seen a gear before? Like this." The tiny Delver shoved the burly blacksmith away from his own anvil and plucked the hammer right out of his hands.

"Hey—"

"You have to talk to the metal." She shook her head. "Look at all those pieces over there. You think I got them working together just by slamming them over and over until they cried in submission?"

Lynniki gestured to her pack sitting by the outside wall. Its open flap spilled copper and bronze bits out onto the flagstones so they glinted in the sunlight. There were a couple large, curved sections that Rowan could imagine covering a limb like Lynniki's arm, but the rest were tiny, little gears or joints ready to be assembled like the world's most complicated puzzle.

Rowan raised her eyebrows. Lynniki had been hauling all that as they'd escaped down the mountain? How fast could the Delver run if she wasn't carrying half her workshop with her?

Rowan pushed between the farrier and the fletcher who watched with growing admiration as Lynniki browbeat the smith into producing the delicate work she was looking for.

The Delver finally caught sight of her and left the unfortunate man to his anvil.

"Tell me you're making progress," Rowan said under her breath. Gavyn could probably still hear, but he didn't say anything.

Lynniki gave her a funny look like she could guess where the comment had come from. "It's all progress. The body is actually the easy part. The transfer is going to be trickier."

"That's the part that will need magic, right? Maybe Lord Karaval knows another mage—"

"It all needs magic, but the transfer is going to need something special."

"Special how?"

Lynniki went to her open pack and dug inside. "Like this." She held out a square stone with a gem set into the middle. It fit inside her palm.

"What is it?"

"I call it a soul anchor. I've been working on it for a while."

"Sanctioned or unsanctioned by the elders?"

Lynniki gave an unapologetic shrug. "What they don't know won't hurt them, and even Delvers are interested in prolonging life. I haven't gotten it to preserve a life past its natural death, but I think I can get it to hold Gavyn. I just need some Eldroi magic to complete it."

"That *will* be the tricky part."

Lynniki waved her hands in a shooing gesture. "Well, it's all moot unless I can get the body going, so go. Let me get this lunk working the way I want him to."

Rowan raised her hands with a grin and backed away, not sure if she was talking about the construct or the smith.

Across the courtyard, another pair of doors opened on the stables with a fence all around.

She set the lantern on a hitching post just outside the stable and hoisted herself up on the fence next to it.

After a night in a bed with no lumps and no strange noises to make her toss and turn, her back felt better than it had in years. She stretched and then leaned forward to brace her elbows on her knees.

"Better?" she asked Gavyn.

"Better." Silence stretched between his words. "Thank you for checking on Lynniki."

She folded her hands once, twice. "You're welcome. Do you want to talk about what happened last night?"

"Absolutely not." He answered so quickly that he had to have been waiting for her to ask it.

"All right," she said. She didn't want to start another argument. And she could picture the mage's body and his bloated face far too easily. The pain of it had to be a lot closer to the surface for Gavyn.

He was quiet a moment.

"It can't happen again, Rowan," he whispered in her mind. "We have to control the Grief Draw. Or we have to be able to defend ourselves without using it. With mundane means. I can't... I can't kill again."

"Do you think spearing someone with a sword is better somehow? If we have to defend ourselves, it might always come down to killing."

"A sword would be far better," he snapped. "One thrust and then it's done. This was horrible. Not enough time to do anything. Too much time to die in blood and agony."

Rowan could think of several ways a sword thrust would result in agony. Her mother was a healer after all, but Gavyn didn't want to hear that right now.

"Then we'll learn to control it. So no one dies by accident." She stared at the lantern. "Besides, we need to understand it fully if we're going to go into a noktum. We can't rescue Patessa and Mellrea unless we know what we're doing."

"Your aunt mentioned that you talk to the lantern a lot." Lord Karaval leaned on the fence beside her.

Rowan stiffened in surprise and nearly fell off the top rail.

Lord Karaval held out a hand to steady her, but she caught her balance before he could actually touch her. "I talk to Gavyn, not the lantern. There is a difference."

"I'm sorry," Lord Karaval said with a little nod to the lantern. "My mistake."

"You've made a lot of those," Gavyn said.

Rowan bit her lip.

"What did he say?" Lord Karaval said, catching her expression.

"Gavyn is angry at you," she said, wondering if she should pull the punch at all.

"He's not alone," Lord Karaval said. "I'm angry at myself. Let him have his rage. It's justified."

Rowan cleared her throat. "We were just talking about how to avoid accidents in the future. And how to traverse the noktum. We need to understand what we're doing."

"You mean understand the lantern. You know more than most people so far."

Rowan looked down at her knees. "It's not enough. I don't know how well any Human or Delver can understand something the Giants made, but we have to do better. Otherwise it might end up killing us too."

"We can start by finding the other pieces," Gavyn said.

"Yes." Rowan raised her chin. "Keinwen seemed to think we'd need them."

Lord Karaval raised an eyebrow, too polite to keep asking her what Gavyn said.

Rowan steeled herself and pulled the lantern from the hitching post. "Lynniki said these slots on the outside of the glass were made to hold extra panes. We know there are more pieces to the lantern that will make it work the way it's supposed to."

"But there weren't any other pieces in the laboratory where we found it," Gavyn said.

Rowan repeated for Lord Karaval's sake.

"So where are they?"

Rowan's brow furrowed. "Somewhere there's darkness during the day and teeth on a hill?"

Lord Karaval sighed. "I feel like I'm following half of a conversation."

"No, no. That one wasn't Gavyn. I was just remembering. There's this nursery rhyme about the lantern. Gavyn's friend Keinwen left it as a message for him. We know what the first verse and the last verse are talking about, but there's another verse in the middle that talks about darkness and teeth on a hill as if it's a place."

"'Healer, Healer'?" Lord Karaval asked.

"You know it?"

"We sang it to Mellrea when she was little, but we always thought it was just nonsense."

"Not nonsense. Just a message meant for someone over a hundred years old, talking about an object no one else had ever seen."

Lord Karaval sang the verse, his voice far steadier than Verner's had been, though the rhyme sounded strange coming from a grown man.

> *"Healer, healer, where do you go?*
> *Dark in broad daylight will bring only woe.*
> *Teeth on the hill, bells silent and still.*
> *Healer, healer, black hides your foe."*

Lord Karaval cocked his head. "You think it's talking about where the rest of the pieces are hidden?"

"Well, it definitely talks about the healer going somewhere and this place hiding something. Then the last verse is about the missing pieces making a whole so…"

Lord Karaval started nodding. "So it stands to reason. Yes, yes, I get it. It's a riddle. Only it doesn't look like a riddle until you're close enough to see the meaning between the lines."

"Yes, but what meaning?" Rowan hopped down from the fence to pace. "What's dark in broad daylight? And how are there teeth on a hill?"

Lord Karaval tapped the top of the fence. "Where did you find the lantern again?"

"In one of the old Giant ruins."

"There's a fair few nuraghis scattered around the valley and more probably hidden in the mountains. It's likely any Giant artifacts would be found in another Giant ruin. Damn. Mellrea would know this in a heartbeat."

"Are there any you can think of that might match the description?"

He gave her a twisted grin. "It could be any one of them depending on how we interpret the rhyme…" He trailed off, his gaze going distant.

"You've thought of something," Rowan said, straightening.

Lord Karaval held up a finger, asking for patience.

Rowan bit her lip.

"There's a hill to the east."

"And there are ruins?" Rowan asked. He was going so slow.

"I wouldn't exactly call them ruins. The walls are still standing, at least as far as you can tell from a distance, but I've always thought the crenellations looked like teeth against the sky." He met her gaze. "It's made entirely of black stone that seems to soak up the light until it's just a shadow on the hill. We call it Blackfall."

Rowan's breath caught.

Lord Karaval knelt and began sketching a rough map in the dirt as if he were a village boy.

"Did someone lose something?" Lynniki asked, stepping up beside Rowan.

Rowan shushed her. "Lord Karaval thinks he might know where the rest of the lantern pieces are."

"It's a possibility," he said from his position on the ground. "But it sounds like we have little else to go on."

"It sounds like it matches the description," Gavyn said.

"I agree," Rowan said. "It's pretty close."

"The 'bells' part still doesn't make sense," Lord Karaval said.

"No," Rowan said. "But you mentioned you hadn't been close to it?"

Lord Karaval shook his head. "The place is like a noktum without the darkness. It's infested with a myriad of creatures, each more deadly than a wounded wolverine. An order of knights from around the countryside guards the place to keep them from overrunning the valley."

Lynniki knelt beside Lord Karaval to study the lines in the dirt. "Are you talking about that big place on the hill all done up in black stone?"

"Blackfall," Lord Karaval and Rowan said together.

"Yes, only we don't call it that."

"What do you call it?"

"Forbidden?" Lynniki shrugged. "We catalog most of the nuraghis we know of, if only to know how to avoid them." She tapped the map. "This one is at the top of the list of places Delvers are forbidden to go. Lots of Eldroi influence and potential for corruption."

"So naturally you'd know all about it," Rowan said.

"Naturally." She tossed her thick braid over her shoulder. "You can't say 'avoid this deadly poison,' and then never tell someone what that poison looks or smells like. They'll just drink it by accident."

Lord Karaval frowned at his drawing. "I don't think anyone's going to wander into Blackfall by accident. The knights will keep people out as well as they keep the monsters in."

Rowan ran her fingers around the rim of the lantern, ignoring the burn so she could feel the ridges of the slots. "They would let someone through if you told them to, right?"

"Rowan," Gavyn started. "You're not actually thinking of it? You really want to help this guy?"

"You think we could find the rest of the panes for the lantern on our own?"

"They might not even be there. It might just be a misleading reference and we're grasping at straws."

"Then we get closer and check out the fortress. See if it matches the rhyme. We have to at least look."

Lord Karaval met her eyes. "Rowan, these are not the ruins you're used to excavating with Jannik. These are not tumbling walls and exciting discoveries underground. This is a place designed to kill you."

Rowan gulped but she didn't lower her gaze. "Like the lantern is designed to kill?"

Lord Karaval winced.

"You think I want to do this?" she said quietly. "You think I wanted any of this? I'd rather go home, but you want your daughter back. Lynniki wants Giant magic to transfer Gavyn. And I need to know how to use the Grief Draw so it doesn't hurt anyone else. We need all the pieces. We need to make it complete, like the rhyme says."

"I don't like sending you into more danger than I'm already asking," Lord Karaval said.

"Too late. I'm already in danger just by carrying it, and I'll be in danger when I go into that noktum to find your family. The best way to lessen that danger is by understanding what I hold and how to use it."

Lord Karaval's nostrils flared like he didn't like what he was hearing but didn't have anything he could say.

"The best way to protect me would be to help me understand the Grief Draw."

Unexpectedly his lips tilted up in a rueful smile. "You're right."

Rowan blinked. "I am?" She cleared her throat. "I mean, I am, but why did you change your mind?"

"I hear my daughter's voice in yours. She, too, had the most reasoned arguments for the most harebrained things." He stood and brushed his knees off. "Captain Tera."

The captain stepped up from the wall where she'd been lingering. Rowan hadn't even registered her presence.

"We will prepare an expedition to Blackfall to see if this is the place referenced by your friend." He nodded to the lantern. "Captain, send a message to Commander Verence. Tell him I'm coming with a group, and we'll require access to the fortress."

"You're coming too?" Rowan asked.

"My lord," Captain Tera said. "You are *not*."

Lord Karaval met her gaze. "I would walk into Blackfall naked and unarmed and alone if it meant having a hope of finding Patessa and Mellrea. I do this for them."

CHAPTER THIRTY

ROWAN

They rode out the gates the next morning with Lord Karaval, Captain Tera, and three guards. A small party for something that felt so important, but it meant they could travel faster and with less chance of drawing attention.

Behind them, Lord Karaval's keep and the surrounding city rose directly out of the flood plain of the river Yffren. Right now, the water ran low, leaving a causeway between the gates and the dry land of the valley.

Lord Karaval caught Rowan glancing at the swampy ground just feet from them. "The river is good for defense, but it will dry up here before winter."

Rowan rode a placid pony that felt a lot like the old family donkey. She wasn't sure that Lynniki had ever been on a horse before, but the Delver sat astride another pony. She used a pair of pliers to punch holes in a broad piece of copper as if she didn't even notice they were moving.

Lord Karaval had taken one look at Rowan's cloak and declared it wouldn't be fit for the journey. He'd given her the run of his attics, and she had found a long, leather tunic, split up the legs to allow freedom of movement. Her belt fit nicely over it, refitted with parchment, ink, quills, and the lantern's case.

At the crest of the first hill that looked over the river valley, Captain Tera pulled up her horse and glanced back along the route where they'd come.

"Anything?" Lord Karaval asked her.

Her lips pursed, but she shook her head. "Just the back of my neck crawling."

Rowan cast Lord Karaval a quizzical look as Tera continued on. "We've caught Lord Hax's spies across our border twice since Patessa and Mellrea disappeared. He grows bolder every day."

They rode until nightfall when Lord Karaval signaled them to stop. "Blackfall is just a few hours more. Would you like to camp here or press on?"

Rowan's mouth fell open. *He's asking me?*

"This is your expedition," Gavyn said in her head. "He might lead it, but he'll at least make a show of listening to you."

Rowan swallowed. Her sweaty hands gripped the reins too hard, and the pony flicked an ear at her.

"We should rest here and approach tomorrow," she said. "That will give us the best advantage."

Lord Karaval gave her an encouraging nod and signaled his men to set up camp.

Rowan forced herself to relax and dismount, wincing at the unfamiliar pull in her back. She wasn't used to riding for so long.

She braced herself against the saddle to compose her face. She had no idea what she was doing, but she had people listening to her now. They were on their way to Blackfall because she'd decided the lantern was worth the risk. She was going to have to learn fast, because she couldn't lead them into danger without having some sort of plan.

One of the guards took her pony with a smile, and she tried to smile back.

Captain Tera checked her equipment loaded on the pack mule a few feet away.

Rowan hadn't talked much with the captain of Lord Karaval's guards. She got the impression that the woman didn't like her much. Maybe because she'd had to track Rowan through the mountains. Or maybe because Rowan was leading Lord Karaval off into danger. She'd clearly served the baron long enough to build a bond of trust with him.

Rowan steeled herself and stepped up to the captain. "Do you have an extra sword I can use? I need something to defend myself with that won't kill everyone in the immediate vicinity."

Captain Tera stared at her, and Rowan just kept herself from wincing. Her gaze traveled up and down Rowan's body, lingering on her high shoulder and the twisted line of her spine.

Rowan flushed, her cheeks stinging with it.

"No," Captain Tera said shortly, and she turned back to the pack mule.

Rowan sucked in a breath and resisted the urge to run. "No, you don't have an extra? Or no I can't borrow it?"

"No, you can't have it. I don't give swords to people who can't use them."

"Then could you teach me?" Although spending more time with the captain while she looked at Rowan like she was something she'd scraped off her boot was not high on the list of things Rowan looked forward to.

"No."

"Look, I'm sorry I dragged Lord Karaval out into the middle of nowhere. I'm sorry it's made your job harder," she said. "But it is necessary."

"Lord Karaval is a grown man with a grown child," Captain Tera said with a glare at Rowan. "He is free to make his own decisions and mistakes."

"Then what is it? Clearly you don't like me."

"I'm not giving a weapon to someone godsblighted. It would just be a waste when the gods are going to strike you down anyway."

Rowan blinked, too shocked to guard her reaction. "I didn't realize you believed in rebirth."

Captain Tera raised her chin. "You mean you didn't realize I was from around here. I'm Demaijos, but I was raised here, in Lord Karaval's barony."

It was more that the captain hadn't struck her as that small-minded, but she wasn't going to say that to the woman with all the weapons.

"If the gods had wanted me dead, there are plenty of times in my life that they could have killed me. Especially in the last few weeks," Rowan said quietly. "And even if they did want me to keel over, I would still fight. If someone tries to make me dead, I'm going to try to make them dead right back. I would think you of all people would understand that."

"Tera." Lord Karaval stepped up beside Rowan, and the captain stiffened. Rowan didn't think he'd heard what she said, because he just nodded to the other guards. "Will you talk Lobbins down? He swears he saw something out there, but he doesn't have the experience in the woods that the rest do."

"Yes, my lord," Captain Tera said and gave him a little bow.

Rowan wrapped her arms around herself as the captain moved away, keeping her eyes on the other woman's back.

"What's wrong?" Lord Karaval asked.

"Nothing." Rowan shook herself and walked to the fire that was blazing merrily.

"Lovely," Gavyn said. "Watch your back around her."

Rowan's lips thinned, and she tapped the edge of the lantern in response. She couldn't help the shiver that raised the hair along the back of her neck.

"Only a few hours to Blackfall?" she asked Lord Karaval as he sat beside her.

"As long as the weather holds and we don't get an early snow."

One of the guards passed around bread and cheese. Across the way, Lynniki ate with her dinner balanced on one knee, fork in one hand and pliers in the other, adjusting some joint or other in between each bite.

"What do you plan to do once we find the panes?" Lord Karaval asked.

Rowan pushed her food around her plate. "They might not even be at Blackfall. We'll have to see."

"Yes, but presumably you'll look for them until you find the pieces you need to make the lantern work. What then? Do you know how they go together? Do you know how to make it do whatever it is it does?"

She scowled at her plate. "No. The Giants didn't leave any instructions."

"And just poking it until it does something sounds like a really bad idea."

Rowan huffed a laugh. "Actually, that's how I learned Gavyn was in there."

He cocked his head. "You poked it?"

Rowan held up her hand. "My gift. I have the tiniest bit of Life Magic. When I touch something, I can see a memory. When I touched the lantern, it showed me a piece of Gavyn's death. That linked me to him."

"Well, then couldn't you just look further and see one of the Giants using the lantern?"

Her mouth twisted ruefully. "It's not as easy as that. I can't control what it shows me. Usually, it's such a brief image that I can barely make sense of it. As far as magic goes, it's pretty useless."

"It might not be big or flashy but it's probably not useless."

She gave him a look, and he laughed.

"Fair. I'm not the one wielding it, so I wouldn't know. But have you ever seen a man move a boulder?"

She frowned at him. "Once, yes, when my da cleared a new field."

"How did he do it?"

"He used a board as a lever, and as he pried it up, he stacked smaller rocks underneath until it tipped enough to roll."

He raised his eyebrows.

Rowan sighed. "I see what you're getting at."

"You do? But I had the lesson all laid out perfectly."

She hid a smile. "Well, if you want to say it anyway, I can't stop you."

Lord Karaval grinned. "That board and those little pebbles moved that giant rock. Your gift might not seem like much, but maybe it will give you that tiny little thing that will move mountains."

"You are *definitely* a father. You have the motivational speeches down perfectly."

She surprised a laugh out of him. "I'll take that as a compliment."

"That's your prerogative. Though I'm not sure Mellrea would."

His smile grew wistful. "No, she'd roll her eyes at me." He paused. "I miss her."

Rowan bit her lip. "I'm sorry."

He shook his head. "They're alive. I know it. They wouldn't let something like a noktum kill them. I hope you learn everything you need to understand the lantern. Because I need to see them again one day."

He stood to take his plate back to the guard in charge of washing up.

Rowan stared down at her uneaten bread and picked at the edges until they crumbled.

"Do you think he's manipulating you?" Gavyn asked in the back of her head.

"Maybe," she whispered. "But only because he really does want to know what happened to them. I'm a poor support to pin all his hopes on. It doesn't mean he's not right."

"About your gift?"

"I don't have many tools at my disposal. It would be silly not to use every single one, no matter how small. It's just..."

"It's failed you so often before?"

"Well, that, and the last time I tried to use my gift on the lantern, I got stuck with you."

Gavyn barked a laugh.

Rowan smiled but there was pain behind it. "You turned out to be all right, but it wasn't a pleasant experience."

"I think my memories were pretty strong and more recent. There's probably plenty buried under those that are far less painful. And maybe helpful."

"Maybe." She unclipped the case from her hip and set the lantern on the ground in front of her. She rubbed her fingers together for a moment.

"Do you need any pointers?" Gavyn said. "Place fingers on handle. Do the magic."

"Is that how your master taught you? Do the magic?"

"Every mage is different. And… well, it's been a long time. I'm not sure I'd be able to remember how to use mine, even if some miracle returned it to me tomorrow."

"Then maybe I won't take pointers from you."

"That's probably wise."

She took a deep breath and grasped the handle, wincing even before the pain spiked up her arm. It was getting worse, building with every touch.

Rowan gritted her teeth and sought out the little spots of warmth her gift showed her. The pain kept trying to break her concentration, but she'd had a lot of practice blocking out the aches of her spine.

As she remembered, the handle glowed under her touch. She stroked her fingers down the metal, seeking individual touchpoints. The spark behind her eyes reached for a spot along the metal between the glass. Dark flooded her vision, quickly replaced by a disorienting view of the lantern, as if held aloft.

Rowan concentrated, drinking in as many details as she could before the vision faded. A rough, broad hand held the handle in front of her much higher than she herself could ever reach. Another hand steadied the lantern's body as if it had been swinging.

She had just enough time to register the fact that the light behind the glass looked so different because the glass itself was different. And then the image faded, and Rowan blinked beside the campfire, the flames dazzling her eyes.

She shook her head and looked back at the lantern.

"What did you see?" Gavyn asked.

"Not much," Rowan said. "As usual. But…"

"I knew there was probably more. But what?"

"Well, it wasn't nothing. Someone was using it. Or at least holding it. And the panes were different."

Rowan reached out to touch the glass, which was smooth and clear, unmarked except for the one that had cracked in the altercation with Jannik.

"The one I could see had a design. Some sort of metal actually worked into the glass. I don't know how it would be done, but it changed the way the light looked coming out of it. A little like the way the case blocks the light. Only much prettier."

"Hmm, beware the beautiful death," Gavyn said. "It'll poison you even as you smile."

"Very poetic."

"Yes, well, Keinwen's inspired me. If I must be stuck forever, I might as well do something with my time, even if it's only write bad poetry."

"I didn't say it was bad," Rowan murmured, but she had picked the lantern back up to stare at it. A single image wasn't much to go on. As she'd thought, her gift still gave her only a brief glimpse. But that glimpse had added something. A small something. But like Lord Karaval had said, even small somethings could be significant.

CHAPTER THIRTY-ONE

ROWAN

As soon as Rowan could see Blackfall in the distance, she knew why Keinwen had passed down the words "teeth on the hill."

A solitary peak rose out of the low foothills. The mountain range behind it stood taller, but they were set apart far enough to make them seem tiny in comparison. A jagged fortress stood atop the hill, as black as a moonless night, the crenellations along the top wall stabbing the sky like the bottom jaw of some slathering monster.

Rowan gulped and followed Lord Karaval through the thin trees that did nothing to hide the monstrous fortress.

The road didn't go directly up the hill to Blackfall. It circled the place, swinging around nearly a mile to avoid it. On the western rim of the circle, they found a semi-permanent encampment. Six tiny tents waited in a neat line beside a firepit dug out of the rocky earth and lined with cut stones. Beside it stood a table of rough-hewn planks.

The knight commander stood beside the road, back straight and shoulders thrown back, with his six knights arrayed behind him, as if they'd been waiting since they'd gotten Lord Karaval's missive.

Lord Karaval swung off his horse and gave the commander a nod. "Commander Verence."

Verence wore a full set of plate armor, well cared for and polished to a high shine, but it had also clearly seen hard use with deep scratches no amount of polishing would remove.

His men wore much lighter leather with metal pauldrons and shin guards, but they were just as worn as Commander Verence.

"How are things, Commander?" Lord Karaval asked.

The armored knight pushed back his helm, revealing a young face seamed with lines beyond its years. "We're in a lull now, my lord. Afternoons are fairly quiet, until it gets dark, but I have to strongly protest your plan to proceed into Blackfall. This is an extremely bad idea."

"I understand." Lord Karaval gave him a firm nod. "But know that it is necessary, and we'll take every precaution to stay safe."

"What exactly do you guard against?" Rowan asked. She didn't get down from her pony. "Lord Karaval said creatures but…"

The knight commander gave her a once-over from where he stood. Even astride, she wasn't that much taller than him. To his credit, his lips only thinned in response to whatever it was he saw. He didn't bother bleating about cripples or godsblighted.

"That's all we know to call them. Creatures. Monsters. They live and breed in the fortress and try to make their way out at night. We keep them from overrunning the countryside."

"What kind of creatures?" Lynniki asked.

She actually got a raised eyebrow, but Commander Verence was too well disciplined to let the sight of a Delver out of the mountains faze him.

"Nothing normal. Giant lizards that spit venom. Cats as large as a horse. Something I swear was a boar before someone gave it horns. We're lucky none of them have wings, or they'd have hopped right over us." Commander Verence swiped at his face. "They remind me of the creatures you find at the edges of a noktum sometimes. Except not quite the same. Most of these are smaller, and there's no noktum here, so we have no idea where they're coming from."

Lynniki stared up the hill, tapping her teeth with her metal fingertip. "This used to be a Giant's laboratory. One of the big ones. The Delvers have strict instructions to stay away because it was a place where they created and experimented with magical constructs."

"What's a construct?" one of the knights asked.

His fellow elbowed him. "The things you've spent the last few weeks fighting, idiot."

"If you know where they are coming from, why wouldn't you storm the place and exterminate them all?" Rowan asked. "There must be a reason you haven't."

Commander Verence grimaced. "There isn't. We have done exactly that. We do it every couple of years, but the things keep coming back. We've scoured the surface fortress, but I fear there's another deeper section we've never been able to access."

"You've done admirably, commander," Lord Karaval said. "We'll need your exp—"

"Incoming," one of the knights screamed, and a dark shape barreled out of the thin line of trees. Rowan had a split second to register four long legs and a mouth full of teeth before chaos erupted.

The knights surged into motion. Three rushed forward to plant the butts of their spears into the ground while three fell back to form a line in front of the visitors.

Commander Verence drew his sword and widened his stance, but the creature—a massive wolf with the shoulders and weight of a bear—went down under the first line of knights' spears.

A shriek split the air, and another shape charged the line, this one low and sleek, moving with a boneless slither. The three forward knights were slow this time, untangling themselves from the previous assault, and the new creature sped past them.

Rowan's pony rolled its eyes at the approaching threat and reared. Rowan cried out as her grip slipped, and she crashed to the ground.

She caught a flashing glimpse of black scales and thick digging claws before the long lizard leaped for the neck of her pony.

Rowan scrambled out of the way as the pony thrashed and tried to dislodge the creature. But the lizard's jaw clamped tighter, a thin line of blood spurting from the pony's neck. It fell to its knees with a groan.

Rowan gagged and rolled further to escape the thick claws.

Shouts rang against the rocks, and Rowan had the brief, blurry impression that more creatures had come out of the trees. Commander Verence was a bright flash to her left, his sword swinging to cleave a great snake in half.

Lynniki leapt from her pony to grab Rowan's arm. "Get up. Get away."

"You think I don't know that?" Rowan snapped.

Tera stalked past Lynniki, her sword drawn, and her expression fixed on the lizard.

The lizard raised its blood-covered muzzle, and its long tongue flicked out as it faced this new threat. It hissed and drew back its head to spit a line of gray liquid at the captain. She dodged, but the ground sizzled where the liquid struck.

She swung her sword, a short blade curved through the middle. Her blow had enough force to slash through a normal animal.

But rocky plates armored the lizard's shoulders and flanks, and Tera's blow clattered off them to strike the ground. She stumbled past it, her momentum taking her an extra step.

The lizard spun and drew back its head to spit again.

"Look out!" Rowan called. Her hand closed on a fist-sized rock, and she hurled it at the lizard. It connected with a meaty thunk, and the spray of venom went wide.

Tera recovered her balance, and she lunged at the lizard while it swung its head in pain. Her blade bit deep in its less armored throat, and she struck again for good measure.

The lizard collapsed in a pool of black blood and bile, its chest caving until it looked oddly flat. Like a terrible rug someone had thrown across the ground.

Tera stared at it for a long moment before glancing at Rowan. "Are you all right?" she asked, voice rough.

Rowan nodded because she didn't trust her lips not to tremble.

Around them, the knights beat back the last of the creatures. Lord Karaval followed Commander Verence, a longsword in one hand as the commander swept across the campsite, making sure no more creatures remained.

The captain joined them.

"You're welcome," Lynniki yelled at her back. Then she hauled Rowan to her feet. "You probably saved her life, you know."

Rowan winced. "There's no honor in being saved by a godsblighted."

Lynniki snorted. "Sure. Whatever you say. Humans can be so stupid."

"Hey, I'm half Human."

"And that's the dumb half."

Gavyn chuckled in the back of her head.

"I suppose you agree?"

"Hey, I was Human once, but I'm not really in a position to argue. My worry is about finding the pieces of the lantern. And also not getting smashed the next time you fall off a horse."

Rowan winced and avoided looking at the sad remains of the pony. "Poor thing."

Commander Verence prodded the back half of the snake he'd severed earlier. "If they're attacking during the day now, we're getting closer to another extermination run. They always get bolder the more there are. If you're intent on proceeding..."

Lord Karaval lifted his chin. "We are. I don't want to wait here for anyone to creep up behind us."

"Then our best bet is to go now, before the creatures gather their strength for another foray. My men and I will come with you as far as the fortress."

"I was hoping to have more time to regroup and prepare, but you're the expert." Lord Karaval surveyed the rest of them, including Rowan and the downed pony. "Are you all right?"

"I'm ready." Her back hurt from the fall, but that wasn't anything new.

They approached Blackfall on foot, and Rowan took the time to draw the fortress the way she had drawn the ruins for Jannik. She mapped the space both as they saw it and how she imagined it would look from above. She would have loved to have time to shade the map and check her proportions, but they reached the black stone walls atop the hill far faster than she had expected.

Huge gates hung crooked, their hinges bent and broken. Rowan reached out to touch the black stone, wondering if it was similar to the black metal arch in the laboratory where they'd found Gavyn. This was just rock polished smooth.

"Basalt," Lynniki said. "Lava rock. From volcanoes."

"What's a volcano?" one of the knights asked.

"A fiery mountain. It's made when the heat under the ground reaches up to the sky and it spews fire and melted rock. I think there's one on an island along the southwest coast somewhere. Clearly the Eldroi had some way of cutting and moving it."

Commander Verence indicated the gates. "We would have hung them back up and locked them, except the damn creatures go right over the walls. At least this way we can get in and out easier."

Lord Karaval kept his sword drawn as he stepped through the broken gates and peered around the corner into the fortress itself. Past his shoulder, Rowan could see the afternoon sunlight filtering down to light up black walls and doors. Buildings and rooms had been jumbled together in a veritable maze of ruination. All infested with the magical constructs the Giants had left behind.

Rowan could hear a scritch-scratching sound, like claws against stone and dirt. She did not like how closed in this place felt compared to the open space of the Grief Draw's ruins.

"I think we will have to start your extermination pass early," Lord Karaval said with a reluctant smile at Commander Verence. "In order to learn if this is even where we should be looking."

Commander Verence scowled. "Except when we go through for an extermination, we bring at least twenty knights."

As they pressed into the fortress, Gavyn sang the nursery rhyme in the back of Rowan's head. A litany of images that only made her heart pound faster.

> *"Healer, healer, where do you go?*
> *Dark in broad daylight will bring only woe.*
> *Teeth on the hill, bells silent and still.*
> *Healer, healer, black hides your foe."*

The fortress brooded dark in the middle of the afternoon sunlight. The crenellations seemed to swallow them like a massive creature. And the threat here had certainly brought plenty of woe in its lifetime. But what about the rest? Was this really the place where Keinwen said the panes were hidden?

How would they be able to tell?

Lord Karaval took the lead, longsword ready in his hand. Rowan followed close on his heels. They came around the corner into a room open to the sky, and a black shape lunged at them.

Rowan swallowed a scream as Lord Karaval lunged. He ducked under slashing claws and used the thing's own momentum to stab the massive cat-creature through the heart. He twisted his body and let the heavy mass of fur slide over his shoulder and off his blade.

Lord Karaval eyed the dead cat and then turned to give Rowan a look, eyebrow raised in silent question, and she scanned the room.

The walls were more intact than the laboratory where they'd found Gavyn, creating more rooms, but they were all open to the sky. Thousands of years of weather hadn't left much of anything intact. If the panes were here, would they have survived all these years?

But Keinwen's rhyme was only a hundred years old. Why would she have directed them here if there wasn't anything to find?

"I don't know yet," she said, answering both his question and hers.

Lord Karaval gave her a tight-lipped nod, and they moved on.

Nightmarish shadows dogged their steps, stretching up the walls in grotesque mimicries of nature. Each corner hid an ambush, and every room became a risk. Rowan left the fighting to the others and filled in her map, trying to get an idea of the shape of Blackfall. If she could see how the rooms were laid out, maybe she could glean what it was the Giants had done here and where they would have hidden their work.

The maze of rooms didn't give her many clues. The buildup of debris and the plant matter that had grown up between the cracks in the floor and the walls obscured everything. Her map grew, but it didn't let her see any clearer.

In the center of the fortress, they came out into an open space. A courtyard stretched between the walls. Or maybe it had been a huge room now open to the sky after centuries of weather.

A yowling, growling sound surrounded them combined with the spine-tingling scratching. Something wasn't happy they'd disturbed this place.

Lord Karaval set his back to the group, facing the threat. Or at least as much of it as he could. Tera, Verence, and his men arrayed themselves around the courtyard, keeping Rowan and Lynniki in the center of their circle.

"Rowan," Lord Karaval said. "We're going to have to make a decision."

Rowan's teeth clenched, and her fingers tightened on her sheaf of parchment. Even Jannik would have needed days and a full team to make a survey of this place to determine its worth as an antiquity site. Rowan alone had had maybe an hour.

But the sounds were getting closer, and she couldn't help remembering the trail of beastly bodies they'd left behind.

Here in the courtyard, the dirt and debris of years wasn't so thick. It piled around the edges but not in the center where an intricate tile floor lay cracked under the bare sky. At first glance, it was circular, but as Rowan took it in in its entirety, she realized the edges were straight. Five sides. Mirroring the five outer walls of the fortress and the five corners.

Five? What a strange number? Why not a square with four?

She raised her eyes, seeking out the corners. Squat towers rose at the five points of the fortress. From afar, they'd blended in with the crenellations, looking like the teeth from Keinwen's rhyme.

Rowan squinted. The tops of the towers were open under their roofs, letting afternoon sunlight shine through, but something blocked the openings, creating a dangling shadow.

"Bells," she whispered.

A stiff breeze must have been blowing above them, blocked by the surrounding walls, because the bell in the northern tower swung back and forth, soundless.

"They don't have clappers," Lynniki said.

Lord Karaval looked back at them and then up at the towers. His eyes widened.

"Teeth on the hill, bells silent and still."

"The missing panes are here," Rowan told him. "Keinwen was talking about Blackfall. They have to be here somewhere."

"But where?" Lord Karaval said.

Commander Verence kept his eyes on the walls around them, but he asked over his shoulder, "What are we looking for?"

"Glass panes," Lynniki said. "For a lantern. About this big." She held her hands a few inches apart. "They probably wouldn't be out in the open though. They'd be in a sealed room like the one in the laboratory Rowan found."

Commander Verence shook his head. "We've been all over this place during the exterminations. I've never found anything as obvious as glass and metal artifacts. Or even a locked room."

Rowan glanced at her feet. "You said the creatures had to be breeding somewhere underground in a hidden part of the facility you haven't accessed yet. We have to go down."

An armored lizard bigger than Rowan's poor dead pony climbed over the nearest wall. Its tongue flicked between wicked teeth, and black stone shifted in plates over its muscles, like it had taken the basalt of its home as its armor.

Lord Karaval started to turn toward it.

"Keep your eyes to your side," Commander Verence called. "Don't let us be flanked."

The lizard slithered down the wall. Instead of dodging, Commander Verence lunged forward and caught the creature against his shield. He heaved, and the lizard rolled away only to spring to its feet and charge the knight again.

Three cat-creatures swarmed over the walls, converging on the group.

"Rowan, how do we get down?" Lynniki cried. "Where are the stairs?"

Rowan flinched away from the fighting, flipping through her drawings. "I don't know. We haven't found any yet."

"Then guess," Tera snapped.

"Based on the shape, that way." Rowan pointed to the north corner. It was a wild guess with no basis except a gut feeling, but that was all she had to go on right now.

The fighters pushed back the creatures, leaving three bodies bloody on the ground, and followed as Rowan and Lynniki raced through the maze of half-tumbled walls.

"Where?" Tera asked.

Rowan came up against the north wall and spun in a desperate circle. There was nothing. Not even a collapsed stairwell like in the laboratory. Nothing seemed to point toward a basement. It was like the whole fortress had been built on one level.

"I don't—"

A huge shape, as big as a bear but with the sloped back and curving tusks of a boar, charged through the nearest wall, showering them with powdered rock.

The group scattered out of the way.

Rowan ducked behind another wall and clutched her maps to her racing heart. This boar didn't just have tusks. Spikes traveled down its spine, and a pair of horns rose out of its skull. It swung its head around, looking for a victim to trample or gore.

It lowered its head with a snort and headed for the knight nearest Rowan.

She flung herself away as the man cried out and leaped out of the creature's path. There would be no meeting its bulk or momentum with a shield this time.

Rowan fetched up against the outer wall of the fortress, the stone smooth under her fingertips. Her fingers flexed against it.

The boar had gone straight through one of the inner walls, but the outer walls were thicker. She'd gotten a pretty good look at them on their way in.

She spun to put the wall at her back.

The monstrous boar pawed the ground and swung its head back and forth, its beady eyes fixing on each of them in turn.

Lynniki lay sprawled nearby, as if she'd tripped while she fled. Tera scrambled to place herself between the boar and the Delver.

The boar grunted and swung around, attracted by the movement. It lowered its head to charge Tera and Lynniki.

"No!" Rowan cried. "No, over here, you great brute!" She grabbed bits of basalt that had landed at her feet and flung them at the boar.

The creature spun, faster than anything that size had any right to move, and charged for Rowan.

She sucked in a breath and leaped aside at the last minute. The creature's tusk ripped through the hem of her tunic as she dodged.

But as fast as it charged, it didn't have time to correct when she lunged out of the way.

It struck the outer wall headfirst with a sickening crack.

The creature staggered, shaking its head. Its horns had left two huge pockmarks in the stone, but the wall still stood.

Unfortunately, so did the boar.

Tera darted in and swept her short sword up and through the thing's throat. Its head might have been as hard as basalt, but at least its hide was soft underneath.

Rowan gritted her teeth but didn't turn away from the spray of blood as the creature slumped and finally lay still.

"Rowan," Lord Karaval called. "Are you all right?"

"Fine," Rowan said and started to push to her feet.

A hand stretched out to help her.

Rowan raised her eyes to Tera.

The captain's expression remained hard and implacable, as if she hadn't just saved them all.

Rowan took her hand and let the captain help her to her feet, but when she tried to pull away, Tera kept hold of her hand.

Rowan's brows came down. "What—?"

She drew a long dagger from her belt and pressed the hilt into Rowan's palm. "Here."

Rowan blinked as her fingers curled around it. She had to clear her throat. "I thought it was a waste to give someone like me a weapon."

"You fight pretty hard to protect someone you have no reason to love. Do you promise to fight like that to find Mellrea?"

Rowan raised her chin. "Of course."

"Then I'm going to give you every chance I can."

"What happened to being godsblighted?"

"Oh, I still think you're blighted. But now I'm wondering if the gods did it to make you stronger."

Rowan screwed up her nose. "That's a pretty poor reason."

Tera's lips twitched like she suppressed a smile. "They're gods. Their reasons don't have to make sense to us." She thrust her chin at the dagger. "That's better than a sword for someone who doesn't know how to use one. It's lighter and faster."

Rowan lowered the blade, knowing she looked awkward doing so. "Thank you. I'll have to practice."

"I'll work with you. For now just make sure the sharp side goes into the other guy."

"This lull isn't going to last," Commander Verence said, clambering over the wall the boar had broken through. "I can already hear them rallying. What are we trying to find?"

"A door?" Lord Karaval said. "Or a stairwell? We have to go down."

"It's locked," Lynniki said. She pushed to her feet, shaking out her wrists with a wince. "I don't think we'll be able to find a way down until we unlock it."

Commander Verence shook his head. "That doesn't make any sense. You can still see doors that are locked."

"This isn't a Human-made door," Lynniki snapped. "This is Eldroi work, and they were tricky at the best of times. If this facility was made during one of their wars in order to house dangerous weapons stolen from their enemies, then I think we can all say it wasn't the best of times."

"Then how do we unlock it?" Rowan said. "Whatever it is?"

Lynniki planted her hands on her hips. "We have to meet certain requirements. Eldroi wouldn't have wanted anyone else getting in unless they had the key."

"Well, I hope we don't actually have to be Eldroi," Lord Karaval said. "I'm tall, but I'm not that tall."

Lynniki ignored him, placing her hands on the stone walls. "This whole place was built to resonate, but with what?" she muttered.

"Resonate?" Rowan said. "Like with sound?"

They all looked up at the bells in their silent towers.

Lynniki sucked in a breath. "Of course."

"They're coming!" one of the knights screamed.

"Get to the bells," Lynniki called. "One to each. They don't have clappers, but there must be some way to ring them."

Lord Karaval, Lynniki, and Commander Verence took off toward the south. Captain Tera met Rowan's eyes before she raced for the northern bell, so Rowan took the one closest.

No one asked if she was capable or if she needed help. They trusted her to get there without them.

It would have been refreshing if there weren't creatures swarming over the walls again.

Commander Verence's knights ducked between Rowan and the creatures, as she raced for the foot of the nearest tower. She plunged inside the black hole in its base.

Her sudden appearance surprised one of the cat-creatures at the foot of a set of steps. Without thinking, she lunged at the beast with a cry and plunged her new dagger in its side. It snarled and snapped, but Rowan kept her head down and shoved.

The cat rolled off the step, away from Rowan. She slashed as it tried to climb to its feet, and it fell back with a hiss. Rowan stumbled back up the first couple of steps and brandished her blade. Then she spread her arms wide and yelled, making herself look as big and mean as possible.

The cat-creature shied away, dripping dark blood, and it slunk out of the opening, back toward the rest of the fortress.

Rowan breathed hard. "I can't believe that worked."

"So you're a warrior now?" Gavyn asked.

"At least I can defend myself without the lantern's light," she said and started climbing the stairs.

"We're going to have to use it if we want to find Lord Karaval's daughter, you know."

"Not until we understand it better."

"Then get to the bell. I have a feeling a lot of the answers are at the bottom of this place."

Rowan didn't bother answering, saving her breath for the climb. The stairs were steep and taller than her legs were used to stretching, and it wasn't just because she was short for a Human. These had clearly been made for Eldroi.

The stairs opened onto empty space. No convenient railing to help her pull herself forward. She kept pausing to gaze up and make sure there were no more surprises on the steps.

Something rang in the still air, more than a sound. This was a feeling that traveled through the stone and up her legs until she could feel it gathering in the base of her skull.

"Someone got to their bell," Gavyn said.

Rowan picked up the pace. The tower seemed to have doubled in height since she'd started.

Another bell rang, making her feet buzz through her boots.

And a third. This one rattled her bones. The sound grew, pressing in on her from all sides even as it threatened to shake her apart.

She hoped Lynniki was right. If not, then they'd just activated some sort of defensive magic.

Light spilled down the last few steps, and the air grew fresher as the fourth bell tolled.

The sound of it pressed on her lungs, and she dropped to her knees under the pressure.

"Rowan!" Gavyn's voice seemed to come to her from the end of a long tunnel. "Rowan!"

Rowan reached to grasp the top step and pulled herself forward with her hands.

Here, at the top of the tower, hung a great black bell. Lynniki would know what sort of metal it was, but Rowan could only guess that it was lighter than normal, for it swayed gently in the breeze. She craned her neck, her head pounding with the combined sound of the other four bells.

There was no clapper inside, just an empty, yawning darkness.

She couldn't stand. She rolled onto her back and stared up. A hammer hung far above, nearly against the roof of the tower. If she stood, she might be able to reach the lever that would release the hammer and ring the bell.

She tried to raise her arm, but it shook with the effort. The sound thrust against her ears and her chest, a constant building crescendo that would never end until it burst her eardrums and turned her inside out.

She had to reach the hammer. But she couldn't stand, couldn't pull herself up, couldn't even push onto her elbows.

Rowan heaved in a deep breath, defying the sound that tried to cave her chest in, and with a scream, she swung her dagger hilt first at the bottom edge of the bell.

The moment it connected, all sound ceased.

Rowan lay on the floor of the tower gasping in the sudden absence of pressure. Healer's Ghost, the sound was gone. It wasn't just that her bell had not rung; the others had ceased just as suddenly.

She waited, heart in her throat, taking in the stillness and the silence. Then, long moments later, a rumble shook the roots of the tower, traveling all the way up its walls to vibrate the floor under Rowan's back. She rolled over and crawled to the open edge of the tower.

Below, she could see the maze of ruined rooms and the creatures which made their home within the walls.

They'd all stopped, frozen in place, turned toward the center courtyard, watching.

The five-sided circle of tile shifted and dropped, one tier of tiles after another until a set of steps led down into the earth in the middle of the fortress.

CHAPTER THIRTY-TWO

ROWAN

owan raised her gaze to the other towers where she could see four figures silhouetted against the afternoon sky.

She dragged herself to her feet using one of the supports for the tower. She didn't dare touch the bell in case it broke the spell of sound that had opened the steps.

As she climbed back down the stairs, she kept one hand on the wall to steady herself and the other on her chest. The pressure was gone, along with the sound, but the memory lingered, and each breath seemed to threaten a repeat of the experience.

Lord Karaval came through the open archway at the base of the tower just as Rowan reached the last step. He moved to support her, putting a hand under her elbow.

"Are you all right?"

Rowan tipped her head back to look up the inside of the tower again. "That seemed like a lot further, going up," she said.

Lord Karaval chuckled. "Yours was probably the longest. Metaphorically anyway. The rest of us felt the pressure, but not until the fourth bell rang. By then our job was done, and we could just lay there until the fifth sounded."

She leaned on his arm gratefully, but by the time they reached the central courtyard, she could stand upright on her own again, trusting her legs and her lungs to keep working.

Another of the large cats crouched at the top of a wall, and Rowan eyed it sidelong. A boar swayed in the opening of a wall opposite them.

"They seem to be docile now," Lord Karaval said. "Or frozen. They haven't moved since the fifth bell rang."

"Let's hope they stay that way," Rowan said as they stepped up to the edge of the newly revealed stairs.

Lynniki knelt at the opening, her metal fingers tapping the top step while Tera and Verence watched.

The steps led into darkness.

"Well, we have a way down, now," Lord Karaval said.

Tera cocked her head. "Yes, but what's down there?"

"More creatures," Commander Verence said.

"Hopefully Eldroi magic," Lynniki said.

Rowan gave her a look.

"What?" Lynniki shrugged. "I'm allowed to dream. This place could be full of useful stuff."

"Let's concentrate on one thing at a time," Lord Karaval said. "We're never at our best if our focus is divided."

"Maybe you can't do two things at once," Lynniki grumbled but she climbed to her feet. "But that doesn't mean the rest of us are dull."

"Commander Verence," Lord Karaval said, and the knight straightened. "Stay here. You and your men guard our rear. I imagine we'll have to come out the same way we go in, and I don't want to worry about any of these things waking up and coming down for us."

The commander's jaw twitched as though he clenched his teeth. "What if you encounter more down there? We know they have to be breeding somewhere."

"We'll deal with them as we come to them. Hopefully the influence of the bells extends belowground as well."

The afternoon sun dipped low behind the walls of Blackfall, sending shadows across the courtyard as Rowan drew the lantern out of its case and held it before her.

Her thumb stroked the touchpoints on the handle, and the spark behind her eyes reached for the lantern. She let her gift flare.

Black closed in on all sides before colors shifted and formed an image. A hand held the lantern. This could have been the same one she'd seen before or someone else. Impossible to tell with this little sliver of vision. Another hand entered from the blackness at the edges of her field of vision and touched the top of the lantern, fingertips moving in a complicated pattern across the filigree. The light suddenly dimmed.

No, it shifted, concentrated into a beam that shot through one of the decorative panes of glass. Shadows sprang up in front of the lantern bearer, shifting and morphing into shapes made of light and darkness.

Rowan had the sudden impression of trees and mountains in a whirling array, before the image faded and the stairs came into view in front of her.

"Are you all right?" Lynniki whispered.

Rowan blinked. Her gift only ever took a moment to show her something, so she hadn't been standing there long, but the brief jumps through time left her disoriented and groggy. How many years had it been since this unknown person had handled the lantern? Hundreds? Thousands?

"Fine," Rowan said. "Just learning more and more."

She shook her head and started down the stairs, holding the lantern so its light illuminated the dark below. "We may not know everything about it, but at least the Grief Draw makes a good lamp."

Someone snorted behind her—she suspected Tera, but that would mean the woman had a sense of humor, and that was harder to believe than any of the fairy stories Stefan had told her growing up.

She descended with Lynniki, Lord Karaval, and Captain Tera right behind her. Lord Karaval's guards followed with more trepidation.

The light gleamed against smooth black walls that lined the stairs.

"Hooray, I always wanted to be a vanguard," Gavyn said, voice flat in the back of her head.

"Really?"

"No. I was a Land Mage. I was meant to sit on a velvet cushion making magical trinkets for rich people while beautiful girls fed me exotic fruit."

Rowan wrinkled her nose. "That sounds boring. Also made up."

Gavyn snorted. "All right, maybe something in between, but let's just be careful, all right. I wasn't made for the front lines of anything."

Rowan's lips twisted, but she concentrated on the way down.

Whispers drifted behind her, stretching and distorting as they echoed.

"How far does this go down?" asked Lord Karaval.

"Who knows?" answered Lynniki. "Eldroi had as many wonderful magics and technologies at their disposal as they had terrible ones. They could have built a facility miles deep as easily as we'd build a stable on the surface."

"Great," Tera said. "So we could be climbing for years and find anything down below."

"Exactly! Isn't it exciting?"

Rowan had to pause for a moment to switch hands with the lantern. The pain made her eyes water. Or maybe that was the light reflecting off glossy black walls.

When she started again, it was only a few more steps before the bottom of the stairs came into view.

The steps emptied into a broad room large enough to fit Lord Karaval's courtyard between its walls.

The black stone underfoot had been polished to a high shine, but Rowan's boots didn't slide across the smooth surface the way she expected. The lantern illuminated a broad desk in the center of the space and dark openings leading off to other hallways.

Tracks marred the shine on the floor, and the place reeked like the back alley of a tavern with no outhouse and a well-used stable.

Movement caught her eye, and she spun, holding the lantern up to see a lizard creature slink into the edge of light. It stopped there, filling the corridor with its armored shoulders, its tongue darting out to taste the air.

Lord Karaval brandished his blade, but the creature didn't advance. He exchanged a look with Rowan. "The effect of the bells must extend down here."

"I suggest we take advantage of it before it expires," Lynniki said. Her boots tapped as she stepped across the stone to rummage in the desk. She had to stand on her toes to reach the top.

"Which way should we go?" Rowan asked. "There are too many hallways."

"I vote the direction away from the massive lizard thing," Tera said, glancing at the creature that still stared at them.

"Really?" Rowan said, eyes on the many doors leading away from the black foyer. "You strike me as the sort of woman who likes a challenge, Captain."

Her lips twisted in something not quite a smile. "Careful. You'll make me actually like you."

"Why would the Giants separate the pieces of the lantern?" Lord Karaval asked, moving to peer down one of the dark, seemingly endless hallways. "Why keep the lantern itself in one nuraghi and the panes in another?"

"It was made by their enemies," Lynniki said. "I imagine it was a precaution to keep the other Eldroi from being able to use its full abilities. Like taking a sword apart or hammering it into a plow." She strode confidently to the back of the large room where an even larger hallway opened up. "This way."

Rowan followed with a frown. "How do you know?"

"I don't, but this hall seems more official. If they built a part of this facility just to house the pieces of the lantern like the other one, I feel like it would be in a place that's more central, rather than tucked in a corner."

"Unless they wanted to hide it. Then you'd toss it down a well," Tera grumbled, but she followed as well.

The walls reflected the lantern's light, bouncing it down ahead of them and illuminating the corridor, long past its normal range. Here, glass windows lined the walls, giving them open views of filthy rooms, long abandoned.

They stopped frequently to search through the remains of these, looking for anything that seemed like a glass pane or lens. It was quickly obvious these had been built for something else.

Most contained long-decayed remnants of misshapen beasts. Bones and teeth and in one memorable case an entire snakeskin big enough to swallow Lord Karaval whole. Some of them even housed creatures who weren't dead yet.

Eyes reflected the lantern's cold light from nests tucked into the corners of the rooms, but none of the creatures moved.

These they left alone.

"This is where the creatures were created and studied," Lynniki said, voice barely more than a whisper as they left a room of monsters that looked like large, hunched men with reddish, wiry fur. "See how the doors could be closed and barred and the occupants could be observed through the glass."

"I would prefer to exterminate these while they're docile," Tera said. "Can't we stab a few? I don't like leaving them behind us."

"Who knows if that would wake them from their stupor," Lord Karaval said. "Better to live and let live, at the moment."

"I wonder if we should go back and try one of the other halls," Rowan said. She swung around and peered back the way they came. "If this was a breeding wing, maybe there's another wing built for the lantern."

"Keep going," Gavyn said.

"What? Why?"

"There's something ahead. The lantern is… singing."

Rowan bit her lip. "What does that mean?"

"I don't know how to describe it. I haven't felt it before, but it's humming."

"All right. Gavyn says there's something ahead. Something that's making the lantern sing."

"Pretty sure I've heard horror stories like that," Tera said. "Ghosts singing people to their deaths."

The corridor continued unchanging, but Rowan trusted Gavyn. After a few more steps, she could feel it too. A hum under her hand that was more of a feeling than a sound.

Ahead, the hallway seemed to end in a black void that ate the light of the lantern, and Rowan held her breath as she approached. She stopped at the opening.

A vast cavern stretched out, reminding her of the Delver city with its size, although the comparison stopped there. This void sat nearly empty in the depths of the earth. A set of floating steps led down to a platform hanging by itself in the middle of the empty space.

"This seems promising," Lynniki said over Rowan's shoulder.

"Yes," Gavyn hissed.

Rowan took a deep breath and started down the steps. With no railings or any visible supports, she took them slowly and carefully. It was a long drop on either side, but whatever magic kept them in place had survived the centuries, and the steps didn't collapse under her weight.

Statues lined the platform on either side of her as she stepped onto the floating floor, huge men and women each with an arm raised. They all held an exact replica of the lantern Rowan carried.

"More than promising," Rowan whispered. "This is it."

"Now, why couldn't I have spent the last hundred years here?" Gavyn said. "The Giant that built that laboratory was clearly a practical bastard, but this one had a flair for the dramatic."

Rowan stepped forward, and the two statues on either side lit suddenly, their stone lanterns glowing from within.

"It's been waiting for you," Tera said.

"Could you make that sound less creepy, please." Rowan followed the corridor made by the statues. Each one lit up as she passed, leaving a path of light.

At the very end stood a black stone table. And in the center stood a stone lantern exactly the same size and shape as the one Rowan held.

Panes of glass beautifully detailed with gold and silver filigree were clamped to the surface of the stone lantern.

Rowan blew out a long breath. Here were the pieces Keinwen had been talking about. It wasn't all just a dream or an ill-advised treasure hunt. They were real, and she stood just feet away.

Lynniki stepped up beside her. "Look how perfectly they'll fit. Once we figure out how to get them free."

Each pane was fitted into the stone face of the lantern and was held there with a black, metal clamp similar to the black arch that had held the Grief Draw and Gavyn's body.

"Do you think there's a spell?" Rowan asked. "The last time there was some sort of magic that kept Gavyn's body in stasis for a hundred years."

Lynniki's lips twisted. "Maybe. Definitely a deterrent for looters. And of course, there's always the metal to deal with. We'll be fine, but don't touch anything you didn't carry in, all right?" she told the full Humans.

"That's a given," Lord Karaval muttered as Lynniki bent to consider the clamps.

Rowan frowned at them and then stared back down the line of statues. This whole place seemed built to recognize the lantern if not welcome it outright. The front of the table held a circular depression the same size as the lantern's base. Lynniki kept twisting her head to look at it from different angles as if that would help her figure it out.

"I don't think it's that complicated," Rowan murmured.

She placed the lantern in the depression.

The clamps hinged back, leaving the panes free.

Lynniki rolled her eyes. "I guess I was looking for something a little cleverer than that."

Rowan gave her a grin and carefully reached for one of the panes. The metal and glass buzzed against her fingertips just like the lantern.

She lifted it free and tilted it so it caught the light. It was a rectangle of glass with gold filigree running through it in whorls and eddies like petals on the surface of a pond.

Rowan slotted it into one of the spots on the lantern, covering the normal pane that protected the flame.

"A perfect fit," Lynniki said.

There were five total. Rowan carefully took each one and slotted it into place. Two, three, four.

As she reached for the fifth, a rumbling, creeping snarl rang from the corridor behind them.

Rowan sucked in a breath as Lord Karaval and Tera spun, weapons drawn. Lord Karaval's guards exchanged a look and moved back down the platform toward the steps.

"That didn't sound good," Lynniki said.

"The effect of the bells must have expired," Lord Karaval said.

Tera glanced back at Rowan. "Hurry that up."

Rowan grabbed the last pane.

"That's mine." A familiar voice called across the cavern, chilling in this unfamiliar place.

Rowan spun.

Jannik stood at the top of the steps, just close enough to be illuminated by the lantern. A figure hulked behind him, light eyes standing out under his dark brows, even at this distance.

Lord Hax.

CHAPTER THIRTY-THREE

ROWAN

Lord Hax glared at them from the top of the floating steps. His face was as sharp as Rowan remembered, like the edge of a hatchet, and he wore his amber and crimson.

Jannik looked tired, and Rowan's heart twisted.

"So much for Commander Verence guarding our backs," Lynniki said. She sidled back, next to the table.

Lord Karaval's eyes never left Lord Hax. "Commander Verence would have had no reason to stop them. He answers to all the nobility, not just one baron. He would have let them through the same way he let us through."

"Hand over the lantern," Lord Hax said. His voice should have been lost in the vast cavern with all its open space, but instead it rang against the stone at their feet, making him sound much closer. "It's not yours. It belongs to me."

Lord Karaval raised his chin. "How do you figure that?"

"It was promised to me as repayment of a debt, long since due." Lord Hax glanced at Jannik who sagged.

"Rowan stole the lantern from me after I rightfully claimed it," Jannik said. "She never had any right to it, despite what she's told you."

"Do you think he makes up bedtime stories to help himself sleep too?" Gavyn asked dryly.

"I do not suffer thieves," Lord Hax said, stepping down onto the platform. Several guards, dressed in his colors, came after him.

Lord Karaval's guards didn't hesitate. The three of them spread out across the platform to block the way.

Lord Hax lifted his hand to point at them. "Kill them."

Rowan sucked in a breath. "What?"

Lord Karaval raised his voice to the guards who had advanced onto the platform. "I am Lord Karaval. By drawing on me or my men, you are committing an act of treason and starting a war."

The guards hesitated.

"Is this worth it?" Rowan called to Jannik. She held up the lantern. "Are you really willing to kill me for this? Have you told Lord Hax it will kill him if he tries to carry it?"

Jannik's hand slashed through the air. "Enough of your lies. You clearly aren't dead."

"That's because of my father, and you know it," she said raising her chin.

His eyes went to Lynniki. "You talked to your mother. And went into the mountains, I see."

Rowan's teeth clenched. She glanced at her aunt, and her brow furrowed. Lynniki was bent over the table, a chisel in one hand, and a hammer in the other. With the tools, she pried at the clamps that had held the lantern's panes.

"What are you doing?" she whispered.

Lynniki just gave her a look and gestured with her metal hand as if the answer should have been obvious. There was nothing left on the table unless she meant to take the clamps themselves.

"Enough," Lord Hax barked out, making Rowan jump. He put a hand to his waist, and Rowan realized the belt he wore wasn't actually a belt. It was a heavy, iron chain attached to a spiked ball. He unwound it and swung the end around so the ball whirred through the air.

Faster than Rowan could track, Lord Hax swung the chain at the closest of Lord Karaval's guards. The chain wrapped around the man before he could dodge, and Lord Hax's yank sent him flying over the edge of the platform.

He screamed for a very long time.

Lord Hax shot a scathing glance at Jannik. "If you want to clear your debt to me, you will get me that lantern. Now."

Lord Karaval's remaining guards cried out and rushed forward, but Lord Hax's vanguard stepped to intercept them. Tera took a step as if she wanted to join them, then hesitated and glanced at her lord.

"Lord Hax," Lord Karaval called, gripping his sword. "Your aggression will be repaid in kind."

Rowan raised the lantern and slid the last pane into its slot so hard it stuck three-quarters of the way in. But her hands were too sweaty and slippery to get it to go in any further.

The light swung around, glancing off the edges of swords, and it swept over dark shapes hanging on the distant cavern walls. Eyes blinked open, reflecting bright green in the cold, white light.

"Senji's spit," Tera said in a flat voice.

Giant figures spread wide ribbed wings and dropped from the walls to soar over the open space to the platform.

A great, bat-like creature with reaching talons swept past them, and Rowan dove behind the table. Karaval and Tera rolled after her.

There was a thud, and a wavering scream faded away. Rowan winced.

"I thought Verence said there weren't any flying creatures?" Tera spat.

Lynniki still chiseled at the base of the clamps. "He's never been down here before, and these are much too large to make it up to the surface the way the others did."

Lord Karaval peered around the table, then ducked again as something large flapped overhead. "Cursed hells, Lobbins is fighting alone now, and Lord Hax's men are still advancing, stupid bastards. They're going to get themselves killed."

"*We're* going to get killed if we don't find a way out of here," Tera said.

"How? They're between us and the door," Rowan said. She raised her free hand to cover her head. As if that would protect her. "And there's bats from hell trying to pick us off, if you hadn't noticed."

"Believe me, I noticed. We'll have to cut our way through. It's the only option." She exchanged a wordless glance with Lord Karaval and raised her short sword. "We'll cover you. Follow the moment it's clear."

She and Lord Karaval ducked out from behind the table and sprinted for Lord Hax's men.

"Good luck," Gavyn called in the back of her mind as if he was wishing them a good day. "We'll just be here."

Claws scraped across the table above her and someone screamed from the platform.

"How are you so cheerful?" Rowan said, craning her neck to see the threat.

"You can only be frozen in terror for so long before you become numb to it. Now are you just going to sit there waiting for Lord Karaval and Captain Tera to die?"

Rowan took a deep breath and peeked around the table. Their two companions stood in the corridor between statues, but they spun around each other, eyes on the swarming flying creatures. Lord Hax's guards left two bodies on the platform and concentrated on the diving bats. Lord Hax and Jannik had retreated to the safety of the hallway.

Rowan chewed her lip. The lantern still burned in her hand, but under the painful tingle, she could feel the warm spots that indicated memories.

She frowned. The last one had shown the lantern actually working, a beam of light shining through one of the panes, concentrating its light. Like a lens. The shadows had warped and shifted looking a lot like terrain.

A map. Could the lantern show what was around it even if it was hidden?

Her breath came faster as she raised the lantern level with her face.

"What is it?" Gavyn asked. "What are you thinking?"

"Don't flare up, all right? I'm going to try something."

"Is that safe? We don't know what it does."

"We have to do something." She spun the Grief Draw, examining the different lenses. There was the one that wasn't seated properly yet, but she didn't have time for that one.

Here. This one seemed to match the one from her vision. Its whorls and eddies of gold reminded her of trees on the one side and mountains on the other.

Rowan reached out to touch the abstract pattern of filigree along the lantern cap. This had been the key. Some sort of combination or code that made the lens work.

With a crack, Lynniki finally broke the last clamp free and plunged the piece of black metal into her pack. "Is that safe?" she asked.

"People need to stop asking me that," Rowan growled.

She touched the lantern, trying to remember the code the Giant had used. It took three tries before the light changed, concentrated through the lens. Shadows and light swirled together until they formed humps and shapes and little spots of color.

Rowan winced as a bat creature screeched above, then she squinted at the light shapes.

"It *is* a map," she said. "I can see rooms."

"I don't see anything," Lynniki said as Lord Karaval and Tera backed toward them. Lord Hax's guards advanced. "But whatever you think you're doing, you'd better hurry."

A mess of rooms and hallways spread in front of Rowan, and her mind reeled at the detail.

Focus, she told herself. *It's just like the maps you drew for Jannik.* Except there were moving parts. Bits of color flashed between the walls.

There, a big, empty space in the middle of it all.

"There's another way off the platform," Rowan said, thoughts racing almost too fast for her tongue to keep up.

"I hate to break it to you, but there isn't, unless you can fly," Lynniki said. She glared up at the swooping creatures. One dove for them, but instead of ducking out of the way, Lynniki swung upward with her hammer and delivered it a solid blow on the muzzle.

It fell with a shriek before recovering and flapping away.

Rowan stood and stepped to the back of the platform. The map clearly showed another set of stairs leading up from behind the table. But Lynniki was right. The stone ended abruptly, leaving nothing but empty space.

As she stepped closer, a smooth piece of black stone at her feet clicked, and stairs slid out of the platform leading up.

"You just have to know they're there. This way. Grab the others."

Lynniki ducked out from behind the table and snatched an arm from each of their companions, dragging them back the opposite direction than they'd been trying to push.

"What—?" Karaval started.

"Run now, fight later," Lynniki said. She shoved him and Captain Tera toward the stairs. "We've got a way out."

Rowan checked to be sure they were following then turned and raced up the stairs. She couldn't manage two at a time, but she went much faster up the floating steps than she did down. It helped to have mortal danger behind as well as on either side.

The steps led up to another corridor, and Rowan rushed inside then paused to let the others catch up and gain the safety of the corridor. She glanced back into the cavern. The lights on the statues dimmed in the absence of the lantern, but she could still make out Lord Hax's men battling the flying creatures. Lord Hax himself was waving and pointing, but with the winged creatures between them, he wouldn't be following anytime soon.

"Where are we going?" Lord Karaval said. His chest heaved from the rapid climb. "How did you know there was another staircase?"

Rowan raised the lantern. "It's showing me a map. I think I can get us out."

Lord Karaval looked between her and the lantern. "I don't see anything," he said, voice uncertain.

"I think it only appears for the one holding it."

"I see it," Gavyn said. "But it's convoluted. You can read this?"

"I've made a lot of maps," Rowan said.

"But what are these colors?"

Rowan glanced over her shoulder at the fighting down below. "I think those are people. People and creatures. Living things."

Gavyn paused. "There are a lot between us and the surface. If I'm reading it right."

"You're reading it right," Rowan said quietly.

"Can we get out?" Lord Karaval's eyes darted like he was trying to see the map still.

"If we're careful. Gavyn, you help me navigate. I'm going to concentrate on the way, you tell me if we're going to run into anyone."

Rowan led them as fast as she dared. She didn't want to get turned around, and even with advance warning, she didn't want to accidentally lead them around a corner and come face to face with a creature that didn't care about the bells anymore.

But she could see the movement of colors behind them and knew that Lord Hax and his men were advancing, and once they were out of the cavern, they'd gain ground against their little group quickly.

Every now and then, Rowan had to send Tera and Lord Karaval ahead to ambush a waiting creature, but so far, they hadn't been swarmed.

The map led her to another set of stairs. This one was much dustier. Dirt tumbled down the steps disturbed by fresh claws.

The staircase led to an opening, long since broken through, and here they found footprints in the dirt where the creatures had been escaping from the facility. They climbed into the clear night air through the hole where a sealed doorway had once been.

"A back door," Lord Karaval said. "Not very secure apparently, but handy for us."

It led out behind the walls of Blackfall, where they could see the bell towers outlined against the sky.

Rowan blew out her breath and touched the top of the lantern so the light returned to its normal glow, not concentrated through the lens.

"We're not safe yet," Tera said. "We can make our way back from here, but Lord Hax could catch up at any minute. And there still might be creatures—"

"Rowan!"

Rowan jumped and spun, her heart hammering in her chest.

Her brother Darryn stood at the corner of the wall as if he'd just come from the entrance to Blackfall.

"Darryn," she cried. "What are you doing here?"

Darryn stalked forward, his face set in hard lines, and Rowan's heart sank. In his right hand, he carried a naked short sword.

"Looking for you, obviously. I'm bringing you back."

Rowan's brow drew down. "Back home? Darryn, there's a reason I left—"

He shook his head, anger making the movement jerky. "Not home. Back to Lord Hax and Jannik. They'll know what to do with a thief."

Rowan cried out. "Darryn, I'm not a thief."

"You took the lantern!" He threw his arms wide. "You took the thing that Jannik was looking for. He promised it to Lord Hax, and you took it for yourself." Creases deepened at the edges of his mouth. "You completely betrayed us. Your family. We could have used that reward. Jannik was willing to pay anything to get that thing, and you just up and left with it, without giving anything to us."

"You were the only thing I was thinking about," Rowan said around the lump in her throat. "Darryn, it was making Esrell sick. I had to take it away."

Darryn made a disgusted noise. "Jannik said you would lie to cover your own greed, but I didn't believe him until now."

"Jannik is the one lying!"

"Who's the one who has the lantern now? And a wealthy patron?" He gestured at Lord Karaval. "You took the lantern and left us with the consequences."

"What consequences?" Rowan said. She'd left her family at home so that Jannik would know she wasn't with them anymore.

"You think Lord Hax is just going to let you get away with this? No. We're all branded as criminals because of you. We're all in debt to him now. That's why I'm here." He pointed his sword at her. "I was conscripted into his army, and now I'm going to bring you back, so *you* can pay for your crimes. Not me."

Rowan's chest went tight, cutting off her breath and for a moment, she feared she would black out. Her eyes darted back to Lord Karaval, Tera, and Lynniki, but none of them had anything to say. They stared between her and Darryn.

What did she expect them to do anyway? She was the one who held the lantern. She was the one who could hand it over or run with it.

She was the one whose family had suffered in her absence and for her actions.

Rowan bowed her head, eyes stinging.

Her fingers clenched around the handle of the lantern. It burned, the pain slashing through her panic, clearing away the questions and doubts.

The lantern burned her, yes, but it would do far worse to Darryn. Whether he knew it or not.

As horrible as he thought she was, she would be ten times worse if she knew it would save him and Esrell and the rest of their family.

"I'm sorry." She raised her head to meet his eyes. "I'm sorry, but I can't go with you. If you'd rather believe Jannik over me, that's fine, but I'm going to keep you safe even if it means you hate me."

Darryn's eyes narrowed, giving her a split second's warning. He lunged for her.

She twisted but he rushed her, knowing she couldn't move fast enough to stay clear of him. She flung her arm out as he struck her, tossing the lantern toward the others so Darryn wouldn't even chance touching it.

There was a heart-rending crunch as the lantern struck rock, and Rowan cried out as she fought free of Darryn's grasp.

He swore at her and scrambled for the lantern, but she kicked his feet out from under him, and he went down with an oof.

Lynniki scrambled for the lantern as Lord Karaval grabbed for Rowan's arm, and Tera advanced, sword drawn.

"Darryn, please," Rowan said. "I won't kill you, but I will go through you if you try to get in my way."

Darryn's lip drew back in a snarl.

Tera raised her blade. "I have no such compunctions."

Darryn grabbed his sword and lurched upright to charge her. The captain turned neatly so Darryn's blade slid past her, and she used his momentum to spin him around.

Suddenly Darryn was on the ground, and Tera held his sword. She leveled the blade at his throat.

"No!" Rowan cried. "Please, Captain. Don't. He's not a threat."

Darryn glared at her, but Tera sighed. She flipped his sword around, his eyes following the edge of the blade.

"If you're going to be a soldier, learn how to see truth. Following orders is one thing, knowing whose orders to follow is another." She drew back her arm and heaved his sword into the distance. It flew like a spear and landed out of sight down the hill.

She sheathed her weapon as Lynniki darted to Rowan's side and handed her the lantern. At first glance, it seemed intact, but as she spun it, one of the panes of glass fell away in shattered pieces, tinkling as it hit the ground. The one that hadn't been seated properly. It must have shattered as it hit the ground.

"Gavyn, are you all right?"

"A little shaken and very dizzy, but I'm still here."

Rowan swallowed and took one last look at Darryn as Lord Karaval and Lynniki drew her away.

His face was hard.

"Wipe that look off your face," Tera shot over her shoulder. "Your sister is the only reason you're alive. Twice over."

CHAPTER THIRTY-FOUR

ROWAN

T he way back to Lord Karaval's keep was made more complicated by needing to dodge Lord Hax's men. They retrieved the remaining horses and ponies from Verence's camp before racing across the countryside, away from Jannik and his patron.

Lord Karaval was quiet during the journey, as was Rowan. One image kept circling her head. She couldn't rid herself of the look on Darryn's face as she'd left. Rage. And deep under that, a hurt she might never have a chance to address.

She had very little time to dwell on it. They'd retrieved the pieces of the lantern and had everything they needed to find Lord Karaval's wife and daughter. So long as it worked with one of the lenses missing.

As soon as they got back to Lord Karaval's keep, his retainers burst into flurries of activity, preparing for the next trip.

"We leave the moment you're ready," Lord Karaval told Rowan.

But how could she be ready for any of it? She'd thought she was ready for Blackfall, but then they'd left so many people behind. And Darryn had speared her with that look.

She shut herself away in the guest room as Lynniki headed for the blacksmith, intent on her own project.

"You've been very quiet," Gavyn said as Rowan paced the space.

She stopped and stared at her hands. "I don't know how to fight him."

"Who? Lord Hax?"

"Jannik. Darryn would rather believe him than me. He'd rather believe I'm a thief and all those horrible things he said. And I don't know how to get him back."

"Prove him wrong," Gavyn said. "You need proof that the lantern is dangerous and Jannik is lying. Big proof, since making your sister sick wasn't enough."

Rowan's mouth hardened. "And unless we want to actually kill someone else, we'll need to be clever about it. We need Lord Karaval's daughter. She can help us with the lantern."

"You know the most about it," Gavyn said. "You know more than Jannik by far."

She couldn't help the small smile that spread across her face. "I guess you're right. But…"

She pulled the lantern from its case and set it on the table beside the fireplace. She braced her hands on either side of it.

"I need more."

The one lens she knew, with its pattern of shapes that made her think of trees and mountains. The lens on its right depicted a repeating wave, its curves bending over and over. The lens next to that gleamed with intricate starbursts. Beside that, the next lens spiraled endlessly toward the middle in swirls of metal. And the last lens was shattered on the hill of Blackfall.

Unique in their glow as Keinwen had said. But what did they do?

Everyone else bustled below, preparing for their journey into the noktum. Rowan owed it to them to make sure she knew what she was doing. She owed it to Lord Karaval, who'd faced down Lord Hax and was still waiting for the answers he sought.

Her gift only ever showed her tiny glimpses into an object's past, but tiny glimpses over and over could add up to a bigger picture. And a bigger picture could lead to greater understanding. Lord Karaval had been right about one small glimpse giving her an advantage she hadn't had before.

What else can I gain?

Rowan rubbed her hands together and braced herself for the shock of pain before she placed her palms on the lantern. The spark behind her eyes reached for the touchpoints, and she closed her eyes, welcoming the black before the vision.

A face, swarthy and broad with thick, black hair. Not much else.

Her sight cleared, and she let out a breath. The metal burned against her palms, but she didn't let go, reaching instead for another point of heat.

A hand. Behind it, an open archway and a burning mountain in the background glowing red against the night sky. Was that a volcano like Lynniki had described?

Another spark of warmth and another vision. Over and over, she let them come, cascading one after the other.

She saw faces, broader, taller, and she assumed they were the Eldroi, but they weren't so alien that she couldn't read the determination in their expressions. The worry. The fear. A myriad of emotions scattered over the centuries.

Forges deep in the heart of a burning mountain glowed with a heat she could feel even through the vision. Molten glass flowing together with metal.

And death. So much death. A body bloated with the effects of the lantern's deadly metal. Another burned away to ash in the heart of its light.

She saw long journeys, passing landscapes dotted with mountains both sloped and familiar and jagged in a way she'd never seen in her life.

The lantern's cold light glowing against a grasping, creeping darkness, spearing through that inky blackness. Furtive forays into forgotten worlds.

More Eldroi yelling. Deep laboratories and hidden caverns. Long centuries underground.

Light and shadow formed into trees and buildings and mountains like the map at the heart of Blackfall. Figures made out of light and the darkness in between. People running. People fighting. A wall undermined with red before it toppled over on itself. A fortress standing, outlined in gleaming blue.

Little glimpses, bits of the past. Swirling so hard and so furious that they made her dizzy. Her stomach churned, and her hands burned, the pain lancing up her arms and gathering in the pits of her elbows and along her shoulders.

Finally, she gasped and stumbled back, flexing hands that felt raw and ragged but looked as normal as ever.

Her head ached, and her vision blurred, the room in Lord Karaval's keep smearing around her until she couldn't tell if she stared at reality or a fragment of past.

Gavyn's voice cluttered the back of her head, but she could only give him half-answers. Yes, she was all right. No, she didn't need anything but food and sleep. Sleep won out.

She fell into the bed, and if Lynniki came and left again while she slept, she didn't notice.

The sun slanted high against the window when she finally woke, head clear at last.

Rowan groaned and rolled out of the bed. Her shoulders ached like she'd spent the last day and a half carrying a weight around her neck.

"As much as I like a woman staring deeply into my eyes, please don't do it again," Gavyn said. "That was more frightening than romantic."

"I'm sorry," Rowan said, rubbing her face. Her hands still felt a little raw, and she flexed them, trying to loosen them up. "I didn't mean to scare you."

She got the impression that if he could have shrugged, he would have. "You're back now. I assume it was worth it. What did you learn?"

Rowan stood and stepped to the table. She stared at the lantern, her fingers rubbing each other over and over.

"Everything," she said.

She knew how to make it work now. Light and shadow formed by different lenses created different effects.

It wasn't a weapon. Or at least that was only its crudest use. Like killing a man by caving his head in with a spyglass. The deaths seemed to be an unfortunate side effect of the Eldroi disdain for life.

She would need time to interpret everything she'd seen, but for now, it was time to take the Grief Draw to the dark and let it shine.

She found Lord Karaval in his study, finalizing his plans. He looked up as she entered, lantern in hand.

"I'm ready," she said.

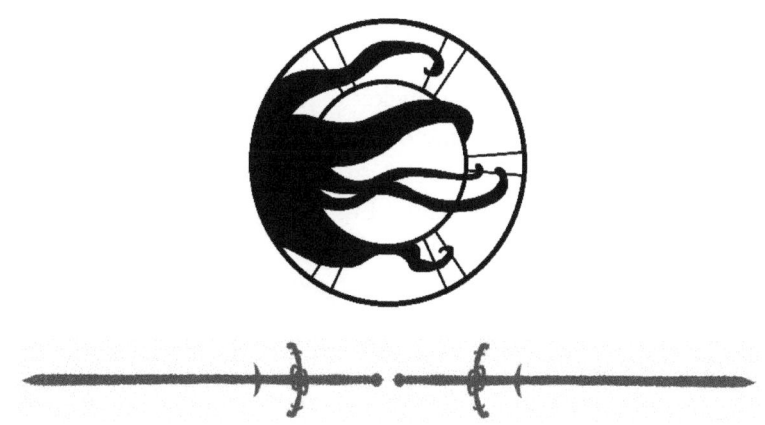

CHAPTER THIRTY-FIVE

ROWAN

Rowan had her meager belongings tucked into the pouches along her belt and the lantern stowed safely in its case. The courtyard rang with the sounds of hooves on flagstones and the voices of retainers calling out for last-minute additions.

Lord Karaval stood to one side, talking with Tera. The bodyguard planted her fists on her hips, as if she needed help looking any fiercer. Her fitted, leather jerkin ended at her hips, giving her a lot more freedom of movement than Rowan's long tunic, and leather guards protected her thighs and calves.

Lord Karaval wore a mail shirt and a simple, black tunic trimmed with silver. His scabbard gleamed in the sun, freshly oiled.

"Any word from our spies inside Hax's keep?" Lord Karaval was saying as Rowan passed.

"Not yet, my lord."

"Then we go now. Before he has a chance to come after us."

Rowan found Lynniki in the smithy. Everyone else was nearly ready to ride out the gate, but the Delver still bent over a bit of glowing metal, tapping it delicately with a hammer.

"You're not ready?" Rowan asked.

"Oh, I've been ready for hours. Everyone else was taking so long, so I decided to finish this one last thing before we left." She dunked the piece into a bucket of water, letting it steam and hiss. Then she turned to snatch a couple of brass rivets from the table behind her.

"It's nearly done," she said. "I'm going to bring it with us, in case I find what I need to finish it."

She knelt, and Rowan finally noticed the shape in the corner. A gangly mass of metal limbs and plates. It looked far more complete than it had the last time Rowan had seen it. All the pieces seemed to be attached now.

Lynniki fitted the little plate over a gap in one of the limbs—Rowan couldn't tell if it was supposed to be an arm or a leg, or maybe a tail—then she hammered the rivets into their precut holes.

"What is that supposed to be?" Gavyn asked from her hip.

"I think it's your new body."

"Wonderful. I suppose a walking junk heap is better than a killer lantern. Er, it does walk, doesn't it?"

"It has limbs so… yes?"

Lynniki squinted up from her work. "Your skepticism is astounding. Don't you know by now I'm a genius?" She stroked her hand across one of the metal plates.

The pile unfolded with a clank, and Rowan skipped back a step. Legs stretched in jerky movements, and the bulbous bit Lynniki had touched rotated in a jagged circle until Rowan realized it was supposed to be a head. The construct wobbled to the center of the smithy, clanking and weaving with each step.

Lynniki spread her hands with a broad grin. "Ta-da!"

Rowan blinked. It looked vaguely like an animal. At least it had four legs and a head held together by half-hidden gears and cogs. Brass and copper plates covered the inner workings just enough to look intentional, and it stood about as high as Rowan's hip.

"It's… nice," Rowan said.

"Four legs instead of two means a lot more stability on almost all terrain, and the best thing about metal and gears is that it can be modified forever. We can always add and upgrade. Unlike flesh and blood."

"Are the front legs on backwards?" she asked, tilting her head to peer at the joints that faced the wrong way.

"They're supposed to be like that."

"Why?"

Lynniki rolled her eyes. "Reasons."

Rowan reached out to touch the thing's head, and it swayed forward on its jerky legs, looking for a pat.

"It moves already."

"Oh, yes. Everything's in place. Like I said, it's almost done. Once we get Gavyn in there, he'll be able to control it like he was born in it. I learned a lot from making these." She held up her metal hand and wiggled her fingers.

"But how do we get him transferred? Did you find anything at Blackfall that will help with your—what did you call it? A soul anchor?"

Lynniki pointed to the back end of the construct, what would be the hips on a cat. There was a pocket there between the hip joints. Rowan recognized the black metal poking out as the clamps Lynniki had pried up in Blackfall.

"I found about half of what I need. These will hold the anchor and attach him in there. I just need to find something to power it."

"Do you know what you're looking for?"

"Of course. You've actually found one already, though we don't have the time to get back there. That preservation spell that you found Gavyn in would be just the thing. I can manipulate something like that to bind Gavyn in the soul anchor."

"And you think you can find a working one?"

Lynniki shrugged. "Or I can get a defunct one working again. Either way."

"Will there be one just lying around in the noktum?"

"Well, they're a bit more common than a murderous lantern, and you literally fell on that one."

"Fair point," Rowan said.

"Look, there are a lot of relics left over from the Eldroi. You just have to know what to look for or how to open the treasure box, like at Blackfall. Magic got Gavyn in there, and magic is the only way we'll be able to get him out. A Life Mage and a Land Mage working together might be able to do it, but if I can find the pieces I need in the noktum, this will be much easier."

There was a sharp whistle from the courtyard, indicating it was time. "Then we'll hope there's another preservation spell somewhere."

"As long as the final product moves, I am completely happy," Gavyn said as Rowan stepped across the courtyard.

The journey to the edge of the noktum took longer than the journey to Blackfall, but Lord Karaval was much more reserved for this ride.

He remained tense until the valley flattened out and a dark smudge spread across the horizon, obscuring everything from the northern range to the ruins beyond Lannasbrook.

Rowan's throat grew drier, and it was harder and harder to swallow as they approached the shadow. The inky blackness draped across the landscape like a curtain.

Her hands clenched on the reins. Had a cloud gone across the sun, or had the looming noktum sent a cold shiver down her spine?

Instead of riding straight for the sheet of darkness, Lord Karaval traveled for another mile south before stopping.

Rowan's gaze swept the edge of the noktum, and her breath stuttered. Black tentacles crept from the surface of the darkness and wavered in the air as if reaching for the people it could sense just out of reach.

"This is about where Patessa and Mellrea disappeared," Lord Karaval said, voice flat. "I suspect Lord Hax drove them into its clutches. Whatever happened, they haven't been seen since."

Rowan bit her lip and raised her chin. Lord Karaval's mouth was pressed thin and hard with grief and worry.

If it was Esrell or Darryn in there, Rowan would have thrown herself at the waiting tentacles. She couldn't imagine the pain he must be hiding.

She unhooked the lantern from her belt and dismounted. Lord Karaval swung a leg over the pommel of his saddle and slid to the ground.

"Let's go," he said.

"My lord?" Tera raised her hand to shield her eyes as she peered back the way they'd come. "Someone's coming. A lone rider."

Lord Karaval stiffened, glancing between the dust rising in the distance and the edge of the noktum. Then he blew out his breath and stepped back to wait for the rider.

As the horse drew closer, Rowan could see Lord Karaval's colors.

"My lord," the rider called as he reined his horse in.

"Benni. What is it?"

"Lord Hax moves. We've had word from your spies."

Lord Karaval threw back his shoulders. "He is too late. He can't stop us from entering the noktum now." He raised his fist to signal the rest of his men.

The rider shook his head. "Not here. Lord Hax isn't following you. He moves on your keep, bringing troops and siege weapons."

Lord Karaval froze, his mouth falling open.

Captain Tera swore. "Coward. We thought he'd come after the lantern. Instead he slips in behind to attack the town while we're away."

Rowan swallowed. "You have to go back." She didn't want to say the words. She'd counted on having Lord Karaval with her for this, but she could see the choice that would tear at him.

Lord Karaval's lips thinned and his eyes darted frantically to the edge of the noktum. "Patessa and Mellrea—"

"We're not abandoning them, either." Rowan straightened as much as her spine would let her. "I'll find them."

"I'm not letting you go in alone."

"Not alone," Lynniki said. She stepped across the ground, the construct following her. Its movements were still jerky, but somehow its back stayed level and smooth across the terrain. It looked like an animal but moved like nothing alive, making Rowan's stomach twist in barely suppressed disquiet.

"I don't doubt your cleverness or bravery, but neither are a substitute for skill. I was supposed to be there to defend you while you worked the lantern. I *need* to be there. And I need to be here."

His nostrils flared and a muscle in his jaw jumped as if he clenched his teeth.

"My lord." Captain Tera swung down from her horse.

They exchanged a long look with no words and then Lord Karaval's shoulders sagged.

"Take care of them," he said, voice quiet and rough. "Find Patessa and Mellrea, please."

"We will. Now go. You'll need time to evacuate the lower town to the keep."

"I'll leave some men here to guard the edge of the noktum," Lord Karaval said, climbing back into his saddle. "I don't want Hax sending a contingent to trap you in there."

Rowan stepped to his side. She reached to put her hand on his, almost out of reach on the pommel of his saddle, and she squeezed.

Lord Karaval squeezed her fingers back before turning his horse to watch them.

Rowan stepped back toward the others. "Thank you, Captain Tera."

"You can just call me Tera. Unless you feel like saluting."

Rowan cocked an eyebrow. "Is there a first name that goes along with that?"

"No," Tera said shortly.

Rowan suppressed a smile and settled her pack on her back before she faced the undulating edge of the noktum.

Fingers of darkness stretched and reached, grabbing for them even as they stood out of reach.

Rowan took a deep breath and held up the Grief Draw. She half expected the tentacles to pull back at the light, but they kept reaching and grasping.

"Here goes nothing," Rowan whispered to Gavyn.

Tera drew her sword. The naked blade and Tera's fierce look made Rowan feel a lot better. She stepped forward into the grasp of the reaching darkness and let it fold her inside. The shadows sank cold hooks into her skin, and the sky disappeared.

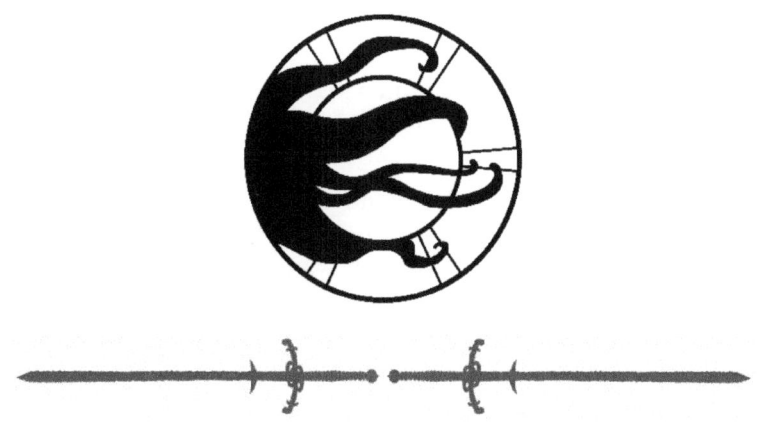

CHAPTER THIRTY-SIX

ROWAN

lack crowded Rowan on all sides, flooding her with panic. She couldn't see. She couldn't hear anything other than her heart thudding in her ears.

Healer's Ghost, what if the lantern doesn't work the way I thought? What if something essential burned out in the centuries since the Giants used it?

"Rowan?" Gavyn said into her mind. "Rowan, say something."

His voice steadied her. "I'm here. I—I can't see yet." Her own voice rang in her ears, proving she wasn't deaf.

She gritted her teeth and raised the lantern.

A glow grew in her grasp, and she blinked fiercely until the glow spread and she could make out her arm. She sucked in a breath, relief pouring through her like warmth, and she swung the lantern to and fro trying to peer into the dark.

Gradually the black faded like ink bleeding from a piece of parchment, leaving the ground awash in a cold, white light that revealed gray terrain.

Grass crackled under her feet, but it stayed an unhealthy shade of gray. *How did it grow without sun?* She squinted up, and the sky remained a near-black, studded with clouds of a lighter gray.

The edge of the noktum undulated like a sheet of dark water, and Lynniki stumbled through, followed closely by Tera, her blade drawn.

Rowan grabbed Lynniki's hand and pulled her closer to the light. Tera held her sword point down so she didn't accidentally stab anyone, but Rowan could tell from the way her shoulders tensed and her free hand shook that she was dying to swing it.

"It's all right," she told them. "I'm here. Give your eyes a chance to adjust."

Lynniki blinked rapidly, spinning one way then another, pulling against Rowan's grasp as she tried to see. Tera waited, frozen, only her eyes darting in rapid movements.

"Oh, I do not like that," Lynniki said, rubbing her face.

"Can you see?"

"Yes? Where did all the colors go?"

"This appears to be it. Welcome to the noktum." The light extended out in a circle around them, and Rowan could now see all the way to the horizon. The very gray horizon. The valley continued down, stretching on either side away from the barrier that led back to the sunlit world.

"Not very welcoming. I don't think I'll be setting up a workshop here," Lynniki said.

"I don't know. It might be homier with some flowers." Tera's lip twitched as she peered around them.

Rowan stared at her. "Did you… did you just make a joke?"

"They'd probably just be gray," Lynniki said, kicking at the grass.

Rowan squinted. "Where are the monsters? Noktums are supposed to be full of them."

"Maybe don't second guess a gift of gears," Lynniki said.

Tera pointed. "There are your monsters."

Far off, over the rolling hills, black shapes wheeled against the dark sky. From this distance, Rowan only got the impression of wings and dark, sinuous bodies.

Behind them, Lynniki's construct stepped through the edge of the noktum. Its movements were as jerky as ever, but it didn't seem to mind the dark, sidling up next to Lynniki.

She gave its head an idle pat. "So where do we start?" She raised her hand to shield her eyes, as if there was any sun to blind her, as she gazed at the featureless landscape.

Rowan bit her lip. She hadn't expected the area behind the edge of the noktum to be so open. It meant nothing could sneak up on them, but she had no idea how to track someone across a featureless plain.

She glanced at Tera, but the captain gave Rowan a little shake of her head before she went back to surveying the landscape, keeping watch.

"This is about where they disappeared," Rowan said to herself. "This is where there would be any signs, if there was anything to find."

Tera flinched, just enough for Rowan to notice before the captain hid her reaction.

Rowan touched the top of the lantern in the pattern that called up the map. Light sprang out in front of her, the shadows crawling into rolling hills just like the ones where they stood. Bits of colors flickered, but only at the very edges, far enough away that she didn't immediately worry about them.

"What do you think?" Tera said.

"I think we should travel along the edge and find the exact place they might have entered. If I was alone and afraid in the dark and I couldn't get back out because of Lord Hax's men, I think I would stay as close to the edge as I could."

"If they could even see." Lynniki planted her hands on her hips.

"Mellrea is smart," Tera said, and her voice wobbled on the word "is" as if she had to think twice about the present tense. "She's her father's daughter. She had all that book-learning with Jannik, not to mention a ferocious curiosity. She trained with me while she was young." She glanced at Rowan, mouth hard. "She's resourceful, and Patessa wasn't exactly delicate either. They would have fought to survive."

"All right," Rowan said quietly. "Let's try north."

They set off, keeping the edge of the noktum on their left and a wary eye on the creatures flying in the distance. So far it didn't look like they'd been noticed, but Rowan was carrying a lit beacon, so that wasn't likely to last long.

Lynniki's construct ranged out further into the noktum, weaving back and forth, sometimes closer, sometimes almost out of sight.

"What's it doing?" Rowan asked.

"Looking for more material made by Giants," Lynniki said.

Rowan's brow furrowed. "It can do that?"

"It can follow simple commands. Run, fetch, follow. That sort of thing."

"You think it'll find one of those preservation spells?"

Lynniki shrugged. "That, or I figured anything left behind by Giants would be a great, big landmark to someone who's lost. We might find Patessa and Mellrea there."

"Good thought."

"Rowan," Gavyn said in the back of her mind. "Look."

Rowan returned her attention to the map, and there in front of them, she could see a break in the featureless landscape. Something ragged and lumpy rose against the smooth rise of the hill.

"I see it," she said. "Just ahead."

She quickened her pace, and the others followed.

Rowan turned her focus to the real ground passing by under the floating overlay of light and shadows. It was hard to concentrate on both at once, but she tried to keep the map in the corner of her eye, watching those colors flickering at the edges.

Five more minutes of walking, and Rowan finally saw what the map had been showing her. The spearing ribs and lonely skull of a dead horse lay just inside the noktum, surrounded by the debris of a burst saddlebag.

They stood, staring for a long moment.

"Something ate it," Lynniki said.

Tera's throat bobbed, and she turned her back to the mess. Rowan wouldn't have expected a seasoned soldier to show even that much emotion over this mess, but maybe Mellrea had been a closer friend than Tera had been willing to admit.

"You were looking for monsters," the captain said. "They must have taken care of the carcass and left the bones here."

Rowan glanced at her, lip between her teeth, but Tera's profile didn't reveal anything deeper than worry.

Lynniki knelt while her construct jerked its way around the edges of the debris field. "Clearly something attacked them. These are claw marks." She held up the tattered remains of a saddle.

Rowan touched the top of the lantern to get rid of the map so she could see better, but she kept hold of the handle, gritting her teeth against the pain.

"I don't see anything that looks Human," Rowan said. "That might be good news." Or it meant that something had dragged off the bodies they were looking for.

There'd been books in the saddlebag. A couple lay open on the ground, tattered pages waving in a slight breeze. Metal glinted in the lantern light, a couple of buckles and the hilt of a broken dagger, the blade sheared off.

She didn't see any tracks or marks to show something big being dragged.

"What happened here?" Tera said under her breath, and Rowan wasn't sure she meant for them to hear her.

"Let's find out." Rowan reached for the dagger hilt.

Rowan ran her fingers down the hilt. Nearly everything but the pommel was covered with the warmth of memory, and Rowan let the spark behind her eyes reach for the past.

The dark that crowded her vision reminded her too much of that first touch from the noktum, and she shuddered, but then colors coalesced into an image. The taut, anxious face of a middle-aged woman. She was caught in the middle of a spin as she turned away from Rowan. She raised her arm to point into the distance.

Rowan drank in every detail before the vision could fade, imprinting them on her memory to examine and analyze later.

The woman's face reflected a warm, yellow light. The horse lay freshly dead at her feet and something large and hulking prowled just out of the corner of her eye.

Rowan blinked the vision away. She still knelt on the ground amid the debris of a broken saddlebag.

"What did you see?" Tera asked. She glanced over her shoulder, her blade still out in a guard position.

Rowan's brow furrowed as she thought. "I saw a woman. Middle-aged with dark brown hair and a long face. She wore blue riding leathers."

Tera let out a breath. "Patessa. So she was alive *then* at least. Was Mellrea with her?"

Rowan let the dagger hilt roll down her hand a little so it caught Tera's eye. "Was this hers?"

"Yes."

"Then I think so. I think it was her memory."

"How could they see?" Lynniki asked. "The only way we can see anything is with the lantern."

Rowan shook her head. "They had some sort of light, but I couldn't see its source." She stood up and tried to line herself up with the memory. Then she peered into the distance, in the direction Patessa had been pointing. "I think they were headed that way."

"What's over there?" Gavyn asked.

She couldn't see anything beyond the rolling gray of the plains. Rowan raised the lantern with a wince and called up the map.

"It looks like… a wall?" Rowan said. "Maybe they thought it would shelter them."

Tera jerked her chin. "Let's move."

Lynniki snatched up a couple of things from the saddlebag. Rowan couldn't see any immediate use for discarded buckles and straps, but then she wasn't the one building new bodies from scratch. Lynniki's construct sniffed around them before pointing its nose in the direction they were heading.

Rowan could no longer tell north from south, but she trusted the map to get them back out of the noktum when the time came.

When they finally reached it, the waist-high wall stretched from their left to their right, but no other details stood out.

"What is it?" Lynniki asked. "Why have a wall in the middle of nowhere?"

"It looks like the ones back home that separate two fields," Rowan said.

Tera frowned. "This was once farmland?"

"Maybe a long, long time ago, before there was a noktum here?"

"I guess I assumed the noktum was forever."

"Heads up," Lynniki said, voice quiet and intense. "Our grace period is over."

Tera's head snapped up, and Rowan turned to follow her gaze. Several sinuous shapes swam through the air as if it were water, and Rowan got the impression of long, sleek bodies with ripping talons and fangs.

She realized with a start that the monsters didn't cast shadows over the grayed-out grass.

"At least we can see them coming," Tera said, placing herself between Rowan and Lynniki and the approaching threat.

Lynniki whistled to her construct. It came tumbling over the wall, and she drew a hammer from her pack.

Rowan tightened her grip on the lantern despite its pain and drew her dagger. The hilt slid in her sweaty palm.

Her breath stuttered as the creatures approached. In this wide-open plain, they could see for miles. This turned into a curse, as it seemed to take the creatures forever to get there.

The map shimmered over the ground, and Rowan's eyes narrowed. It wouldn't do them much good when they could see everything coming. She reached for the cap to switch it to a more general glow but hesitated.

The lens facing her had swirls of gold swimming through the glass, forming intricate starbursts with dead areas in between.

Rowan bit her lip, an image of a wall undercut with red coming to her mind.

"Here they come," Gavyn called. "Rowan, what are you doing?"

The first of the flying, slinking creatures with their long sleek bodies dove for them, fangs bared.

Tera gave a fierce yell and threw herself at the creature. She dodged its lunge and swept her blade around to strike it in midair. It tumbled away but then rolled and righted itself with a hiss as if she'd only angered it. It certainly didn't look like the blade had even split its fur.

Lynniki swung her hammer, striking a creature square on the snout. It swerved around her, landing on the other side of the wall. In one smooth motion, it planted its feet and twisted back on itself to come at Lynniki from behind.

Rowan grabbed Lynniki's collar and pulled, yanking the Delver out of the way at the last second. Neither creature seemed to care about the blows that had been dealt.

Rowan reached for the lantern cap, already recalling the pattern that would activate the starburst lens.

Light shot out in front of her in a white arc, bathing the attacking creatures in a clear glow.

The one that crawled half over the wall turned black eyes on her and bared its fangs. Rowan gulped, but her gaze was caught by the stripe of red down the center of the thing's chest, a flickering bit of color among the white light.

What's the lantern telling me? All those images she'd seen back at Lord Karaval's keep swam through her head, a jumble of puzzle pieces she'd only just started assembling. The crumbling wall appeared with that spot of red underneath it, nudging her with a possibility. To one side, Tera was caught in a fragment of the light. Her sword arm glowed blue, and red shone in the spaces between her armor.

Rowan swung the lantern at the creature's snout, a feint to make it jerk away. As it batted at the light, Rowan lunged in close and low, gambling everything on her hunch, and slashed her knife along its underside from neck to hip.

Its thick fur parted along its belly, and it screamed in pain as Rowan's dagger struck home. Hot blood coated her hands, and she rolled away, avoiding the creature's death throes as it flopped against the wall. Her breath rasped in her ears, but a swelling heat rose in her chest, a feeling she didn't recognize.

"Underneath," she called to Lynniki and Tera. "Strike them in the belly where they are weak."

Lynniki nodded, but Tera didn't even pause. She dove forward, her blade slashing as she kept the worst of the swarm from reaching Rowan and Lynniki.

The Delver took the right side, sweeping her hammer to knock the sleek creatures off their feet and then landing the final blow against their chests. Her pile grew, each one sporting the caved rib cage of a hammer victim.

Rowan kept her dagger in front of her, letting the lantern illuminate the creatures coming after her from the left. She ducked around the swiping talons that glowed blue and followed the red streaks, showing her the vulnerable bits of her enemies.

Her heart hammered, but it never drowned out Gavyn's voice in her head.

"Behind you—another one on the left—Duck! Strike now!"

The flurry of claws and teeth and furry bodies seemed endless, Rowan's lips pulled back unconsciously until she realized she was grinning. Was this how people like Tera felt while fighting? This fierce surge of heat that beat in her pulse. Like pride, only brighter and steadier.

I control this place! Terror still tried to drown out the confidence, but Rowan clung to the feeling that for the first time in her life she knew what she was doing.

The creatures kept coming until, all at once, Rowan looked up to find the next target and there was none.

She sucked in a breath and checked her companions. Tera winced and touched her neck where a long scratch bled freely while Lynniki pushed her way through the pile of bodies that threatened to swamp her.

"Here," Rowan said, reaching for her pack. "I think we brought bandages."

Tera pulled her hand away to examine the blood. "How did you know they were weak underneath?"

"The lantern," she said. "It has different lenses that do different things. The map is only one of them. I'm trying to figure out the others."

"Being able to see an enemy's weaknesses is certainly helpful."

Rowan dug for the long rolls of linen, and Tera didn't bother protesting when Rowan tried to wrap her wound and ended up with a sloppy mess that barely staunched the bleeding.

"I'm sorry," Rowan said. "I'm usually better at that." She couldn't keep her hands from shaking, even now when there was nothing attacking.

Tera shook her head. "Good enough. We need to move. If the noise didn't attract more enemies, the smell of blood certainly will. Which way?"

Rowan pointed. "Past the wall. That is if they kept going in the same direction after reaching this point."

"We have nothing else to go on." Tera grimaced and climbed to her feet once more. "Let's go."

Rowan exchanged a worried glance with Lynniki before they clambered after Tera. Rowan pulled the map up again so they wouldn't be surprised by anything.

The plain wasn't so featureless now. There were bits of tumbled stone where walls had crumbled, and at one point, the square foundation of a ruined outbuilding interrupted the wide-open space.

Rowan kept her attention divided between the map and the skies around them, watching for more creatures. Lynniki concentrated on the remains of civilization they found, examining each stone and ruin for something only she would recognize. Tera watched their rear, making sure nothing snuck up on them.

Rowan's gaze sharpened on the horizon. Off to the right of their trajectory, a dark smudge marred the gray landscape. She didn't adjust their course right away, keeping them moving forward, but as they hurried ahead, the bit of darkness grew clearer and clearer, becoming a mass of bodies.

Wings flapped over the sleeker forms of the creatures they'd just fought. As if giant bats competed with the flying fanged monsters.

"They're swarming," Rowan said quietly, pointing into the distance.

Lynniki's mouth tightened. "Yes. Like they've found something."

Rowan exchanged a look with Tera.

"Better hurry," the captain said. "Before there's nothing left of whatever it is they've trapped."

Rowan didn't stop to wonder if it was a good idea or not. At this point, anything that was an enemy of the creatures and had them in that much of a frenzy was a friend, in Rowan's book.

Rowan's back ached, and her left arm burned all the way to the elbow, but she kept her feet moving and her dagger drawn in the other hand. As they ran, she touched the cap so the map disappeared and the starburst lens activated.

Giant bats with talons as long as Rowan's forearm swarmed the crumbling walls of a house. A villa to go with the fields they'd spent the last few hours crossing. It held wide windows, boarded over with debris, and makeshift barricades, and Rowan couldn't even see where the ancient door had stood.

More sleek creatures ducked and wove through the bats, scrabbling at the ancient tile roof, making horrendous screeching noises as they struck. The fliers reminded her of the ones in the depths of Blackfall, except these were much larger, as if the Eldroi had taken those first attempts and improved them.

Several large bodies littered the uneven ground leading up to the villa. Some were fresh, while others had been picked over for a time. Whoever was trapped had been here a while.

Tera didn't stop to plan or issue orders. She charged up the broken path, silent and ready with her blade already drawn.

"So cut a path through, then knock on the door," Lynniki said, racing after her. "I guess that's simple enough."

"Go for the undersides again," Rowan called to them. Several creatures spun at the sound of her voice, but she was already moving into position behind the other two. "The bats are weak in the neck and along the wings. Ground them, and we should have a chance."

Lynniki yelled, racing up a fallen pillar. She leaped from the top, swinging her hammer, and a bat met her in midair. Her blow cracked against the base of its wing, and it screeched in pain. The Delver followed it to the ground to cave its head in.

Tera screamed at a bat diving for her. She fell to her knees to slide under it, and Rowan caught the startled creature across the neck with her dagger.

One of the sleek ones with the fangs fell on her, and Rowan stumbled with a yell.

Talons scrabbled at her torso, cutting into the leather of her tunic, and she swung her arm around so the lantern connected with the thing's thick skull.

It winced away, its black eyes narrowing, and Rowan got the impression it hated the light more than the blow.

Red crawled up its belly like before, but another streak caught her eye from its shoulder. Under the revealing light, its sleek fur was seamed, as if it hid an old scar.

Rowan twisted to slash at the seam.

It hissed and ducked away, long enough for Rowan to scramble to her feet. She didn't wait for it to pounce again, following her movement up with another slash. The creature scrabbled back a step.

The pathway opened before her, and Rowan darted for the villa. Lynniki was already there, clearing a space with her hammer.

Tera darted after her, then spun to catch Rowan's attacker with a thrust from her short sword.

"Now what?" Lynniki panted. "There's no door."

Rowan backed up against the wall and waved the lantern at the bats stooping from above. One veered off course when the light struck its eyes, and the other screamed. It wove, as if partly blinded, and Rowan struck for its wing.

As it fell at their feet, Lynniki bashed its head in.

Rowan sidled along the wall to the nearest boarded window and hammered at it with the pommel of her dagger. "Hey! Is anyone in there?"

Wings fluttered above her, and the sleek creatures hissed through their fangs, but Rowan thought she heard a muffled voice through the cracked wood.

A creature raked claws down the tile roof, and Rowan winced back under the eaves.

Tera pushed through Lynniki and Rowan and pounded on the boards. "Mellrea. It's Tera. Let us in."

A surprised cry pierced the barricade, and something began attacking the boards from the other side.

Rowan raised her dagger and faced the bats that lined up for another dive. "If that's not Mellrea…" She slashed at a bat and ducked as Tera finished it off.

"Or if she takes too long to let us in…" Lynniki added.

"We're dead, I know," Tera said. "We're dead anyway. Inside is our only hope of survival."

Rowan bit her lip and ducked back, panting. The eaves provided a little cover, but there were still at least twenty creatures up there. Only three of them, and they were already wounded and exhausted. Tera was right.

"Here come more," Lynniki said.

Under the flutter of chaotic wings, Rowan made out the stalking shadows of large cats creeping up on the villa from afar. Again, these reminded her of the ones from Blackfall. Only bigger and worse.

Tera squared her shoulders. "All right." She blew out her breath and then said a little stronger, "All right. Keep your blade up. Don't let them get behind you. Watch your heads and stay under the eaves."

Lynniki brandished her hammer, Tera flicked blood from the tip of her sword, and Rowan resettled her grip on the burning lantern. The dagger hilt was sticky against her palm.

Three bats wheeled above and dove in concert, falling on them at the same time.

Rowan raised her dagger.

The boards fell away from her back, and hands dragged her through the window.

CHAPTER THIRTY-SEVEN
ROWAN

Rowan tumbled to the dusty floor of the villa and coughed before she scrambled to her feet. She whipped around to find whoever it was that had grabbed her, and her gaze latched on a young woman stepping back with her hands raised in a placating gesture.

This was not the middle-aged woman Rowan had seen in her vision by the dead horse. She was only a year or two older than Rowan and had thick, dark hair that escaped from a once-elegant knot, as if she hadn't had a chance to fix it in a while. She wore a sword at her hip.

"Who are you?" the young woman snapped. "Where's—"

Lynniki sailed through the window as if someone had heaved her, and Tera jumped in after her.

"Tera," the young woman breathed.

Tera spun. Her breath caught, and she stepped forward. "Mellrea."

The two women met in the middle of the room, throwing their arms around each other.

Rowan blinked as Tera and Mellrea murmured to each other, but Lynniki swore as she threw herself at the window. The construct scrabbled over the windowsill before Lynniki snapped a board against it.

"A little help?" she called.

Rowan handed her pieces the Delver then nailed into place. Claws scrabbled against the barricade, and Rowan smashed a talon that tried to sneak through one of the cracks.

Her heart didn't slow until Lynniki hammered the last nail in and stood back.

"It'll have to do for now," she said, tight-lipped. "But I don't know if it'll hold against a concentrated effort."

"We have to replace it every couple of days," Mellrea said, finally pulling free of Tera's arms. "Hours, if they decide to go at it in a frenzy, which happens sometimes."

Rowan turned to meet Mellrea's eyes. This was Karaval's daughter. They'd found her alive, but all Rowan could feel was the dull panic in the back of her mind, pounding home the fact that they were trapped.

Mellrea's gaze dropped to the lantern. Her eyes widened, and she glanced between it and Rowan's face, recognition creeping across her expression.

"You work with Jannik," Mellrea said softly.

Rowan winced. "Not anymore. It's a long story."

"Mell…" a breathless voice called from the back of the room.

Mellrea started and turned.

Rowan hadn't even realized in the light of the lantern that there was another glow spilling out through the room. They stood in the bare space of some kind of dining room or parlor, the furniture long since decayed with only the walls remaining, and huddled on a couple of blankets in the back, lay a young woman. Her long, delicate features were pulled taut with pain and sweat dampened her loose golden hair. Hair that glowed with a golden light.

She was the source of light in the villa.

Healer's Ghost, Rowan had never seen a person glow before. Was it a spell? Or some quality of the woman herself? Like the Delvers' immunity to Giant magic.

The woman turned her head as Mellrea knelt beside her, revealing the sharp tip of a pointed ear.

The stories about Luminents were even more rare than the stories about Delvers. Delvers at least lived in the mountains near Monclaren, but Rowan had assumed Luminents were a myth, like unicorns and sprites.

Mellrea leaned forward and drew back a dark cloth that covered the Luminent's side. Rowan hissed when she saw the three long gashes that bled sluggishly in the light.

Tera's lips thinned, and she gestured to Rowan who turned so the captain could dig in her pack. Tera pulled out more bandages and a jar of astringent salve, then handed them to Mellrea.

"Where is your mother?" Tera asked quietly.

Mellrea's lips thinned as she applied salve to the bandages and changed the dressing on the Luminent's wound. "She's gone."

Tera sucked in a breath. "I'm sorry."

Mellrea rubbed her face one-handed.

"How long ago?"

"Several days. At least I assume it's been days. Impossible to tell here. Sometimes I think it's been forever."

Rowan stepped closer as Lynniki ranged around the room, checking the barricades on the other windows. Her construct sniffed at the corners.

"Allianne saw Lord Hax's men drive us into the reach of the tentacles, and she came in after us. She's the reason we've survived as long as we have. The monsters pushed us further and further in and we holed up in here for safety. Mother fell during our first attempt to escape. We've been fighting to stay alive ever since."

Rowan knelt on Mellrea's other side. Allianne lay her head back and closed her eyes.

"I'm sorry we didn't get here sooner," Rowan said. "We weren't exactly sure how the Grief Draw worked, and we had to find the missing pieces in Blackfall before we could come into the noktum."

Mellrea glanced up at her, brow furrowed. "Who are you? Don't get me wrong, I'm damn glad to see someone else in this place, but what the hell are you doing here?"

"My name's Rowan," she said. "And that's Lynniki. We struck a deal with your father. My part was to help find you."

Mellrea rubbed her forehead. "Congratulations. Here I am."

Rowan smiled grimly. "Yes. Now to get you home."

Mellrea snorted. "Good luck. You're as trapped here as we are now."

"She's just a ray of optimism in a dark place, isn't she?" Gavyn said in the back of Rowan's mind.

"I'll admit, that swarm outside is terrifying," Rowan said. "But you have more tools at your disposal now." She set the lantern down between them.

Mellrea's eyes glinted in the light. "You say that so casually, like that thing is just a shovel or a torch. Do you even know what it is you bear?"

"I know more than Jannik did, but that's one of the reasons I wanted to find you. I have a feeling you can tell me more."

Mellrea sighed and sat back on her heels. "My knowledge is piecemeal. From things I put together before Jannik completely cut me off from his research and from what I've discovered here."

"Here?" Lynniki said. "You mean there are clues about this thing here in the noktum as well?"

Mellrea nodded. "It's actually not surprising that so much of the Giants' focus went into the lantern and what it could do. It was made by their enemies, and from what I've read, it worried them. A lot."

"They definitely put a lot of effort into hiding it and keeping the pieces separate so it would be harder to use," Rowan said.

"Yes, well, how would you feel if a spy from Triada brought a magic artifact to infiltrate Usara?" She waved a hand. "What if we were at war and this artifact could tip the balance in their favor? You'd kill the spy and bury the artifact as deep as you could, right?"

"Something like that," Rowan admitted.

Mellrea stared at the lantern in disgust. "We might not know exactly what the Grief Draw does, but if the Giants were that afraid of it, I certainly don't trust it."

Rowan sat forward. "That's why I took it from Jannik. He didn't acknowledge its danger. He just wanted to give it to Lord Hax, even though it was killing people."

Mellrea slumped. "So it is a weapon."

"No. No, you were right. It's something far more complicated. The danger seems to come from how it was made and how it's used. The metal is… toxic for lack of a better word. As long as people don't touch it, they're safe. And as long as it's used well," Rowan spread her hands, "it can be used for good things too."

"Like rescuing people from the noktum," Lynniki said.

Mellrea pursed her lips, her eyes narrowing. "I'm not sure the ends justify the means."

Rowan cocked her head. What means? Using the lantern? This woman didn't value her life very highly it seemed.

Mellrea gestured to the lantern, her lip curling. "Who did it drain in order for you to come get me?"

Rowan's brow drew down. "What do you mean? It killed Gillfry, but that was an accident. We discovered that if the light flares, it acts as if whoever was in the way touched the metal. Only the effects are more accelerated."

Mellrea's hand slashed through the air. "No, I'm not talking about that. I'm talking about who is powering it? The death that supplies its energy."

The bottom dropped out of Rowan's stomach. Lynniki turned to her, her mouth falling open.

Mellrea gaped. "You never thought about what was powering it?"

She had, but the mystery had been buried under the urgency of Jannik and Lord Hax's pursuit.

She swallowed. "What powers it?"

"Human lives." Mellrea's words fell into the quiet villa like a rock into a pond, sending out ripples to disturb everything. "The texts I read said it drained the energy out of a person and left nothing but dust."

"That hasn't happened," Rowan said quickly. "The only time it kills people, they get sick with boils and sores. Their insides melt, and there's too much left over to ever be called dust."

"Rowan," Gavyn said quietly.

"What?" She turned to the lantern.

"The treasure hunter. When I tried to destroy the lantern and it sucked me in, it turned my captor into dust."

Rowan's heart beat in her throat, choking her.

"Whatever I did must have triggered the lantern to drain him. To gather more power."

"Healer's Ghost, I should have figured it out." She'd even seen people turning to dust in all those visions. Just like Gavyn's body had.

Gavyn… oh gods. Her hands crept to cover her mouth.

Mellrea looked at her askance. "Are you talking to the lantern?"

"She does that," Lynniki said as Rowan's mind whirled. "We should introduce you to Gavyn. He's the one living inside the lantern. Rowan talks to him all the time…" Her voice trailed off as the blood drained from her face.

"What would—" Lynniki started and then had to swallow. "What would happen to someone who was trapped inside it?"

Mellrea's eyes flicked between them and the lantern, her finger tapping an uneven rhythm against her thigh. "I didn't even know that was possible. The texts said the lantern would seek a new source of energy when the last one ran out, so the Giants kept a steady supply of Humans nearby."

"Humans," Lynniki said, cocking her head. "Not just *any* people then?"

"It was originally carried by a Delver. So they must be immune to all its effects, including the draining. Everyone else seems to be forfeit. Including your friend?"

"It must store power," Lynniki said. "If it takes more than one life at a time."

"That's not what's happening." Gavyn's voice was sharp in Rowan's head, making her wince. "This was completely different. My body was there. In stasis."

He didn't know. The lantern hadn't been nearby when they'd buried his body. "Gavyn."

"What?"

"Your body. It turned to dust when we tried to bury you."

"But it was my Land Magic that trapped me in here." His voice lost its vehemence. "The treasure hunter isn't in here with me. We can't hear *his* voice."

"Maybe it consumed too much of him. Or maybe you're only able to talk because of the magic that put you there."

Gavyn remained silent, and she desperately wished she could see his face.

She vividly remembered the way he'd collapsed at bottom of the grave. His body had remained long enough for her to find his ring, but it had crumpled just like the husks of the people in her visions.

"So it ate me?" Gavyn's voice shook. "The Grief Draw ate me!"

"But what does that mean?" Lynniki said.

"It means that the lantern will start consuming your friend," Mellrea said. "If it hasn't already. One day soon, even his voice will be gone."

A final death for Gavyn, a hundred years after he saved Keinwen. A hundred years after his body had died, his mind would finally die too.

CHAPTER THIRTY-EIGHT

ROWAN

Rowan's hand clenched in the leather of her tunic, her eyes locked on the lantern. *Healer's Ghost, what did I do?*

Every moment the light shone, every time she activated one of the lenses, it chipped away at Gavyn's life. He was trickling away right before her eyes and she hadn't even noticed.

He'd always seemed slightly immortal. The man who had defeated death, but that was a lie.

She opened her mouth to say she'd never use the lantern again, to preserve him for as long as she could, but they were still in the noktum. They were trapped here with monsters trying to get in. Even now, they could hear the yowls and scratches at the wood barricades.

Her gaze darted to the wounded Luminent who'd opened her eyes again and was watching them quietly. So far, she hadn't said anything more than Mellrea's name.

Rowan couldn't put the entire weight of the group's survival on Allianne's shoulders, even if she wasn't wounded. They knew nothing about her. They needed the lantern, and Gavyn would die just as surely if Rowan and Lynniki perished here in the noktum.

Rowan ran her hands up and down her arms. Gooseflesh dimpled her skin under the leather. "Say something, Gavyn."

"What do you want me to say?" His tone was neither flippant nor angry. He sounded weary. "Did your mother ever give bad news to one of your neighbors. 'I'm sorry, but you only have a month to live. A week? A day?' This is like that."

Rowan stood abruptly. Her legs itched like she wanted to run. To leave the problem behind or go back to those previous few moments where she'd felt strong and powerful. In control of her life and the lantern.

Instead, she scrubbed her hands over her face. "We have to get out of the noktum. As fast as we can."

Mellrea raised her eyebrows. "What do you think we've been trying to do?"

"We'll get out, Rowan," Lynniki said. "Don't panic."

Rowan glared at her. "Yes, but even if we do, we'll go on living. However every moment we spend in this place shaves time off his life. We need to get him out of there but we can't until we're out of the noktum and we don't need its light anymore."

"Look, I'm sorry for your friend," Mellrea said, tilting her head back to meet her gaze. "But Allianne is still hurt from our last escape attempt. I'm not risking her life by rushing things."

Rowan shook her head. "You said the lantern seeks out another source of power once its current reserve runs out. If we're still in here when Gavyn expires, it will go after one of us. One of you. Maybe her. She'd be just as dead then as if she died from her wounds." She hid a wince and nodded at the Luminent. "Sorry."

Allianne took a deep breath and struggled to sit up. "I agree," the Luminent said, voice soft and lyrical. "For many reasons, including the chance to help someone I've never met." She flashed a smile at Mellrea whose lips firmed. "But also, because I'd rather not die in the dark."

Lynniki tapped her foot, hands planted on her hips. "We might be able to prolong the time he has."

"How?" Gavyn asked at the same time as Rowan.

"If the lantern works anything like other creations of the Eldroi or even other things I've made, then the power it uses varies based on what it's doing. The low-level light it provides is the bare minimum. You haven't even been able to turn it off, and it lasted over the centuries without anything else to feed it except one measly treasure hunter."

"True."

"When the light flares or shines through one of the lenses, it's using more power. Probably a lot more."

"So we avoid using the lenses."

"If we can," Lynniki said with a shrug. "This place is dangerous. The only reason we made it this far was because of the lenses and the advantages they gave us."

Tera gave a grim smile. "I'd like to say that's not true, but that would make me a liar."

"Even the light will eventually use him up," Lynniki said. "So Rowan's right. We have to get out of here. More than that, though, we have to get Gavyn out. As soon as we leave the noktum, if possible."

"Do you think you can find that spell you need here?" Rowan's gesture took in the rest of the villa lying dark and mysterious behind a couple of open doorways.

The construct snuffled around the edges of the room like a clanking dog. Its square jaw opened, and it grabbed something that glinted from the rubble in the corner. Then it trotted to Lynniki and dropped it at her feet. Rowan noticed it had already started a pile of trinkets there.

"It's more likely to be here than out there in a field," Lynniki said, jerking her chin at the window they'd come in. "Preservation spells were used for all sorts of little things like food storage. I just need to find the kitchen."

Rowan swallowed. "And if you can't find one?"

Lynniki met her eyes and raised her chin. "Then I'll have to cobble something together from scraps." She looked directly at the lantern. "I dare you to tell me I can't do it. I work best when the naysayers are at their loudest."

Gavyn snorted in Rowan's mind. "By all means, tell her I'm skeptical if that helps, but I'm not going to doubt the only person whose given me any kind of hope in the last hundred years. Besides you, Rowan, of course."

"Don't worry, I know where I stand," Rowan told him. She looked back at Lynniki. "How well do you work when everyone believes in you?"

Lynniki's face went clouded and full of pain, and Rowan worried she'd said something wrong. But Lynniki cleared her throat, and her expression grew fierce. "I don't know. No one's ever believed in me before."

CHAPTER THIRTY-NINE

ROWAN

ynniki started immediately. "Give me two hours. After that, we leave regardless. May I take this with me?" she asked, touching the edge of the lantern.

Rowan gave her a tight-lipped nod.

Tera and Mellrea exchanged a glance before Mellrea stood and dusted off her knees.

"We'll need a way out of here," Tera told Rowan. "Mell and I will make sure we have a clear path to escape when it's time."

"Then I'll make sure everyone is fit enough to travel," Rowan said quietly as Mellrea gripped Allianne's shoulder before leaving.

They all disappeared into the rest of the villa, leaving Rowan alone with the Luminent.

"Are you a healer?" Allianne asked as Rowan settled beside her, digging in her pack.

"My mother is," Rowan said. "I'm a poor substitute, but I suppose I'm the best we have right now."

"I'll take it," Allianne said.

Rowan peeled away the new bandage Mellrea had applied and found the wounds had at least stopped seeping.

"What got you?" Rowan asked. Nora would probably have wanted to sew the wounds closed, but Rowan wasn't nearly skilled enough for that. She decided to work with the bandages and wrap the area tightly to keep the Luminent from bleeding any more than she already had. Perhaps with time and care, the wounds would close and she would recover.

"One of the Kyolars," Allianne said with a wince. "This morning? Last night? I'm not sure anymore."

Rowan gave her a quizzical look. "One of the what?"

Allianne waved toward the window. "The big cats. It was waiting to ambush us and got me as we tried to get out the window."

"I didn't know they had names," Rowan said.

Allianne shrugged. "Kyolars are the cats. They seem to be attracted to blood and meat. Those sleek otter-like things that swim through the air are Sleeths. There are more that have never been named. And I'm sure there are some that have only been seen once before the observer dies."

Rowan's lips thinned as she wrapped the bandages tight around Allianne's torso. "We found a lot of creatures the Giants created in Blackfall. I wonder if that place supplied the creatures found here."

"Possibly. A long, long time ago maybe."

"Are all Luminents this knowledgeable about the noktum?"

Allianne snorted. "No. Most of them know enough to stay away, but there are some of us who think it's our duty to protect people from what the Giants left behind."

She went silent, her lips pressed in a thin line, and Rowan sensed there was some old bitterness there.

"I think Mellrea appreciates that more than anyone right now."

Allianne seemed surprised enough to huff a laugh, wincing when it jarred her side.

Rowan finished tying off the bandage and checked to make sure it wouldn't slide or cause more pain. "How does that feel?"

"Better actually," Allianne said.

"I think you'll be able to move, now. It'll be better when we can get out of here and get you to a real healer, but hopefully this will get you there."

"I'll run if I have to," Allianne said. She met Rowan's eyes. "Thank you. If I don't end up making it, would you tell Mellrea to send a message to my family? To tell them what happened. She knows where they are."

Rowan swallowed.

"I will," she said.

That seemed enough for Allianne, who settled back to close her eyes and rest for the little time they had left.

From the way her stomach rumbled, Rowan guessed it had been nearly two hours when Lynniki stomped back into the room, the lantern in one hand and an armful of odds and ends in the other. She dumped her finds on her growing pile and handed the lantern back to Rowan.

Rowan's shoulders relaxed a little the moment she picked up the lantern again. She trusted Lynniki, but it still felt better to have the handle back in her hand, even though the shock of pain made her jerk.

"Did you find what you were looking for?" Rowan asked quietly as Lynniki knelt to sort through the pile.

The Delver turned a coin over in her hands. It reminded Rowan of the fire charges, except this was clearly meant to be more permanent.

"Yes," she said, but her face and voice remained grim.

"What's wrong?"

"It's out of power."

Rowan blew out her breath. *Damn the Giants and their creations. It can never just be simple, can it?*

"Too bad you can't hook it up to me," Gavyn said. "I'd light it up like the sun."

"I like the idea of using the last of the lantern's power to get you out of it, but I'd worry that it would eat you too," Rowan said.

Lynniki's mouth twisted in an amused grin. "That's very convoluted. But no. I found some other things that I think might be able to power the preservation spell that I can then use to bind Gavyn to the soul anchor. I won't know for sure until we try it, though, and we can't do that in here."

Rowan bit her lip. "Which means it's time to go."

She stepped to the open doorway into the rest of the villa. Tera and Mellrea stood at the other side of the room, staring at the boarded-up entryway.

"It's time," she told them. "Are you ready?" She couldn't tell what they had done, but several ropes crisscrossed the cracked ceiling.

"As ready as I can be without a troop of guards and a siege engine," Tera said with a grumble.

Mellrea laid her hand on Tera's arm and gave her a smile.

"Go with the others," Tera told her quietly. "I can handle this. I'll cover our escape, and catch up with you."

"Be careful," Mellrea said.

Tera touched her cheek. "When am I not?"

Mellrea's mouth went tight and hard, but she left Tera there and slipped her shoulder under Allianne's arm to help the Luminent to her feet. Lynniki shoveled her pile of finds into her pack, which was nearly as big as she was already. The brass and copper construct waited obediently beside her.

"What's Tera going to do?" Rowan asked Mellrea.

The young woman helped Allianne to the window they'd originally came in. "She's going to draw the creatures around the villa so we can get out this side."

Rowan blew out her breath. "Oh." She hoped the captain knew what she was doing. They wouldn't be able to come back and rescue her. This was going to be all or nothing.

"Yes," Mellrea said and didn't bother elaborating on any of their worries. "Get ready to run."

Rowan and Lynniki pried the nails from several of the boards so they were ready to tear them from the window.

Just in time.

A crash came from the other side of the villa, and Tera started yelling incoherently. Rowan jumped in alarm, but Mellrea grabbed the first board from the window and yanked it down.

"Now," she said between her teeth.

Rowan and Lynniki tore at the boards, trusting that Tera's distraction would draw enough of the creatures away from the window that they wouldn't be caught half in and half out.

Sure enough, the moment it was clear enough to see through, Rowan found nothing but a tail or two disappearing around the edge of the building.

"Fast," she said and tumbled through the window, ignoring the sharp pain up her spine and the burning that crept up her arm from the lantern.

She helped Allianne over the sill, and Mellrea leaped out after her. Lynniki climbed out after them and gestured for them to move.

As Rowan raced down into the nearest field, the villa rumbled behind them. It groaned and buckled, and the ceiling collapsed with a roar.

Healer's Ghost, what had they rigged?

She kept running, heart in her throat. Her legs pumped, keeping her moving, but she checked behind her to make sure the others were keeping up. Allianne moved mostly on her own, her face twisted with pain while Lynniki huffed and Mellrea ran half-turned, watching for Tera.

"Do you know where you're going?" Gavyn asked.

Rowan panted. "I'm doing this mostly by memory."

Gavyn was silent a beat. Then he said, "You don't have to, you know."

"Yes, I do," she said through gritted teeth. "I don't want to use the lenses."

"Rowan, you're going to have to."

"Not yet."

She could get them to the edge. It had been nearly a straight shot, and in these mostly flat plains, she would see the horse's skeleton easily enough. She hoped.

Here was the first wall around the fields of the villa. She vaulted over it.

"Here she comes," Mellrea called from behind. "And not alone."

Rowan turned to see Tera sprinting for them, one hand on her hilt to keep the sheathed sword from hindering her.

Behind her a mass of writhing bodies swarmed, both on the ground and in the air.

"Why are you stopping?" she cried as she drew even with them. "Keep going. I took out as many as I could, but there are still more."

Rowan turned to keep running. Lynniki was keeping up just fine, but Allianne flagged more and more as they went.

"You need the second lens," Gavyn said. "You won't make it to the edge in time."

"Gavyn, no," Rowan said between heaving breaths. "I'm not knowingly killing you."

"You only came in here because you knew you could use the lantern to keep you all alive. If I take that away, *I'll* be killing *you*."

"Then I guess we're arguing about who gets to die first."

"Rowan, I want you to use it. If I'm going to disappear forever, I want it to be protecting someone. I want it to be protecting *you*."

She sobbed, and she wasn't sure if it was because she'd never run so hard in her life or because of Gavyn's words.

"Trust me, Rowan."

She glanced over her shoulder. Allianne stumbled, and Tera hauled her to her feet, but the creatures behind them were gaining. Rapidly.

"How do we even tell when the lantern runs out of the power it got from the treasure hunter?" she asked. "How do we tell when it switches over to drawing from you?"

"I'll be able to tell," he said, and something in his words sounded certain and final. "I can control the light, can't I? I could sense the lenses when we got close. You said it before. In a lot of ways, I *am* the lantern."

That just made her want to separate them more but that couldn't happen until they could get out of here.

The swarm of creatures closed on them, the growls and snarls crawling up Rowan's spine and raising the hair on the back of her neck. Lynniki screamed, short and sharp.

"Rowan! Use it!"

She spun with a cry and touched the cap, activating the starburst lens.

Tera turned, sword drawn to face the threat. A Kyolar fell on her.

"Tera, left shoulder!" Rowan called.

Tera didn't hesitate. She sank her blade into the Kyolar's left shoulder, and it sprang back with a yowl.

Rowan drew her dagger to swipe at the nearest Sleeth, following the line of red along its flank. "Lynniki, above you. Go for its left side."

The Delver lunged with a full swing of her hammer.

Rowan called out directions, trying to keep her eyes on everyone and everything. Claws and talons surrounded them, but so did the red streaks of weakness and the blue of strength. Rowan slashed at as much red as she could find and twisted out of the way of the blue, warning the others back when they strayed too close to the creatures' strong sides.

She panted, trying to catch her breath even as she spun. Gavyn called out the openings he saw, and Rowan did her best, but there was so much. How could one mind and one set of eyes keep track of it all?

The colors blurred before her, and her limbs ached, but if she slowed even for a second, one or all of them would be lost, dragged away under ripping claws or torn in half by huge talons.

Allianne stood, one hand clutching her side, the other darting back and forth with a rapier, protecting their right. Mellrea handled the left, and Tera bore the brunt ahead of them.

A Sleeth dove for Tera, too quick for Rowan to call out. She lunged forward, plunging her dagger into its side, using the red glow of the lantern as a target.

The Sleeth fell with a scream, slashing her with blue-wrapped talons. She twisted aside so they scraped down her leather clad arm, drawing blood but not tearing her apart the way they could have.

In that moment, blue washed over her companions as the remaining creatures fell back, regrouping beside the wall of the field. There were far fewer of them now.

"Now," Rowan gasped. "Now's our chance. Get to the edge of the noktum. Go!"

She urged them on, touching the cap so that normal light spilled out. She took the rear, this time, keeping the rest of them in sight ahead of her.

There. Far ahead, the jagged white of a horse's rib cage rose and beyond that, a curtain of inky blackness.

"Almost there," Rowan panted, mostly to herself. "Almost there."

The light in her hand sputtered.

"Gavyn?" Rowan gasped.

"It's fine," he said in her mind. "I'm fine."

"Is the power used up? Is it draining you?"

The briefest hesitation. "No. I'm fine. Keep going."

They pelted for the edge of the noktum. Rowan kept her eyes on the edge of the darkness, straining her ears for the sounds of claws and growls behind them. They were coming. The sounds of pursuit raised the hairs on the back of her neck.

Tera was only feet away from the curtain. She paused to make sure the others were there with her.

The light flickered in Rowan's hand, black warring with white and gray.

"Go!" Rowan called. "Go now!"

The lantern went dark, and Rowan was plunged into a black, thick enough to choke her.

Panic crawled along her skin, and it was all she could do to keep running. Forward. The edge had been just ahead of her. She could make it.

Her eyes strained to see anything except black, the ache of effort crawling into the back of her head. A snarl ripped through the air right behind her.

She screamed and threw herself forward.

Light pierced her eyes, and colors whirled around her. Black tentacles stretched in front of her, and Rowan realized she'd breached the edge of the noktum. She rolled away from the questing tentacles. She would not be drawn back in there now.

As she rolled, she lost her grip on the lantern's handle, and the burning stopped for a brief, euphoric moment. She'd have to grab it again, but at the moment she relished the absence of pain.

The light stabbed at her eyes, blinding after so many hours in the noktum, and she buried her head in her arms.

"Gavyn?" she said into her sleeve. "Gavyn, are you all right?"

The light had died. That had to mean the power from the treasure hunter was done. The lantern would be feeding off Gavyn now.

"Here," she heard in her mind, but his voice was thin as if coming from a greater distance. "I'm here. Just—" He gasped. "Rowan!"

Rowan raised her head and found herself staring up the length of a sword. She sucked in a breath and lurched up onto her knees.

Soldiers in Lord Hax's colors surrounded her. Lynniki lay beside her, hands in the air to show she was weaponless, though her hammer lay within reach. Tera was the only one standing, glaring at the guards that held her at sword point. Mellrea knelt beside Allianne, who panted in the grass.

Lord Karaval's guards lay dead in a pile beyond their captors.

There beside the dead guards stood Rowan's brother. He held the lantern in his left hand, a naked sword in his right.

"Darryn?" Rowan gasped. "Darryn, put it down right now."

Darryn's mouth thinned. "I don't listen to liars who use deceit to cover their weakness. I have what I came for. Now you can't hurt our family anymore just so you can feel powerful."

"Darryn!" Rowan lunged forward, but the guard in front caught her with a kick to the chest. Rowan fell back, gasping for breath, her lungs burning.

"What do you want to do with them, sir?" one of the guards asked Darryn.

Darryn turned to a horse standing just beyond him. "Lord Hax is busy with the siege against Lord Karaval. He has no opinion about these, and I care even less." He sheathed his sword and mounted one-handed. "Kill them if they try to follow."

He kicked his horse into a swift gallop.

"Darryn!" Rowan screamed as he rode away. "Darryn, you don't know what you're doing! Please!"

CHAPTER FORTY

ROWAN

Lord Hax's guards advanced, naked blades glinting in the setting sunlight. Rowan swung between the nearest two, dagger raised across her chest. As if that would protect her. Without the lantern's light, she had no idea where to strike or when to dodge.

The others shuffled closer together, watching the guards approach.

Healer's Ghost, she couldn't let Darryn escape with Gavyn and the lantern, but she couldn't let the guards slaughter them all either. Trapped between the approaching men and the edge of the noktum, she didn't have a choice either way.

Mellrea glanced between them, eyes landing on Rowan's face before seeking out Lynniki's grim determination and Tera's fierce frown. Then the baron's daughter blew out her breath and unsheathed her sword.

Tera started. "What are you—"

Mellrea darted forward and spun, catching the nearest guard off-balance and stripping his weapon. She trapped his arm under hers and thrust her blade into his chest. He collapsed with one last surprised breath. Then she slashed her sword across his throat so blood spilled out onto the dry grass.

Rowan cried out.

"Wait for it," Mellrea said, face calm and implacable as the guards yelled and surged forward, rage written in their expressions.

Rowan opened her mouth to cry, "Wait for what?" but the curtain of darkness separating them from the noktum parted, and a dark shape made of muscles and teeth leaped out of the black.

Rowan staggered back as the Kyolar fell on the dead guard, its mouth wide in a snarl.

The guards screamed and lunged at the beast. Two more Kyolars and a Sleeth poured out of the noktum, looking for prey.

Rowan and the others scrambled back, leaving the predators a clear path to the guards. Tera hauled Lynniki along with her as Mellrea helped Allianne.

Tera snapped, "Go!"

The guards were preoccupied with the giant creatures now searching for their next meal, lured by the smell of blood.

Rowan didn't look back, ignoring the screams and snarls behind them as she followed Tera.

The captain led them swiftly out of sight of the noktum and the slaughter happening in its shadow. Rowan assumed Tera knew where she was going and let her mind go blank as they ran yet again. Her legs burned but not as much as her arm had burned when she'd held the lantern. Her skin seemed cold and numb in the absence of pain.

They followed a path across the valley that Tera and Mellrea seemed familiar with, avoiding the main road. As night fell, Tera led them to a darkened building at the edge of a dirt track. Another wayrest with a lean-to piled high with dry firewood and a couple of sealed barrels.

The windows were dark, but Tera checked inside first to be sure they were alone before gesturing them all into the building.

The interior reminded Rowan of the wayrest where Midge and her son had tried to steal the lantern, with shelves full of supplies and two cots in front of the fireplace.

Allianne collapsed on one of the cots as Mellrea went to toss a couple of logs into the fireplace.

Tera stopped her with a hand on her arm. "No fire. Not if Lord Hax's men are out looking for us."

"Why would they be?" Lynniki asked, voice short and succinct. She pulled her pack from her shoulders and dropped it beside the empty cot. "He got what he wanted this whole time."

Rowan collapsed against the closed door and slid down, covering her face with her hands.

"He has the lantern," she said into her palms. "Lord Hax has Gavyn and the lantern and my brother."

Tera cast a look at Mellrea. "That's bad enough, but also your father's under siege. You know Lord Hax will try to use the lantern against him."

"I'm sorry," Rowan whispered. "Healer's Ghost, if I could have talked to Darryn, made him understand. Now he has Gavyn, who will die in hours."

Lynniki stepped across to kneel in front of Rowan. "We'll get him back, Rowan."

"How?" She barked a laugh. "How, Lynniki? Are you going to traipse in there and ask him for it? Go ahead. Maybe you'll be better at it than I am. I can't even get my own brother to believe me."

She pushed herself up to stand, looming over Lynniki who remained kneeling.

"I can't *do* anything. Every time I try, I make things worse. I try to protect my family, and they think I'm a monster. I try to keep people safe from the Grief Draw, and I just let them take it! I held the lantern, and it hurt, but... for the first time I felt in control of something. Mellrea was right, the lantern's power is false. It's not worth the price."

Rowan's hands shook, and she stared at them. Still no blisters but the numbness was spreading in the absence of remembered pain.

"I used it, and I put Gavyn in even more danger than he was in before. If he'd just stayed down in that laboratory, who knows how long he would have lasted. Years more? Decades?"

"You couldn't have known—"

"I could have found out! I could have waited until we knew more before using it. Now Gavyn's nearly dead, and my brother might be next!"

Rowan put her hands to her cheeks, her cold palms shocking against her flushed skin. "The lantern went out right as we crossed from the noktum. It's used up all the power from the treasure hunter. Gavyn is next, and after that it will look for another source of power. Darryn is the closest. If he even lives that long after holding the lantern."

Rowan spun for the door and pushed through it, out into the night. None of them tried to stop her.

There was nothing outside for her, save for an expanse of dark plains almost as gray and featureless as the noktum. But at least the others weren't staring at her, the author of all their problems.

So much pain. The first thing she'd set out to do was keep the lantern from hurting Esrell or Darryn. And she'd failed on both counts.

What was she supposed to do now? Walk away? Go home and tell Nora and Stefan that Darryn would be the next victim of the Grief Draw? She could just leave Lord Hax to break down the walls of Lord Karaval's keep. It was a squabble between barons anyway. She didn't belong in it.

Except she was the reason Lord Hax was such a threat now. How much damage could he do before the lantern killed him?

And Gavyn…

She sat on the bare ground throwing her arms over her head to quiet the screeching of her thoughts. Her back ached, but it was an easy pain after the lantern.

The racing guilt made her breath come faster and faster, and she had to concentrate on breathing. In and out. Slow, so she didn't pass out.

The lantern case at her hip hung flat and empty, and she tore her belt off to fling it across the ground. The last few fire charges spilled out, and a bottle of ink popped its cork and poured a dark stain into the dirt.

If the Delvers had just taken the lantern like she'd asked, none of this would have happened. If anyone else had found the lantern, they wouldn't have been able to figure out how to make it work, and so many people would have been safe from her decisions.

She'd felt so lost after running from Jannik, like a kite with its string cut. And that was the truth of her. That was truer than the confidence she'd felt while fighting in the noktum. Control was an illusion.

Moonlight glinted from the sad, little pile of fire charges and ink. Rowan's brow drew down, and she pulled out a polished, wooden ring from among the clay disks.

Gavyn's ring. *I nearly forgot about that.*

Bits of warmth flared under her fingertips. Memories trapped in the wood, over a century old now. Once she'd thought to use it to see who Gavyn had been. She knew him so well now, but her heart ached with missing his voice, and then, before she could think better of it, she let the spark behind her eyes seek the memory, connecting with the touchpoint on the ring.

Black surrounded her like the noktum before an image formed. A blurred view of the lantern in its stasis spell down in the laboratory. Hands reached for the gleaming metal as if casting a spell.

Gavyn's hands. This could have been when the treasure hunter forced him to work with the lantern. To make it safe for others to use. Or it could have been the moment when Gavyn tried to destroy it by thrusting as much magic into it as he could.

Rowan's eyes burned. He'd been through so much already by then, but still he'd tried to destroy the lantern in order to keep anyone else from misusing it. To keep Keinwen and all the other mages like her safe.

He'd lived for so long with so much of his life in shambles. He'd endured death and loss and a powerless half-life. He'd lived trapped, forced to watch others around him repeat mistakes over and over with no voice and no power to change anything.

But *still* he was strong. Not in the way Rowan had always thought of strength. His strength came from his endurance. From being tested past the breaking point and surviving regardless.

Rowan could recognize it because she'd endured too. She'd carried pain her entire life. Even now, her twisted spine sent aches down her back and legs. She'd carried her family's unspoken disappointment. She'd carried the label "godsblighted" and the villagers' loathing and that little bit of doubt that maybe she really had done something to earn all this. That she wasn't who she was supposed to be.

That was what made her so good at carrying the lantern.

She scrubbed her hands down her cheeks, rubbing away the guilt and the anger to make room for clarity.

If I'd left the lantern in the laboratory, Gavyn would still be down there slowly dying. He'd never have seen the sun again or spoken to anyone or learned Keinwen's fate.

If I hadn't found the lantern, Lynniki would still be in the Delver city, feeling stifled and frustrated and like no one believed in her.

If I hadn't learned how to use the lantern, Mellrea and Allianne would have eventually died in the noktum. Tera and Lord Karaval would never have known what happened to them.

Darryn thought Rowan's weakness had driven her to steal something powerful, but really her weakness had shown her she was the one to carry it.

She'd made mistakes, yes. But there was no one better suited to bear the lantern, and the pain it brought, than her. She could handle the burning when she touched it. She could handle the mistrust and misunderstanding from others. She'd done all that before.

She'd stepped into the noktum and survived. She knew what it was like to keep going when everything hurt.

She knew pain. It didn't scare her.

There's still work to be done.

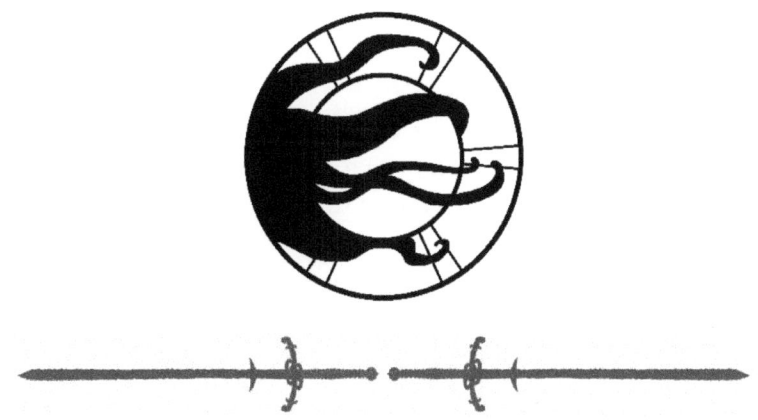

CHAPTER FORTY-ONE

ROWAN

She pushed back into the wayrest, steeling herself to meet everyone's gaze. Tera and Mellrea sat with their heads together. Allianne rested with a fresh bandage around her middle. Lynniki squatted on the floor, her finds from the noktum spread around her while the construct that was supposed to be Gavyn's body shuffled around the corners.

"I'm sorry," she said to all of them, but she made sure to hold Lynniki's gaze. "You've done nothing but help me so far, and I yelled at you for it. I'm angry, but not at you, and you didn't deserve that."

Tera and Mellrea were silent for a moment, and Rowan held her breath before Tera finally snorted.

"Your brother would make me yell too," she said. "Seems like a habit with him."

Rowan's mouth twitched. "There's a reason I used to call him Little Beast." Her gaze shifted to Mellrea and Allianne.

Mellrea shrugged. "I know nothing of siblings, but you were the one to pull us from the noktum. I think that earns at least a little tolerance."

Lynniki still didn't look up. The Delver's hands fiddled with one of the pieces she'd picked up in the villa, a black, metal rod with lines etched into it, spiraling from the base to the tip.

Rowan knelt beside her.

Lynniki's lips thinned. "I don't have time for dramatics. I need to know if you're going to follow through with whatever we come up with next. I promised to get Gavyn a new body, and time is running out to make that happen."

"I'm in this till the end," Rowan said. "No more dramatics. We work until he's rescued, and that's it."

Lynniki gave her a grim smile. "Then you're forgiven. Let's make this work."

"Sneaking into Lord Hax's camp is suicide," Tera said. "You're crazy."

"Well, we can't let him use the lantern against Lord Karaval, so we have to get it back. Now rather than later. I don't know if you've noticed, but we don't exactly have an army to wrest it away from him so sneaking it is." Rowan cocked her head at Tera. "You'll just have to work to give me every advantage you can."

Tera's eyes narrowed. "Like what?"

Rowan unhooked the pouch from her belt, which she'd retrieved. It rattled. She tossed it to Tera. "This is a war, right? Make Lord Hax think he's under attack."

She frowned and pulled open the drawstring, then poured the last of Rowan's pilfered fire charges into her palm.

Tera sighed. "All right, fine. I can make enough noise to draw his attention for maybe a few minutes. What then? You'll be caught almost immediately."

"The point isn't to avoid capture," Lynniki said. "Just to avoid capture long enough to use this on Gavyn and the lantern." She held up the stone with the inset gem that she'd brought from the Delver city.

"The soul anchor," Rowan said. "Will it work now?"

Lynniki's lips thinned. "There's only one way to know."

Mellrea rolled her eyes. "We're risking everything by sneaking into an army's fortified position just so you can 'test' your theory?"

"It's not like I have any other subjects to try it on," Lynniki snapped. "Unless you happen to have a hundred-year-old mage trapped in *your* pocket."

Mellrea held up her hands to concede the point.

"I'm not a mage," Lynniki said, shoulders sagging. "I can only adapt the magic that I find to work with the things I can build." She held up her metal hand and wiggled her fingers.

"We don't have a choice," Rowan said. "Either we transfer Gavyn out of the lantern, rendering it inert, or we smash the lenses so at the very least Lord Hax can't use them. Either way, we have to get close enough."

"What happens after Gavyn is freed?" Allianne said quietly. She still lay on the cot just behind Mellrea's shoulder. "Or gods forbid, he's completely consumed? Won't the lantern seek another power source? How do we keep people safe?"

"The lantern goes after whoever is nearest, right?" Lynniki said, turning the stone over and over in her hands. "So, we just make sure that when we make the switch the only people nearby are the ones we don't like."

Rowan coughed while Mellrea and Allianne looked at Lynniki in horror.

"You're not serious," Allianne said.

"I'm just saying, Lord Hax seems like a great candidate," Lynniki muttered to herself.

"No, we have to keep it from consuming anyone," Rowan said. "That's the point. The Grief Draw must be inert so no one can use it."

"Well, you two are Delvers," Mellrea said. "Or at least mostly. You'll be safe. If you're the only ones around, then it should be safe enough to transfer Gavyn out. But afterward, anyone who comes near will be forfeit."

"Is there any reason to keep it?" Allianne asked. "I mean, I'm grateful for what you've done with it so far, but…"

"But now that you two are out of the noktum, it seems like more trouble than its worth," Tera said. "We should destroy it."

Rowan swallowed against the sudden dryness in her throat. The main reason she hadn't wanted to smash it had been Gavyn, but if they managed to rescue Gavyn was it worth keeping the lantern? In its inert state, it would always be looking for the next Human life to drain. It would be even more dangerous than it was already.

"It's a fitting tribute to all the people it's consumed or killed," Rowan said slowly. "To make sure it can never do so again."

"I say take a hammer to it." Mellrea raised her chin. "I'll bet Lynniki has one you can use."

Lynniki winced. "If you must, but it hurts me to see anything useful broken."

"Friends," Allianne said from her cot. "Destroying it is the goal, of course, but according to the plan so far, Rowan and Lynniki are still stuck in Lord Hax's camp. Even if they manage to transfer Gavyn, they will never get away before he captures them."

Mellrea blew out her breath and ran a hand over her head. "That's where I can help."

"What are you planning?" Tera asked.

"If I can get to my father, and if you can guarantee the lantern is out of the picture, then we can make that diversion attack a reality. We'll ride in and break Lord Hax and his army into a thousand pieces."

Lynniki tapped her lip. "Um, how are you going to get to him? Isn't that the point of a siege? No one in or out."

"There's always another way in besides the front door," Mellrea said with a laugh. "Nobles don't like feeling trapped."

"Hmm," Lynniki said. "Neither do Delvers."

Tera shook her head and surveyed them all sitting in the darkened wayrest. "This is crazy."

"Oh, come on," Rowan said with a grin. "Don't pretend you don't want to take on Lord Hax and his army single-handedly."

Tera sighed but then a grin tugged at her lips. "All right, I won't." She cracked her knuckles.

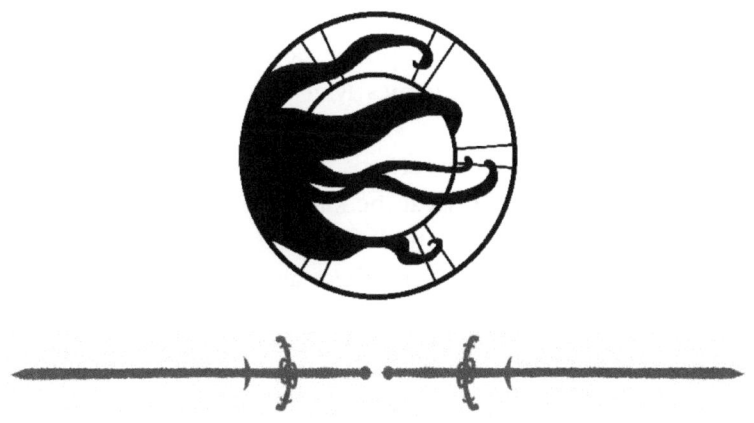

CHAPTER FORTY-TWO

ROWAN

Lynniki and Rowan waited at the edge of Lord Hax's camp, watching for the guard walking the perimeter. Tera had gotten them there, pointed to the ground like directing a dog to sit, and then disappeared into the night to guide Mellrea and Allianne to the other side of Lord Hax's camp.

She'd also spent the last few hours traveling back to edge of the noktum to retrieve the uniforms of Lord Hax's dead guards. She hadn't said much when she got back, but what she'd handed them was a few pieces of tattered surcoats and some chainmail that they could cobble together into two uniforms between them. Rowan guessed there hadn't been much left after the creatures of the noktum were done.

"I will never pass for a Human, let alone a soldier," Lynniki had said, eyeing the uniforms dubiously.

"No, but you might pass for a messenger. Some of them are very young." Tera had tilted her head. "So long as you don't get too close to anyone. Ideally, they'd be nearsighted too."

The point was just to get them close to the lantern. Tera's distraction would hopefully take care of anyone else.

Rowan fought the urge to fidget as she lay flat in the grass just beyond the perimeter where Tera promised the guard would appear. Behind the line, campfires glowed between rows and rows of tents. A sea of enemies lying between them and Lord Karaval's keep.

It couldn't be the thousands that it seemed. Lord Hax couldn't keep an army to rival the king's, or he would have been fined into poverty long before this—if the king even let him live. But the troops that lay between them and their only ally seemed like plenty to Rowan.

Lynniki breathed quietly next to her, the bronze construct ducked down beside her.

"There," Lynniki whispered.

A shadow, dark against the glow of campfires, marched into view. The guard paused and looked out over the plains where they waited.

"Don't kill any guards. It'll leave a hole in Lord Hax's perimeter," Tera had warned. "Someone will notice. You're sneaking in, not bashing your way in."

Rowan held her breath and made sure her head was below the screening grass.

Then the shadow turned and moved on, continuing his rounds.

"Now," Rowan said.

She and Lynniki stood and hurried forward, bent low and moving as quietly as they could. Lynniki carried the construct under her arm, swathed in a blanket. She'd found some grease in the wayrest and insisted the joints wouldn't squeak anymore, but the shiny, brass amalgam of gears was still too conspicuous to let it wander around by itself, so she carried it.

Beyond the perimeter of guards, they plunged between rows of tents. Here they stood straight and walked like they had a purpose, counting on the fact that it was the middle of the night before battle. Hardly anyone was awake except those soldiers standing guard, and they avoided the pools of light around the campfires.

Time seemed to tick away in Rowan's head. They only had so long before Tera started her distraction and they had to be in place. Which meant they had to get close enough to the lantern for Rowan to hear Gavyn.

She aimed them toward the center of the camp where Lord Hax was most likely to be, and every so often she stopped to whisper, "Gavyn?"

It felt silly to call for someone so far away, but Gavyn had heard her before in Lord Karaval's keep. She just had to be close enough.

"Gavyn?"

"Who's there?" Not Gavyn's voice. A soldier stood up from the nearest campfire and turned toward them.

Rowan and Lynniki ducked behind a tent, and Rowan held her breath. Footsteps approached.

Lynniki plunged a hand in her pocket before flicking her wrist and tossing something away down the row of tents.

It clattered against a crate, and the soldier turned toward it.

They slipped by, and Rowan waited another five breaths before whispering to Lynniki. "What was that?"

"Spare gear," the Delver said. "It's always worth it to carry an extra."

"Rowan?" *Finally.* Finally Gavyn's voice came into her head, sounding weary and faint.

Rowan swallowed down a surge of relief that made her legs shake. There'd been a persistent nagging at the back of her mind telling her that Gavyn was already gone, consumed by the lantern in his final, prolonged death.

"You won't believe how glad I am to hear you," she said, casting Lynniki a relieved grin. "Guess what we're doing."

There was a pause. "No. Rowan, you cannot come get me."

"Too late. You just need to tell me where you are, and we'll come to the rescue."

"There are guards everywhere—"

"I'm sure there are. Tera's distraction should take care of those."

"Lord Hax is right next door—"

"Not for long."

"You'll be captured."

"That's kind of the point."

Gavyn laughed helplessly in the back of her head, and she wouldn't trade that little undercurrent of hope for all the certainty in the world. "This is ridiculous, you know."

"I know. This is the last time I'm rescuing you, and that's a promise."

He caught the tone of her words and went quiet.

"Now where are you? We're running out of time here."

"Beside Lord Hax's tent. He's near the cook tent and the armorer. There's a crimson standard flying from the peak."

"Coming," she said. It wasn't hard to follow the smells of burning porridge. Clearly, the cook was already hard at work ruining breakfast for the army before they tried to break Lord Karaval out of his keep.

A hammer rang against an anvil beside the cook tent, and Rowan finally saw Lord Hax's standard flying from the peak of canvas behind it.

They avoided the front, where the cook and the blacksmith worked, and sneaked around behind.

Here was Lord Hax's tent with the crimson standard, and beside it…

She would have asked Gavyn if he was on the right or left, but she could see a cold white light coming from under the canvas on the right.

"Gavyn, I thought the light went out in the noktum," she whispered. There were barrels stacked at the back of the cook tent, and she and Lynniki hunkered down beside them.

"It did. It… came back. I can't turn it off. Believe me, I tried."

So he could stay alive longer.

"I'm sorry." It must have been switching between the treasure hunter and Gavyn. That moment when Gavyn had said he was fine, he'd been lying.

"We're here. And it shouldn't be long now."

"Long until wha—"

A boom echoed across the plains from the direction of the keep.

Rowan exchanged a grin with Lynniki. "Until Tera takes on Lord Hax and his entire army."

"What?" Gavyn cried.

"Just wait."

Gavyn had been right before. You could only live in terror for so long before you stopped feeling it entirely. A flippant confidence rose in her, and Rowan chuckled as she watched the faint glow of flames rise from the north, orange and red flickering against the walls of the distant keep.

Cries rose from the sentinels at the front and spread through the tents until soldiers poured out into the walkways between the canvas walls. A hundred footsteps echoed around them, heading for the edge of camp, where the fire raged.

Lynniki and Rowan pressed their backs against the barrels and held their breath as booted feet made the ground rumble.

"Gavyn?" Rowan whispered. "What about the guards?"

He laughed, voice incredulous. "They've gone. What did you guys do?"

The moment there was a break in the noise of the soldiers, Rowan peeked around a barrel. "Now," she said.

And they slipped across the way into the tent.

This was a space meant to house one thing. There were no bedrolls or camp chairs or packs. Nothing except a table for the Grief Draw.

Rowan rushed to grab it. It sent a wash of pain up her arm the moment she touched the handle, and she sighed in a strange sort of relief to feel it again.

"Are you all right?" she asked Gavyn as she checked that each of the lenses was intact and still in place. Nothing seemed broken or misplaced.

"You always ask me that," Gavyn said, and his voice had gained its old strength. "And I always say the same thing."

"As all right as you can be as a disembodied voice trapped in a piece of metal and glass?"

"Something like that."

Lynniki knelt on the bare ground and set down her construct. She pulled the soul anchor from the black metal clamps.

"Are you ready, Gavyn?" she asked, staring at the stone.

"You'd think that would be a stupid question, but does it make any sense that I'm nervous?"

"Considering your last hundred years or so, I'd be nervous too," Rowan said. "But don't worry. Lynniki knows what she's doing."

Lynniki barked a laugh.

"Ready or not, we have to try it now, before anyone comes close," Rowan said.

"Right. Give me a moment."

"Before anyone comes close?" Gavyn said.

"We have to get you out, but once we do, the lantern will look for its next power source. Lynniki and I should be safe as Delvers, but anyone else—"

"Will just be sucked dry and power the thing up again."

"Right. And before that happens—well, our best plan is to smash it."

Gavyn choked. Despite having no throat or lungs.

"Are you all right?"

"Yes, it's just… that's what I died trying to do. To finally see it done…"

Lynniki propped the soul anchor against the lantern. "All right," she muttered. "Let's see if this works."

She traced the edge of the stone, outlining a pattern of lines Rowan hadn't noticed before. Lynniki might not have magic, but the Giants did, and this was more like a fire charge. Something a mage had created, and anyone could use with the right combination of tools.

"Should they really be touching?" Rowan whispered. Two powerful objects in such close proximity made her nervous.

"Well, normally I'd have the person hold the soul anchor. But…"

"Right, no hands. All right. Carry on."

Lynniki turned the gem in the stone until lines etched into its surface lined up with the pattern along the edge. The whole thing lit up, and Lynniki flinched back, like she was expecting something big.

Rowan opened her mouth to ask what was supposed to happen, but there was a flare of light and a sizzle. The wood of the table started to smoke.

Lynniki yelped and snatched up the soul anchor. A square of scorched wood sizzled beside the lantern, and Rowan's nose burned with the stench.

"Oops," Lynniki said.

Rowan's breath hissed through her teeth. "What do you mean 'oops'? It didn't work? What happened?"

"I told you it might not," Lynniki whispered back. "That was only the first test. You can't expect me to get something completely new right on the first try. That's not science, that's luck."

She set the soul anchor down and crouched to rummage through her pack, pulling out some of the odds and ends she'd brought from the noktum. She stood and balanced the black rod with the etchings on top of the soul anchor.

"I'll try again. I don't know how many more chances we'll have at this."

"None," Darryn's voice said from the tent flap.

Rowan gasped and spun. Lynniki snatched up the soul anchor before it could activate again, and Rowan loved her for that one little damning gesture.

It meant their failure, but it also meant Darryn's life.

"Darryn," Rowan said, voice weary. She didn't even have the energy to be angry at him anymore.

"I can't believe you," Darryn said. "You would risk your life to come back for this thing just so you can take it away from me. Do you care about this power so much that you would betray me and Jannik for it? That's not like you, Rowan. I don't know what happened to you."

"You're right," Rowan said, meeting his eyes. "It doesn't make sense, does it?"

Darryn's eyes narrowed.

"A lot of what Jannik says about me doesn't make sense. When would I ever steal anything from you or him, for that matter? All I ever cared about was you and Esrell. But you'd rather believe that I threw all that away for some sort of weapon? Why would I care about that?"

"It makes you strong," Darryn said. "You've never been strong before."

"I've always been strong," Rowan snapped. "It's not my fault you can't see it."

"And now you have a wealthy patron. What did he give you for it?"

"Nothing."

His eyes narrowed.

"I made a deal with Lord Karaval to find his daughter because family is all he cares about too. He didn't give me anything for it. You're the only one who keeps bringing up money, Darryn."

He snorted and crossed his arms.

Rowan sighed, swallowing down all the arguments that crowded her throat. None of them had worked. "I'm done, Darryn. All right? I'll never stop trying to protect you. Even from your own stupid decisions, but I'm done trying to get you to listen to me. Because in the end, how you feel about me changes nothing about how I feel about you."

Darryn's face went stricken, and he took a step back as if he couldn't help it.

Rowan gestured to Lynniki who packed the soul anchor back away. Then Rowan grabbed the lantern's handle.

"I'm not letting you go," Darryn said.

"Oh, I know," Rowan said. "I didn't expect you to believe me this time either. I wish I knew what I did to you to make you think I'm such a horrible person."

Darryn flushed. "Running off with the lantern without saying anything the first time was a pretty good start."

Rowan nodded. "I did do that, but I've told you why."

Darryn shook his head. "It was stupid to come here. You were supposed to be the smart one, but here you've gotten yourself caught."

Lynniki huffed a quiet laugh, and Rowan gave him a sad smile. "Getting caught was always the plan."

By now, Mellrea would have gotten back to her father, and Lord Karaval would be leading the real attack. Any moment now the charge would sound, and he'd come riding through Lord Hax's line. Since Rowan currently held the lantern, she wouldn't let them use it against him. She'd defend herself and Gavyn if she had to.

She raised her chin and smiled at Darryn.

He stared back at her, lips pulling tight in an uncertain frown.

Then the tent flap flipped back, and Lord Hax stepped inside, Mellrea dangling from his grip.

CHAPTER FORTY-THREE

ROWAN

I knew this was a badly executed feint," Lord Hax said as Rowan's breath froze in her chest. He shook Mellrea, who barely kept her feet on the ground since he held her by her collar. He carried her sword in his other hand. The chain with the spiked ball was wrapped around his waist, but a bloody bruise spread up Mellrea's neck as if she'd been struck with the weapon once already.

She glared at him, fists bound ineffectually in front of her.

Rowan clutched the lantern with both hands as if that might keep him from yanking it away from her. Lynniki crouched beside the table making herself as small as possible.

Jannik squeezed into the tent beside his lord, blinking between Rowan and Lord Hax.

"I knew this one would go crawling back to hide behind her father if given half a chance. Luckily, we knew where to look." He cast a glance at Jannik. "Have we found the one who set the flames yet?"

"No, my lord," Jannik said.

Rowan and Mellrea exchanged a swift look. At least they hadn't caught Tera in all the confusion she'd caused, but where was Allianne? She'd been with Mellrea, last Rowan knew.

"Traitor," Mellrea said, jerking her head around to snarl at Jannik.

He flinched. "My dear, you don't understand. Yours is not the only family at stake. I finally have the chance to make up for my great-grandfather's failure. Lord Hax's promises—"

"You're right, I don't understand. I don't understand how someone so smart can be so dumb."

Lord Hax shoved Mellrea, and she fell to her knees, catching herself with her bound hands. Rowan just kept herself from reaching to catch her, but she had to keep her grip on the lantern. If she could just find an opening, maybe she could activate one of the lenses and get them all out of this. But she'd have to be fast. Faster even than she'd been in the noktum.

"Your knowledge of the family let me catch this one," Lord Hax told Jannik. "You'll get everything I've promised after the siege. Help ensure my success, and you will be my personal scholar, with all the comforts that entails."

"You know you have my loyalty, my lord," Jannik said, eyes downcast.

"At least now we've made up for *your* mistake," Lord Hax said to Darryn. "For letting Lord Karaval's daughter escape the first time."

"I didn't know she was a noble," Darryn protested. "I didn't know you would want to capture her."

Lord Hax's lips thinned. "That's the problem with promoting farmers."

Darryn flushed a dark red but bit his tongue against any more arguments.

"Have you figured out how to use the lantern yet? Your crippled sister managed that already; surely you can best her."

Rowan's teeth clenched so hard they creaked, but inside, a tiny spark of hope caught fire. They didn't know how to activate the lenses.

"I figured out how to hold it without danger. That's more than Rowan managed." He held up his left hand, and Rowan realized it was gauntleted from finger to elbow in overlapping plates of iron. Sloppy work compared to Lynniki's deft craftsmanship, but if he wasn't getting blisters or feeling ill from the effects of the lantern, then clearly it worked.

Rowan's thought kept getting caught on the fact that Darryn had bothered with the gauntlet in the first place. He must have listened to her at least a little. Or remembered what happened to Esrell when she'd held it. Maybe she hadn't been screaming into the darkness for no reason.

Lord Hax frowned at Darryn. "Hardly impressive when we're ready to march on Lord Karaval and press the advantage. I have the Grief Draw. I have his daughter. It's time to make the man beg."

Mellrea pushed up on her knees and spat at Lord Hax.

His face remained passive and serene as he backhanded her with the hilt of her own sword.

Rowan cried out as Mellrea sprawled unconscious across the ground.

Lord Hax turned on Rowan, and she backed up a step, running into the table. Her fingers tightened on the lantern. She'd smash it. She'd sacrifice Gavyn if it meant keeping Lord Hax from using the Grief Draw. It would mean all of their deaths, because she couldn't imagine him leaving any of them alive after that.

"Maybe I have everything I need after all," Lord Hax said, thoughtfully. "I have my enemy's daughter, and I have someone who can use the lantern."

Rowan's stomach clenched. He thought he could threaten her into activating the lenses? She swallowed. Was she ready to destroy it? Smash it into a million pieces and consign them all to death.

She raised the lantern to stare into its light.

"Rowan?" Gavyn said in the back of her head.

She took a deep breath and lowered it again. Not yet.

She exchanged a look with Lynniki. The construct wasn't anywhere to be seen. Lynniki must have sent it out the back of the tent while everyone was distracted with Mellrea.

She hoped the Delver could call it back, because their only choice now was to find a way to transfer Gavyn and destroy the lantern. Hopefully before Lord Hax took down Lord Karaval's walls.

● ● ●

Lord Hax gestured to Darryn. "Keep a hand on her. If she escapes now, it'll only add to your debt."

Rowan's lips thinned as Darryn grasped her shoulder.

"Don't make this harder for me," he hissed in her ear.

Lord Hax barked an order out the tent opening, and two guards appeared. One slung Mellrea over his shoulder, and the other headed for Lynniki.

Lynniki held out her hands to appear as non-threatening as possible. The guard rummaged through her pack but apparently didn't make much of the bits of brass and copper she'd stashed in there because he returned it to her with a shrug, though he did strip the hammers from their holders on the outside. They might not look like weapons, but she could still cave in a head with one.

Lynniki smiled at the guard, her grin showing off way too many teeth to be friendly. Rowan didn't envy the guard if Lynniki got her hands on another hammer.

Lord Hax swept out of the tent, Jannik scurrying behind him. Darryn prodded Rowan into movement, and she stumbled forward, hands clutched around the lantern.

"Well, unfortunately this seems to be a step in the wrong direction," Gavyn said dryly.

"Just wait." Rowan kept her eyes straight forward as her thoughts raced. She just had to find an opening. She could still make this work, still find a way to free Gavyn. And if she could get away from the rest of them, she could do it without hurting Darryn.

She watched Mellrea's head sway over the guard's shoulder and glanced back at Lynniki. The Delver shuffled forward, her hands working at something Rowan couldn't see.

Jannik trotted in Lord Hax's footsteps.

Rowan's chest tightened, and her stomach clenched. Every kind word in her memory, every encouraging smile her mentor had given her was overlaid by the look on his face as he'd struck her. His intelligence and his enthusiasm were overshadowed by the lies he'd spread about her and the way he'd turned her family and her village against her.

She'd respected him once. She'd cared about his opinion more than anyone else's, including her parents.

"You know using the lantern will kill Gavyn, right?" she told him. The guards around them gave her funny looks, but Jannik's shoulders stiffened.

"It's powered by Human life. It's consuming him right now, and when it's done, it will drain someone else and kill them in the process."

Jannik said nothing. She couldn't see his expression from this angle, but his shoulders remained tensed.

"I used to respect you," she said quietly. "I used to think you knew everything and cared about more than just power and money. Cared about people."

"That young man we found died over a hundred years ago," Jannik said. "If he's taken this long to fade, then hurrying his final death along is nothing more than a blessing."

"Thanks," Gavyn said. "And your ancestor is still a murderer."

"What about whoever the lantern consumes next?" Rowan said. "It could be you or Lord Hax or anyone here." She flung out a hand, and the nearest guard startled away from her.

Finally, Jannik turned his head enough for her to see his face. His lips were white where they were pulled tight in disapproval.

"You seem to think I'm a villain, Rowan, but the dangers you describe just aren't that bad," he said. "Lord Hax is a powerful patron, and his support makes my work possible. I'm not going to destroy that partnership over one or two lives."

Rowan reared back at this, and Darryn pinched her shoulder to keep her moving.

It wasn't that Jannik didn't believe her. At least not anymore. He believed her, and he didn't care.

She caught Lord Hax smirking at her over his shoulder at her. "Well, my dear," he said. "You got what you came for." He gestured at the lantern burning in her hands. "I hope you are prepared to use it."

He stopped walking, and his guards halted with him.

Rowan raised her gaze with a start. They'd reached the edge of camp.

The fires had been quenched, but Rowan could still see blackened pits in the grass around them and scorch marks that stretched on either side. Ahead of them stood the army, called from their beds early and now arrayed in orderly lines on the flood plain outside Lord Karaval's keep.

The river stood dry, leaving a flat, open path to the walls of the city, which rose against the dawn. At the top of the hill, the keep itself stood silhouetted on the vivid pink and orange sky. Armor and weapons gleamed on the battlements, signs of Lord Karaval's preparation.

Lynniki worked away, head down. Rowan was on her own to distract Lord Hax. Delay him until Lynniki could get the soul anchor to work.

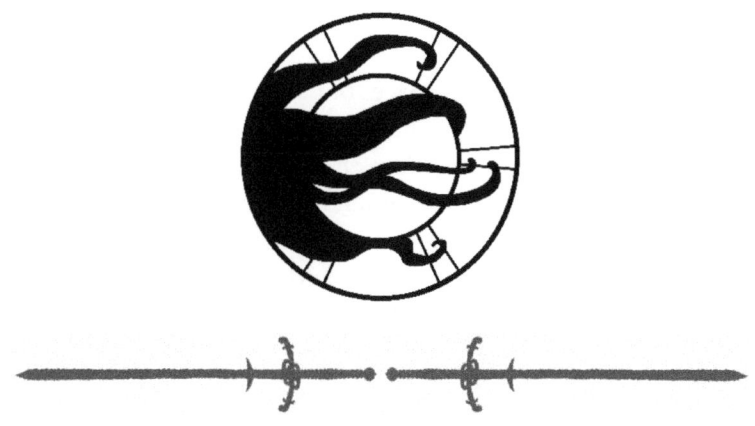

CHAPTER FORTY-FOUR

ROWAN

ord Hax directed the guard to toss Mellrea on the ground right there in the grass. She tumbled to one of the blackened spots.

Rowan's teeth clenched. "Be careful," she said.

Lord Hax cocked his head. "Her safety is squarely in your hands, lantern bearer." He gestured and the guard dumped a waterskin over Mellrea's head.

She spluttered and came up gasping, struggling to sit up with both hands tied.

A soldier in gleaming armor rode up to them and saluted Lord Hax. "We are in position, my lord."

"Sound the attack. We break Lord Karaval open today."

Mellrea shook her head to clear it and looked out at the army in dawning horror.

The soldier rode away, and Lord Hax turned to watch as horns blared and the army advanced across the dry flood plain.

A rumbling from behind made Rowan spin. Three siege engines rolled across the plains, pulled by teams of oxen, and the soldiers parted for them, letting the great catapults arrange themselves before the walls.

Lord Hax grabbed Mellrea's dark hair and pulled her head back. Her lips pulled in a grimace, but she remained silent.

Rowan hissed through her teeth.

Lord Hax met her eyes. "Aim the weapon at the walls."

Rowan couldn't help the bitter mocking laugh that left her lips. "You haven't been paying attention. It's not a weapon."

He yanked Mellrea's head back and lowered her own sword to her throat. "Lying will not save your friend."

"Stop," Rowan cried. "I'm not the one who's lying here. I have no reason to."

Lord Hax's eyes narrowed. "You think someone here is lying?"

"I think you're very intimidating, and it's in people's natures to protect themselves as much as they can."

"Stop wasting time."

"Who promised you a weapon in the first place?" she snapped back. "Who has the most to lose if he doesn't deliver on his promise?"

Beyond Lord Hax, the army advanced. The first catapult fired, and a boulder cracked against the thick walls. Mellrea winced.

Lynniki stood with her head down, hands concealing her work in front of her. She didn't look up.

"Just keep him talking," Gavyn said.

Lord Hax turned his eyes on Jannik.

"My lord," Jannik said, glaring at Rowan. "You already—"

"Jannik knew the lantern wasn't a weapon. Mellrea told him ages ago. I told him when we found it. But he needed to deliver what he'd promised, so he told you I stole a powerful artifact and sent you scrambling after me to save his own skin."

Jannik flushed a deep red as Lord Hax scowled.

"If it's not a weapon then why do you keep claiming it kills people? You can't have it both ways."

"Just because it's not designed for killing doesn't mean it's not dangerous. It hurts the one holding it. It's not something you can fire or stab with."

Rowan fought not to flinch at the distant booms and cries from soldiers. The men at the gate carried a battering ram, and it echoed across the valley.

"The metal it's made of is poisonous to Humans. That's why you can't touch it."

Lord Hax's scowl deepened. "Then what does it do? Why were the Giants so afraid of it?"

Well, he'd paid attention to at least some of its lore then. Either Jannik had told him, or he'd come to his own conclusions in Blackfall.

"Its power is knowledge," Rowan said. "The Giants used it to spy on one another. They used it to gather information about their enemies, and the one who has knowledge beyond the ordinary is the one who has the power."

Lord Hax smiled, lips pulled tight across his teeth. "Then what knowledge can you give me? You found the lenses. You've been using them. What do they tell you?"

Rowan's heartbeat sped up with every word she wove. None of it was a lie. *Yet.* She wanted to be very careful about lying to this man.

"One is a map," she said. "It shows the lay of the land and where people are. Another is… I don't know how to describe it."

"Try."

She raised her chin. "It shows weaknesses and strengths. Where to strike and what to avoid."

"There," he said. "That wasn't so hard, was it? Now. Activate it and show me where to strike Lord Karaval."

Rowan huffed in indignation. "That's not how it works. You can't see what the lantern shows me."

"Then tell me where to strike."

"It's more complicated than that. I can't just turn it on and see. I would need time to figure out what I'm looking at."

Lord Hax drew a line across Mellrea's cheek with the tip of her sword. She screamed.

"Stop making excuses and tell me. I know you're stalling. Try it again, and she dies."

Rowan cried out, "I'm not—"

He shook his head and pulled Mellrea up by the hair. He laid her sword across her throat. "First this one, then I cut the Delver too."

"Wait," Mellrea choked out. "There's a spot on the bottom of the southwest wall."

Rowan froze. What was Mellrea thinking?

Lord Hax looked down. "What did you say?"

Mellrea knelt there, eyes closed as blood dripped down her cheek. "She's not the only one who knows weaknesses. There's a spot on the bottom of the southwest wall. A tree grew into the mortar from the other side and cracked it all the way from the bottom to the top. We never got around to fixing it."

Lord Hax sniffed. "Jannik said you were smart to see you're outmanned."

He turned to issue an order to a runner standing nearby. The boy darted off to relay his orders.

Rowan stared at Mellrea. *What did she gain by giving Lord Hax the advantage?* She couldn't think of anything except that she didn't have to use the lantern right away. Giving Gavyn more time.

Maybe Mellrea was thinking of Allianne, plunging into the noktum to save a stranger.

The young woman raised her head to meet Rowan's eyes, blood running along her jaw to drip into the dry earth.

"Get him out," she mouthed. "Smash it."

She gave Mellrea a jerky little nod and glanced at Lynniki.

The Delver didn't look up from her hands, but her lips moved as if in a chant. "Almost, almost, almost."

A crack echoed across the valley. Then another and another. And a rumble made the ground at their feet vibrate.

Lord Hax's men raised a cheer that sent a shaft of ice down Rowan's spine.

Across the undulating sea of soldiers, the wall crumbled under the onslaught of the siege engines, sending cut stone tumbling across the grass below.

Mellrea stared at the destruction, face grim and tight.

Rowan's hands burned, a familiar pain, but it seeped into her mind, making her grit her teeth, her breath coming faster and faster. She wanted to use the Grief Draw in her hand. She wanted to turn it on Lord Hax while his back was turned and decimate his soldiers from behind.

But they'd never get through the entire army, even with everything the lantern could do, and Lord Karaval would not thank her for getting Mellrea killed now.

Lord Hax gave the signal to move out, and Darryn and the other guards prodded them toward the break in the wall where the army poured into the city.

CHAPTER FORTY-FIVE

ROWAN

Darryn and the guards dragged Rowan, Mellrea, and Lynniki over the broken tumbled wall into the city. Screams echoed down the streets as Lord Hax's soldiers marched up the cobblestones, chasing guards in Lord Karaval's colors.

That didn't mean Lord Hax's men had free rein of the city. Lord Karaval's soldiers retreated slowly, throwing up barricades in their wake, keeping Lord Hax's men from storming right up the hill.

Rowan's nose burned with the acrid scent of smoke and the tang of blood, and she coughed as Darryn hauled her over the last of the stones and down into the street.

Lord Hax hesitated at the edge of the road, staring right, then left.

Rowan saw her chance. "What? You're storming a city and you don't even know where to go from here?"

Lord Hax's heavy frown pinned her where she stood on the broken cobblestones. "That's where you come in, little lantern bearer. Show me the way to Lord Karaval."

Rowan pretended to hesitate for a moment, but Darryn's fingers dug into her shoulder.

"Do it," he hissed in her ear.

She yanked herself from his grasp with a glare. Then she stepped forward to the middle of the street. She didn't dare glance at Lynniki or Mellrea, trusting that they'd be watching for an opportunity as intensely as she was.

She took a deep breath and touched the cap of the lantern, but she didn't use the pattern to activate the map. She activated the starburst lens.

The light sprang into focus, flooding them all in a white glow interspersed with red and blue. Rowan didn't pause for another breath, and she didn't have a weapon to draw anyway. She sprang for the red smear across Lord Hax's middle, tucking her good shoulder into the soft spot just under his ribs and ramming all of her weight against him.

The air rushed from his lungs in a surprised oof, and he collapsed, too winded to yell.

Mellrea did it for him. She screamed a battle cry and leaped to wrench her sword from his shocked grasp. Her bound hands didn't seem to slow her as she swung around to cut down the guard who rushed to catch hold of her again.

Lynniki's guard started forward, but Lynniki dropped to the ground, tripping him. He fell with a grunt, and Lynniki spun and struck his head with a vicious kick. He went limp.

"What are you doing?" Darryn cried. He lunged forward, drawing his sword.

Rowan intercepted him, following the red glow to show her where to strike. She grabbed his free arm and brought it down against her hip. His elbow crunched, and he dropped his sword with a cry. She ducked under his arm as he swiped for her and grabbed his fallen sword. Then she swept his feet out from under him with the flat of the blade.

Rowan spun to find Jannik scuttling around the corner, away from the fighting. Lord Hax clambered to his feet, face red.

Mellrea drew back her sword, ready to charge.

The sound of boots rang from the broken wall mixed with the cries of soldiers, and Rowan changed to the map overlay which sprang out to show her Lord Hax's men approaching.

She jumped in front of Mellrea. "No, wait. We'll be surrounded in moments. Better to escape and destroy the lantern. Come on."

She couldn't grab Mellrea's arm, since she had the lantern in one hand and Darryn's sword in the other, but she crowded Mellrea back until the other woman finally relented and turned with a frustrated cry.

Lynniki was already at the mouth of an alley, gesturing to them frantically, and Mellrea and Rowan ducked after her.

Rowan took the lead, keeping an eye between the map and the streets around them. They kept to alleys and back roads, losing Lord Hax and his men behind them, pausing only to cut Mellrea's bonds.

"I can't believe that worked!" Gavyn crowed in her head as they ran. "You are a fiend, Rowan, and I love you for it!"

She huffed a laugh. "Thank you, I think. It won't be long now. We just have to find a clear place where we won't be interrupted. Then we can transfer you out and smash this thing for good."

"No arguments from me."

In fact, he sounded stronger than he had in days. Hope must have bolstered him. Especially since the lantern would be draining him directly now.

She would have stopped using the lenses to conserve what little time he had, but the map was the only thing keeping them from getting captured again.

Rowan stopped just before crossing another street. Groups of soldiers patrolled both ends. If she led them across, they'd be spotted for sure.

She swore under her breath.

"We need to split up," Mellrea said, peeking around the wall. "I can't be around when you transfer Gavyn anyway, right?"

"Right," Lynniki said.

"And I need to find Tera and my father."

Rowan bit her lip. "Do you think Tera's still alive?"

Mellrea jerked her chin up. "I'm not going to count her among the dead yet. If anyone could single-handedly take on Lord Hax's army, cause a diversion, and escape into the night, it would be her, and if she did, she'll be somewhere in the city, leading the defense."

"What happened to Allianne?" Rowan asked.

Mellrea smiled grimly. "I left her at the entrance of the back door, before I was caught. She was supposed to make her way to my father."

Rowan gulped and stared around the sacked city. "If Allianne had made it, wouldn't Lord Karaval have attacked Lord Hax, according to the original plan?"

Mellrea shook her head. "I knew the plan was messed up as soon as I saw Lord Hax. I told Allianne to tell Father to fortify his position."

"You think he'll be up at the keep?"

"Not anymore. He'll issue a challenge to Lord Hax, I'm sure of it. Something to stop this bloodshed before it kills too many of his people. I need to get to him." She pointed to the lantern. "And you need to destroy that."

"Let's quit talking about it then," Gavyn said.

"You get to your father," Rowan told Mellrea. "We'll do the rest."

Mellrea beamed and gave them a jaunty salute with her sword.

Then she stepped out into the street. She deliberately kicked a broken chunk of cobblestone, sending it clattering away down the road. There was a distant yell, and Mellrea turned to race away from Lord Hax's men.

Lynniki and Rowan ducked to avoid being seen as the troop clomped by, chasing Mellrea.

"I suppose that's one way to do it," Lynniki said. "Now, where are we going to do this?"

Rowan was already studying the map. "I don't know. There are people everywhere."

Lynniki frowned. "We just need a few clear minutes. It might not be ideal, but find a spot, and let's hurry."

Rowan blew out her breath. "All right. This way."

Another troop cut them off on the other side of the alley, and Rowan dragged Lynniki into a nearby building. From the stained vats, it was a dyeworks. Rowan almost stopped them there, but then she saw the flickers of light above them on the map. Someone was hiding upstairs. They didn't dare try to get Gavyn out here.

Nowhere was safe. And how far away did someone need to be to be out of range of the lantern's malevolent reach? They would just have to guess. Rowan hated guessing.

"Here," she said.

She'd stopped in an empty square. It was much more open and exposed than she liked, with streets leading in all directions, but the map showed a blank space around them for more than a hundred yards. That was the best she'd seen so far.

Lynniki slung down her pack and hauled out the soul anchor.

"Where's the construct?" Rowan asked. She set the lantern down on one of the stone benches that ringed the square. The cobbles ended at the edge of a patch of green in the center of the square where a statue of a horse reared in front of a flagpole. Any other time, it would have been a pretty spot.

"It's trying to find us. I made it plenty capable, but navigating a war is hard for anyone."

Rowan turned off the map and hesitated, her hand hovering over the lenses where they rested in their slots. Then, as quick as she could, she slid them up and out and stacked them, so they fit in the case at her hip.

"What are you doing?"

"I don't know. We have to destroy the lantern, but a part of me thinks that if we keep the lenses, we could find a way to use them someday. Without a Giant's artifact that does its best to kill people."

Lynniki huffed a laugh. "Well, you know my opinion on dangerous technology."

She propped the soul anchor against the lantern on the bench. "Ready, Gavyn?"

"I feel like we've done this before."

"Yes, but this time it'll work," Lynniki said with a grimace that undermined her words.

"Do it," Rowan said. "I can't see if anyone's coming anymore. Who knows how much time we have?"

Lynniki twisted the stone, lining up the etchings so they glowed again.

This time nothing exploded. Or caught fire.

"Oh, that feels odd," Gavyn said, his words slurred.

"Is it working?" Rowan whispered to Lynniki.

"Shhh, it might take a minute."

A jingle echoed from one of the cross streets, bouncing around the square. It sounded like chain mail. Rowan's heart sped up.

"Someone's coming."

She spun, trying to pinpoint the sound. Boots tromped the cobblestones, and she finally saw a troop of Lord Karaval's men emerge from the street closest to the keep. Lord Karaval led them, dressed in a studded leather jerkin, his longsword at his hip. Allianne limped at his side, her rapier drawn.

"Healer's Ghost," Rowan whispered. "Lynniki, stop the transfer."

"I can't!" Lynniki cried. "That might kill Gavyn."

"No, no, no." Rowan raced toward Lord Karaval. "Get back," she called. "Lord Karaval. Stay back."

He froze in his tracks, his hand signaling his men to stop. "What is it, Rowan?"

"The lantern. We're trying to get Gavyn out, but it will try to consume anyone nearby. You have to go."

Lord Karaval pointed, and his men trotted back up the street without a word, but Lord Karaval and Allianne stayed.

"Lord Hax will be converging on this spot. He won't let my standard remain, and I thought to challenge him when he got here." He pointed over her shoulder.

Rowan spun to the center of the square where the flagpole stood. A blue banner with a red horse snapped from the top.

Gavyn's voice called out in Rowan's head, a mixture of pain and relief.

The lantern gave a brief, blinding flash. Beams of sickly, silver light sprang out, ranging over the square like the tentacles of the noktum, searching for a new victim.

She hadn't seen this in her visions, but she could guess what they would do easily enough.

"Don't let the light touch you," she cried to Lord Karaval as she raced back across the square.

Lynniki scooped up the soul anchor and stepped back.

Rowan snatched the lantern, and before any of the worry and doubt and fear could come crashing down on her, she raised her hand and swung it as hard as she could against the ground.

Glass shattered, sending shards across the cobblestones. Several ricocheted hard enough to slice her arms.

But the lantern stayed lit, the wickless flame steady within the glassless metal frame.

Rowan stared at it in horror. Her gaze met Lynniki's.

She'd spent so long worrying about breaking the thing and killing Gavyn that she'd assumed this would work.

The beams of light traced over the square, seeking out someone to consume. Lord Karaval dove behind a barricade just as a beam swept toward him. "What's next, Rowan?" he called.

Rowan raised the cursed thing and tried to shield the wickless flame so the light wouldn't pass her, but it went right through her hand as if that didn't matter. "I don't know!"

"Karaval!" Lord Hax's voice rang around the square.

Rowan spun. The invading lord stalked into the square from the south, Jannik and Darryn behind him. Darryn held his arm limply at his side, and he had a black eye, which Rowan hadn't had any part in.

"Stay back," Rowan called.

"Senji's ass, girl, you don't know when to get out of the way."

"Lord Hax." That was Mellrea's voice coming from another street over. "You get one warning. Leave this place or be slaughtered."

Rowan's heart thumped as Mellrea and Tera stepped into the square, a whole host of Lord Karaval's guards behind them.

Across the way, Lord Karaval's eyes went wide as he saw his daughter. His lips moved in the shape of her name.

Healer's Ghost, there are too many people.

"Get your sister out of the way," Lord Hax growled to Darryn. "I'll deal with Karaval and his girl."

He unslung the chain from his waist as Darryn stalked toward Rowan.

One of the beams swung around toward Rowan's brother.

"No!" Rowan flung the lantern to the ground and lunged for Darryn, tackling him out of the way of the beam.

They hit the ground with a thud.

"Rowan, you're ruining everything!" Darryn cried.

Rowan pushed herself off him.

Lord Hax drew back his arm and swung the chain with its spiked ball directly at Mellrea. She tried to dodge, but the chain wrapped her around the waist, the spiked ball locking it in place.

Lord Hax yanked, pulling her off her feet.

Tera yelled and raced for him.

But the danger wasn't Lord Hax.

He hauled Mellrea across the square, as a beam swept toward her from the other direction.

Tera wouldn't get to him in time to save Mellrea.

Across the square, Lord Karaval's stricken face went calm and still. He stood from behind the barricade and stepped into the path of a beam.

He met Rowan's wide eyes as the silver light lit up his features. "End this," he said to her and her alone.

And then he crumbled to dust, wisps falling away to eddy along the cobblestones.

CHAPTER FORTY-SIX

ROWAN

ellrea screamed, the sound tearing through Rowan like the slash of a burning knife. She caught her breath, staring at the pile of ash.

But even as her heart ached and the back of her mind played the moment over and over again, wondering if she could have changed it, she stepped forward, her legs steady.

Lord Karaval was gone, his energy sucked into the lantern which glowed with that familiar, steady white light. But his sacrifice had given her a range of choices, and she could use them to honor his last wishes.

A bronze and copper gleam caught her eye as Lynniki's construct weaved its way across the square, swerving back and forth like a drunken soldier.

Lynniki knelt to meet it and slotted the soul anchor into the clamps at the back of its hips.

Rowan went for the lantern.

But Jannik got there first.

Healer's Ghost, she'd nearly forgotten about him, slinking around in Lord Hax's shadow.

The old man swept the lantern up in his bare hands, the stupid man.

Rowan's heart burned as Jannik raised the lantern with a happy smile. Like a child with a forbidden toy. He reached for the filigree on the cap as if he even knew what he was doing.

Rowan leaped on him. "No!" she cried. She did not endure the pain of this malevolent thing for months, she did not endure Jannik's lies or watch Lord Karaval pay its price, only to let Jannik have it after all of that. He'd done nothing to earn it, letting everyone else suffer for his hubris and stupidity.

Jannik snarled and yanked the lantern out of her reach while she kicked at him. He brought the lantern down to smash her over the head with it, but she twisted out of the way so the blow landed on her high shoulder.

She cried out and lost her grip on him for a moment.

He lashed out again and struck her across the face, the edge of metal tearing into her cheek.

She fell to the cobblestones, blood dripping to her chin.

A gleam of bronze didn't exactly streak across the square, but Jannik was still surprised by the considerable weight of a metal construct hitting him in the back of the knees. He tumbled backward over the four-legged mechanical beast and sprawled across the cobbles.

"Ha," Gavyn's voice said in Rowan's mind. "I've wanted to do that since I met you. Now drop it, you stupid man."

"Gavyn," Rowan gasped, relief sweeping through and making her limbs weak at the sound of his voice. The bond forged by the spark of her magic must have held even through the transfer.

"This is harder to control than I thought it would be."

Gavyn's new body staggered out from under Jannik's legs and hopped, bringing his full weight down on the antiquarian's wrist.

Jannik cried out and dropped the lantern.

Rowan snatched at it and hissed at the familiar stab of pain. Now—Now she could end this nonsense.

She reached in her pouch to pull out the four remaining lenses and slotted them back into place over the empty space where the glass had once been.

To her left, Lynniki had a hammer in each hand—where she'd gotten them, Rowan had no idea—and she had taken charge of the barricades, hauling them into better position and adding wreckage and debris to keep any more soldiers from invading the square.

Across the cobbles, Tera attacked Lord Hax, forcing him to drop the end of the chain and relinquish his hold on Mellrea who scrambled to free herself from its coils.

Jannik struggled to his knees.

"This is your last chance," Rowan said. "Go home or I will treat you the same way they're treating him." She gestured to Tera, Mellrea, and Lord Hax.

Jannik's mouth thinned in a sour scowl. "It's not yours—"

"Wrong answer."

She activated the second lens. It washed him in white light, shot through with red and blue.

Rowan picked up the sword she'd dropped. Tera was right about it being too heavy for her. Her wrist ached with the weight, but it felt good to hold a weapon. It felt good to be able to face the man who'd made her life miserable for the last two months.

Jannik's eyes widened as she faced him with a naked blade. "You really think you're going to wield that? Rowan. We are scholars. We fight with words, not weapons. We study history, we don't repeat it."

He ducked for a loose cobble and flung it at her head.

She saw the blue light shining along his arm as he threw and avoided it easily. She lunged in, sweeping the sword in a cut designed to slice across the red glowing from his midsection. He spun away too slow and fell clutching his middle. Blood leaked between his fingers.

"Rowan," he gasped.

She hesitated. He was down and wounded. She didn't need to drive a blade into his back to end his tyranny over her life, did she?

Then he jerked and the blue light shone around his hand so bright she nearly missed the dagger he threw.

"Rowan!" Gavyn threw himself in front of her, and the blade clattered against his metal body, falling harmlessly to the ground.

Jannik growled and stood. He kicked out at Gavyn's low form.

Rowan screamed and slashed, her sword following the arc of red across his throat.

Jannik couldn't even cry out. He fell to the cobbles clutching at his neck.

Rowan sobbed and dropped her sword so she could catch him before his head hit the street. Though she kept a firm hold on the lantern, even now.

Jannik gurgled and finally lay still, eyes staring at the sky.

Rowan swallowed against the tears that spilled down her cheek, stinging where they flooded the cut he'd made earlier. "I'm sorry," she whispered. Despite everything, she found the words were still true. She lowered her forehead to touch his. "I'm sorry. I *am* a scholar. I deal in truth. If it's true that we come back in different lives, please do better next time."

Gavyn limped up to her. One of the plates lining his body was dented and scuffed. "Rowan, there's no time. Mellrea and Tera—"

He didn't have to finish. She left Jannik dead on the cobbles and rushed for the fight at the edge of the square. Lynniki had trapped a troop of Lord Hax's men behind a barricade, and there was some sort of metallic pinging going on that made the soldiers duck and dodge. But Tera and Mellrea faced off against Lord Hax, who kept them at a distance with his chain.

As Rowan raced for them, Lord Hax snapped out with the chain, and the spiked ball smashed into Tera's leg. She crumpled with a cry of pain, and Mellrea lunged to cover her. Another hit could kill either one.

"Lord Hax!" Rowan cried.

She expected him to turn or flinch or show distraction somehow. Instead, he spun the opposite direction, sending the spiked ball in a wide arc that wrapped around and speared straight toward her.

A heavy force hit her from the side, and she fell underneath Darryn's weight. Lord Hax's weapon struck his head with a sickening crack.

Darryn slumped across her, eyes closed. Blood seeped from the gaping wound across his temple.

"Darryn?" Rowan choked. She touched his face, stroking her thumb down his cheek, the way she had when they were little.

His chest rose and fell, but he didn't respond, knocked cold.

Her breath came in staccato gasps through her teeth as she yanked herself free of her brother and stood to face Lord Hax. Rage battled in her breast, but none of it reached to cloud her thoughts. She raced ahead, noting the red and blue glow along Lord Hax's limbs revealed by the light of the lantern.

Lord Hax spun the chain round and round in his hand, building momentum.

Rowan raised the lantern. "It's time, Lord Karaval." She knew he couldn't hear her the way Gavyn had. He was as gone as the long dead treasure hunter and all the others the lantern had consumed before him but it felt good to speak to him one last time.

She touched the cap in a pattern that corresponded with the third lens, which pictured a repeating pattern of waves. A lens she hadn't used yet.

Instead of a focused beam, the light sprang up around her in concentric circles, the shadows from the filigree in the lens twisting and turning between the light. Then five other figures of Rowan stepped into place beside her. Exact copies of herself designed to trick the eye and the mind.

Whispers crept across the square, and Lord Hax faltered, the ball at the end of his chain striking sparks from the cobbles.

Rowan stepped forward, and the copies all moved, weaving around her in a shield of confusion.

Lord Hax shook his head, and then growled, striking out at the nearest copy of Rowan.

It dodged as if it were real.

Rowan watched, lips pressed tight as she waited for an opening.

The lantern dealt in knowledge. Between the map and the illumination of weaknesses, it was easy to see how a spy might use those to gather information about their enemies. But this lens dealt in the mirror image of that. This was the spread of falsehood. The dissemination of doubt.

Lord Hax twitched and lashed out at another copy of Rowan. Behind him, Gavyn slunk, his jerky movements bringing him closer and closer to the lord.

Rowan raised the lantern, and the false Rowans converged on Lord Hax, making him stumble back. He struck out with the chain, sweeping it around to hit all five copies. Except at that moment of unbalance, Gavyn darted in and tripped him, his bulky body the perfect height to strike someone behind the knees.

Lord Hax fell, and Rowan stalked up to him. She struck his right arm with the flat of her blade, along the red glow she remembered from before. He dropped the chain, and she kicked it out of the way.

She held her blade to his throat, and he gazed up at her, lips twisted in a grimace. His gaze flicked between her and the five other figures around them, his head flinching and jerking as if to shake away the whispers that crept across the cobbles.

"You are magnificent," he said, startling her.

"What? Not godsblighted?" she said.

"You hide your strength so well. Let me up and you can take Jannik's place on my staff. You will run his digs, disperse his funding. You can be my scholar and wield the lantern for me against my enemies. In return I will care for your family forever; they will thrive under my children's protection for the entire length of my legacy."

"No, thank you," she told him, voice brittle and cold. "I am already loyal to a noble far more honorable than you. Lady Karaval," she called.

Mellrea helped Tera sit up against one of the benches. She looked up, face grim, then she stood to approach.

Gavyn circled the fallen lord. Lynniki stepped up to Rowan's side as she deactivated the lens, and the copies of herself winked out of existence. She kept her sword though.

Lord Hax glared at Mellrea. "Congratulations," he said, his lips twisted sourly.

"Thank you." Mellrea didn't waste any more breath on this man. She stepped forward, and her sword flashed in a smooth, quick arc, striking Lord Hax's head from his shoulders.

Lord Karaval's daughter had tearstains on her cheeks, their tracks crisscrossing the blood that smudged her face, but her voice didn't waver. "Bastard."

She looked over at Rowan. "Thank you. For your help." She nodded to the lantern. "He's not in there, is he? Like Gavyn? We can't make him a new body and get him out?"

Rowan swallowed and shook her head. "I'm so sorry. Gavyn was a special case. He tried to destroy the lantern with magic, and it did something to him. It trapped him at the same time that it consumed Jannik's great-grandfather. Lord Karaval is gone."

Mellrea's throat bobbed, and she blinked.

"This isn't over," Lynniki said quietly. "His soldiers are still all over the city."

Mellrea nodded. "Will you help Tera? And Rowan's brother?" she asked Lynniki. "Rowan, with me." The words might have been a command, but her voice rose at the end as if she wasn't quite used to giving orders.

"Yes, my lady," Rowan said. "I'm right behind you."

CHAPTER FORTY-SEVEN

ROWAN

Rowan and Gavyn trotted down the halls of the keep. Gavyn's movements were still jerky, apparently a feature of the construct's design and not due to his lack of control. Lynniki had promised improvements, but she had also offered to help rebuild a lot of the city after the battle.

The Delver had so much work lined up for her, they'd barely seen her in the last few days. She hadn't mentioned returning to the Delver city once, and Rowan couldn't imagine her trying to fit herself back into that tiny mountain when she'd expanded so much out in the world.

"I know Lynniki said four legs is more stable than two but maybe she could make me taller. I'm tired of being mistaken for a dog," Gavyn said in her head. Another improvement would be some sort of voicebox so he could talk to other people, but even Lynniki had looked daunted by that challenge. So, for now, he was stuck communicating with everyone else through an elaborate series of charades.

"Eventually," Rowan said. "I think she has a lot of plans. Most of them require more Giant magic."

They reached the door of Lady Karaval's study, and Rowan tapped on the wood before entering.

Mellrea sat in her father's chair, and Rowan's heart twinged at the sight. Mellrea had every right to be there, and she had her own sorrows about it, but Rowan couldn't help remembering the lord as he'd sat there and promised her the help she'd never thought she'd get.

Tera sat at her right, holding her hand, wounded leg propped on another chair.

Lynniki stood in front of her, gesturing to the injured limb. "I can make it better for you. I promise it only hurts a little at first. I've done this dozens of times now."

"Dozens?" Mellrea asked.

Lynniki waved a hand. "Well, half a dozen, including my own, but you'd make it an even seven."

Tera's lips twitched, and she folded her arms over her chest. "I think I'm going to wait a little. I still have hopes that it will heal enough to let me fight again."

"Your loss," Lynniki muttered.

Mellrea met Rowan's eyes as they settled themselves in front of her desk, Gavyn circling the rug before folding his joints into a semblance of sitting.

"How is your brother?" she asked quietly.

"He hasn't woken up." Rowan's jaw clenched. "They're not sure he ever will."

"I'm sorry," Tera said and Mellrea nodded.

Rowan nodded with them. She tried to distract herself in the times when she wasn't actively sitting with him, otherwise she drove herself crazy with wondering. Why had he jumped in front of Lord Hax? Had he forgiven her? In her memory, he was frozen with that look of betrayed contempt, his mouth forming the word "liar." He'd taken Lord Hax's blow for her, and that had to count for something.

She cleared her throat. "Allianne said she would watch over him as long as they're sharing the infirmary, but I imagine you called us here for something more urgent?"

She drew the lantern from its case.

All the eyes in the room locked on it. Gavyn's mechanical head tilted to face it.

"It's been a very long time since I've seen it from this angle," he murmured.

"Ah, yes," Mellrea said and chewed her lip. Just like her father. "I thought it time we dealt with the problem."

Rowan placed the Grief Draw on the edge of the desk and sat back. Her breath escaped on a huge sigh.

"It's still dangerous," she said. "And powerful. And now more people know about it and what it can do."

"Which means it's only a matter of time before someone comes looking for it, hoping to take it for themselves," Mellrea said.

Tera nodded to Lynniki. "The improvements to the city's defenses are coming along nicely, but of course it would be better if we didn't have to deal with outside threats at all."

Gavyn stood to pace from one end of the desk to the fireplace and back. "You know my opinion on this," he said, voice short and sharp.

"What's he saying?" Mellrea asked.

Rowan winced. "Gavyn wants to destroy it. He's always wanted to destroy it. That's what he died doing."

Mellrea nodded. "Yes. Until the battle, I saw it his way."

Lynniki cocked her head. "But the battle changed that?"

Mellrea's lips thinned. "It's my father's sacrifice that is powering it now. Is it so selfish to want to honor that? Destroying it made perfect sense when it would have been an inert object. But now... it means he would have died for nothing."

"Not nothing," Tera said quietly. "He saved you. And the lantern helped us defeat Lord Hax."

"Still," Rowan said. "You're not selfish."

"I just keep thinking maybe his sacrifice made it worth keeping. We don't have to use it as a weapon the way everyone thinks. We can use it to defend ourselves. Or protect Usara." Her voice rose. "We'd be able to do just about anything. And who knows what the fourth lens does. It has endless possibilities." She stopped, hands raised in the air, and she winced. "I sound like Lord Hax, don't I?"

"No, but you don't sound like your father either," Rowan said. "He knew its power would corrupt. It's a noble idea, but I think we need to be very careful about using the lantern."

"Are we really considering this?" Gavyn said, stopping with a jerk beside Rowan's chair. "This thing has ruined all of our lives, to some degree, and you want to keep it around?"

"We're just considering the possibility that maybe destroying it isn't the best option, Gavyn."

"If we even could," Lynniki said. "Magic didn't do it, and smashing it didn't work. What's left to try?"

"Melting it?" Tera said, and Lynniki looked suddenly thoughtful.

Rowan glanced between Gavyn and Mellrea, torn. She'd spent so long working toward destroying it, but in the end, they'd failed to do so. And Lord Karaval's sacrifice had allowed them to defeat Lord Hax. It had saved Mellrea and the rest of them. How much did that balance out the Giants and their carelessness with life?

"I think I'm not willing to throw everything away yet," she said slowly. "It's too powerful to use, but it's also too powerful to destroy. And just because it was made by people who could have been evil, it doesn't make the lantern itself evil. It's saved lives now too. Not just destroyed them."

"A tool is just a tool," Lynniki said. "It's not good or evil."

Rowan gave her a smile. "You're very good at walking that line. Maybe I can learn from you."

"The world is full of people who will tip that balance the wrong way," Tera said.

"That's why we should hide it. Protect it. Make sure it never falls into the wrong hands again. I think it's the only way to move forward right now."

Gavyn didn't say anything. He just jerked over to the fireplace and lay down with his back to them.

Mellrea sat back. "I think my father came to the same conclusion."

"What do you mean?" Rowan asked.

She pulled a sheet of paper out from under a book on the desk. "Many years ago, he started construction on a sanctuary deep in the mountains. A simple retreat for those who wanted solitude, but the project always got pushed aside for more urgent matters. A few weeks ago, he started work on it again. As if he was rushing to finish it as soon as possible."

Mellrea turned the page to face Rowan. "He sent the new orders just after you headed into the noktum to find me."

"We made a deal." Rowan examined the drawings. "I would help him find you if he helped me keep the lantern safe." She hadn't known for sure that Lord Karaval would keep his promise.

"He must have come to the same conclusion. Hiding it and protecting it is our best course of action. It's remote," she added. "It's isolated. And the only ones who know it's there are the builders and those of us in this room. It's perfect."

Rowan's fingers twined around and around themselves as she pictured how they'd found the lantern. *Hidden away so it couldn't be found or used. We saw how well that worked.*

"It's *almost* perfect," she said.

Mellrea raised a quizzical eyebrow.

"We can't just lock it away and expect the best this time. Someone needs to guard it. To prevent the same thing that happened last time. To Gavyn and to us."

Gavyn raised his head, but he didn't turn to face them.

One by one, their faces went stricken as they stared at her.

She tried to smile. "I've carried it this far. What's a little further?"

Tera swung her injured leg down and sat forward with a wince. "This is the rest of your life, Rowan. Are you prepared to give that up?"

"There wasn't a lot of my old life I was willing to go back to," she said. She didn't admit that she'd wanted desperately to see who she was now that she didn't have the lantern or Jannik to deal with. But she liked who she was, even if this sense of duty trapped her into a future she hadn't chosen.

"I'm the best one to hide it," she continued. "The same way I'm the best one to hold it. I know how to use it, but I don't want to. I'm strong enough to carry it, and with my Delver blood, I'll likely live a lot longer than the average Human."

"You'll be alone," Mellrea said. "For centuries maybe."

"What? You won't come to visit?" She huffed a laugh even as her heart contracted. "No, I know it's better if no one comes with me. The fewer people who know about the lantern and its whereabouts, the safer it is. Isolation is just another kind of pain, and I'm used to pain."

"One day you can train a replacement," Lynniki said. "A Delver who can hold the lantern. You won't be alone forever." She gestured to the drawings which Mellrea gladly handed over. "And I can make improvements—"

"Of course, you can," Tera muttered.

"That'll make life a lot more comfortable." Lynniki finished as if Tera hadn't said anything.

Mellrea bit her lip then nodded decisively. "Then I gift the sanctuary to you," she said. "To keep you and the Grief Draw safe. I'll spread the rumor the lantern was destroyed so no one will even bother to look for it."

Lynniki bent over the drawings, and Mellrea rummaged for a quill to write out the deed.

Gavyn remained silent and still beside the fireplace.

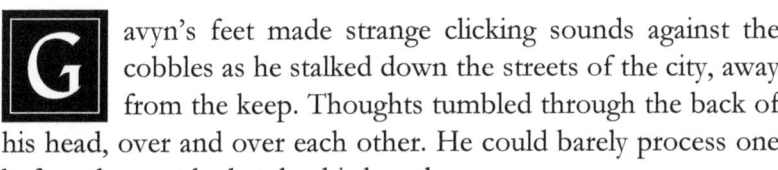

CHAPTER FORTY-EIGHT

GAVYN

G avyn's feet made strange clicking sounds against the cobbles as he stalked down the streets of the city, away from the keep. Thoughts tumbled through the back of his head, over and over each other. He could barely process one before the next had stolen his breath.

Imagined breath. Lungs hadn't been part of the new body Lynniki had crafted.

He had gone through so much grief trying to destroy the lantern, and now they were just going to keep it? If anyone knew firsthand why it was called the Grief Draw, it was him. The thing brought pain like a malevolent magnet, and now even Rowan had fallen for the lure of power, ignoring the hurt the lantern had dealt her.

He shook away the thought that he was maligning her just like Jannik or Rowan's brother and wove across the street.

His body twitched, and the legs with their backward joints always wanted to bend the wrong way. Especially when he was irritated or angry.

He'd never thought he'd have to get used to using a body again. Somehow, it had always gone better in his head, a seamless transition where he settled into the metal like an old leather glove. But his brain had different ideas than the gears, and when his emotions ran high, the joints did what they wanted while he yelled from inside.

At least that part he was used to.

A woman with a basket of laundry on her hip skipped out of his way, lighting on a doorstep to let him pass. A man carrying a saw over his shoulder stepped to one side, and after a brief hesitation tipped his hat to Gavyn.

He'd become something of a local legend himself, following in Keinwen's footsteps. Karaval's people had seen him around often enough, and tales of his exploits during the battle had softened his way, and now most of them treated him with wary, and sometimes confused, respect.

His halting movement finally brought him to the city gate, where the bridge extended out over the dry flood plain.

Five more steps and he would have left the city. *Finally.* Finally he could move without being carried. He could make his own choices and break from the people he'd been beholden to.

It made sense to go. A hundred years old and he hadn't seen much except the inside of a laboratory and all the dark sides of the sentient races, Human, Giant, and Delver alike. He finally had a chance to live and make the most of the second chance he'd been given. He could live the life he'd wanted to live for Keinwen.

Alone.

An involuntary shudder traveled up his disjointed legs, and his gears rattled.

There would be sights and experiences, yes but no one to talk to. No one to share them with.

And even if he could speak, what would he say? What stories would he tell that weren't tinged by his journey and the pain he'd carried for this long? The grief, fear, and despair that had been such a part of his life until just a couple of months ago.

No one would understand him. No one knew what he'd lost and gained.

He hung his head.

Back at the keep, Rowan would be wrapping up the last of her business. She'd be packing. She'd be saying goodbye. To the family she'd been born into and the family she'd chosen.

He'd wanted to go out and live. For Keinwen's sake.

But Keinwen was gone. She'd lived and she'd loved and she'd died. She'd had a life because of him. But she was gone.

And Gavyn had another friend who still lived. She was making a mistake, choosing to protect a thing that had only ever harmed. But he understood her choice.

He understood her.

I don't have to agree with her to care about her.

CHAPTER FORTY-NINE

ROWAN

Rowan stood beside Darryn's bed, her pack straining against her shoulders, the lantern tucked safely in its case at her hip. She wore a new leather tunic, cut to allow her legs the freedom to climb and run.

"I'm leaving," she whispered. "I'm sorry I can't stay. Lynniki returned from the sanctuary days ago. Gavyn still isn't talking to me, but every moment I stay, someone might rediscover the lantern, and then Mellrea will have to deal with the consequences."

Darryn lay still, his face as pale as his pillow. The bandage had been removed from his head, leaving a massive scar, but his eyelids remained closed as Rowan spoke.

Rowan's throat convulsed, and she had to swallow before going on. "I just couldn't leave without saying goodbye. I hope you forgive me. I hope you know I love you. I did everything for your sake, yours and Esrell's, but I have more people to think about now. More to take care of."

"Rowan?"

Rowan's heart caught, but the voice didn't come from the bed. She turned and found Esrell in the doorway of the infirmary.

Rowan choked, and her sister stepped forward to wrap her arms around her. Rowan held on for dear life.

"You're all right?" she said. "Healer's Ghost, you look well."

"I'm much better," Esrell said, pulling away only after a long moment. "Still a little weak, but Ma says that if I work the muscles gently, I should be back to normal soon."

Rowan kept her hands locked around Esrell's elbows, unwilling to let her go just yet. "I'm glad." So much feeling contained in those too words.

"How is he?" Esrell asked, gaze straying to Darryn's pale face.

"The same as my letters, but I can't wait any longer. I have to leave."

"You're still determined to sacrifice yourself for this?"

Rowan's lips twisted in a sad smile. "I am. It's not just you two who might be hurt now. There's Mellrea and Tera and Lynniki and—"

"The world?" Esrell raised an eyebrow.

Rowan winced. "I know it sounds conceited."

"No," Esrell said and twisted her arms so she could grip Rowan's elbows too. "It doesn't. I know what you've done for us. What you gave up and what you're going to be giving up for the rest of your life. Because you're the one who can do this. I'm proud of you."

Rowan fought to breathe, her chest aching with the words.

"Ma is on her way, and we'll care for Darryn." Esrell looked up and met Rowan's eyes. "I'll tell him the truth when he wakes. And I'll make sure he believes it this time."

Rowan blinked. "Thank you," she said, voice thick.

⬟　⬟　⬟

Mellrea's guards left Rowan several miles away from her destination on the assumption she would be continuing to Monclaren alone.

In reality, she turned in the opposite direction and traveled deeper into the mountains to a secluded bend of the path rarely seen by travelers. Now that Lynniki had had her way with the trail, it was nearly impossible to find for anyone who hadn't been there before.

Rowan drew her hood up against the snowflakes drifting down. Winter was even further along up here, and given the color of the sky, she would be snowed in very soon.

She sidled between the deceptively rugged outcroppings that marked the entrance to her new sanctuary and stopped on the other side of the barrier to stare.

The narrow, little cut between the rock was just wide enough to admit her, but on the other side, it spread into a wide track between the cliffs and eventually became a wide flight of stairs carved into the tumbled stone. The steps led to a terrace already decorated with its own layer of snow. Delicate stone balustrades lined the space where one could stand and survey the tiny valley between the cliffs.

Beyond the terrace rose the facade of the sanctuary built directly into the mountain. The front half of the building stuck out from the mountain, topped with a steeply pitched roof designed to shed the snow and ice, but the rest of the sanctuary disappeared back into the mountain. Diamond-paned windows lined with bright brass and copper glinted with a welcoming light. Lynniki must have left the lights on for her, even knowing it could be days or weeks before Rowan arrived at her final home.

She took a shuddering breath as a flurry of feeling clogged in her throat. It was beautiful, and it looked warm and even cozy.

Her prison. Her exile away from her family and the friends she'd only just made.

Lynniki was scheduled to check her improvements every couple of months as the weather allowed. Mellrea and Tera had promised to visit when they were sure they wouldn't be followed or observed. But the majority of her life would be spent alone. And Gavyn had been quiet and terse after they'd made their decision. He'd disappeared so thoroughly before she'd left that she hadn't even been able to say goodbye.

She swallowed down the overwhelming mix of emotions and traipsed up the steps. The cold made her back ache, and the sun would be down soon.

At the top of the steps, an asymmetrical lump atop the balustrade moved. It stood, shedding snow until it became a strangely squat and square four-legged construct. The melting snow gleamed from copper plates, covering a selection of complicated joints.

"Gavyn," Rowan breathed.

"You sure took your time getting up the mountain."

Her mouth hung open for a moment before she gave him an indignant laugh. "You're one to talk. Do you know how much time I wasted trying to find you before I left?"

He had no facial expressions, his head a strange amalgam of smooth metal and the gaps between. But he ducked his head as if ashamed to meet her eyes. "I'm sorry. I had to think. Then by the time I'd decided, you'd left, and I had to race up here. I thought for sure you'd beat me."

Rowan bit her lip, staring at him. "Gavyn…"

"Come on. Let me show you inside. The best part of getting here before you is that I get to give you the grand tour."

The doors, big, carved panels of wood hauled up from the valley somewhere, opened at her approach.

"Lynniki got them to recognize the lantern," Gavyn said at her soft gasp. "I had to push them open, but the sanctuary will open like a flower for you. This whole place is a combination of Human architecture, Delver ingenuity, and Giant magic."

A puff of warm air enveloped her, smelling a little damp. Copper pipes lined the stone entry hall, and she recognized a bit of the steam heating system from the Delver city. Hopefully that meant hot water too.

The foyer ended in another set of doors that led to a large hall. Rooms opened along either side that Rowan was starting to get excited about exploring. In the center, a pedestal waited with a familiar circular indentation. A notebook lay beside it. Lynniki's spiky handwriting scrawled across the first page. "I'll be back in a month, but these notes should get you started."

Gavyn said, "The pantry is stocked for several months in case of snow. But once spring rolls around and the garden outside gets growing again, this place will be mostly self-sustaining. The shutters for the windows can be locked down at a moment's notice, and Lynniki's hidden more traps and defenses that I don't even know about."

Rowan stepped forward and placed the lantern in its place on the pedestal. It fit perfectly, and as it slid home, lights around the great hall sprang to life, flooding the whole area with a warm glow that drowned out the cold, white light of the lantern.

"Don't worry, it's all powered by steam," Gavyn said. "I don't think Lynniki wanted it drawing anything at all from the lantern and Lord Karaval. The Grief Draw is just like the key to a lock."

Rowan took a deep breath and tipped back her head to stare at the ceiling, beautifully carved with peaceful little flowers, interspersed with the gleam of copper pipes.

"It's actually not a bad place to spend eternity," Gavyn said. "Much nicer than the laboratory."

"Did you come to wish me luck?" Rowan asked, when what she really wanted to ask was "when are you leaving?"

"No," he said quietly.

She lowered her chin to look at him. "No?"

"I mean, of course, good luck. I just meant... that's not all I guess."

Rowan waited, heart in her throat.

"I still think the lantern is too dangerous. I'd rather find a way to destroy it. But Lynniki's right. I didn't succeed the first time, and you didn't succeed the second. It'll take me time to figure out how. And for now..." He jerked his head at the sanctuary. "Maybe this *is* better."

That didn't answer the question, but she was too frightened to ask it. She would not admit to being that selfish.

"You have your life now. At least you have movement and eventually communication. You can go *live*."

"You know, I thought about it. I got about as far as the gate and realized the reality wasn't nearly as exciting as the thought had been. Out there wasn't where I wanted to be." He turned to stare back at the doors which still stood open. "I'd rather be here. With you."

She bit her lip hard.

"You were the only one who heard me. You were the only one who fought for me. And now you're the only one who knows what it's like to have your life usurped by an object."

She huffed a laugh.

"I know what it's like to face forever alone because of a choice that you've made," he said. "And I didn't want that for you. So, I'd rather spend a lifetime here with a friend, than an eternity out there by myself."

She didn't have words. Definitely not any as eloquent as his.

"Thank you, friend," was all she managed to say.

"Yes, well." He stood and shook his head as if trying to settle it properly on his neck. "Now you can help me draw up some ideas for Lynniki. If this is going to be my body, I'm going to need some changes."

She smiled. "Ah, now I see. You just want me for my hands."

"Hands!" Gavyn cried. "Opposable thumbs. Great idea."

"I'll get some paper," Rowan said.

Then she turned and closed the doors behind them, shutting them in.

ABOUT THE AUTHOR

Books have been Kendra's escape for as long as she can remember. She used to hide fantasy novels behind her government textbook in high school, and she wrote most of her first novel during a semester of college algebra.

Older and wiser now (but just as nerdy) she writes fantasy with main characters who have disabilities. If she's not writing, she's reading, and if she's not reading, she's playing video games.

She lives in Denver with her very tall husband, their book loving progeny, and a lazy black monster masquerading as a service dog.

She writes comedic fantasy under the name KM Merritt.

IF YOU LIKED...

If you enjoyed this novel and the world it's set in, then the creators of the Eldros Legacy would like to encourage you to don thy traveling pack and journey deeper into the mysteries of the world Eldros and all the myriad adventures set therein.

The mortal world of Eldros is coming apart. The Giants, who once ruled its five continents with draconian malice have set their mighty designs on a return to power. Mortals across the globe must be victorious against insurmountable odds or die.

Come join us as the Eldros Legacy unfolds in a growing library of novels and short stories.

You can find all the novels at:

www.EldrosLegacy.com/books

Our website is, of course:

EldrosLegacy.com

The Books by Series

Legacy of Shadows
by Todd Fahnestock

Khyven the Unkillable

Lorelle of the Dark

Rhenn the Traveler

Legacy of Deceit
by Quincy J. Allen

Seeds of Dominion

Demons of Veynkal

Legacy of Dragons
by Mark Stallings

The Forgotten King

Knights of Drakanon (Forthcoming)

Sword of Binding (Forthcoming)

Return of the Lightbringer (Forthcoming)

Legacy of Queens
by Marie Whittaker

Embers & Ash

Cinder & Stone (Forthcoming)

The Dog Soldier's War
by Jamie Ibson

A Murder of Wolves

Valleys of Death (Forthcoming)

Other Eldros Legacy Novels

Deadly Fortune by Aaron Rosenberg

The Pain Bearer by Kendra Merritt

Short Stories

Here There Be Giants by The Founders (FREE!)

The Darkest Door by Todd Fahnestock

Fistful of Silver by Quincy J. Allen

Electrum by Marie Whittaker

Dawn of the Lightbringer by Mark Stallings

Milton Keynes UK
Ingram Content Group UK Ltd.
UKHW041951031123
431812UK00001B/43